S0-BDQ-830

"Kudos... for the fine sense of menace... interesting characters..."

—*Houston Chronicle*

"... the author pulls out all the stops in a clever conclusion..."
—*Booklist*

"THERE IS INTEREST IN YOU.

Russian interest. *American* interest. *British* interest. God knows who wants to know where Schaefer Braun is going next. You are the most exciting thing in years."

His voice was low, and angry. "The reason for telling you this is obvious. I am your friend. There are spies out there, and they have an interest in destroying you. We are a bunch of very tough, very nasty, very determined and competitive people, Schaefy, and we are getting bored. And I do not wish you swatted like a bloody blackfly. God help me, if you were anyone else, I would see you go down without a quiver."

"Posey maintains suspense and manipulates his characters with ease."

—*Publishers Weekly*

"This is truly a stunning work. Mr. Posey has done something with the genre that no one has done in... well, maybe ever."
—Dan Sherman, author of
The Man Who Loved Mata Hari

By the same author:

KIEV FOOTPRINT
PROSPERO DRILL

Carl A. Posey

Red Danube

WORLDWIDE®

TORONTO • NEW YORK • LONDON • PARIS
AMSTERDAM • STOCKHOLM • HAMBURG
ATHENS • MILAN • TOKYO • SYDNEY

To the good, good P.

RED DANUBE

A Worldwide Library Book/September 1988

ISBN 0-373-97082-X

First published by St. Martin's Press Incorporated.
Originally published in Great Britain by Robert Hale Limited under
the title *Dead Issue*.

Copyright © 1985 by Carl A. Posey. All rights reserved.
No part of this book may be used or reproduced in any manner whatsoever
without written permission except in the case of brief quotations embodied in
critical articles or reviews. For information, address St. Martin's Press,
175 Fifth Avenue, New York, N.Y. 10010.

® are Trademarks registered in the United States Patent and
Trademark Office and in other countries.

Printed in U.S.A.

Author's Note

The people and events depicted here are imaginary, and any resemblance to actual persons, alive or dead, is entirely coincidental. However, as I have borrowed Vienna for my large backdrop, I have borrowed for my smaller one the settings and some of the essential lunacy of the international research community. But none of their people appear. To paraphrase Mr. Waugh, I am not I, she is not she, they are not they, it is not it.

Vienna 1984

PROLOGUE

ORDINARILY, IT WOULD HAVE fallen to Trulov to handle—to "tackle," as the Russians like to say—the matter of the chairman's death. But, with Trulov gone, the task went to Ivanov, the Bulgarian assistant, and the memorial gathering had been shifted out of the dry elegance of the castle to the gloomy corner of the village cemetery where the local Soviet dead of World War Two are remembered in gilt cyrillic characters on an oblong of polished granite. More than a hundred of us surround the little monument now, nearly everyone from the Centre, huddled against the sudden rotary gusts that spin ribbons of dead yellow leaves skyward, and make even the strutting Ukrainian crows pause, and fluff, and mutter against the chill.

I like their size and confidence and wariness, their raucous, determined voices, and the way they seem suddenly all to arrive from Russia at the same instant in autumn, and to vanish as quickly in the spring. Today they perch in skeletal trees along the cemetery, balance on the waving turrets of windblown poplars, their heads drawn into a dark puff of feathers, their big feet locked. Some try their wings against the wind until fatigue forces them down on the dark farmlands that surround our little garden of death. One clings to a cross where a dwarf iron Jesus suffers, watching us with empty metal eyes. And from my own apparatus of pain, and grief, and anger, I tell myself: there, watch the crows.

Ivanov's pudgy yellowish face pops up here and there on the edges of the crowd, the watery golden eyes asking everyone, over and over, if everything is satisfactory. There are scientists I know, and the mix of secretaries and report editors, minions, the directors, but no one recognizes me. Or almost no one. I see Trulov's wife, her eyes damming a flood of grief and hatred. Her daughter, a girl about ten, stands next to her, the image of Trulov himself, except that his round, flat face has become beautiful on this child; she glows like a moon. The mother's shining eyes meet mine, hold an instant, then flee. Vera, I think, her name is Vera. For the moment I cannot think of the child's.

Yes, and the men I am really here to see, the spiders, are present, diametrically across the crowd from me, ageless, compact, composed. They seem not to notice me, but I know they have, that they will come over finally and want to talk. I hope they are a little frightened of me, but cannot read them. They have always seemed to me to feel...nothing. Simply, nothing.

So, of them all, only these men I've called spiders, and Trulov's wife and possibly the child recognize me, the person behind the blonde beard and stringy blonde hair and thick smoked glasses in metal rims, the ill-cut costume of an ordinary Russian male in winter. It is just as well. I am in my ninth month of death, and want no resurrection here.

The Japanese director of the Centre stands near the granite oblong, a slender man with the long, large-mouthed face of a gentle clown. His voice, so thickly accented that he seems to strangle there before our eyes, rises and falls on the wind, no doubt persuasive, intelligent, charismatic, but also unintelligible. Well, we are here to listen to such things, to demonstrate, by our willingness to be cold and drenched and rheumy-eyed, our admiration of the dead chairman. It doesn't matter that we hear, in this voice gasping at English, the hollow vocabulary of superlatives in which we marinate at the Centre for Analytic Studies, or that, listening closely, we hear behind the grinding, false sincerity and impossible enthusiasms his hatred of what this death will mean to him. There is no Centre without its Soviet chairman, and, so, no Japanese director. None of us knows this failed, ebullient man has run out of tether; the voice can still hide its despair. His suicide three months from now will surprise all but his Danish wife.

The chairman. Andrei Borisovich Pastukh. My thoughts hang upon him, they are his winding sheets. No more long walks in the birch forest, no more sprawling in the summer heat that trembled along the banks of great rivers, to talk and talk, to go beyond the central single fact with which we had begun, and make ourselves visibly detailed to the other. He would remain for me a virtual silhouette, whose shape comes from what we put around it—a man for me to illustrate with memory and reflection. He might have said the same of me.

Andrei Borisovich Pastukh. Another dead Russian in a city that sees at least its share of them, this one discovered two days ago seated at the wheel of a rented Mercedes sedan, sedately parked at Schwechat—death pins him there, suspended between Vienna and the Aeroflot desk. Because he is Russian, the Centre's organs of gossip beat and twitch like hearts. Some whisper of fatally depressing trouble at home, given the demise of Andropov, and murmurings of cyanide pellets, pushing the death toward the unmentionable, dark side of the place. But I know that he had come to Vienna to die, to be pulled down by the greedy men who could not rest for wanting him dead. I look across the crowd at them standing imperturbably among the others, riding the gale of wind and sentiment with equanimity, gazing calmly toward the speaker. These are the men who kill you, and leave you in a car at Schwechat. My fingers touch the metal of the heavy Makarov automatic weighing down one pocket of my greatcoat. These are animals who will want to talk, later...

The director finishes his elliptical praising of the dead, and, with the ominous humility of a priest, turns aside, making room for a Polish mathematician who can drink all reason from a congregation of reasonable men. Others follow. I drift, hearing only snatches. Tales of this kindness, or that demonstration of wit, the certainty he would have followed old Aleksandrov as president of the Soviet Academy of Sciences. One of the Russians speaks glowingly of the chairman's war record. Another hints of fresh proximities to Chernenko's throne. An American describes a humanitarian act he would have noticed only in a Russian—we expect so little from them. An Austrian sycophant, eyes brimming, tells us that his late chief had been like a son to the chairman, and would have felt the loss of him more keenly than anyone alive. Looking up, I see one of my men, the older, taller one, giving a wolf grin, remembering how this "son" had died. On and on they come, shuffling into position like shy players, these people who believe they knew the chairman, and had not. Not at all. Not in the least. Of those assembled here, only these two men and I know our lost man, and even we know too little.

Suddenly the ceremony is over. The silence at the center of the group is like an explosion sending everyone back toward the castle in small bunches of different nationalities—a pod of British secretaries, a free-form of mixed Poles, Hungarians, East Germans, and Bulgarians, a cluster of Swedes, Americans, and the Russians, always by themselves. The crowd disperses toward the castle, vanishes in the gathering darkness of a late November afternoon. Lights flash along the village streets. On the approaches to Vienna one would see the sudden, progressive illumination spread across the city, like pale lightning. In a moment I am left almost alone.

The spiders come over then and for a time we stand like three comrades, silently regarding the monument. Both are about the chairman's age, give or take a year or two, and neither is yet seventy. Time has marked them very gently. The taller of the pair is a bit overweight, but glossy, the sleek dark hair thinning but still black, going down to distinguished white tufts at the sideburns. The face is a block of scalded granite, small-featured, the little eyes clever and penetrating and cold as death. His stubby, hairy hands still look strong, and he has the wrists of a bouncer in a low bar. The other is stocky, but still strong, his face bland as a wrinkled boy's; he wears a mask of sleepiness and his hair is thin and grey. Age pries away at their power. One senses that, and their reluctance to let go, their selfish regret.

"Schaefer," the taller one says. "I didn't expect."

"I had the impression you sent a message to me." I will not look at him, for we have begun a game at which I am the rankest beginner, but one he has played well all his life.

"*He* sent for you."

"He didn't have time."

"I . . . we . . . made time."

"How much?" My anger kindles, and I relax into its flow. I will be all right with these men, these greedy killers. "How much time?"

"We never have enough, do we?" The familiar, sneering voice.

"You robbed him."

"Of a few weeks, and a hell of a lot of pain."

"The choice might have been his."

"But it wasn't. We can't have someone like that drugged and helpless and mad with pain in a hospital. It's too . . . unstructured. He understood that."

"Why leave him in a car?"

"Why not? But that's a detail. He *understood*. That's the important thing. Let the rest go. At the end . . . he didn't bend or break."

"Jesus. You should have told the people that today. At the end he did not bend or break." And yet, the news heartens me; he knows it, it was supposed to. I veer away. "Then you sent for me."

"We had to see you. You understand?"

"What, that you have to kill me? I don't like the way you solve your problems."

"Ah," and he smiles broadly, the eyes glimmer. "You talk about us, but here you are ready to pop both of us with that anvil in your pocket. Where do you go afterwards? The moon? Where?''

"I can go back.''

"Not without Andrei.''

"You mean, you won't let me.''

"I mean, our deal is off. Everything's over.''

"It isn't up to you.''

"The hell it isn't. I created all of this!'' His eyes sparkle with sudden mad light. "And I can destroy it, you, everything, and I can do it in Vienna, or Moscow...all the great world capitals,'' he ends sarcastically.

"Then why bring me over?'' There is a crack in this old spider after all. He is always less than one expects.

"It's easier to...handle you here.''

"Kill me, you mean.''

"We don't need that. There's no reason for it. No need...now.''

"Bullshit. You want it ended. You would've had me run over if you thought you'd get away with it. But you began to worry about insurance...''

"Insurance?'' he asked, transparent as a guilty child. The other man cannot look at me. "What insurance?'' The granite face is older now, the eyes dull, the skin loose and pale. He could answer his own question.

"Andrei gave me everything.'' I smile. "We have again, what he called a Siberian standoff. How do you solve your problem now? Anyone for more killing?''

"Jesus,'' he whispers. "We had a deal, he promised...''

"You promised. If you'd let him have his life, what was left of it, we wouldn't be talking now. But you can't keep a bargain. Well, neither can I.''

"We need to talk. This isn't the place.''

"I know. You want me in the Belvedere gardens or on the Danube quayside, a target in a quiet place. An uninsured target, I mean.''

"Schaefer,'' he murmurs. But both men have seen, in my slightly altered stance, perhaps in my face, my eyes, that they are out of time, that the internal switch has moved that last increment of travel, and I am ready. "Schaefer, he *understood*."

"He understood you boys can't keep a bargain. But you don't understand anything yet. It isn't just Andrei, although that would be enough. It's everything...what you say *you* created."

And, remembering everything, I think: Really, it is time for you to die.

PART ONE

1

LOOK AT IT as a terrain map, a sand-table exercise, with various units deployed. Two large hills stand upon a rolling plain that is time; they are separated by nearly four decades, the interval in which my life was passed, a temporal land in which the relief is typically small and scattered, although, like short battles, even small features can be important to those closest to them. Shrouded in the mists rising from the flat terrain of time, stands the death of Franklin Delano Roosevelt, on the evening of April twelfth, nineteen forty-five. Look closely and you will see a small hillock not quite a year this side of it, marking my birth. The other large feature is the death of Leonid Brezhnev, on November tenth, nineteen eighty-two. Ah... one other should be noted: there, in the foreground, where the plain of time runs out, there is my own.

But we begin with Brezhnev.

Word that he had died rose on the morning tides of gossip at the Centre for Analytic Studies, the diurnal speculations on sex and intrigue and hirings and firings abruptly marked by an extraneous event of genuine importance. Word had come on Blue Danube Radio that morning, and, in somewhat denser form, on the BBC world service at eight: the long-time leader, imitating Franco, had *really* died in the night. Heard in America it might have caused one to shake one's head, induced a rising curiosity about the vectors of succession. But learning of it at the Centre, where half the people's fortunes tied them in some way to the regime, was... thrilling.

Twice each year, the score or so of delegates to the Committee for the Centre for Analytic Studies came to our sprawling yellow castle to vote on finances and research directions, and to honor retired, moribund, and dead participants. There were Britons in dark rumpled suits, and Bulgarians dressed like comic book gangsters, in green suits with yellow ties; tieless, leather-elbowed Americans in jeans and corduroy coats, and the woman from Paris, large-pored but pretty, like a pink butterfly among the men; Germans from east and west, the Polish delegation, whose faces spoke of martial law that year, and worse to come... It was a circus, an entertainment, a fairy tale of science, and yet, on that November day, we had the rare opportunity to experience the intrusion of actual events. As I say, the prospect thrilled.

But no one gave a sign that anything had happened anywhere. The Russians appeared to cluster more than usual out in the parking lot, out by their terrible Ladas and Soviet-built Fiats, talking covertly, as they always seemed to do. Apart from that, there was not the slightest indication, except one knew it probably *had* happened, having been about to happen for so long. So that, crossing to the castle through the Indian summer morning, the tan grasses and yellow leaves, the noisy squadrons of crows, one could think, Ah, if it is true, we shall be among the first to know it.

The possibility of this added another increment of tension in the meeting room, already charged by the prospect that some member nations would today question the Centre's work—its quality, its content, its relevance. Put another way, the conference was expected to challenge the ability of our little think tank to think thoughts worth a hundred million Austrian schillings a year. Another ugly intrusion by the world outside.

I refer to the Centre as "ours," but I never felt it was "mine," or that I was one of "them." As a scientist I knew about the Centre's work, about its successes and the joke science there, but I had a latecomer's immunity to the sentimentality and nostalgia that had become the main forces holding the place together, like love and guilt in an O'Neill play. The world had changed, but the Centre had not, and everybody in that room on that November morning knew it.

A dozen years before, it had been a promising child of east-west détente, a showpiece of good intentions of the United States and Soviet Union, and the ancillary good intentions of nearly everyone else. The Centre had attracted some very good people from both sides, and its explorations of certain difficult human problems had been sincere and occasionally successful. Certainly the setting, an elegantly renovated Habsburg Schloss near Vienna, was as conducive to think-tank thinking as a large accelerator would have been to particle research. The Centre's computers were old but large enough to run most mathematical simulations developed there—the models were not terribly complex—if they could run them slowly. And there was support for all kinds of work, some of it so far out as to be called daring, or silly, depending on your point of view.

But if you compared the place to a research lab in the real world—to the ocean chemistry lab I'd left in La Jolla, for example—the Centre was small, somnambulistic, dreadfully run, and disconnected. There were still abundant good intentions when I arrived that spring, but it was clear that the Centre had become an exclusive club for gentlemen scholars, bound together by congenial tennis, cocktails, ritzy "retreats" to distant Schlösser, everything softened by droning methodologists from the east, who blurred this world with abstractions like allegorical Night drawing grey veils across the land at dusk. A club, then, but also a kind of slick asylum, in which the main perspective was an introspective one, like a catatonic studying himself in a cocoon of silence, while the real world turned outside.

Like a lot of people in this funhouse, I had come over to begin a new life, feeling bereft of all but my experience as an oceanographer; if science were the price of starting fresh, then science we should do. But, to be truthful, the Centre was more a hospital than a lab for me. I arrived there with the peculiar sensitivity of a convalescent, in which the sound of a cornball Austrian band, or a shaft of brilliant spring light, or a V of storks transparent against the sky, could fill my eyes with tears. The external signs were few...a tendency to drink too much at parties, to fall quickly into bed with people barely named, or, on days like this November, Brezhnevian one, to keep to the fringes of the gatherings.

I drowsed around the edges of the group, sat in the warm light that slanted in through the big double windows along the southern wall. While the delegates milled around, getting their coffee, finding their seats, pressing familiar hands, at their square of gilt and white French desks, I watched the park. The autumn sun beat its golden wings upon our corner of the castle, and a gang of Austrian boys danced around a soccer ball outside, kicking up small clouds of yellow leaves. Young girls walked the pale gravel paths of the park, arm in arm, in the pretty Viennese custom. An old couple shuffled among the trees, led by a greying dachshund in its tan plastic muzzle, the people clinging to one another with affectionate tenacity. The light was really all you saw, though, the sun-angle so low that even the interiors of trees vibrated with grainy, ochre illuminations. A soft breeze swept the fields, recently gone a creamy brown, and the only birds in sight were a band of Russian crows, dark and smart and brassy, in Vienna for another season.

A sharpening of sounds brought me back to the conference room. Chairman Pastukh had still not arrived, nor had Trulov, the big Russian who accompanied him perpetually when he visited the Centre. Andrews, who was the Centre's liaison with the delegations, opened the meeting, his high, rapid-fire British voice calling us to order. He was one of those very pale Brits whose small, blonde head wears tiny faces, the mouth a mere scratch beneath the

nose, the eyes hooded and pinklashed. He must have been
in his early thirties, and one heard he was out of his depth
at the Centre, although he had become a kind of institution there. One also heard that he acquired his buoyancy
from the chairman, to whom, everyone used to say, Andrews was like a son. Watching him now, I wondered
whether the Brezhnev rumor were true, and whether that
death would bring the chairman crashing down, and Andrews with him; or whether it could go the other way, to a
bureaucratic heaven of some kind. What are you thinking, Andrews? You could never tell with him.

Completing the preliminaries, and still without a chairman, Andrews passed the helm to the Centre's director,
who rose and began a speech he had given, in one form or
another, three times I knew of in the past year. One
strained to understand him through the drowning noises of
his accent as he kept crashing against unpronounceable
sounds. He spoke English with a gargle and enthusiasm.
But he seemed to sense the approaching death of his or-
ganization, for his voice, while always convinced and optimistic, was that of a doctor who has given up. Describing
the present litter of proposed new projects, his voice rose
to that elevated, dishonest note one hears from salesmen.
A car, sold in that voice, would have something mortally
wrong with it. Listen to them.

"...A momentous opportunity to connect to the international dissemination process and also to the developing
world..."

"...A quantitative study of the processes of international negotiation..."

"...An unparalleled opportunity to express..." he
raved, flashing viewgraphs on the overhead screen, waving arms. He gave us the Carnival Project (the persistence
of religious long waves in periodic secular celebrations),
and more. "Hunger!" he shouted, and "Energy!,"
"Structural economic change in Lebanon!," "Min-
erals!," "Amazon Ecosystem!" The members leaned away

from the crazed speaker, scared to death by the bullshit reverberating through this mad list.

"A crucial piece of mammoth puzzle of atmosphere, ocean, and climate change over host of temporal and spatial scales..."

Jesus, I thought, embarrassed. He was talking about *us*.

"I am pleased to introduce to the committee Doctor Schaefer Braun, from the National Ocean Chemistry Facility in San Diego." He gestured and I stood up and nodded, the members bowing toward me with blank, friendly, curious faces—the faces, I supposed, fish see from the aquaria. "Dr. Braun spearheads oceanic side of study, with aid of Doctor Gordon Dexter, from United Kingdom, whom you all know..." A general nodding of heads. "...and Doctor Valentina Orlovsky, of Institute of Oceanology in Moscow." My skin prickled. Where had she come from? "Dr. Orlovsky will arrive in few days, but unfortunately not until after committee meeting ends. You will meet her at later date, no doubt."

I knew her work. She was a physical oceanographer, widely published in the journals, and highly regarded as a specialist on air-sea interactions. I'd expected a third partner on the project, and someone from the east, since we had Soviet data, but both Dexter and I had also expected some consultation on the matter. Valentina Orlovsky. I knew she was good, but wondered now what she looked like. Probably, I thought, one of those big, hairy-legged Soviet babes, with odors and a voice and even a face rather more like a man's; hearty but guarded, a hard-eyed dyke of a girl. I shook my head, and thought how sad it was that, needing warmth and beauty, we would have only a cool, possibly outsized, Soviet bosom to cry upon. Jesus, Gordy would be eloquently enraged when I told him.

The director was introducing someone else. "...Lincoln, of Physical Science Foundation in United States. Mr. Lincoln has been instrumental in finding continued support for us over there... and is rectifying a bad situation in America. He comes here often, but never before at time of committee meeting...I like then to introduce this benefactor and marvelous man to you." He gestured grandly toward a far corner of the room, where a dapper, dark-suited man in his sixties stood up, stockily poised, and nodded at the assembly, murmuring, "Thanks very much," in a harsh but not unfriendly New England accent. The director added, "Mr. Lincoln is with us, off and on, through next year, to help us consolidate incredibly successful efforts..." and he was off again.

Looking back at the moment, I have tried to coax some significance from it. But nothing comes. Lincoln looked around the crowd for the time it took him to turn his head ninety degrees, and sat down. Our eyes may have met, but I don't think so. I keep searching, though, for it seems incredible to me that, seeing him for the first time, I felt nothing, and had no sense of who he was, or what he meant to me.

Andrews chaired the meeting once more, the small face flicking anxiously toward the entrance door, then proceeding with the agenda, in which each delegation would comment upon proposed new programs in research. The tough delegate from Finland declared that it all sounded "woolly" to him, and that a poor nation like his had to be careful in spending its money. "Woolly" became the catchword of the morning, as they pursued some reassurance that all of this was still worth doing.

I guess I was ambivalent about the woolliness of the work there. I was used to casting sensors into a nearly opaque liquid that devoured most materials, a dark world of crushing pressures which we sampled from a floating platform, like blind scientists in a balloon. The backs of my legs have some big blue veins from heaving all that metal over the sides of research ships. And there was the wonderful brainwork, trying, as a chemist, to tell you how much oil nature put into the global ocean, or the age and origins of a continent-sized lens of sea water, or, more or less, where chemistry shaded into biology, physical pro-

cess into life. Of course the Centre sounded woolly to me—
what is more real than the sea?

Musing in this way, it took me a moment to feel the
sudden stillness in the room. The meeting poised expec-
tantly. Against this suspension, like a powerful actor oc-
cupying his stage, a large, agile man in a fine pinstriped
grey suit strode to the table, taking the seat next to Andrews. He was a handsome man in the way movie stars
used to be, well-made, somewhere in his sixties. His steel-
colored hair was brushed back from his forehead in the
Russian manner, but that was the only thing Russian about
him; his dress, manner, everything suggested good schools
and family in the west. He was about my height, a shade
over six feet tall, and heavier, as the years had fleshed him
out—you could sense the muscles like hanging ropes under the good suit, the stomach beginning its contest with
the belt, the hands missing some of their former strength.
His mouth glittered with Russian steel, but the teeth were
his own. You could hardly look at his eyes, eyes buried in
dark caves beneath heavy black eyebrows, eyes of a peculiar softness and luminosity, but penetrating too. He was
not an easy man to observe, and one guessed that his grey
aviator glasses were intended to subdue the effect of his
eyes on others.

I had never seen him in person before, and yet there was
that vague sense of having seen him again and again, faint
as the fragment of a distant dream, that face, and the un-
forgettable eyes. It unsettled me, for we had never so much
as been in the same building together before today. But
there it lay, down in the dark, untraveled mnemonic al-
leys, beating like a heart . . .

No. I ruled it out, deciding it had been some spurious
residue of old and tangled memory. Or perhaps it had
come from an effort to remember something else. The
poised silence of the room just before his arrival had reminded me of . . . what? Now I remembered: the room had
gone still and quiet, like a busy reef suddenly swept by a
large shadow.

Pastukh leaned toward Andrews, who whispered information into his ear. For a moment, the Russian eyes seemed to rest on me (I emphasize *seemed*; there is retrospective significance in every lifted eyebrow), then swept the square of tables and silenced delegates. "I am very sorry to be late," he said in a voice kept almost to a whisper, an odd voice for a large man, deep but not oratorical, the sort of sound one can lose in background noises. His English was almost unaccented, with more of an American flavor than a British one, except that it emerged slowly, with care, and without English contractions: always cannot, never can't. "What I propose now is that we continue with the discussions..." he said, picking up the thread of the meeting. For an amazed instant I thought he would ignore the Brezhnev rumor. But he added then, almost as an afterthought, "We are all aware of the tragic rumor circulated this morning. I am in touch with the Soviet embassy. They will let me know when they have more information." And that was all. The room began its murmuring once more, and the Dutch delegate restored the term "woolly" to the proceedings, as did the man from West Germany and the lady from France.

While she spoke, a cloud of warm, garlicky breath enveloped me, and I turned to find Trulov in the next chair. He squeezed my shoulder and I grinned a greeting at him. I knew Maxim Trulov better than most of the Russians there, partly because he was more outgoing than most, but also because he led a computer information project that gave us some machine help with our pile of raw data. He was a big man who could be very funny, and who laughed a lot, his large, round, flat face a happy coin beneath the pompadour of dark hair he kept always slicked straight back, like someone in the 1930's. His eyes were large, dark brown, and glowing, against the Asiatic ivory of his skin. Today, as always, he wore a tailored woollen suit, looking for all the world like an American lieutenant of homicide. In fact, the word on Trulov was that he held the rank of major in the KGB, but that he was also human: there had been an affair with one of the Austrian secretaries before his wife and daughter came over. It gave him an aura of harmless fallibility, and perhaps it was a deliberate effort to moderate a competing aura of raw strength and ugly temper—like the grey shades covering the chairman's piercing eyes.

Now Trulov leaned toward me and whispered, "Schaefer, what is this 'woolly'?" His English was very American, and almost perfect, but with unexpected idiomatic gaps. To my ear his accent was North American, but unstable, ranging widely from New York to California, with touches of Boston and Quebec thrown in.

I laughed. "The polite terms would be obscure, fuzzy. Really, it means they think it's bullshit."

He grinned. "So what else is new?" Trulov liked coming from The Other Side, enjoyed telling Americans about what he called Life Behind the Iron Curtain, lacing the terms with heavy sarcasm and contempt, and how we both came from revolutionary societies, and about the eighteen months he'd spent at Stanford, getting laid, learning that all grass was not in lawns, studying systems management, and becoming knowledgeable, as well as humorous, about the United States. He liked to give the impression of being independent, a Russian on his own. He turned to me again. "Are you going tonight?"

"Where?"

"We have a *Heuriger* evening for the Committee. Even if our leader dies, the *Heuriger* goes on, although with perhaps a little vodka thrown in on top of that Austrian wine. All the project scientists are invited, of course."

"Maybe I will." The prospect of an evening's drinking in company pleased me, and it was a hell of a lot better than gnawing away on my bottle of Stolichnaya alone. "Where is it?"

"Here," he said, taking out a folded sheet of paper. "Take my map. I can find these places with my nose. It goes from nineteen hours to infinity."

"I'll try to get Dexter to go."

"You might come with Emil Dashko and me, but, you know, someone might think we were friends. I like you, Schaefer, but not enough to spend so much time eating rock soup and sawing trees." He chuckled, folded his thick arms, and leaned back, taking in the meeting with apparently boundless good nature. But in this repose, you could see the iron in him, the easy cruelty of the cop.

That peculiar stillness settled over the group once more. The chairman had been summoned by Wöber, Andrews' gofer, and hurried out of the room. Moments later he was back in place, to tell us about death. Without sitting down, he lifted a long, pale hand and said, "I must now interrupt our proceedings with very sad news. The Soviet embassy has just informed me that President Leonid Ilyich Brezhnev died last night at eight-thirty Moscow time. Now, if you would, please join me in standing for a minute of silent tribute to this great leader." We stood, linked by the faraway passing of a powerful tyrant, in a country that was then as remote to me as the moon. That was all the chairman said about it. A tough man, contained, without a single outward sign that he saw what would come: the secret chaos beginning to unfold at home, his fortunes rising or falling with the result. He seemed to take the darker possibilities with equanimity, as medieval earls in Shakespeare's histories stare unblinkingly at the end of everything.

Something else happened in that minute of silence. It might have been just the collective energy with which everyone there was forced to think of large, impending changes, of dangerous instabilities ahead. It might have been some reflexive exchange between people in the room—a look, a twitch, a scratch. God knows. But something had just barely flickered, there had been a faint, electric signal that told you, if only you'd been able to read it...what? That things were not what they seemed, I guess. The way a light skin of phosphorescence tells you the night is not simply a black sphere, but half ocean, with move-

ment and watery terrain. It was that kind of hint, that
vague. Then we all sat down. The moment passed.

But when Trulov turned back to me, his large, velvet
eyes had ice in them for an instant before the cheerful
warmth returned. Max was a cop, and he had seen something dimly illuminated the way a cop would, completing
some Gestalt his unconscious had floated near the surface. At the time, knowing nothing, I felt merely bewildered by his change, and chilled. Only much later did I
understand that, in our minute of silence for Brezhnev, in
that random juxtapositioning of figures, Max Trulov had
made the mental leap everyone had always been afraid
of—made it, mistrusted it, but began to *think* about it.
When the killing started, I would remember that change,
that chill, that minute given to an old man's death, when
Max and I began a steady journey toward our own.

2

I FLED THE MEETING before we broke for lunch, fleeing
both the heavy mid-day meal of pork, dumplings, and
dessert, but also the nonsense; for, after their mild cen-
sure, the delegates would be mesmerized by a big lunch, a
few liters of local wine, the cozy feel of a good men's club,
and the crushing nostalgia, and would conclude their sessions with a strong endorsement of whatever happened to
be going on. The Centre would close, I guessed, when I
was back in La Jolla. There would be the five lines from
the Associated Press, or perhaps nothing beyond a few
sentimental contributions to Op-Ed pages in Washington
and New York, and a mock-bereaved editorial in *Science*.

Still, I believed, and I think most of the other scientists
there also believed, that my own work at the Centre was
worth doing, that the nonsense emanated from somebody
else. I thought our little carbon dioxide project would finish in a year or two with something interesting—nothing
definitive, just interesting—and I know Gordon Dexter did

too. However, the morning's hollow superlatives and critiques had left me feeling silly and uselessly employed, so that I was also running toward the rough, rational sound of my ursine colleague.

I found it in the two high, narrow rooms we shared in the west wing of the castle, where angry grunts emerged from a huge rat's nest of computer printouts and weather maps. And there, prowling around on all fours went my meteorologist, grumbling ferociously about something. "Bloody wogs," he was growling, "bloody culture-bound *idjits*," and on and on, as he hunted for whatever he had lost in the mess.

The solid reality of him cheered me immediately. "Lose a contact lens, Gordy?"

He reared up in an explosion of paper, standing like a grizzly with his large arms spread in fake despair. "The goddamned woman's gone and hid my pipe," he wailed. "My bloody pipe. I can't work without a pipe, you know that, Schaefy." His tangled hair, the mixed orange, black, and white of a collie, was more tangled than usual, his green eyes more red rimmed, his stubbly chin more stubbled. He wore a light woollen turtleneck that had begun to change color from oatmeal into greasy grey, and Levi bushpants with all six pockets bulging full, and blue thongs. I thought, as I had many times before, that what he needed was a hyacinth macaw on one shoulder, and a couple of four-inch golden earrings, and perhaps a black patch over one of his rabbity eyes.

"I'll help you look," I said. "Have you tried your desk?"

"None of your damned cheek, now," Dexter mumbled, returning to his burrowing.

Our project rested on a mountain of paper. My corner of the office had carbon dioxide data taken during three major ocean surveys, one by the U.S. in the equatorial Pacific a few years before, another, by the Soviet Union in the Barents Sea, and a third international project in the Atlantic. Our getting the Barents Sea data out of the Russians was seen, especially by our excitable director, as a major gift to the Centre, but it virtually guaranteed us a Russian partner on the project. "Exciting news, Gordy," I began, as my hand swept through the litter on his desk, feeling for the large curve of the missing meerschaum.

One could tumble into the silence generated by Dexter's powerful listening. Now the office entered such an interval, the rampage through rolls of paper ceased abruptly. Into this attentive pause I said, "The director announced who our Russian colleague will be."

"God, man, go on, go on, can't you see I'm all ears?"

"Valentina Orlovsky, from the..."

"Institute for Oceanology of the USSR Academy." He drew himself up into an immense half-lotus on the brown carpeting. "That's quite good, you know. She's right out of the top drawer...for a, um, Russian, of course. Do you know her?"

"Only by reputation."

"Ah," and he gave a great laugh. "That explains it, you poor ass. I know exactly what you think, with your idiotic American preconceptions. Exactly what you think. Hairy legs, you think, and bad teeth, and big bazooms, and kind of stupid in a peculiarly Mongolian way, and probably not quite up to her reputation, like a Russian athlete, you know, pumped up a bit with steroids and gold. So you're just the slightest bit disappointed..."

"Some, yes." But he had begun to make me pout.

"Come on, now, bear up. We can't be messing about this way. We need to find my pipe."

The material we searched through was a complex set of data, much more really than a score of us could handle easily. Three people could only scratch the surface, but we thought we could scratch it productively.

It's a dull schoolboy who can't tell you about the so-called "greenhouse" effect of carbon dioxide in the atmosphere, and how too much carbon dioxide could shift climate patterns, change lives, and possibly add a few fathoms of ocean from melted polar ice caps. But nobody knows for sure what to expect, whether the expected change means a global desert or a global garden; everybody would like it to be more predictable.

What we wanted to do, in a very modest way, was develop mathematical techniques for estimating the rates of CO_2 exchange between the ocean, atmosphere and ocean, which is the planet's second largest reservoir of carbon, and, a powerful wild card in the climatic deck. We had no thought of being able to exceed the abilities of the big computers at Bracknell and Princeton. We had in mind the fashioning of a primitive predictive tool, something mathematical with about the complexity of a rake, say, that would help the regiments of scientists looking at the problem. It seemed modest and do-able.

Dexter and I considered it very much worth doing, especially on those days when the Centre's trick mirrors reflected us as terribly tall and thin, or grotesquely fat, or smiling when sad. For the Centre was an administrative nuthouse even more than a scientific one. We barely knew from one day to the next what our funding would be, or how long it would be there, or when some political shudder would cut us loose for reasons totally unrelated to our work or abilities. Because the CO_2 problem was, for the Centre, kind of sexy and newsworthy, we had been protected from the worst of the fiscal insanities, but many had not. Emil Dashko, a Soviet economist and strong friend of ours, spent his life waiting for the axe to take another slice out of his dwindling pie, as the Powers slowly forced him out, no one knew why, at a time when the Centre had hired its first *astrologer* to help with the Carnival Project.

"You know, Gordy, I think it may help us, having a Russian."

He stood up in another shower of paper. "You do, do you? Well, good. At last the Yank begins to see how the stuff is spread over here. But you're right, Schaefy, they don't mind shitting on us Anglos, but they're loath to do it on a Russian..."

"Emil's case to the contrary..."

"Yes, notwithstanding poor Emil. In general, though, Russians keep things pretty stable. God, if the Soviet Union dropped out, she'd take the whole bloody east bloc with her. The west should enjoy such *solidarnos*, eh?" He added with a twinkle, "So we should be happier with our hairy whoor of a Russian . . ."

"God, what a bastard I drew. What a . . ." But I'd seen something. "I'm going to crack you, Dexter."

"Aye, are you now?" His eyebrows arched; he drew himself up, ready as a bear to be angry, wary of this new tack.

"Crack you, sir. Yes. I've found your pipe, sir."

"Where . . . ?" He glanced around wildly.

"To find out, you must do a *spawt* of work."

"Yes?" His voice contained the muted snap of the rather annoyed.

"I want you to go with me to the committee's *Heuriger* thing tonight.

"Well, perhaps if we don't stay till all hours . . ."

"Thanks."

"My pipe."

"Pipe? *Pipe?*"

"Listen . . ." His face went rosey.

"Look in your pants pocket, lost person. No . . . not the side pocket, the one below." I had noticed the pistol shape of the meerschaum in the lower pocket of his bush pants. He patted it now, and grinned shamelessly for me.

"You know, I can't imagine its having been there all along. Did you plant it on me, Schaefy? Did you now?" He took it out and began to stuff it from his pouch, which had mercifully not been "lost." "I believe," he said when the pipe exhaled its huge, sweet cloud into the room, "you must have planted it on my person. Perhaps you sedated me. Or hypnotized me. Hypnotism's catching on with the police, *New Scientist* reports. Not that a bobby could hypnotize a rock, but among the Higher Services it's regarded as something of a tool. I imagine that's how the Centre got into its latest abyss of shit, that poor bastard

Ivanov let himself get hypnotized." Dexter made his pink eyes go large and empty. "By a chicken, no doubt, or a child."

"What abyss?"

"The American CIA's leaked a secret report to the *Washington Post* saying the computers here are probing classified western ones. Of course, a man in your position, would've heard about it, but I'm reporting anyway, patriotic duty, and all that."

I waved away his silliness. "That's going to kill American funding."

"Not to worry. Nobody believes it, really. Everybody knows we're not clever enough for such work. But if there weren't something going on, then we wouldn't have this Russian kneejerk response crying 'CIA smear campaign'."

"Seriously, what do you think?"

"Difficult to be serious with you, but I shall try. I suppose that what the CIA say they *think* we're doing is the purest sort of cock. But you don't get smoke without something on fire, do you? And the Russians *always* have something going on. It's their greedy nature. They always go home with more—more wallpaper, more data, more tennis balls, more anything at all—than they came with. We just don't know what kind of more this is. Perhaps you were dropped in to find out, eh, Schaefer?"

3

WE SHARED AN ODD, quickly forged friendship, Gordon Dexter and I, one based mainly on his good instincts, which were deep and perceptive, and healing. His clowning in the office had been more than just his search for a "lost" pipe; it had also been his way of acknowledging that I'd picked up some burden at the morning meeting, and he would help me clear it all away. Now, watching the big man bent intently over the steering wheel of his maroon and silver Citroen, what he called his Wee Froggie, I was struck by how little I knew about this shaggy friend.

In his Real Life—which is the way we referred to life before and after the Centre, like infantry soldiers overseas, speaking of The World—he was a research meteorologist at Bracknell and a scientist of some high reputation, which he took pains to screen with eccentricity, in the English manner. One sensed he had been painfully conditioned in some profound and lasting way, so that there had not been time or heart for families or a host of friends; he gave the impression of having even fewer people in his life than I had in mine, which may have encouraged our affinity. He had hated it when I'd moved into the wreck of his office. But then, as we recognized that neither of us budged in our determination to have the place to ourselves, we decided to make an accommodation or two, and began to speak, and take lunch together, and eventually share rides back to Vienna. Then we were drinking buddies, stopping for a cold *Krügel* of beer or two of an evening. And finally we arrived, in an oblique and hard-humored way, at that point where we would extend ourselves for one another. Still, while he talked about himself night and day, he revealed nothing.

He seemed to drive through life the way he drove his car, with the near-sighted, unhappy concentration of a trained bear on a motorcycle, and hardly ever faster than seventy kilometers an hour. Driving with him in Austria, with its madly careening cars, was like running an artillery barrage—exhilarating, but with some doubts about survival. The other cars whizzed around us like bright bullets, some playing a long, descending sneer upon their horns. "Goddamn them all," he muttered now, noting a fresh pair of agitated headlights barely a meter behind his rear window. He had muttered since we'd begun our slow progress across the Danube bottom lands south of the city, and climbed slowly up through the rolling vineyards to the west, rendered in pale greys and pools of black shadow by the November moon behind us. Beyond these sparsely lighted foothills one could see the larger darkness of the Alps, and the bright sky. "Ah, but we've not very far to go with these lunatics…" A glowing, honking burst of traffic sped by, and away through the vineyards, as if they chased each other.

One night we had decided to force Vienna to prepare a decent martini, and had consumed several glassfulls of vermouth slightly tainted with gin in the training process. Reeking and with a slight spin, we had arrived at the Blue Bar of the Sacher Hotel, where, tieless, we could only be served in the crimson, tapestried sitting room next door. But the English-speaking bartender understood our needs, and fed us a quantity of good martinis while we talked— or, rather, while I talked, for Dexter slipped quickly into his powerful listening mode. And having this dedicated ear, this intent audience, and too much gin, triggered in me that conversational reflex one has after a long ocean voyage, returning to the world, its tributaries and mainstreams. Then one finds a bar and someone to talk to for the evening. For oceanography is, among all the other things it is, a sanctuary for the solitary. You find a lot of stammerers among us, stammerers of the kind whose efforts to utter the unutterable make you hold your breath in sympathy. Well, you also find a high incidence of poets and musicians, and people who have had too little warmth from the world, people who at their centers are chilled and alone and unconnected, as though they sprang from eggs buried in the sand. "Their susceptibilities are crippling," I had told Dexter. "They take their loneliness to the ocean… because nothing else *holds*."

I had paused, then, assessing whether to continue. Beyond this point were monsters. Easy as she goes. Soft. Yes, and I had also wondered why this man listened so hard that he drew words out of one. "Their susceptibilities," he'd cued me then, reminding me that he listened. We might have been in the latticed cage of a confessional, so easy was it to move on to admissions of chasms and cracks.

So I told him about all the death in my life, death that made one's mental horizons shiver with a fearful light, one's stomach ache and gnaw upon itself, one's brain go over and over and *over* the loss, singing an ordinary name the way a bell sings its single note. I told him about Nancy, who, two years before, had come into my shipboard lab as a colleague. She had been one of those golden California girls, but without the pout of starlets, genuine and smart and strong, with the integrity of a drilling rig, a way of welcoming everyone and everything, of bringing it all in. She joined me in the business of reading chemical secrets in seawater, and all the crew and scientists and no doubt the seagulls and dolphins themselves fell in love with her; but I most of all. God knows, it was mythical and unexpected, like being plucked from a storm by a mermaid. One can't be critical, when a woman strikes a chord way the hell down in one's center, completes some fundamental process that must have germinated in my marrow, in the embryonic I—something terribly, fearfully, deep within. I handled all this carefully, nervously, turning it over and over in wonder, afraid I would finally break the charm, like a monster, delighted by a bird, crushing her between enthusiastic hands.

We threw in together, as we put it, on that same cruise, the rejected shipload of admirers all still in love with Nancy, celebrating our happiness, unable *not* to celebrate hers. We seemed to have no dark side. Sometimes, seeing us reflected in a shop window angled so that recognition is delayed. I would marvel at their happiness, *those* two...ah, *we* two. She filled and warmed those cold and empty regions of mine that had been given to the sea. She embodied intellect, talk, sex, home, hearth, everything. There was neither shadow nor complaint. And then, one day, she was gone. Everyone was gone, Nancy, my parents, everybody, suddenly wiped off the coast highway, leaving behind a world turned cold and silent. "Nothing holds, finally," I told him, "nothing is intelligible. What chord was it that

Nancy touched, that made it all seem so predetermined? I'll never know.''

Dexter had nodded, knowing I talked myself into a kind of spell, not wanting to shatter it just then, but also not wanting it to stand too long. "There is nothing to be done for loss," he said after awhile. "The world has really neither joy, nor love, nor light, nor certitude, nor help for pain, as the gentleman says. Parents and children, men and women, why we're all like drums and bells for one another, and the world is very silent when the playing stops. Still, I do know this, too. We have women in the world with us, and, whatever else they may do, you can trust them always to *say* the necessary, *do* the necessary, to draw another woman's poison, or mitigate our loss of one. They're wonderful in that way, really," he went on, letting his features mobilize a doggy grin, leading me gently back from my boozy confessional. "At least, for awhile, you're safe for the combat of romance." He laughed gently. "And now you're in one of the very best posts available, a veritable *Burma* of sexual intrigue. It's a flaming *aviary* of English birds, and Austrian ones, and Germans and even a Japanese if you must, or an Indian, or, if you are very self-defeating and discreet, *Russians*. Sample them all. Sample them until your heart begins to feel like a great thumping lump of tantalum carbide and you can't quite remember the name of that shadowy, fine-smelling silhouette being humped. And then, my friend, you will be ready for the Real Thing again. Or, not." He shrugged philosophically. "One might get to liking the Unreal Thing, follow?''

But my memory of that night was not so much of what I said, or that I said too much, or of his grand good humor and help for pain. No, what I remember most clearly is seeing him, after his hardhearted monologue, after our relieved laughter, after another martini, turn away from me, hiding rusty eyes that ran with tears. Detecting my interest, then, he'd croaked, "Ah, me, we've had a *lot* to drink this night, have we not?''

No doubt we would again tonight, I thought, rousing myself from revery to glance at the big, wildhaired man who stared fixedly into the flashing lights of passing cars, and drove as tentatively as an animal, trained to do it without understanding why. All his talk of combat and sampling girls, the endless crucifixion of a world of "wogs," and all the rest was just a smokescreen. Under the grumping lived a lonely, sensitive man with a heart of gold. A delightful phoney.

That night's *Heuriger* was high on the hill where the touristy old town shades suddenly into more vineyards, the land then running sharply up to sky. We entered beneath the hanging bunch of pine twigs that tells you a *Heuriger* is open, past an iron gate into a broad courtyard. A barricade of noise met us at the entrance door, loud laughing voices yelling in German. Near the center of the crowd, a man who must have been in his eighties yodeled from behind an accordion. Only the waitresses were quiet, determinedly, stoically, sailing back and forth between the customers and the wine, big, plain, middle-aged blondes, half-beautiful in their *Dirndls*, that pretty peasant dress in which no one is ugly, and a beautiful woman can take your breath away. The bodice does it, tightly hooked, rising beneath the breasts, which hang out into the atmosphere, covered by a starched, often very low-cut, white blouse. The costume invites familiarity of a certain type—the impulse is to take the proffered breasts very gently in your hands—while also exuding the innocence of a christening dress. It attracts lewd men, but may protect the wearer from them; although, the costume is unquestionably made for haystacks, meadows, country matters. Well, perhaps I was a bit of a *Dirndl* buff, but I could hardly take my eyes off any reasonably pretty costumed female. Noting this, Dexter snarled from a corner of his mouth, "You're a flaming *embarrassment*, Schaefy."

"Sorry." But, roughly slapped back into reality, I asked one of the women in very bad German where the people from the Centre were. She gave me a tolerant smile and replied in faintly accented English that we should be in the next room. Dexter heard, and led us off toward an arched doorway cut in the thick, cream-colored plaster, into a long, narrow room where a blue tile stove glittered like a ceramic throne. Heavy, unfinished beams crossed the high ceiling, and, on the stucco of the walls, hung a cemetery of game, stuffed rabbit, boar, and beer, and dozens of tiny antlered skulls, taken from the dog-sized deer. A dozen small, whiteclothed tables had been arranged end to end to form a long line that bowed around the stove, set with vases of carnations and liter pitchers of white and red wine, and glasses.

We got there early, but the place was already crowded with delegates and colleagues, all kept on their feet by the uncertainties of protocol, unable to calculate the proper distance from the chairman and director. The latter had a glass and a cigarette in one hand, and made grand gestures with the other, as he talked animatedly, in a rush of superlatives, to the American named Lincoln, who watched the room like a conductor matching bodies with tickets. Andrews bent deferentially toward old Hydeminster, the U.K. delegate, who was speaking in his elliptical, impatient way of the Centre's poor work. Wöber, always the minion, trembled just beyond, living on scraps of important conversations. Across the room, the Polish deputy had cornered poor Morely, the melancholy little man from Ottawa, and wrapped the Canadian's brain with opaque cloths of logic. Small, national clusters had formed here and there in the room, Scandinavians with Scandinavians, Czechs with Czechs, Spanish with Spanish, so that the air teemed with odd tongues.

"Dr. Braun?" someone said almost inaudibly behind me. I turned to find the chairman regarding me with those strange, caved, brilliant eyes. His voice was barely more than a whisper, and yet it had a kind of clarity, even against the noise of the room. "I am Andrei Pastukh, unfortunately absent today when you were introduced."

I extended my hand. "Very good to meet you."

He gave me a firm, warm handshake. "I am afraid we shall not have much chance to talk here . . . may I call you Schaefer?" I nodded. "Good," he said, without asking that I call him Andrei. "But I would like to make time before I return to the Soviet Union. Perhaps tomorrow?"

"Sure. Do you want Gordon Dexter, too?"

"I think you will be enough, thank you. I want to hear more about your work, both at the Centre and in the United States. You are the first oceanographer we have had here, you see."

He smiled his imperturbable smile once more; but there was something troubled and nervous in his manner too. So, I thought, the death at home has him worried after all. I said, "That was bad news this morning . . ."

"Yes, it was. Even when such things are anticipated for a long period of time, the actual event can be quite sad." He frowned suddenly at something across the room. "What is Maxim up to?" he asked rhetorically. He gestured almost imperceptibly, as a master might to a well-trained dog, and Trulov pushed away from the wall and eased his large bulk through the crowd of smaller men. "Maxim," the chairman said, "you look awful. What is the matter?"

Trulov grinned sheepishly. "I was . . . I was just thinking about things," he said. "You know, drifting with melancholy thoughts."

But Pastukh would not let him off. "You worry me when you look like that. Where is your joy?" As he asked this, one heavy eyebrow raised, the bright eyes twinkled, the broad, thin mouth gave a slight lift. It was interesting to watch, like a trainer with a big cat, like Prospero running Caliban—one felt the deft, gentle application of power.

"I shall put on a happier face," Trulov said, forcing an exaggerated smile. He was obedient, but you could see he didn't like to go through a hoop in public. If Caliban, he looked capable eventually of hurling his magician into the sea.

"Good, thank you," Pastukh replied dryly. "Well, you are incorrigible after all." He turned away from the Russian and said to me, "Now please excuse me . . . I need to circulate, as you say. But I look forward to our talk tomorrow." We shook hands again, and he moved away into the crowd. Trulov stayed with me.

"Something wrong?" I asked him, deciding to be direct.

"Nothing, Schaefer." The cold light had gone out of his eyes, but he watched me interrogatively, asking me a question I could not understand; something like: have you anything to tell me, before it is too late?

"I thought maybe a word in invisible ink had appeared on my forehead."

He gave it a brittle chuckle. "Nothing like that. I am just . . . drifting, as I said. The President's death, changes ahead, the condition of the Centre. The usual things. Vera's headaches."

"Is she here tonight?"

"No, she stayed home after all."

"Hope she feels better."

"She will. But thank you, Schaefer." He made a shallow bow and walked into a Bulgarian group which the room's currents had brought within reach.

Dexter had percolated around until he'd found a corner, where he camped, watching the players, listening powerfully, and sucking up all the wine in sight. I poured myself a *Viertel* of red and decided not to join him, wanting suddenly to be alone. I found a nearly vacant window that admitted a whisper of cool night air into the overheated room, and simply stood there, cooling off, watching distant lights, sipping my wine. My mind idled about the next day's talk with the chairman, which, for reasons I could not have explained, made me slightly anxious, like the examination which faces the dreamer who has not attended class all year; and an awareness I could not quite shake of something sour between Trulov and me. Suddenly chilled, I gave a shiver.

"Somebody walked on your grave." It was Lincoln, smiling a cold greeting when our eyes met.

I said, "Sometimes I think my grave's under a shopping mall."

"Know what you mean. Fact is, the American hypothalamus can't handle the European tendency to overheat and underair." I nodded, being friendly, but also reluctant to spend much time with Lincoln. "Fascinating man, isn't he?" he volunteered, as if determined that the conversation should proceed.

"Who?" I was still with Trulov.

"Academician Pastukh. The chairman."

"Oh. Yes, he is. Very."

"Had you met before?"

"No."

"I guess you and I haven't either, at least not formally. I'm Baker Lincoln. And you're Schaefer Braun." He extended a plump, hard hand, which I shook; it felt like hairy wax. "You must miss the ocean," he said.

"I'm enjoying Vienna."

"A pretty old girl of a town."

"Yes."

"Good team they've put together, you and Dexter and the Orlovsky woman. Do you know her?" I thought I saw an ugly creature move behind his eyes, but shook my head. "I've only seen her at a distance, read some of her work. I think you will find her a...an interesting colleague. I mean, *you* will in particular."

"Good," I said. I could feel his forcing, his manipulative impulse. It made me uncomfortable, and I moved to leave. "Well..." I began, extricating myself.

But Lincoln wouldn't let me go that easily. "It always amuses me that we think of Pastukh as *ours*. I mean, we seem to think this little hobbyhorse is all he does, when, in point of fact, he is a rather large figure at home. He's almost certain to succeed Aleksandrov at the Soviet Academy of Sciences, no matter how the present transition goes. I'm frankly surprised he finds any time for the Centre."

"People need their hobbyhorses."

"Yes. He likes the Centre. He got it going, really, got it through that Soviet resistance to new things. And he's sentimental about it."

"Everyone is."

"You've noticed? It keeps the place open."

"Probably." I kept as quiet as I could, wanting more and more to be free of this man. He emanated manipulation, you could feel him clutching at you in some ulterior way. I shivered.

"Beneath a shopping mall, as you said." He flashed an opaque grin that told me he missed nothing. "But maybe the chairman is in this for Vienna. Something to lighten the Russian gloom." He gazed across the room at Pastukh, who had joined Andrews. The two men spoke with easy, respectful camaraderie, a son in the company of a powerful father. "Look there," Lincoln said. "They seem happy enough, don't they? But how close are they really, I wonder." Then, after a pause, "Have you been there?"

"Where?"

"Russia."

"Not yet."

"You'd find it interesting. But gloomy. Too little play," he added. His eyes told me something else: you'll never see Russia, forget Russia, Russia's not for you. Then, before I could turn away, he nailed me in place with a burst of confidence. "Look, Schaefer, I'm not being very candid with you."

Trapped and curious, I said, "I don't understand."

"I've approached you as a total stranger. Fact is, I know quite a lot about you. It was rude of me not to show my hand more clearly." Nothing in his face cared the slightest damn about candor, or courtesies, or me. He would lick the queen mother's hand at court and coldly hold her eye afterward, all brass, for no little canary of conscience lived within this Lincoln. "I brought your article on the carbon dioxide problem to the Centre's attention, and also did a little homework on you."

"Homework?" I rose to the new note of self-satisfaction in his voice.

"You know, a superficial background check."

"How would you do that?"

"It's very easy to do, unless you want to know somebody's innermost thoughts."

"I imagine that's more difficult."

He laughed harshly. "Yes, but everything's possible, you know. But, seriously...in the interest of supporting your recruitment by the Centre, I wanted to have a little information. A credit-card company would have probed deeper than I did. No offense, I hope."

"There's not much to reveal," I said. "It's kind of a blank book."

"I found it so. Born in California, parents dead about a year, school, work. Not much except work, actually. And yet..."

"And yet?"

"You'd expect there to be more. More play. More people. More...continuity, maybe. Your life looked like one blind alley after another. And camouflaged, desert dun."

I laughed through my discomfort. "I guess there's no law forcing people to be colorful."

"Of course there isn't. And, please, I hope all this personal talk hasn't offended you. I sometimes get carried away, being an, um, amateur. You understand."

"Sure."

"Perhaps I feel proprietary about you...being a patron of what is very likely the only ocean chemist in all of Austria." He added then, "In a way, I guess you'd say I discovered you." He seemed to draw pain from the idea, which he quickly concealed.

"Well...thanks."

"You like it here?"

"Very much."

"I hope it works well for you."

"I'm sure it will."

"Better than La Jolla did."

I bridled. "La Jolla was fine. I'm returning when this is over." Nothing happened to my work, Lincoln, just to my life. My empty, colorless little life, you preening bastard.

"Well, more play, perhaps."

"Maybe."

He hesitated, loath to leave me, and reflected upon some detail in the tile floor, some speck, some moving thing. "I wonder if this is just natural antipathy or something more."

"Something less."

"But, you see, you know exactly what I mean. You hardly know me, and yet I can feel your strong dislike. Odd. One wonders if it's hereditary or something... why would you have that reflex?"

"I think we've talked enough, Lincoln."

"Not nearly. If I didn't have a plane to get tomorrow I'd tell you why... but it can wait."

"Forever."

"Oh, we'll have our talk, all right." He gave a smile that had nothing in it but cruelty, a cold uplifting of the mouth's grim corners, almost a snarl of his small white teeth. His face was what a puppet would see, glancing up its strings toward the cruel master, illuminated from within by... hatred. Hatred of the puppet, hatred of the strings. My own immediate dislike of him was just a reflection of his larger hatred of me, that burned behind his eyes. But *why*? Jesus, *why* such hatred?

"Have a nice flight," I said, stained by the encounter, and shaken by the growing realization that this cold stranger, this man who so visibly hated me, knew far more about me than I did. It left me chilled and, if confusion can be fear, frightened. In all my lonely life, that dun-colored life in which so little moved, I could not remember feeling more alone.

4

A GENERAL MOVEMENT in the room pushed us all toward
the tables, freeing me from Lincoln. I searched for Dexter, my lifeboat in these floods, and found that he had
shifted position and now knelt in the extraordinary company of Emil Dashko, the Soviet economist whose projects were being eroded by the gradual withdrawal of
support. In a way, erosion was what Emil was all about,
for he lived in the closing fist of one of those rare but effective diseases that reduce you finally to nothing but
thoughts, and then to nothing at all. Dashko's barely au-
dible voice seemed to speak directly from his vibrant mind,
which glowed from eyes so vividly intelligent that they
imparted to the small, smashed man a luminous beauty.
He spent his life crumpled into an electric wheelchair, able
to drive it with a small panel of control buttons; able to
see, and think, and converse if one could get close enough
to hear. He was Gordon Dexter's favorite Russian, of
whom he had said, "If all Russians were like Emil, why,
they could *have* Europe and no problem." The two of
them spent hours together at the castle. One saw them,
Dexter huge and deferential, kneeling or sitting nearby, the
great tousled head tilted close to the murmuring voice; the
other, tiny, looking as though God had pressed him into
place with a big cruel thumb.

Perhaps Dashko drew some physical strength from the
presence of large, healthy men, for his other close friend
was Trulov, who oversaw the ministrations of the Russian
nurse one knew Emil must have at home, who made it
possible for Emil to work outside the Soviet Union, and to
escape into evenings like this one. The two men were very
close, and there was a kind of love between them. Even
Dexter, joining them occasionally, could not connect with
the molecule they formed; you would see the three of
them, moving slowly like figures in a pastoral play across
a sweep of open park, and then Dexter falling behind,

watching, turning away, while the other two continued their quiet progress.

My own relationship with Emil was good but shallow. We knew and noticed one another, and occasionally talked along convergent interests—climatic change was one of the unsynchronized features of the Soviet system that people like Emil hoped to bring into better synchronization. I thought that, if he lived, and I did, we would become friends, and the three or four of us would perambulate in the park, talking, exchanging jokes; odd comrades. I wonder now how much of this kind of speculation came from liking Emil Dashko, and how much from a fundamentally sentimental view of the Soviet Union.

To many western Europeans, Russia was eternally Russia, a great nation to the east, run by lunatics and gangsters, an outlaw nation you could depend on only for bullying and subversion. Calling it the Soviet Union merely acknowledged that the powerful had exchanged one corrosive ideology for another, the idea of communist domination in place of the old Russophilic God. "A bunch of bloody criminals, that's all you can say about them," Dexter would say. Such views sounded blind and irresponsible to me. A few international experiments had given me a glimpse of great good fellowship among the Soviet scientists, unbelievable generosity, and wonderful humor, sentiment, affection. Of the other side, the paranoid, secret side, where Russian hospitality becomes the guest whose throat the host has cut, the Gulag side, the bullying side that spied and subverted and killed as willingly as any servant of a Mahdi—of that side, I had no knowledge beyond the wildly conspiratorial ones you find in thrillers. By that November, I had just begun to feel the encroaching ideology, which ruins science as surely as it ruins art and agriculture, and a kind of greed, perhaps induced by the eternal shortages back home, and almost an eagerness to abuse any institution. But on the whole, my view of Russians then was not a balanced one, but inclined toward them; so that it took me an ungodly long time to think they could be my deadly enemies.

But Emil Dashko drifted free of all this, a crippled compliment to his own system. I carried two cherished memories of him, one demonstrating his integrity, the other his belief in the Soviet system. The first was when the Czech began tweaking the Soviet nose with the old story about Russia taking over the Sahara ("A month later word is coming back: we have run out of sand.") Against the laughter came the purr of Emil's chair; he left the room in protest.

The other memory was of his impassioned speech, at the same retreat, when, parked in the center of a U of tables, he raised his thin, breathless voice in a plea for less abstraction, more concrete, focused research on more tangible problems, "so that we can find *consistency*," he cried, almost with tears in his huge, bright eyes. "We need to have *con-sis-ten-cy*." It rang like a minister's plea for a sign from God, and, really, Dashko was that kind of communist, a person who believed in his system the way a priest believes in Jesus Christ—that is, to a degree that outsiders can scarcely credit. He had begged us to join his search for consistency, for repeatable results, for a predictable and workable system, so that Soviet planners could finally tune the outsized Russian economic engine.

Emil, Dexter, and I took three seats side by side, far from the director and the chairman, with Dashko between us.

"Hello, Emil," I whispered to him, shaking one of his little claws.

"Hello, Schaefer. How are you?" he hissed.

"Good, thanks." You never asked him how he was.

"We have been watching the crowd," he told me, painfully rotating his head to hold my eye. "Very interesting."

"Very," Dexter confirmed. He had begun to help his plate and Dashko's to portions of sliced ham and chicken, bread and cheese, and I undertook to refill our glasses with red wine. "For example," he said, continuing to serve the food that traveled toward us along the table, "he knows the chairman from the war."

"Is that right?"

"We did not really know each other. But we were at the same place at the same time. I was very young then, and only a rifleman. My only talent was in accepting discomfort..." If his blood had been moving as it should have, he would have blushed at this oblique reference to his condition. "I mean, in accepting cold. In winter I would go along the bunkers, doling out vodka to my comrades. Very long ago." He cocked his head away, and stared up the table at the chairman, who, catching the gaze, returned a smile of general friendship, but without any special recognition in it. "Ah, you see," Emil said, "he also remembers nothing. Not that we are what you call army buddies. Hardly that. He was a young captain. We are rounded up together, the day that we liberated Vienna, and photographed for Soviet newspapers. That is what I meant, we had this slight contact." He paused, and you could almost see him stopping some thought, wanting to clarify it further, to fix the idea within. He laughed now. "What I remember is that I remember nothing of him but that, and then, of course, moving northward to Berlin, our paths would cross from time to time. So," and he laughed self-deprecatingly, "my memory is a kind of non-memory, after all."

Dexter had listened closely, and then looked at the chairman, who, noticing this again returned it in a friendly way; he seemed to feel the passing glances of people the way aircraft sensors feel a pulse of radar. But Dexter was attending once again to Dashko's plate, cutting small squares of ham and forking them into the barely open mouth, which, like a carnivorous reef plant, would gently masticate the material, swallow, and begin to wait for more. And I, deciding to participate, held a *Viertel* for Emil while he drank. In this way, we got through the meal almost in silence, feeding our frail Russian plant his meat and bread and wine, gentle as apostles. When he had enough he shook his head and said, "You are neglecting yourselves, my friends," and smiled his gratitude for being so thoroughly fed, with so little fuss. I was pleased at being included. For Dexter, such aid was an old reflex; he often ate with Dashko. We turned to a second liter of wine, and thought of pork chops.

"It is odd how memory works," Dashko mused. "You sit here, month after month, and old comrades come and go, and you recognize some of them, but just barely. And then, one moment, you remember...something. Some chemical, perhaps, makes you suddenly clarify...in the end everything is finally borne to the surface."

"Upwelling," I said.

"You oceanographers, always talking shop," grumped Dexter.

Dashko rambled along. "Tonight, seeing Andrei Pastukh for the first time in months, but also after bumping against him in the scientific hallways of the Soviet Union for many years, I realize he is *not* the familiar face I thought he was, but actually someone *else*..." He hesitated. He had spoken in his quiet, mashed voice, but it had fallen into one of those conversational troughs that stalk all banquets, so that everyone within earshot turned to learn who was "actually someone else." Emil felt the listening going on around him, and finished, "Suddenly you see he is that Russian captain, from the day we freed Vienna."

I thought I saw a shudder of relief run along our segment of the table, touching everyone but Lincoln, whose eyes gave back less than a shark's, and Trulov, who ate busily and paid no attention to us. But all of this is retrospective construction; the incident would have passed out of memory, except that Emil muttered then, barely loud enough for Dexter and me to hear (and I think not intended even for us), "I remember *not* remembering." He gave a tiny wrinkled smile of satisfaction. Another inconsistency had been smoothed. "Schaefer, may I ask for a little more wine, please?"

As I held the *Viertel* for him, we heard the ringing of a spoon against a glass, asking for silence. We all turned to look at Pastukh, who had stood up, obviously prepared to make a speech. Meanwhile, the waitresses hurried along the table, depositing small, chilled glasses of cold vodka.

"Thank you," he began, encouraging our silence. "It is a peculiar thing for us to do, perhaps, to meet like this on the same day we have heard of the loss of a great Soviet leader." Most of us, I think, had forgotten the morning's news, lost it in liters of wine and the evening's conversation. "I believe we are here to offer our toasts to his memory. But also we are here to reassure ourselves. Changes in leadership, especially in the superpowers, can bring intervals of great turbulence. But, in neither system, is this turbulence permitted to destroy the state. When the Centre for Analytic Studies was formed, the climate was right for such a combination of efforts from eastern and western scientists. Tonight, we find ourselves alone. Only we, of all the cooperative efforts instituted in the past two or three decades, still stand, a monument to the desires of the Soviet and American people, and the right-minded people of all nations, that there should be peaceful competition, and cooperation, and friendship between us. But we have turbulence of our own. The global mood has changed. Accusations of abuses from one side or the other have already begun to erode support in certain countries." He pointedly avoided looking at old Addison, the departing American representative, who, like a good delegate, fiddled with a spoon, listening abstractedly. "We must survive our period of turbulence too. The world must have these shelters, where we can discard our ideologies for a time, and speak without politics. I now propose a toast..." He raised his vodka glass; the rest of us bounced up like musketeers. Dexter stood by to feed Dashko his. "I toast the continued spirit of the Centre for Analytic Studies in the name of the late Leonid Ilyich Brezhnev, under whose regime that spirit took root within the Soviet Union. He was a powerful believer both in the Soviet system and the ability of competing nations to live in peace, side by side. We see in his continued personal support for the idea underlying our own Centre a broad, humanist vision, the vision of a great Soviet leader and also of a great Russian soul. Tonight let us toast the memory of this lost leader, demonstrating the depth of our respect for him by the dryness of our glasses when we lower them again. Leonid Ilyich Brezhnev—his bright memory will always remain in our hearts!"

Our arms went up and we tossed back the triple-shot of Russian vodka, the good stuff from their embassy store in Vienna, and let it burn down and down. Before anyone had lowered a glass, I heard Dashko's crash to the floor. He looked at the star of shining fragment. Pastukh, seeing what had happened, said, *"Brezhnev!"* and let his own glass fall to the tiles, where it smashed to dust. Trulov followed suit, immediately, like a soldier. Then the four other Soviets, and then Ivanov and the several Bulgarians, the Polish deputy, the director, a demographer from Israel, the Hungarians, Scandinavians, French, Americans, East Germans, Dutch—one by one, or in staccato bursts of three or four, gleaming powder that settled around our feet. I think some of them were truly commemorating Brezhnev; but most of us had been thrust into this satisfying round of destruction by what we took to be Dashko's embarrassment over an accident. An accident indeed! Looking at him now I saw the ruined face was beaming, and that his eyes were full. God, so were mine, and Dexter's.

When at last the room lay totally silent, caught in the aural shadow of the crashing glass, Pastukh said very softly, "Thank you for that, Comrade Dashko." It was the kind of moment for which I had come.

Of course it ended the evening. Patrons in the outer room had peeked in at us, and the management had complained about the breakage, and the waitresses were grim, cleaning up the mess. But nothing could spoil our moment. Dashko, Dexter, and I went out together, the chair's rubber wheels crackling and sparkling with glass shards, and then Trulov came out to take Dashko home. We said our goodnights and Dexter and I went off down the cobbled streets, searching for the Wee Froggie. And, having found it, Gordy turned it like a galleon for the long expedition back to Vienna.

5

THE CHAIRMAN'S MESSAGE had set our meeting for lunch, at noon, in front of the Schloss. I arrived a few minutes early, but he was there before me, standing with Lincoln between the French vanilla façade of the castle and a black Mercedes sedan, where a big, sad man whose arms were too long for his jacket waited uncomfortably. Pastukh and Lincoln were both dapperly done up, the chairman in his dark diplomatic costume, the American in a traveling kit of tweed, ascot, and an Austrian cap with a spray of feathers in it. I saw them as I rounded the south end of the castle, and from that distance they looked like any pair of successful businessmen, talking golf, or some minor but amusing deal just culminating. But they looked...*familiar*, I mean, familiar with each other, as though there had been a great deal of golf, a lot of deals. Fascinated, I slowed my approach to observe them. I heard Lincoln say, "I told you it was remarkable."

The chairman nodded, but said nothing in reply. Closer to them, I noticed he looked pensive and sad, as if the animation I had seen emanated entirely from the American. "But you believe it, don't you?" Lincoln said then, his voice carrying the harsh note he had used with me the night before.

"I shall let you know." Pastukh paused, seemed to test the air; as he had last night, he sensed and turned toward the faint optical pressure of my interest. He smiled a welcome and when I had come within reach extended a warm hand, which I took, finding it perfectly right, somehow,

our meeting like two old friends. Perhaps that was just his
way of bringing people into his magnetic field, I thought,
this instant familiarity—perhaps that was what I'd seen
between the two men. "Good morning," he said to me.
"Have you met Mr. Lincoln?"

I nodded, and shook hands again with the American,
feeling his dislike around me, ambient as humidity.
"Looks like you had a late night, Schaefer," he said in his
tough voice. It came to me then that he was hanging
around, wanting to get the flavor of this meeting between
the chairman and me. Why? What did he care? There he
stood, radiating his hatred of me, but also curious about
me, wanting to be around me and the chairman. Something drew him, but I couldn't see what it was.

So it relieved me when the miserable driver called, *"Herr
Lincoln, bitte."* Lincoln did not want to let go. I saw him
twitch at having now to leave, at having to yield up whatever it was he'd wanted. The driver fidgeted with a big
digital wristwatch, and finally got out to hurry Lincoln,
whom he almost but not quite walked, police-style, into the
back seat. The American leaned forward, waved unhappily to us; then this evil spirit was accelerated rapidly away,
as though exorcised.

Pastukh almost slumped with relief. He saw me notice
and gave a grin that twinkled; and at the same time he was
surprisingly shy. "Well, now we shall have our lunch," he
said, and led me toward the gate to the park. "I thought
we could have a sort of Habsburg luncheon if you do not
mind a short walk to the lake." Yes, he was very nervous.
Was the lunch an opportunity to tear up my contract? Had
I been *that* bad at the Fourth of July picnic? Later he
would tell me, "It was a desperate move, you understand.
Something had to be done, but where did one begin?
Really, a desperate move. And I had believed most such
moves were behind me by then."

It was another Indian summer day, the air not quite hot,
not quite cool, like the air along the California coast. The
haze that usually filled the Danube River valley had been

flushed away by a small weather system crossing just before dawn. The mountains were visible off to the west, the sky pale blue, the sun dazzling, the park a forest of bewildered trees, caught between summer and their winter sleep. "Beautiful day to be out," I volunteered as we scuffed along the gravel paths.

"Yes, a perfect day."

We arrived at the artificial lake that decorated this corner of Maria Theresa's park, a place surrounded by enormous plane and lime and chestnut trees, and rows of poplars. Across the lake squatted a small castle, built perhaps a hundred years ago by a wealthy Austrian. We had the park pretty much to ourselves, beyond the few old couples laboring around the shoreline, and the patrolling squadron of hungry swans. There would be crowds on the weekend, as everyone squeezed the sun for just one more day or two of summer.

"This is the way to spend November," he said. "It will not be easy to go home."

"What is Moscow like now?"

"It has had freezing days already. We are into our winter, which we generally are even before this." He grinned. "But, you know, one does not mind it so much. It is quite a special winter, dreadfully cold. We like to think it is too cold for any other people."

"That's its reputation."

"Have you visited the Soviet Union?"

"Not yet."

"It is best to go there from the Centre. We are quite welcoming to our colleagues here. We do a great deal of toasting. Well, *most* of us are welcoming, I should say. Let me talk about something to you, if you do not mind."

Ah, I thought, there *is* a reason for all this. It relieved me, to have an explanation on the horizon.

"Maxim Trulov and I had a row about this lunch of ours today. He was quite exercised over it. He told me that this was just the wrong time for me to be having a private lunch with an American, and he even invited himself along. I told him he could not. But he became quite excited." Now he gave me a measured sideways glance. "What do you think of that?"

"I know something's bothering him. I have no idea what."

"Are you someone with whom I should not be seen?"

I laughed. "God, I hope not."

"Good," and he left the little shadow in our conversation quickly and went on to other things. "I have been looking forward to this...this talk with a chemical oceanographer, and I did not want it clouded with politics."

"I have hardly any."

"I take that to mean we can speak our minds here, today, and tomorrow it will not be all over the Centre. That would make it a valuable interlude for me."

"But one can't help but wonder..." I began.

"Why I would ask for this meeting, a friendly walk and lunch, in privacy, with an American I have never met before? Yes, I imagine you do. Well, what are the possible explanations? I wanted to get out of there for a few hours and also wanted to talk about your work, so this seemed a chance to do both. There is something about you I wanted to explore? Perhaps this is an opportunity I have created in order to get to know you better...I mean, to explore an interest I sensed we had in one another..." He caught the flicker of distaste on my face, and amended quickly, "No, of course I do not mean anything like *that*." He passed a large thin hand before his eyes, a gesture of fatigue, and of embarrassment. "Will you do me a particular favor, Schaefer?"

"Of course," I said, still guarded.

"Just take this at face value. Trust me. It is nothing terrible." The expression he turned to me was earnest, deferential again—it was, I realized suddenly, the face of a panhandler, or, no, a salesman who needs very badly to make a sale. When we talked about this moment later, Pastukh would accuse me of making his life that much more difficult. "It was very important that we be on the same level...by which I mean to have us not deferring back and forth and wondering why there was no curiosity, and bridling and perpetually going on guard. God, how you did go on guard, thinking you were out with an aging Russian queen!"

And so I did. But I said, "Face value it is."

We rounded the far end of the lake, and took a bridge that led us back toward the folly. "How do you like the Centre?" he asked.

"I like it."

"After what?...about six months here. If I were to guess, I would say you like it but cannot take it very seriously."

"That would be close to the mark."

"Well, you know, it is not intended to be taken all that seriously. It is not the real world, it is a simulation of it, a funny little model. But, you see, one thing it does provide—you can come here, you can, Soviet scientists can, the world can, and discard ideology, and politics, and even suppress one's keenest sense of his own nation's interests. Not entirely—but to a large degree. I think that makes it worth doing."

"The prevailing view is that it's your scientific...child, I guess."

He looked off across the lake, and I worried for a moment that this had been too frank. "No," he said finally, wearily, "the Centre is not my child. It carries some prestige. I like the absence of ideology. The western contacts are good to have." He gave a very eastern shrug. "And it is good to come to Vienna now and then...like the crows leaving the Ukraine in winter, eh?" Then, "How do you like the old town?"

"Very much. It's..."

"What?" He emanated a strong interest, which surprised me.

"A time machine. It's like living in 1890."

"Ha," he responded. "I know what you mean. People who have known the city for a long time think it is going to hell with the *Autobahns* and cars and those terrible blocks of *Stadt*-financed flats. But I think it...*she*...does not change a great deal. She is very similar now, really, at heart, to what she was when I first saw her. There was something grim then, but there is something grim now. There was also something very beautiful, as there is now. She is a regular Cleopatra of a city."

"When were you first here?"

"In 1945, with the Soviet army. And then, after the war, with the occupation." He looked around the park. "The Schloss was our headquarters, and over by the parking lot we used the meadow for a firing range for the tanks. But, listen...I have spoken with Austrians who were little boys then, living in the village, more or less ignoring the fact that the Soviet Union occupied their town. This park was more a forest, a wilderness. They would sneak out, for we forbade them, to go into the park. The growth was quite dense then, especially if one were small. Imagine, going through this forest as a boy and coming suddenly upon the old bridges, the old shrines and archways, this *castle*, this lake...they told me they played knights out here. A very magical place, or at least it has seemed so to me." And, in the gesture he made with his arms, he seemed for a moment to be the resident magician of the place. "A very magical place."

"Did you know Emil Dashko then?"

"Dashko? No." A new tension touched his features. "Why do you ask?"

"At the *Heuriger* last night, he remembered you from the army. He said something about a photograph the day Vienna fell."

"Ah, *that* photograph. Yes, it is quite a famous one for us, like the flag-raising on Iwo Jima for you. And not entirely spontaneous, either, also like yours. There are half a dozen of us on the roof of the Hofburg, with the stone figures, and we are raising the Soviet flag. So he is there too. Amazing." He gave me a puzzled look then. "But Dashko could not have been there..."

"He was well once."

"Of course."

"He's almost nothing but brain now. As he describes it, memories just pop up to the surface. Rather wonderful, to have such access...but also sad to see him going down..."

"Going down is a bad situation to be in," he said, oddly abstracted.

"But you don't remember Emil?"

"Not from the war. The photograph, yes. That was on April thirteenth, the day Vienna was ours. I remember that day...most vividly."

"What was the city like?"

"A bit damaged, although not nearly so badly as they would have you believe. Nor like the German cities...Aachen..." He shook his head sadly, seeing rubble. "Vienna was only a bit scarred by comparison. And there was that peculiarly Viennese point of view, that cheerful acceptance of adversity masking perennial despair. So that, even then, the flowers were coming out..." He drifted, remembering.

"An Austrian friend says living here now is like living in Russia before the revolution," I offered.

"Russia before the revolution. Hmm. That's quite good. I like that. I believe it explains a lot about the place. Yes, that's quite good. A time machine. You evoke those warm Chekhovian afternoons, you know, with friends in the garden, drinking wine and eating pastries, and exchanging ideas on...what? Novels? Plays?" He frowned. "But also on something just on the horizon. What you may be seeing is not time arrested, but time about to crack. The thing that is like old Tsarist Russia here may not be just people living the good life, but also people who are about to lose that life. Remember that, in a turn-of-the-century political map of Austria, you would have had to color Vienna red. That is one reason it is so comfortable for me and my colleagues, why we occupied her so resolutely for so long—there is that long socialist tradition here. Those ugly Karl Marx Strasse flats were built by the socialist movements of the twenties and thirties, after all, not by the Soviet occupation.

"So it may be your time machine does odd things. Instead of making time stand still, it introduces odd jumps and retreats. It may not be a very efficient machine. And you may find that the period you feel you are in, 1890 you said, is really more like 1917—not Russia before the revolution, but Russia twenty minutes before the revolution."

In this way, talking like students, we crossed the far end of the lake, and arrived back at the miniature castle, where we took a table near the water, but well away from the scattering of other diners. We sat in the sunlight, with chestnut trees going up and out like huge yellowing explosions around us. "I suppose," he said, when we had ordered wine from a small, plain girl in a totally unrevealing, high-necked *Dirndl*, "we should talk about your project."

So I told him what I could, without denigrating the other work at the Centre, and at the same time without claiming too much for us. We were working on some algorithms for the ocean-atmosphere carbon dioxide exchange. The Orlovsky woman, as I still thought of her, would be the bridge between us, so to speak.

"Do you know her?" he asked.

"Only by reputation. Do you?"

"Only by reputation, as you say."

I told him there was no chance at all for us to achieve what the director had advertised, but that I thought we'd be able to do some good with our handling of a small piece of a large problem. "Anyway, we aren't going to solve the CO_2 question at the Centre. They'll do it at Scripps, and NOAA, and Woods Hole. But I imagine they'll find our work useful."

"Well...a serious man. I have to say I would like for the director to be less boyish in his enthusiasm. At the same time, I find that good scientists do their work whether they are well directed or not.''

We took time out then to study the leatherbound menu, so that when the girl brought our *Viertels* of red wine we could order. Then, for a moment longer, we drank our wine in silence. It had relieved me, finally to talk about work, for I could see the utility of it, the *reason* for our meeting. There would still be a mild sensation at the Centre, the day's gossip would percolate with all sorts of speculation, and I would begin to hear odd, untrue things about myself. ''I wonder what they'll make of this?''

''At the Centre?'' He shrugged. ''I am a legendary eccentric. I am fortunate in being able to do what I want.''

''Is that just here, or in general?''

''In general.''

''Will that change?''

''You mean because of the change in leadership? No, not very much. The new man will almost certainly be Andropov, although you will not find everyone so ready to give up on Chernenko. But it will be Andropov. We know one another, and I like him, although he can be quite cold, and I believe his health is not very good. I would expect my star to rise a little under his regime.'' He paused. ''I am gambling with you, you know.''

''I know. Don't worry about gambling.''

''Thank you. In any event, I think my life will go along as it has, perhaps a trifle better. I think I shall direct the Academy of Sciences when the incumbent dies...'' he laughed, then. ''We do not retire, do we?'' He looked at the dregs of his wine. ''But you seem interested in the Soviet Union. Is that right?''

''I'm curious about it.''

''I suspect you may share a view of us that many Americans have, namely that there is something called Russia, which is good, and the Russian people, who are wonderful and warm, and the Soviet regime, which is a big criminal, ruled by political gangsters who are stupid but not really all that bad. You see the bad side and discount it a bit, and you see the good side, and like it, and as for our ability to take care of ourselves economically, well that is just a kind of joke." He held up a hand, anticipating my protest. "Of course I oversimplify, and I apologize for that. But it is almost true, is it not? Despite what you hear of our shortcomings, there is, on balance, a sentimental view. Liberated serfs, those charming but rather selfish Tolstoy families, and the warmth and good humor. And there is also the love affair, which we both have, with great spaces, Alaska and Siberia."

"But the thing to remember is this: this Mother Russia, the focus of all such feelings about us, is a fiction, and she may even be a destructive one, a way of tying us up emotionally. Old Russia has vanished down the river of time. Whatever happens in my country—and I think nothing much will change beyond material improvements—we will never return to that hazy, pretty old Russia. Finally we may come to another Russia...call her Blue Russia...that will surprise us, and perhaps will be better. But the old one does not live on inside a Soviet cocoon, waiting to fly free once again. She is dead. What you see, good and bad, is what is there."

It was a long speech, for him, and a shock for me, to have my general view of Russia be so transparent, and so shallow. I said, somewhat deferentially, "I think we're sentimental about it . . . the view you describe . . . because we think of ourselves as being greedy and wasteful, compared to anybody else. And we think that whatever her faults, Russia can't be the devil. No country can."

"Of course not. Please do not misunderstand me. I know the sources of your point of view, and I have moments when that is the Russia I also see. I was only trying to clarify things a little." He retreated to the shyness with which we had begun. "Blue Russia," he said then. "That gives us something to look forward to."

The girl brought our food, and he ordered more wine for us, and then we set to eat, both discovering a large appetite. After a few minutes' serious consumption, he looked up to say, "I do not mean to make you my philosophical biographer or anything. But we are speaking with unusual candor today...that was the 'deal'. Besides, you just admitted to being a serious man."

I laughed. "Too serious, to hear Lincoln."

Something moved behind his face. "What do you mean?"

"Oh...we were talking at the *Heuriger*. He said he'd put me forward as a candidate for the CO_2 project here."

"That is true. At least he did approach the director."

"And you."

"Yes, he approached me too."

"I still wonder why."

"I think...he was impressed by some of your published work. I really could not say."

"When I came up to you in front of the castle, he was telling you that something was 'remarkable.' What was that?"

"Nothing. That is, I do not even remember. It must have been very inconsequential."

I remembered his reply to Lincoln: *I will let you know.* And wondered why, having been so level with me on sensitive issues, he would become evasive on this trivial one. "It couldn't have referred to me...the only remarkable thing he found about me was that nothing remarkable happened. He thought there weren't enough people in my life."

"Ah. I see." He fidgeted with his food unhappily, as if, suddenly, he were alone, and old, and not handling his life as he wanted to. Then, in a voice which contained a note of failure, he asked, "What was your sense of him? Did you like him?"

"I felt we hated one another on sight."

"But...why would you?"

"I don't know."

"He could be an easy man to hate," he whispered. He might have said more, and changed everyone's world right there and then; but suddenly, as though acknowledging the right to hate Lincoln brought swift punishment, his pain flowered within. You could see it give a great pulse, a shake, like a waking reptile, and fill him utterly. His mouth compressed into a thin horizontal line, his eyes squeezed shut, his hands pressed white upon the table. I leaned toward him, frightened but wanting to help. My touch upon his arm only seemed to amplify the storm within. He shook his head vigorously, driving me back. It left him slowly, returned to its fitful nap somewhere in his body. The brilliant eyes sharpened once more, until he regarded me with the tranquility of strong men who know they are dying. The only signs of trauma were a dew of perspiration across his forehead and upper lip, a tremor of pale hands, a soft panting for breath.

"Jesus," I whispered.

"Yes, and Joseph and Mary too."

"What is it?"

"Something... internal. Some bug. I need to have it looked at."

"You need a doctor."

"A doctor is just what I do *not* need." He raised a restraining hand that shook. "What I need is for you not to expose me as a sick man."

"What does your family think?"

"My family." He smiled with a kind of wonder. "I have not had time for that." The pain had altered him though, imparted the raw emotions of the convalescent, a greater susceptibility to that second *Viertel* of wine. His eyes glistened, as though he were about to cry. I drew back guardedly, to wait, and watch, glad to have a long dish of schnitzel and potatoes to pick at, glad for the silence that flowed in around the severity of his attack. And he, his emotions vulnerable as a girl's, was nevertheless able to wait me out, to let me get rid of my tension, and that reawakened sense that our having lunch was a bizarre thing to do.

At last he said, "I have visited San Diego and La Jolla. It was very beautiful, so Mediterranean. I have taken an entire afternoon to walk along the beach, at low tide. A wonderful beach.''

"When was that?''

"Oh, many years ago.''

"You'd find it greatly changed. But the beach is still very beautiful.'' I didn't like our taking this turn toward me. Nancy and I had walked that perfect beach all the way up past Torrey Pines to Del Mar, and done some diving there, and made love. I didn't want to talk to him about my lost Nancy.

"You grew up there, in La Jolla?''

"No... farther north.'' And, fleeing memories of my vanished girl, I told the chairman a little about my life, about growing up on the avocado ranch southeast of Newport Beach. "As Lincoln said, not many people in my life.''

"Do you still see your parents?''

"They've been dead about a year. An auto accident. I think that was one reason to come over here.'' But that gave out more than I wanted.

"What were they like?''

Speaking of them forced a closer memory: of my mother, large and loving, the flesh hanging down from her soft, sweet-smelling arms, and the long wheat-colored hair she braided, and her bright blue eyes and troubled smile—always a troubled smile, as though she waited for the calamities that must come. And my father, one of those German farmers with huge hands made out of a material that looked tougher than wood or leather, the fingers permanently curled from implements laid down years before, the face large and big-toothed and full of sun and character. They had taken good, quiet care of me, in a house that was large for the three of us, and white, and full of light and the sounds of dogs and cats, green shadows off the big avocados near the house, chickens out back, and, not ten miles west of us, the Pacific Ocean, running out from the high cliffs and beaches below Newport. They had been in their late forties when I arrived, old enough that I used to wonder, the way most children do, whether I hadn't been left on their doorstep. Except there was not that imperfect fit in our relationship: we shared genes, you could tell.

That had been the good life, a life with someone in it who took and gave affection and need, and connected you to something, saw you graduated from high school, saw you through college, saw you married, if you married, and sewed you back together after the slide down the razor of divorce. Ah, I had cried like a baby the day they died, both together, as they had always been, and Nancy with them, the old, indestructible Pontiac swept off the coastal highway by a jack-knifing rig; and they, dressed up to meet me for dinner at a good place in Balboa, had gone fluttering down to the sea, and death. But I didn't tell the chairman all of that—just the facts, as they say.

"Braun," the chairman mused. "Braun sounds a German name. You must have many relatives over here, somewhere. Have you looked for these...other people in your life?"

"I have an uncle and aunt in Vienna."

"I find that very interesting. Many of the people who come here, ostensibly from nowhere, as far as Austria is concerned, turn out to have an Austrian wife, or mother-in-law, or aunt and uncle...some reason to be here besides just the Centre. And yet, without the Centre, many of them would never have come."

"Kismet."

"Yes, you are all fated to be here." If he saw that my remembering had begun to get me down, he gave no sign. "But did you not marry?"

"My girl...got away."

"I am sorry."

I shrugged.

"What was her name?"

"Nancy," I replied. Then I held up a palm and asked, "Why are we doing this?"

"What?"

"Everything." I leaned toward him. "Why are we having lunch? Why are we talking so personally about one another? I don't know you. You don't know me. We mean nothing to each other. So why are we here? Why tell me about Andropov and Blue Russia and then show me a secret illness that looks like it goes all the way down to your toes. Why? What am I to you?"

"Nothing," he said, seeming in that moment to yield something up. "We are . . . nothing."

"Come on. Something's going on. I feel like a lab animal. Trulov notices something about me, God knows what, and goes colder than a cop. Lincoln, this stranger, looks at me and hates me. Worse, I hate him back. Jesus. Am I in some elaborate experiment, or what?"

"You must . . . do me the favor of simply taking the lunch. It is a memory. Nothing can alter the fact of it, or that it is remembered." His voice had diminished, as he had himself. The pain had devoured some of him today. The pain and something else.

"But why?" I persisted. "Why have the memory?"

"I am sorry," he said. He sounded very weak.

"You won't tell me."

But he had closed his eyes. "No more, please." A flickering visit of pain shuddered through him, drawing him into himself for a time. When he returned he smiled wanly and said, "We both seem to have our demons. I do not know which is worse, mine or yours."

"Mine don't kill."

"*All* demons kill." He signalled to the hovering girl, and, when she announced the amount, paid her with a larger figure that included a small tip. "Perhaps we should get back."

"Can you walk?"

"If we walk slowly."

We returned almost in silence, both, I think, slightly embarrassed by the encounter, and I sensed that something had gone wrong—Pastukh radiated mild, unsurprised disappointment. Finally, he said in a melancholy, controlled voice, "I apologize for all this mystery over something as simple as a lunch. Of course I wanted to feel you out ... against some future opportunity for cooperative study at one of our marine institutes. We are often at pains to provide new ways to get your people and my people together, you see. That kind of thing. I regret that it became more mysterious than that."

I laughed with relief. "Thanks for telling me. I'm sorry I bridled back there. Demons, as you said."

But it was clear we both felt some relaxation between us that had nothing to do with a lifting of mystery. It had to do rather with the fact that something had not happened, as if we had both failed some unstated test. The difference between us was that he knew what.

I walked him to the front of the Schloss, and we began our leave taking, both diffident now, both ready to have it over. "I enjoyed our lunch, thank you for coming, Schaefer. Perhaps we can do it again some time." But neither of us saw the slightest prospect of that.

"Yes, thanks," I said vaguely, wanting also to utter my goodbye. But as I took breath, the big wooden door in the yellow wall opened to yield first Trulov, and then a tall, grim blonde woman. At first I couldn't speak. Then forming the important word very carefully, like a stutterer approaching *that* unpronounceable sound, I blurted, *"Nancy?"*

The woman looked up, perplexed, and I knew I had never seen her before. But my heart still cracked in exactly the same way it had cracked that other time, when the lovely mermaid entered my life, as it would crack whenever that person appeared. I felt my spine turn into something like warm wax at its base, a column of sweet powder, a door sprang downward in my breast, and, beyond that single word, that cry of *Nancy!*, my throat prevented speech.

I looked at Pastukh, my lips pulled back in frightened anger, the lab animal surprised by yet another grid. And he, suddenly knowing it all, knowing *everything*, flinched away, pale and stricken. "I did not know," he whispered. "Believe me."

Trulov stepped forward. "Andrei, Schaefer," he said. "I want you to meet Dr. Valentina Orlovsky."

I took the woman's long, cool hand and told her, in what voice I could command, "Welcome aboard," and smiled and tried to stop that shaking. And inside...inside I was running...

PART TWO

1

"Schaefer, Schaefer," Lisa mumbled, rocking her baby, her lids shut, interrupting the pained stare of her opaque grey eyes, her angular and almost unlined face drooping toward repose. With one scabrous hand she swept back her long golden hair, running more to silver than before. For her, the aging process had been a gentle bleaching, turning her whiter and whiter with the years, drying her out, as though time mummified but did not destroy. Time had stopped for her; in the deep grey forest of her brain, where she lived, it did not even exist.

Except . . . one had to feed the baby.

Clumsily now, with shattered fingernails, the cuticles sawed raw by the quiet, steady rampages of other fingers, she spread the sides of her white cotton smock, exposing breasts that also had been almost untouched by time. Gently, she squeezed the dry, erect nipple of one, then of the other, and nodded with satisfaction. She lay back upon her cot, her spine curved into that corner of the room, and folded her thin, furry legs up beneath her, pulling the baby down upon her breasts. She stroked the red yarn of its hair, and straightened its little sailor costume, and thought how handsome he was, with his rosy cheeks and perpetual smile and alert black eyes. "Schaefer, *Schae*-fer, Schaefer," she hummed, swaying rhythmically.

Afterward, she would put her little son to bed, and make herself beautiful in a fresh *Dirndl* and wait for Schaefer, and he would come, and he would come . . . Lisa frowned. *He would come.* Her mouth became a bitter line. "Schaefer," she growled. She looked down at the baby. It seemed to sleep, although when she raised it before her the big black eyes were open, and the smile was there, as always. He would come, and they would walk out into the vineyards with the low hills rising into the evening, and the fields full of poppies and deep grasses. "Schaefer," she said, almost smiling. They would return to their rocky enclosure up beyond the vines, on the ridge in the forest, and lie together, and make love. He would unhook her bodice and scoop her breasts into the air, and kiss her there, and there, and there. He had only to touch her, to brush her arm lightly, and she was wet, wanting nothing but him. "Hmmm," she murmured. The first time she'd seen him, she had known it, his walking boldly into the Gasthaus with the other, little man, and then... One look, one touch, and she was his forever. She reached beneath her thin pillow and brought out a ragged square of paper, and said, "Schaefer," looking at the man there, faceless, although unchanged to Lisa. His clever hands would stroke her downy legs, and cup her breasts, caress her nipples; they would spread her legs, and enter her, and she, sliding toward the madness of that pleasure, would draw them into her quickly, her whole body quivering like the wing of a bird, uncontrolled, beating...

No.

He would not come.

He never came any more.

"Schaefer, Schaefer, Schaefer," she began, her voice rising toward the scream. "Schaefer, Schaeferschaefer-schaeferschaefer..." Her arms contracted inward, crushing the baby against her, and reminding her she held him. For a moment she regarded the small figure almost with affection, but then her eyes went hard and cold once more, and she hurled it away; it landed as a tangle of arms and legs in a corner of the empty room. Lisa hugged herself with wiry arms, drew her knees up under her chin until she was a tightly coiled little animal, her eyes open but empty, her mouth a horizontal line. She waited. One day, he had been there. One day, he was gone, and it was as if he had unplugged the great machine of time in leaving, in disappearing, without a word, a sign, a trace. He would return when the war had ended, by September he said, and then the war had ended, and then September and he had not. And then the time machine stopped turning. One day he would return and set time once more in motion. Lisa thought such things in a kind of circular prayer, rising toward the good, then diving toward all that frightened, that made her hide within herself, waiting, she and the baby. A closed circle of a prayer, impenetrable and eternal.

She waited in a white room, a room without darkness, almost without shadows, perhaps twice as wide as her cot, and half again as long. She and the cot and the baby were the only objects there, apart from some long scratches she had inflicted, digging at the plaster walls when They had first moved her there, and the small wet mound of waste she had spilled upon the white concrete floor. Light entered through three mesh-covered windows at one end of the room, and from a small fluorescent panel in the ceiling near the door, which was white, like the room it sealed, and metal. The place stank of incontinence and madness.

Lisa had been there a little more than a year now; her other time at Camarillo had been spent in a larger room with women who, Lisa had known (they *all* had known), were hiding in similar ways. All day they'd watched one another, occasionally babbling their sentence, their stanza, their obsessing single word; but mostly they had sat upon their cots, rocking, hiding, waiting. And then, one day, Lisa had been moved in here, alone. At first she thought they brought her there to be ready when Schaefer returned. But he had not. Men had come to her, to talk, her door opened and shut, day after day, night after night; but none of them was Schaefer. Still, she preferred her new room, for the only other watcher here was a black video camera, peering down at her from above the door as stonily as she looked back at it. But Lisa also watched the world observing what happened to others. It was just that

she didn't care about it. Externals were... external. And
what was a world without time?

But... the baby still had to be fed. She had to emerge
long enough to feed him. When Schaefer came (the prayer
wheel turned within: he would come, but he would never
come, but he would come...) she would leave her hiding
place to be with him. He would switch on the time again.
Life would resume. Meanwhile, Lisa would wait.

Outside the room, outside the low white stuccoed
building with its red tile roof, a cold winter rain puddled
the neat rays of concrete sidewalk, clattered on avocado
leaves and the fronds of palms, smeared the crisp neat-
ness of the Camarillo State Hospital. Off to the southeast, beyond the dun-colored mounds of the Santa
Monicas, which rose almost at the edge of the sea, suddenly, shaped like the hips and loins and breasts and tor-
sos of a quartered browngreen giant—beyond this line of
mountains, the ovaloid glow of Los Angeles beat against
the storm. A strong onshore wind rattled trees and shut-
ters and the roofs, and, even at this distance, one could
hear the drumming surf, plangent and powerful on the
night. Now and then another inmate would call out, the
voice frail and frightened, rising against the sounds of rain,
rising from some passing internal disturbance.

But those were out there. Lisa waited within. The tap of
rain, the spattering spray of raindrops blown across her
wall, the distant pulse of ocean—none of these mattered.
She lay, coiled and silent, suspended in time that would not
move, in time that held her like an insect in amber.

The building murmured with the muted voices of
whiteclad attendants, roaming the wards in pairs and sin-
gly, using the same earnest tone to speak of their broken
patients, and of their own more ordinary realities outside.
Lisa sensed some pressure at her door, and, without emit-
ting the smallest signal of attention, watched while the spy
slit in it opened to reveal a moist brown eye framed in
large, false lashes; the eye quivered there for a moment
before the slit clicked shut. A moment later the door

opened to admit the attendant Lisa knew was Shirley, a stocky white woman with the arms, shoulders, and face of a powerful little man, the eyes feminized with two spiders of black eyelash, the mouth painted into a wound. She had a hard, scalded look, and wore her hair in tight hennaed coils, reminding Lisa of her baby. (The baby. Where was the baby? She looked around quickly, saw it crumpled in the corner: it slept.) She curled, blankly watching the attendant.

"Hi, Lisa," the woman said, beginning to rinse the wastes into a drain that perforated the floor like a metal navel. Lisa watched her. "We're quiet tonight, aren't we?" Shirley went on. "Yep, real quiet." She turned to the baby. "How 'bout you, Raggedy Andy? How's things?" She strode to where the doll lay, and made a fuss of arranging the limp arms and legs for comfort, with the round smiling face turned toward the madwoman. "There. Always a nice smile for your mom, that's the way."

She talked more than usual tonight, and her body gave off signals of frightened preoccupation, which made Lisa twitch internally. She hated the smell of other people's fears.

Finished with her cleaning, Shirley straightened up, listening. Then, apparently satisfied by the present stillness of the building beneath the roar of rain, she stepped closer to Lisa, who coiled more tightly into herself. Shirley looked nervously at the round eye of the camera, then put herself where it could see only her back. "Lisa," she whispered, "Lisa, look." She held up and unfolded a page from a magazine showing a photograph of men, a dozen or so of them, mostly in dark suits, posed against a kind of antique European (or maybe southern Californian, Shirley had decided) façade. "Look at the men, Lisa," she whispered.

Lisa's eyes flickered warily: it could be a trap, a way to get her outside, something they were always trying, although it never worked. At the same time, she was attracted by the idea of examining male faces. You never knew, she might come to some clue that would tell her more about her location, and his, and when he would return... Like an animal not quite tame, she leaned forward and grabbed the clipping.

Shirley protested, clutching at it, but Lisa snarled, and hugged the paper closely against her breasts. The attendant would have pressed the matter, except that she had become afraid of bites—one bite too many, as she explained it to her colleagues. "Look at the men," she whispered.

Lisa lifted the scrap and stared at each face carefully, without blinking, without a sound. A pulse surfaced in her throat, a mist of perspiration condensed along her brow. The possibilities of learning more began to frighten her, and, as each face touched no memory, she felt increasingly reluctant to go further. After each examination she would pause and gaze at Shirley, looking a question she would not utter. Then she returned to the clipping, to pull the next man into her grey hiding place, make it into memory.

Suddenly, her face distended with surprise, and pain. She smashed the paper between her blasted hands, and curled her body around the fists in which she held it. She had seen him. He was *somewhere*. "Schaefer," she whispered, the whisper rising to the scream of, *"Schaeferschaeferschaeferschaefer..."*

Frightened, the woman backed away, saying, "It's okay, Lisa, it's okay, I'll check on you later, bye-bye Raggedy, bye-bye..." and so on, out the metal door, which she shut with a clang behind her.

2

LISA HAD SEEN SOMETHING in the photograph. "But we'll never know what," Shirley whispered, wondering why the encounter had scared her so, leaning against the metal door while her heart rate dropped to normal levels. Although, she knew her problem: it frightened her to be suddenly a thief, in here, trying to steal from poor Lisa. A lot of attendants took stuff from the patients, but not Shirley Morgan, not once in all these years employed there. Oh, sure, an occasional magazine these people couldn't read, or a piece of candy, something like that. But never anything important. She'd never *betrayed* them, for money.

She wiped her wet forehead. What did it matter, what she'd done? What did it matter? The poor dummies, God help them, had no idea of anything (except that Shirley could sometimes *feel* Lisa watching with perfect comprehension some small cutting of corners in cleaning the room, some minor shift of attention toward or away from her). "Look," she told herself in an angry whisper, "you don't betray a bell if you ring it and tell somebody it went ding dong." You *couldn't* betray a bell, her mind went on in the same admonitory tone, just like you can't betray a catatonic, either. And yet, she had *felt* Lisa's grasp of some change, just then, she had felt Lisa take another tiny increment of pain from that photograph, and it was her, Shirley's, fault.

"Jesus," she murmured. "Oh, Jesus." It isn't a matter of hurting anyone. It just isn't. If a guy pays you two hundred bucks to hear what a bell says, that's his problem. So I'll tell him, okay, I did what you said, I showed her the clipping, and she looked at it, she said: *Schaefer*. Shirley sighed with relief, now her problem had been, if not solved, at least spread into layers too thin for guilt to root in. And she would protect the mad woman further, she decided. She wouldn't tell him that "Schaefer" was all Lisa ever said. She pushed away from Lisa's door, and down the linoleum tiled hall lined with cutouts of turkeys and muskets and pilgrims. Thanksgiving. Good God, try to give these people a Thanksgiving dinner!

The rain had dammed up behind every convex surface on the hospital grounds by midnight, when her shift ended. Long scarves of water fluttered on a cold wind puffing off the sea, the dark palms and eucalyptus trees bent and banged, and now and then a frond would tear away with a cry and flutter into the darkness. Shirley watched the weather from the lighted rectangle of the locker room door, drawing the yellow slicker more closely round her thick body. She'd bought it only last summer for the sail to Ensenada that had not happened as promised after a night in an Oxnard motel. But, what the heck, that was the Navy for you. Chilled through the yellow plastic, by the rain, by the disappointments in her life, she shivered like an animal. Then launched herself across the sodden grass to her green Tercel, feeling the icy penetrations of water where the slicker leaked some in. The moment it took to unlock and enter the car soaked her further, so that by the time she was in the driver's seat she was very wet and very cold, and beginning to be frightened of the wild night.

It must be that it preyed on her, this thing she did, this thing she knew was wrong, bad, possibly immoral, or worse—against the law. A drop of water descending her bare neck caused her to give another mighty shiver, as if the drop *were* the cold touch of the law. "Brrrr," she said, glad to hear the human voice. God, but she'd be glad to have this over, and the money in hand. "Don't worry," she told the night, or God, "I'll get Lisa some flowers," and thought good-naturedly of the possibilities, a few pansies, or daisies, or maybe a pretty longstemmed red rose, "something she won't try to eat." She started the car and got the wipers and defroster going, and waited while the warm air melted a hole in the fog covering the windshield, then switched on the lights and drove into the storm. She took it slowly, hardly able to see through the bright spikes of falling rain that filled the white cones before her. The scattered nightlights of the hospital gave way quickly to black, lightless night as she crossed the bridge, the water roiling and high beneath it, and headed down the long, narrow road that would take her, for perhaps the ten-thousandth time, out of the hospital grounds. The dark, spare eucalyptus trees passed like ragged sentinels, sombre but unbowed. At the entrance, instead of taking her ten-thousandth right turn toward the town of Camarillo and home, she turned toward the sea. The move against old habit revived her uncertainty, made her drive even more slowly along the curving track that took her toward the deeper darkness of the hills shielding Carillo Beach, where he would meet her.

He. That morning, before it had started to rain hard, before a day on duty had ground down her spirits, the request, the whole deal had been...acceptable, she'd call it. Never more than that, really. But at the same time, she'd known from the outset she would acquiesce in it, in anything he wanted. She had seen him peripherally, the big male form sliding onto the counter stool next to hers at Randy's, where she took her *Times* and doughnut and juice and coffee. Although he did not touch her, his presence crowded her, in the way that very lonely people are crowded by an inability to ignore the proximity of others. She slid her paper and coffee a little to one side, listened to him order in a big, happy voice she thought had a little Pennsylvania in it. Then, surprising her, and also prodding her heart into a low leap, he asked, "Excuse me, but are you Shirley Morgan?"

"Yes...yes, I am," she replied, turning to look at him squarely. A great kindness resided in his large, pale face and warm brown eyes, the band of black hair swept loosely across the broad, smart forehead. She wanted to ask what she could do for him, but did not, fearing he would reply, Nothing.

But he said, "I am going to ask a favor, not anything very special, and pay you a hundred dollars for it."

Shirley shook her head, dismayed that the approach had turned dirty so soon. "Sorry, pal," she said in her tough voice, "I don't do things for money."

"Wait..." He restrained her with a hand that communicated a strength much greater than hers. "Please," the kind voice insisted. Shirley relaxed, succumbed, and watched him. "Here is all I want, Miss Morgan," he began. She noted that his voice was deliberately pitched well below the background clatter of the diner—it was the voice you used in a ward. "I have a clipping here, with a photograph on it. I do not want you to look at it. But, sometime today, I want you to show it to one of your patients...to Lisa...and tell me what she says. And I want you then to return the clipping to me. A hundred dollars."

Shirley knew she would do it to see this man again. Although she shook her head and told him she couldn't do such a thing, it came out in a weak, unconvincing voice. Something about this stranger touched her, made her want to do him a favor. "I just couldn't do that to Lisa," she said, almost unable to look at him, so afraid he would say, Okay, forget it, and vanish from her life. She saw a dangerous movement behind his gentle gaze, one she had seen hundreds and hundreds of times in the wards, but ignored it. "Really," she murmured, extending a protest that held no conviction.

His eyes told her he knew she would do it, that he held her in his big, hard hand; but he said, "Two hundred, then." She had seen it coming, like a slap, but it made it possible for her to accept. With a couple hundred you could *buy* something, *do* something, and it would mean nothing to Lisa; in a way, it had nothing to do with Lisa, since she had decided to leave the world in which it would occur. But when Shirley had accepted, when they had agreed to meet at the beach after her shift ended, she understood clearly that it had nothing to do with anything else except pleasing this big man, who made her want, and hope to be wanted, and warm, and attractive, all at once.

Now, driving to meet him in what had turned into the rainstorm of the year, she wondered whether he would have a drink with her—she would have to drag the story out, like Scheherazade, to keep him interested—and whether they would go back to her place for a nightcap, or... A wave of desire stroked her like a man's hand. "Boy!" she whispered, feeling herself begin to melt below. Well, better horny than afraid. Knowing what she wanted, she began to drive with more confidence, as the road entered the clefts separating the low hills which loomed around her in the storm. She took the turns swiftly in the little machine, the rain smearing the world in around her headlights. Soon she pulled into the parking lot, and took a space near the blurred boundary of asphalt and sand. A few other cars were there, young lovers devouring one another's faces in the glow of radio dials. Across the pale band of the kelp-freckled beach, Shirley could see the vague phosphorescence of incoming waves, their clawing at the land. She turned on the radio, which awoke at its customary country station, where a guitar-player lamented his sister-in-law's sexual attraction. Shirley lighted a cigarette, and waited in the isolating metal capsule of her car.

He seemed to materialize out of the night, suddenly there, tapping on the passenger side, which she had forgotten to unlock. She unlocked it swiftly, afraid he would be put off by her not doing it before, and the stranger crammed himself into the passenger seat. He wore a khaki trenchcoat with all the tabs and buttons secured against the rain, but his trousers clung to his calves and he had no hat, so that his dark hair lay glistening as though freshly painted on the large curve of his skull. Completely unperturbed, too, she thought with admiration. "Hi," she said.

"Hello," he replied, rubbing his hands and pushing water back from his forehead and out of his hair. "What a night."

"Yeah, it's something. Lot of people think it's the volcanoes."

"Volcanoes?"

"I don't know why they would, but that's what the paper says. Personally I couldn't care less, just so it quits after awhile." She was so glad to be talking to someone whose eyes contained attention, in a normal voice. "Where's your car?"

"Oh . . ." he shrugged. "I parked it . . . over there." He gestured vaguely up the beach.

"You had a terrific walk, then."

"Yes, it was farther than I thought."

"Where you from?"

"Uh . . . Philadelphia." He said the word carefully, pronouncing each syllable.

"I *thought* I heard a little Pennsylvania in your voice," she teased. "I'm very good at placing people by the way they sound."

"Yes," he said in a tone of genuine admiration, "you do that quite well."

"Thanks."

For a time they sat with only rain sounds and music, as though, she thought, they were on a first date, which, in a way, she guessed they were. The singer spoke sadly of murdering his stepfather's mistress. The ocean boomed. Now and then a new car would arrive, and take up a position as far as possible from the others, and the lights would dim and there would be another pair or quartet of lovers in the glow of their dial. Shirley wondered when it would be her turn, thinking: The answer is yes, oh . . . *yes*. She said, "You must be soaked."

"I am quite wet . . . but I don't mind." She thought some of the kindness, the laughter, had gone out of his voice.

"I was thinking," she began.

He smiled in the dim radio light, watching her. "I think you need to give me a little report, Miss Morgan."

"Oh, sure."

"You showed Lisa the paper?"

"Yes."

"And . . . ?" Slight impatience.

"She looked at it. And then she said 'Schaefer.'"

"And that was all? Just 'Schaefer'?"

Shirley nodded vigorously.

He pulled what looked like a green cigarette from his shirt pocket and handed it to her. "Here are two hundred dollars, as promised." He handed the money over and she took it reluctantly, fearing that their commerce was at an end. "And now...the clipping, please?"

Her hesitation triggered something in him, for the look he gave her suddenly had no kindness in it at all. He sensed her hesitation before she did herself. "The clipping." His voice had gone quite cold.

"I...threw it out," she lied, her mind beginning to race him toward a more convincing story. "She dropped it..."

"You let her hold it?"

"She grabbed it, but it fell...after she said what she said...it fell in some mess...her floor's always full of mess...so I just threw it away when I cleaned up the mess. I knew you wouldn't want it back if it had mess all over it." She could not look at him, and when she did she saw *Liar* in his gentle eyes. She was suddenly afraid of this man.

But he seemed then to draw the coldness inward, pulling it out of his eyes, his voice, cleansing the car of fear and tension. He gave a reassuring laugh. "Yes, you are quite right, Miss Morgan. Who wants an old clipping covered with...mess? Of course you did the right thing."

Tears of relief sprang to Shirley's small, wet eyes, running her mascara slightly, giving her the beginnings of a clown-face. "I'm sorry, but..." She had begun to believe her story. It made sense, and perhaps, by now, Lisa really had dropped it in some mess on the floor. But he seemed to have reached the end of his business with her. She wanted him back. "I can tell you more about her," she said, ignoring the interior accusations of betrayal. "I mean, I'm with her as much as anybody, maybe more."

"I would like that," he replied. "I have a suggestion for us. Why don't we return to town and have a drink together...I am very wet, as you say, and am beginning to feel the cold. It would be excellent to dry out a little..."

"It's late...I mean, most of the spots'll be closing." Then, feeling she dived from a high bridge, she said, "We...we could go by my place. Have a drink. You could put your things in the dryer. You know." The thought of having this man in her condo without his clothes on brought a rush of desire that made her worry about odor.

"That would be very kind," he replied. Ah, he was gentle again, and, God, maybe he *was* attracted to her, and anyway, it meant there would be a man in her life for a while tonight...

She switched on the engine and backed away from the sea, turned, and sped back the way she had come, silent, determined, frightened that this interlude would crack suddenly, letting him escape, leaving her alone. She thought of his car, which he said was somewhere "over there," and quickly forgot it—keep him close, don't let him get away. "You know," she said as she drove, "I would have done that for you without the money."

"But you did not have to."

"No. But you can have it back, if you want."

"Keep it. It belongs to my, uh, corporation."

"What is that?"

"I am here on confidential business and would rather not say, Miss Morgan."

"Call me Shirley."

"Shirley."

"But," and she laughed lightly, sounding to herself like a girl, "I don't even know your name."

"Brown," he replied quickly.

"*Mister* Brown?" she teased. The way to a man's heart, she believed, was teasing, although she had never received the slightest confirmation of this.

"Cleveland Brown."

"That sounds *very* familiar."

"It is a very common name in Phil-a-del-phi-a."

"I imagine that's true." But she had heard of him, she was sure she had.

The lights of the state hospital passed off to their right, scattered as distant stars, twinkling through the rain. "What about Lisa?" he asked now, as though the faint lights had reminded him.

"I wasn't going to tell you this," Shirley said, conscious that she would tell him anything if it meant getting him home with her tonight. "But that name..."

"Schaefer?"

"Right...that's the only word she ever says. She says it softly and she yells it, she says it loving and she says it hating. She croons it to the baby..."

"Baby?"

"She keeps a little Raggedy Andy doll..."

"A Raggedy Andy?" He frowned.

"You know, one of those little rag dolls...they're real famous."

"Of course, with the red hair."

"Yeah, and the little overalls. Well she has one that's her baby. Lots of them have something like that."

She felt his attention on her, warm as love, although of course she knew *that* wasn't it—he was just listening to her very carefully. "She's only been where she is now about a year, maybe a little more. Before, they had her in with a bunch of others. They'd just sit around, staring past each other. But for some reason the doctors moved her where she is now. They keep a camera on her, and she's by herself. Except for Raggedy Andy, of course."

"A camera."

"Yeah, like she got important or something. Maybe somebody's doing a thesis on her. I don't know."

"Tell me how she reacted to the clipping."

"Sure. I didn't read it, okay? But I could tell...I couldn't help but tell...it was a photo of some men. Will you forgive me?" she asked, teasing again.

"Sure."

"Well," Shirley went on, determined to warm up his neutrality, "she'd look at one face, and then she'd look up at me, and then she'd look at another one, and so on. Like she was looking...you know, careful, I mean, really *looking*, you know? So when she came to one..."

"Which one?"

"I don't know. She's looked at maybe six or eight of them...it looked like she went from right to left, but that's all I can tell you."

"Then what?"

"Then she said it."

"Just the one word?"

"At first...and then began yelling, like dingding-dingding...like that." You can't betray a bell. Remember, you can't betray a bell.

"Ah." And that was all he said. Shirley was disappointed; having gone so far, having finally done precisely what she had promised herself she would not do, she'd wanted more from him than that. Her confidence sagged. She wondered what she was doing with this mysterious Mr. Brown, and whether he would find her condo pretty, as she did, or tacky, as she sometimes suspected it was, and how the night would proceed, beginning, as it had, after midnight. I mean, she thought, I don't really know him. But then, glancing across at him, seeing him thoughtful, abstracted, beautiful, in a way—she was touched, and pleased to have him in her world. Maybe he would stay the day, too, she thought, expanding her claim. Maybe they could take a late lunch, before she went on duty. She thought of her body, of its muscular stomach and the broad shoulders and arms roped with muscle, and the hair that too much treatment had turned brittle and thin... Don't think about the hair, she told herself.

The scattered after-midnight lights of Camarillo came into view as they crossed the Interstate, and she turned off to the north, through the unfinished roads of her development until she came to her own single block of condominiums. The concrete had been made to resemble adobe, with no hard edges; the two-storey structure looked like a pound cake melting in the rain. The development was called Los Arboles, and the grounds were dotted with recently planted saplings that cringed in the cold wet wind. She'd bought the first condominium offered and for a time there had been other buyers—two couples and a black

guy—for the three other units that her building comprised. But the development had come upon an empty
money wheel and had stopped developing. The others
could afford to move out, but Shirley could not, and so the
recession left her isolated in her Spanishy condo at Los
Arboles, looking across the arroyo, which coursed with
water tonight, out to sea. It was beautiful, and kind of
wonderful to be alone in such a setting. But it also meant
that her daring, too-expensive move to Los Arboles had
made her even more isolated than before. "Well," she
said, after she'd let the Toyota coast into her narrow drive,
"This is it." She turned to look at him, and was surprised
by his apparent interest in the building.

"It is...quite large," he said. There was something like
wonder in his voice, which surprised and pleased her.

She laughed, "It's not all mine. Just this end. There're
three other units in it. Plans were to put up about a dozen
of these, and a pool and tennis courts and everything. But
I guess this is hard times, and the developers decided to
wait. So...I'm sort of waiting with them." She opened her
door. "Come on." He followed her into a small enclosed
area where a stunted bougainvillaea struggled up a string,
and a few thin roses drooped beneath the pounding rain,
and then to the dark wood-compound entrance door,
which she unlocked and swung open for him. "Welcome," she said, adopting a tone she thought might be that
of a pretty girl, and let him stalk into the place ahead of
her. When she'd closed and locked the door, she said,
"Welcome to chez Morgan."

She watched him take it all in, the small living room full
of plants, a corner fireplace and high ceiling, a bedroom
and bath in back, stairs going up to a loft, an arched par-
tition leading off to a small dining area and the kitchen.
The walls were white, with framed prints and photographs from Mexico and a holiday in Aspen. The litter of
single life lay everywhere in the form of stacked newspapers and magazines and old television programs, dirty
snackplates, glasses. She'd forgotten the place was so

messy. "I'm sorry about the mess, but I wasn't expecting...company...tonight."

"I think you have a very attractive home," he replied. What a nice man!

Shirley disappeared into the back bedroom, and emerged minutes later with a lavender terrycloth robe. "Put this on," she said, naturally taking command of anything resembling care and feeding. "We'll put your wet things in the dryer. You'll catch your death, sitting around so wet and cold."

He nodded and went into the bedroom. She had most of the litter picked up by the time he returned, embarrassed and huge in the woman's robe, but somehow more or less covered almost to his knees. His chest hair sprouted from the top of the gown. She assumed he had his underwear on; but he might be what he seemed, huge and strong and hairy and naked, right there, in her living room. "Here," he said, handing her his trousers, shirt, and socks. "This is most kind of you."

"Well," she began, hurrying off to the tiny utility room where the stacked washer and dryer were hidden, "you get off at midnight, wide awake, and the town's just about shut down. I'm glad for the company, frankly." She threw the clothing in and slammed the door. Soon the place throbbed with the cycling of the dryer, rumbling like the engines of a ship. "I put them on permanent press," she announced, back in the living room. God, she thought, all this is making me a little giddy. "Just make yourself at home...Cleveland. May I call you Cleve?"

"Sure." He sat in a soft leatherette chair that seemed almost to topple backwards, over-accommodating the sitter. He steadied himself, and smiled. "A *very* comfortable place you have."

Shirley had been stripping off her yellow slicker, which she hung in the hall to drip on the tangerine tiles there. "Now we can have that drink? What's yours?"

"Vodka, please."

"Ice? Tonic?"

"Just vodka." He watched her steadily, and she could not be certain what she saw there. Desire, perhaps. Yes, it must be the budding of desire. God, she thought, it will be like screwing with a bear! She shivered, thinking of the act... Oh, God! Her hands trembled as she opened a bottle of Smirnof, which she regarded as her best stock, and poured him a tumblerfull, to relax him; and made a bourbon and Seven for herself. She would have to stop thinking about his schlupping into her... really, she thought, *really*. But she could not quite put it out of mind. It looked like it was going to happen. Oh, God!

She handed him his vodka and sat down on the beige carpet near his chair, and regarded her home, her evening, with satisfaction. Some nice modern, and some Mexican stuff, and one or two things from when her mom had died in Pasadena, lots of color, plants to talk to. A nice nest, someone had told her. You make a real nice nest, Shirley. She tried to remember who it had been. But Brown was pensive. "Penny for your thoughts."

"What? Oh yes. I am just drifting. And tired. It is quite late. But this is very pleasant."

"I could make a fire."

"No... I do not think we need one."

"Some music?"

"Yes, good."

"What do you like?"

"Anything. Anything you like is fine."

Shirley crawled over to the stereo console and fumbled around in a pile of cassette tapes. Then she selected one and in a moment the place filled with the sounds of soft Mexican mariachi. "Goes with the decor," she explained, grinning happily, excited. She had forgotten about her fears, or betraying poor Lisa (you can't betray a bell), about everything. Brown watched her with something like affection—sympathy would have been closer, she decided, but, what the hell, at least it was warm.

"Come here, Shirley," he said then.

Ah, God bless, it was really going to happen. She couldn't believe her luck. "Yes," she replied. *"Yes."*

3

WHEN HE HAD FINISHED with the woman, with this Shirley Morgan, the big man emerged from the living room, carrying his empty glass. This nurse, or, rather, this less-than-a-nurse, lived quite well, he thought, hearing the hum and thump of the dryer, and noting, for the first time, the pattern of city lights beyond her windows. A lonely life, but not a poor one. Not a grinding one. He padded inquisitively around the place in the short, lavender robe, getting a sense of how Shirley Morgan's condo operated. A gas kitchen, he discovered, and, in another closet, the gas furnace and water heater. The furnace roared, warming the place automatically against the storm. He found the switch that turned it off, and stopped the sound; then, bending down, squinting at the instructions, he extinguished the pale-blue pilot lights on the furnace and water tank.

In the kitchen, he washed, wiped, and put away his glass, and the bottle of vodka. Then he found a freezer bag and unloaded all the ice from the refrigerator into it, added some water from the tap, and patted it into an oblong shape before returning it to the freezer. From his own small pile of possessions, made when he emptied his wet pockets, he drew a Swiss army knife and a pair of thick rubber bands, and set to work, his large hands deft and quick. Unplugging the refrigerator, he took the end of the cord with the wallplug on it and stripped and separated its shorn end, careful to keep the insulation almost intact except for the slit made to peel it neatly back. His fingers twisted the shining copper wire into points. Finished for the moment, he blew out the pilot lights on the stove, and got his things out from the dryer. They were better than they had been, but, beneath a superficial warmth, still cold and damp.

With the dryer silenced he could hear the music playing in the living room. Very beautiful. Peasant music. The music of the people, of Mexico, which he would have to visit some day.

Dressed, he returned to the kitchen. It had everything, coffee machines and electric juice-squeezers, a machine that opened cans, another that crushed the trash, destroyed garbage. The gas range and oven were shiny, and of a terracotta brown, along with the refrigerator. Plates and plastic containers and aluminium foil and ceramic mugs and God knew what were everywhere. The clutter was awful, in a way, but also very rich. How could a nurse, or someone not even a nurse, have so many things? She was an exploited class, and yet she seemed to have everything. Worse even than in Vienna.

He turned on all the burners and the oven, which he set to the control marked BROIL. "No pun intended," he murmured pleasantly. The scent of gas quickly rose in the room. Now he focused entirely on the mechanical task at hand, and forgot about standards of living and clutter and the urge to laugh aloud, which always overtook him on an operation like this one.

The stripped ends of the severed electrical cord he fashioned into a long Y-shape, the hot side going up one arm, the ground wire going up the other, the base of the Y ending with the plug. Then he got the ice block out of the freezer and spread the Y of wires around it, fastening them in place tightly with the rubber bands. He arranged them very carefully on the floor behind the refrigerator, the two ends of the Y bent inward, like copper snakes poised to strike at one another, one from above, one from below. The rubber bands pressed them together; the ice block kept them apart. But, as the block melted, the bare wires would approach until a spark leapt the gap, and the gas-filled condominium, the only completed structure in Los Arboles, would disappear. "Except for plumbing, of course." He smiled and plugged the modified cord into the wall outlet, his eyes half-shut against the possibility that, given the odor in the room now, there would be an accidental spark, a limited explosion. But of course nothing had happened. He knew what he was doing. He did not make mistakes—well, hardly ever.

He returned to the living room to switch off the stereo, but then thought better of it. The soft Mexican music on the running tape added a certain verisimilitude to the proceedings. "Do you not agree, Shirley?" he asked the dead woman. She stared back from the black ovals of false lashes, her small moist eyes as blank tonight as Lisa's. A faint bruise marred her throat. If a man were very strong, he could hold a person gently, and, almost without seeming to do anything, turn vision grey, turn it off, kill a brain; it was almost a caress, if one were very strong. He looked at her for a time, and thought, Well, you will not be needing that money after all. On the way out he plucked the two hundreds from her purse and stowed them in a wet pocket, and wiped the surfaces where he thought he might have left a legible print, and then stepped out into the night, walked the half mile to where he had parked his rented Fairmont earlier that evening, and got in. The blowing rain had chilled him, he felt as if he had never been quite dry in his life, or warm. It was worse than deep winter, in its way. Rousing himself, he muttered, "It is just that I am not a bloody polar bear." He cranked the car and drove downhill, keeping the heater on high and the blower going full blast, crossed the rising flood that surged down the arroyo, and drove another two miles to a point where he could park and watch the valley, the ridge above the abortive Los Arboles a dark, even line blocking the city glow.

He lighted a cigarette and waited, with the engine and heater going. For a paradise, California had gone very damned cold, he thought. And it had gone very damned sour, also, that business of the Morgan woman losing the photo. He knew she'd lied about it, but wondered how big the lie had been. Had she lost it? Had it gone down a drain? No, she had let the madwoman have it. What did such people do with paper? She might eat it, and the problem would go away in what Shirley Morgan called mess. But perhaps Lisa would treasure it and no one would know, or she would reveal it, and they would learn of his probing. Learn that his side had developed an interest. Ah, *that* was the one he did not want, not yet. At the moment he was working very swiftly, faster than they were, he believed, and he wanted to preserve his lead until he had it all, objective and ironclad. Even with that error with the clipping, he had come farther than he would have dreamed. To notice something unimportant, and to recognize suddenly that it was extraordinary, was one thing; that was his, and it was much more, he thought, than having talent for smelling smoke. Still, landing at Los Angeles that morning he had arrived with nothing much more than a very prescient nose full of smoke. For the rest, he must credit the technicians at headquarters. Without more information than some scraps from a personnel folder, they had reconstructed not merely the *apparent* history, but key elements of the real one as well. They had been able to peel back time to reveal the people killed in traffic the year before, and peel it back still further, still more deeply, to reveal a missing woman at the state hospital in Camarillo; and now, this Lisa had closed another loop for him with her single word: *Schaefer*. And yet, even with such confirmation as he had his own suspicions were still too fabulous for him to take home. He could loose the technicians upon the problem, in a general way, without their knowing whether they looked for a fox or a mole or a wolf, and they would gallop happily off in pursuit. They were as excited as a bunch of hounds, and they would do what they could with their forensics and electronic memories. In a matter of days, a week or two at the outside, they would have positioned Lisa in time, over there, then; and they would have dates, times, coordinates, a real childhood, real parents, everything—everything but the smoke itself; the talent part was his.

He believed in himself to the extent that he had acted on his own, coming over, using the Cleveland Brown identity, an almost untraceable flight over, driving across the Canadian border as a U.S. citizen, the Seattle plane to Los Angeles. He would return the same way. Two days gone, and the right thing falling more quickly than he would have dreamed, right into his broad, hard hands. On his own...they would not like that. Well...he would not tell them. He would let the technicians draw the outlines, and then he would render it into art, and present it, this fabulously improbable linkage he had sensed, sensed like an animal reading entire libraries upon the wind. Yes, and *he* would be the accuser, the first to see the power suddenly impotent, the commanding presence unable to look into the bright light of the truth. And the anger that moved within? The rage? What was that? He shook his head. Of course you would hate being fooled, of course you would hate spending time under some false thumb. You look at the icon and see suddenly that the whole thing is false, that God has no children, that death is as flat and empty as it seems...well, you would feel some of this, he thought, feeling the monstrous rage begin to pace within. He controlled it, but it was there. He smiled in the gloom. It would keep him warm.

A distant light bloomed across the arroyo, below the ridge, abrupt, blue-white, a sudden star; it shrank immediately to a fire that licked against the storm, too hot for the rain to put out quickly, although it would not last as long as he would have liked. Had he, after a near-perfect career, begun making mistakes? Is that what the rage would do now, have him bungle a little here, a little there, until it all hung from his hands like a raveled scarf? The clipping was bad. The rain was bad, they might find enough of her to autopsy. But even that, even finding her intact with that bruise across her jugular, connected to nothing beyond the well-known hazards of a woman's life alone. No, it was the continued existence of the clipping that worried him. He hoped the madwoman had eaten it, and that he could maintain his narrow edge, and that when the time came he would go with what was real, and end all of this... what was the American term? "Cowshit," he murmured.

4

PERHAPS THE RAIN would never stop. Perhaps we are at the end of everything, he thought, and it ends in the rain. He wrapped his black Burberry more closely around him, cinched up the belt. Come on, come on. The plane had been heard from over L.A., and was letting down into a standard instrument approach to Point Mugu it seemed hours ago. "Come on." His voice was harsh, touched with New England and bad temper, and the beginning of a cold.

As if in response to his muttered summons, a light broke through the rain, sputtering and intermittent, like a flare, and then was swallowed up by cloud and water; then reappeared, then vanished, a moving light jinking around to line up with the runway. Beneath the roar of rain he heard the scream of the Navy bomber. Abruptly there it was, beaked, its wings swept back, a sinister grey bird, flying onto the runway with one wing held down into the gusts of wind and water blowing across the flickering of lights. The A-3D bounced, caromed back into the air, and then seemed to fall to the ground on its narrow undercarriage, the drag chute flung out behind it like an exclamation of surprise, or fear. It rolled out of sight and he waited, wondering whether they would have to go winch it out of a ditch full of water. But, no, here it came, the chute blowing aimlessly around behind it now, the narrow wings folding like the other birds' today. Even in the rain, the crew cracked open the greenhouse to raise the blue and white two-star flag on one of the antennas just aft of the cockpit. "Frigging pirate's flag," he murmured, musing, as he often had before, on the inequities that permitted American admirals to travel—hell, to live—better than most heads of state. He waited with his shoulders hunched up like a pair of stunted wings, cold and demonstrably miserable. The A-3D trundled up to the operations shack on its ungainly gear, and pivoted broadside to the building. Then, as its engines died, a hatch opened just forward of the bomb bay and Carney dropped lightly to the apron, hesitated a moment to gauge the downpour, and walked briskly forward. He had never run for or from anything. When he saw the man under the light he gave his bored half-smile and extended a hard little hand. "Hello, Baker. Good to see you. It's been some time now."

"Yes, it has. How are you?" Lincoln's voice was harsh, and contained no hint of real concern for how the admiral was. But the civilities were observed.

"Can't complain. And you? You look well."

"As well as can be expected, as they say."

"I think I liked my fifties better too." Carney swept water off his leather flight jacket with the two white stars on the collar and slapped his cap against his thigh. "Like being in the submarines," he complained. "Damned interesting approach, though. Things awfully bad going into LAX."

"Were you flying tonight?"

"Needed some instrument time. Better than a simulator."

"I bet so." But Lincoln had heard that note in the voice which said: a little too much better than a simulator.

"The others here?"

"Yes. We're meeting at the hospital, have a room there."

"Good. Want me in mufti?"

"Doesn't matter at all." He gestured at the storm with a plump, hairy hand. "Not in this."

They waded out to the black Chrysler drawn up under the building's metal roof, with the motor and heater going. Both men hurried into the back seat, and Lincoln ordered, "Hospital." A silhouetted driver nodded, the car already in motion, the big headlamp beams slicing through

the dancing streaks of rain. It was warm in the car, and
dry, and both men seemed almost to doze; it was a rite of
non-aggression, each man impressing his sleepy harmless-
ness upon the other.

"How many came?"

"Only two. Most of the architects are dead, by now."

"Just us spring rams, right?"

A pool of light floated to them through the water, and
the Marine inside it saluted as they passed. Carney returned it, a sharp but barely perceptible snapping of a stiff
hand. He believed in military courtesies, but he believed
more in the conservation of his own energy. He glanced at
the man beside him. Getting along, like the rest of us. You
get in your sixties and you begin paying for every damned
little thing. Don't brush your teeth as a kid, they begin to
come out in your sixties. *Adios,* prostate. Testicles in great
shape but that scrotum's gotta go. He chuckled softly,
causing Lincoln to look at him interrogatively. But Carney only shook his head. Getting along and beginning to
wear down. All of us do. He touched his knees, which still
trembled faintly. That landing tonight had been one hairy
son of a bitch, the runway flashing at you through the
storm, a bad crosswind on that dinky little undercarriage,
landing hot, bouncing . . . *Jesus!* But the bad part was that
he had felt the cold touch of fear while sitting in the pilot's seat of an airplane under his control. Never had before. You just begin giving things up.

Daylight made the world ugly, nothing but the grey rain,
the city lights pretty much extinguished, and no glow in the
east, no line between sea and sky, land and sea, not a
damned thing but grey. Carney shook his head at all this
bleakness. It's like being in *Bulgaria*, he thought.

They turned off down the long straight road that led into
the Camarillo hospital grounds, past a bridge where a few
maintenance people in yellow slickers were installing
sandbags, hoping to keep the flooding arroyo from
blocking the highway, watched by a handful of silent inmates wrapped in olive drab ponchos that flapped and

cracked in the wind. Carney had spent *mucho* time, as he
would have said, in such facilities. These were where you
went to find the cracks, the loose wires, the obsessions and
nightmares and unhealing wounds that, when you thought
about it, pretty much made his world go round. Yes, and
these were the hospitals you went to, these and the military ones, to visit the remnants of your people, after another house of cards erected by some brilliant architect had
disintegrated in the evil, easterly wind. On a bright morning, Camarillo would have been pretty, manicured and
open, really more of a campus than a hospital. There
would be women who had not spoken for fifty years sitting placidly on benches in the sun, and men lying alone
upon the grass, in endless argument with themselves, and
attendants helping the hopeless and the very old creep
about in the light, clumsy and frail as creatures brought
suddenly up from the deep sea... Carney passed a hand
before his eyes, feeling that inner fatigue that seemed to
reach down into his very soul, a seed of death, perhaps, or
that cynicism which makes your interior a place where
nothing grows, which makes you take news of death and
pain and shattered love, of loss too much for man to bear,
with equanimity. Finally, nothing mattered but one's
work. Everything else became... external.

"Tired."

Carney shook his head. "Not in the usual sense of the
term."

"Ah." Then, "Here we are." He led Carney out of the
car and into a long, low building with white walls and red
tiled roof, appointed in the shabby linoleum tile and off-
green partitions of government facilities everywhere. The
office set aside for them was at the far end of the building, and apparently used only occasionally for consultation and the visits of relatives frightened about a patient's
condition, or possible return. It was a small room made
smaller by the rain pressing in upon its one large window,
lighted by an oblong fluorescent bank hanging from the
ceiling, like the light above a pool table. A small rectan-

gular wooden table, scarred hospital maple, stood in the center of the room, the captive of a half dozen wooden chairs. The pale green walls were bare except for a picture of the Governor of California and a wild, troubling abstract painting done by a resident child. The room stepped out of another time, the thirties, perhaps, so that the video console against the inside wall clanged with strangeness, like a visitor from the future.

The man and woman waiting there rose when they entered, and Carney looked them over. The man was in his nineties, the oldest of the architects, and, Carney thought now, the one who will outlast us all. His tall, thin body and narrow, squinting face seemed made of paper, paper old enough that an unexpected gust of wind would blow it into dust; but the bright eyes and the immutably captivating voice had not changed, not in all this time. He was like a man of forty trapped in a ruined container. "Carney," he said warmly. "How good to see you again."

"Dr. Spendahl, yes, it's good to be here. You're looking well."

"Well, that goes too far, admiral . . . but I do feel well, yes."

"Admiral Carney," the woman said now, placing a thin, firm hand in his. Had she changed very much? Carney did not think so. The ebony hair had gone to silver, and today was worn in a braid around the temples, held in place by tortoise combs, perhaps the same tortoise combs that he, with trembling hands, had once removed. Looking into her clear eyes, he saw his own memories of intimacies exchanged, of longings extinguished, all long, long ago. "Cybelle," he said. "It's good to see you." He could not release her hand.

She withdrew it gently, let him have the contact, the brush of old memory. He thought it might have warmed her, but it made him cold, as the difficult instrument approach had done in the airplane, as the rain had, and the sense of being on the far slope of one's powers. Time had scarcely touched her face, the eyes still brimmed with intelligence and humor, with that sure knowledge of all that is droll in the human condition, and her figure, at sixty, had survived.

"I think we should begin," Spendahl said. "As the senior person here, let me inject some front matter, and then we can go on to the business at hand. As we see, there are just the four of us architects left, and we can, in the normal course of things, expect that number to diminish. Our cooperative project began as a national initiative, and we have had the generous support of our government in it, both in restricting all knowledge to the highest levels, but also in providing material and expert help to sustain the project.

"I wish now to express my own fear that we have been at this too long. I understand we are very close to having a major success in the Shepherd Property. But a cursory knowledge of actuarial tables leads me to remind us that it can be successful now only for a short time, and that it could very soon become utterly useless from a national viewpoint. When we reach that point . . . well before we reach it, I will urge that we put an end to the entire matter, and remove it from all memory, official and otherwise."

Lincoln watched Spendahl with mild contempt, this old true believer, this genteel spy and trader in grand initiatives, whose hands had no blood on them, nothing under the mottled fingernails. He, Lincoln, had been the worker, and Carney, and Cybelle. And he had created it, made it happen, kept it happening when it looked as though it could not turn through one more chug; and now, when they finally had what had been intended, Spendahl's nerve began to fail, he began crying about national purpose. Fuck the national purpose, Lincoln thought. We've made it go, we keep it going. *We're* not ninety, or afraid. Now he leaned toward the others and said, very gently, "I think we can make that a matter of record, if you like, Dr. Spendahl. But it scares me to think we would begin dismantling that particular property at this point in time, when we are close to achieving a success far beyond what we, as the architects, could have anticipated.''

"Inclined to agree," muttered Carney, like someone talking in his sleep. The woman nodded too, but looked apprehensively at Spendahl.

"I shall withdraw my comments, then," the old man said, beginning faintly to whine. That was no forty-year-old in there, Carney thought. What we see is what we got. "I merely wanted to note..." Spendahl went on.

"Your concern has been noted," Lincoln finished for him. He looked at the other three. They were like a closed club, but not a very good one. They shared a shallow root system of places like Stanford and Annapolis and parents or grandparents driven toward America by famine and repression. Nothing very long term, nothing very solid among them, whereas his roots went down and down and *down* into an America of Pilgrims and money, and thick maroon blood. "We are meeting now, as we did last year, because something has changed...and every change carries some new risk for our property. Last year, when it was clear Brezhnev was finally dying..." He met the old man's eyes, and held them, as if to say: Yes, Goddamn you, I used that filthy word, *dying*. "...we met to evaluate the effect of that event upon the value of our holdings, especially that of the Shepherd Property. We decided, given our information on the probable line of succession, that we would see a considerable appreciation in that structure. At the same time, we wanted to look at the possibility that added security was in order."

"There were seven of us then," Spendahl said, unable to forget death.

"Bad year for architects," Carney put in.

"A very bad year." Christ, these people, even one with the legendary taciturnity of Carney, had a reflex for chatter. "But...moving along...Cybelle, you were the architect who urged that we go back for one last sweep for loose wires. And you were the one who found them."

The woman nodded, but modestly. "I don't want to sound abnormally prescient about this. In a way, it was quite a routine procedure. It's just that our Cray can handle so much material in a relatively short time, all sorts of odd patterns and combinations emerge with a clarity that you just don't see using a smaller machine with simpler programming. That's why we didn't see the loose wire, as you call it, Baker, in the early sweeps. The machine couldn't get down into the noise level of people's lives, which is where we had to go. What we did was set up programs that would probe at increasing multi-dimensional radii from the Shepherd Property, straddling the date of 13 April 1945..."

"The day after FDR died at Warm Springs," Spendahl remembered.

"The property was in transition then," she continued, talking to Lincoln and Carney. "We swept toward and away from that point in time. You'd already told us that there had been some interaction during the Kitzingen stop..."

"It was unavoidable. I had no control at that point."

"But in the end things came right again."

"Yes. But I was surprised they *stayed* right."

"You know, they almost didn't," she said brightly. "Did you know he was in Kitzingen in November of forty-five?" Carney shook his head. Cybelle went on, "That's the kind of detail the Cray can give us. It let us pick up her trail, and at about the same time an anomalous pattern of communication between this hospital, and a ranch south of Los Angeles, with old, apparently inactive ties to Kitzingen. These discoveries caused us to focus down on her, tracking her in October 1945 to California, a short interval with German-American 'parents,' and her installation here at Camarillo in 1947. And, of course... the baby."

"Yes," Lincoln said. "The baby." The reference brought that autonomic surge of hatred he had felt from the first moment he heard of the baby from Cybelle, from that first instant in which it appeared that their structure, their property, had a crack in it. No, worse than that. Hearing of the baby he had known that this crack had been inflicted deliberately upon the operation; Shepherd had *hoped* something like the baby would happen. The love of continuity. Now, gazing down at his short, strong, hairy hands, he found them shaking in a way he could see but could not feel. Sometimes, these days, his fingertips seemed to die. He hated, and yet, he was loath to kill merely, as he would have put it, as a convenience. The baby, the hated residue of a hateful and malicious indiscretion, had its uses after all. In return for x he had produced it. For x plus something rather good he would even plan, *intend*, to leave the baby alone. For awhile. For as long as one could. This hated infant had no memory, no way of tracking itself back and back through all the layers of time across those gaps where living people used to be.

"But also," Cybelle went on, "the fixation on the name, Schaefer. As the doctors reconstruct it, and she gives them nothing to go on, that is the name used during the interval of contact with the woman. Of course it is obvious it had great impact upon her..." Cybelle looked away and Lincoln thought, Yes, lady, some of us have shared that impact, that peculiar magnetism, more than others. He grinned at her coldly; she stared back with a hatred something like his own, into his unresponding face.

"A person should survive the disappointments of having people enter and leave one's life," she said almost bitterly.

"She popped," Carney said, snapping his fingers with a sound like a shot.

"At the time," Lincoln ventured, picking up his chairmanship once more, "it seemed a relatively simple corrective. Our queries indicated that Lisa had no extant ties with Kitzingen. We voted to remove a crucial segment of the mnemonic circuit, and sever Lisa from the baby for all time. That was accomplished last year."

"That damned truck business," Carney put in. "Don't see why we needed quite so much equipment and so many players. Can't kill memory by forming new ones."

"And such fear and pain," said Spendahl, mournfully.

"No new memory was generated by the accident," Cybelle said, interrupting quietly and decisively. "And, as a matter of coincidence, the truck driver died some months later in an operation in Nicaragua."

"What would we do without coincidence?" Lincoln asked rhetorically.

"Still, we went forward with the plan. The crucial wires were removed from the circuit. We believed that the confinement here, given Lisa's catatonic state, would contain all residual memory. And, of course, the baby knew nothing, had no memory to be removed. All things remaining equal, it would have been enough, what we did."

"Yes," said Lincoln then, "but things have not remained equal. We discover now that Lisa has only suspended her life, with no loss of memory. In fact, her point of suspension appears to be exactly at that point in her life we would like her to forget. And now . . . we seem to have drawn the attention of others. We get whiffs of British interest, for example. And Soviet interest." He hesitated. "There has even been, I believe, a murder."

"Ours?" asked Carney.

"No."

"But this is very serious," cried old Spendahl, like a man in a dream.

"What happened?" asked Cybelle.

It pleased Lincoln to have them thus surprised. A little showmanship went a long way in these meetings. "Last night, or, rather, early this morning, a condominium in Camarillo was destroyed by a gas explosion. Faulty refrigerator wiring. Woman with too much to drink. Explosion followed by a fire that, as it happened, did not completely consume the premises, or the complete body of the woman, whose name was Shirley Morgan. The autopsy indicates she was dead before the explosion, with negative lung tests for inhaled gas or smoke. She was dead before the event. Probably murdered, although it will go in as accidental death.''

Lincoln looked around at his audience, pleased to be the first to unfold this new element in the project. ''How does she connect? Shirley Morgan was a ward attendant here at the hospital, and Lisa, *our* Lisa, was one of her responsibilities. Now . . . let me show you something, and see if we can't reconstruct what happened.'' He flicked off the lights in the room, and switched on the video player. The picture oscillated wildly for a moment, then steadied. It showed a mad, wide-angled view of Lisa's room, seen from above the door. The woman sat on her cot, curled up, watchful. The Raggedy Andy doll lay on the floor nearby.

''Poor baby,'' Cybelle said.

Now, leaping like a giant from the foreground beneath the camera, Shirley Morgan entered, gave her greetings, and began to clean the floor. ''This is the dead woman,'' Lincoln told them. Lisa did not move. After a time, the attendant looked around, her apprehension amplified by the wide-angle distortion that lengthened her nose and face, then approached the madwoman. ''Lisa, Lisa, look,'' they heard her whisper. ''Look at the men, Lisa.'' Suddenly the catatonic moved, snatching something away, bending over it; their view was partly blocked by the Morgan woman's broad back. ''Look at the men,'' she whispered, and they could hear the trouble in her voice. The tape continued in silence. Now and then Lisa would look up, then go back to whatever she examined. Abruptly, they heard her say, ''Schaefer,'' and then the rising scream of the repeated name. Lincoln switched off the machine.

''Here's what Lisa was studying. Pass it around.'' He handed the scrap, now badly frayed, to the woman, who shook her head and passed it to Spendahl, who did the same. ''Jesus Christ,'' said Carney, when he saw it.

''A page from last year's annual report of the Centre for Analytic Studies. The men in the photograph are senior scientists, delegates from member nations, the committee...*everyone*. It is exactly what we have hoped to avoid all these years...that chance encounter, a newspaper photograph, a television show, whatever...and her response triggering memories, intuitions, in others. I think it is obvious that the Morgan woman was approached, perhaps paid, although no notable sum of money was found, to show Lisa this clipping and report back what she said. I am sure the person who gave Shirley Morgan this clipping wanted it back, and her murder may be in part punishment for failing to do so. Except for returning the photo, I believe she did as requested. Well...she apparently did *everything* requested.'' He watched his colleagues. "But this other person," he said then, "had no real information at that point. A very strong, very acute intuitive leap, but nothing firm."

"You mean he was improvising." Carney slid the clipping across the table.

"But what would trigger the intuitive leap, as you call it?"

"I think I know," said Lincoln. "I think it was seeing two or three people in a particular way, and having the subconscious say: Hey, *look* at that! Something like that. And then, on top of this, you have another man remembering some odd thing...memory, you see, bubbling to the surface. The man who reached Shirley Morgan is good, very very good, to have got there. He is following connections that are not obvious."

"Or provable," said Cybelle.

"Still...you are saying we have a situation that demands the whole thing be dissolved, now," Spendahl said, shaking his head miserably. "I wish we did not always come to this same bottom line."

"The British are not very far behind," said Lincoln.

"Then all the wires have to come out." Carney did not even look up; his stubby index finger drew imaginary doodles on the wooden table. Then, "How do we proceed?"

Lincoln looked at them, unaware that his face had stretched into its habitual sneer. Now, he thought, we are all going to get our hands dirty. All of us, not just me. Everybody. "We have to limit memory, that's our first imperative. That means we have to do everything ourselves."

"Jesus, we're a little old for field work," Carney complained.

"You're never too old," Cybelle countered, her voice saying that you were never too old for a lot of interesting things, and one of them was field work. Her eyes bright with excitement, she turned to Lincoln. "Tell us about our field work, Baker."

"The immediate problem is Lisa. However, we understand that surgery has been indicated, by a local physician who has performed numerous lobotomies on inmates for whom that seemed the most beneficial treatment. I think we should go with his diagnosis."

"But a lobotomy..." Cybelle began to argue.

"I know, a lobotomized person carries the same risk as a catatonic one, perhaps more. Her memories must be...disconnected. Our surgeon is an experienced man, but possibly not infallible. To get where he now is, he performed in the past a number of private, uh, gynaecological treatments. In discussing the possible career impacts these would produce if brought to light, I found him reasonable and reliable." Sensing further protest, he held up a hand. "And, no, this is not adding to our troubles in the long term. As far as he knows all of this derives from the wishes of powerful relatives. New memories, yes, but all false, irrelevant."

"One wire out," the woman said.

"The others will come out," Lincoln went on. "All but the property itself."

"Their probe?" Carney asked.

"All of them."

"Even the baby," Spendahl gazed at the floor.

"No...we wait on the baby, the baby has its uses, and it will bring the whole goddamned temple down if we touch it. The baby has to be...I don't know, something damned clever."

"It has to be criminalized, dead at a distance from us, and the property discredited," Cybelle volunteered. "All the sentiment has to come off it."

Lincoln chuckled. "Cybelle, you are altogether too good at this."

"It's a living." But her eyes glowed with the prospect of action.

Carney leaned forward, still drawing invisibly with his finger. He did not look up. "So, okay, we have the Lisa circuit out, and we've neutralized their probe...assuming that a bunch of geriatric ops can handle this kind of field assignment...what if we still haven't got this thing under control? I mean, do we just wait for it to hit *The New York Times*, or what?"

"Don't be sarcastic, admiral. If it doesn't come back under control we do what pilots do."

"We bail out."

"Abandon ship," said Spendahl his hands nervously washing one another.

"Everything comes out."

"Property and all?"

"Property and all."

"Even the baby," Spendahl echoed.

"Yes, even the baby."

"Poor Raggedy Andy," said Cybelle.

5

LISA HAD KNOWN this would be the day even before the attendants began to fuss over her, cleaning her, preparing her, making her beautiful again. She had known it as the black rainy night had been displaced before her unblink-

ing eyes by a grey, wet dawn. Today was the day. Today
Schaefer returned. She knew it. Absolutely.

Would he be as he had been?

No. She had seen him, among the other men in the
photograph. He had been living in time that moved, that
worked, away from her and the baby. Acknowledging this
difference between them hurt her, for she had always assumed he waited somewhere, locked in a moment like hers,
a prisoner of broken time. But the photo had contained
him, an older man, broader, a man who lived in the flow
of time, not its crystalline alternative—and yet, unmistakably, her Schaefer. Her heart surged at the memory of
seeing him there, on that page . . . perhaps he had been im-
prisoned in that photograph . . . ? The implications of that
flew at her brain like a swarm of bees, and she flinched
away . . .

How would it be?

As it was before.

Before.

Before the end of time.

First she would hear him, the deep, soft voice, approaching the doorway, just *there*, and she would rise, radiant, pretty as ever. Then the door would fly open and
there he would be, his large, handsome former self, crisply
uniformed in olive-colored twill, his hair a bit shaggy,
silky, in back, his eyes going into her . . . *into* her.

They would walk out of this place, this *Gasthaus*, this
home for the afflicted, whatever this place was (*What
place?* Quickly, Lisa turned away from the question,
trembling.), and outside there would be the vineyards
curving up the hill above Kitzingen, as they had been before, crisscrossed with tank tracks, the vines here and there
shattered by explosions, and they would hold hands and
happily ascend through the vineyards to the line of forest
that boiled at the top of the hill, as they had before, and
there they would find a place, a perfect place, the pine-
needled forest loam like a bed in an upturned palm of
granite, and together they would lie there, and kiss, and

touch . . . ah, *how* they would touch. Off to the northwest, with the afternoon light streaming under low clouds, like the light of autumn, they would see the castle at Würzburg, and smoke, and off to the southeast there would be the smoke and sound of Nürnberg, and Regensberg... She smiled, wanting to say *Würzburg, Nürnberg, Regensberg,* like a child. But she could not. They were not what she said. They were not her word . . .

Lisa started, aware suddenly of a new presence, the new attendant with a wheelchair. "Come on, Lisa," the woman (Where was Shirley? Shirleyshirleyshirleyshirley.) said in a kind voice. "Time for us to do your hair, get you all spruced up. Make you feel nice, light and cool."

She shut her eyes when the big black woman began to cut her hair, shut her eyes and let herself be touched by the gentle fingers that smoothed the tangled strands of silver and gold, that brushed out the snarls, and turned her head a little this way, a little that. *He* would find her beautiful, and they would lie on the Earth and it would spin wildly beneath them and he would touch her, his long, skilled fingers playing her like a lyre, causing her to forget everything, the war, the nuns and priests, Heinrich, Kitzingen, everything except that she had spent her life waiting for this man with hands that made her forget . . . everything, that made her want only to have him, there, have him *there* . . . Lisa leaned back dreamily, rubbing her thighs together, the warm galaxy of desire turning ponderously within. Then, then, she would pull him into her soft red world, creating the song of incomparable pleasure that burst from deep within . . .

"Best leave her alone, honey." The black woman pulled Lisa's hand out of her soiled muslin panties. "You still so pretty, you get ever'body hot doin' that." She moved her big, dark head back and forth in a sympathetic rhythm. "I sure God hope they know what they're doin' with you. Cause I hate those brain cutters, I truly do."

Lisa heard her as a soothing song, the husky voice gentling her, as though she were a golden horse, frightened by...no, she did not want to know what had frightened her. The strong competent hands prepared her for Schaefer. "Schaeferschaeferschaefer," she murmured. The hands finished with the scissors, and now soaped her scalp with foaming cream, and shaved away the golden stubble. It left her feeling light and free, her head cold and clean. Then the woman peeled off Lisa's smock and panties and helped her into a bath, where Lisa sat, blank and pretty, while the woman soaped and rinsed, soaped and rinsed, while Lisa, her eyes shut, thought of Schaefer and their touching, their afternoon and night and morning on the hillside above Kitzingen, with the war going away down the Donau, and their touching, ah, their touching, those cries of delight, of hers, of his, the lovely illusion that they had been put on Earth for one another, their movements, their feelings, reflecting from one to the other, like light, back and forth, the certainty of reciprocation—for, in her opaquely coded memory, there resided her own deep certitude that she, *she*, had been exactly as powerful and permanent for him as he had been for her, and that wherever he had lived, out there in moving time, he still cleaved to those same memories of Kitzingen, to that *intended* intersection of their lives...

Her hand ceased, she drew it away from soapy genitals...

If all that were true, why had he left? asked a clear and unfamiliar voice within. Why, with promises to return, had he not come back to Kitzingen? September had come and gone. But he had only gone, gone... Tears spilled from her closed eyes.

"Poor baby," the black woman said. "Oh, you poor old baby." Then, "Come on, now," helping Lisa from the tub, beginning to towel her dry. "You still so pretty, such a pretty Lisa, after all this time, and after today you got nothing to worry you, hon," and Lisa, hearing this confirmation that today was indeed *the day*, stopped her tears, abandoned doubt, let a bright joy expand across her heart. *"Schaefer!"* she whispered, happy again.

The woman spread her out on a wheeled table, and covered her with light green sheets. It seemed to Lisa she must glow with cleanliness, everything clean, clean (cleancleanclean), her head smooth; she needed flowers, but they would find them in the fields beyond the forest and vineyards, where vermillion smears of poppies bloomed, and wood roses lurked like moths in the shadows...

Again, she seemed to fly down the halls. Her heart lifted toward what lay ahead, she felt like a joyous bird, a lark rising on the dawn, above the vineyards, to announce...to announce that, at last, he would be with her again. He would lie with his head on her lap, as he had before, and whisper with a sad smile on his handsome face, *"Ich bin dein Schaefer, Lisa."*

Another room, one she had never entered before, broad and brightly lighted. Was he to meet her here? Her nose twitched at an antiseptic odor, a mild smell of gas; the place evoked the war, something about the war (*Kriegkriegkrieg*) and...the baby! Schaefer would want to see the baby. But where was it? Her jaws convulsed, unable to say the word, and spat out finally: *"Schaefer!"* The baby, she had to find the baby before Schaefer got there, had to find the baby... She tried to rise, but her wrists and ankles had been strapped down. *"Schaefer,"* she screamed, crying out for help to the man who, today, would return, and want her, and want to see their baby, babybabybaby, but where was the baby, what had happened to baby, and where was the man, and why had they, the enemy *They*, bound her hands and feet, why was she naked, were they raping her, was this her punishment for letting herself think of Schaefer in the forest above Kitzingen, and why had they bound her hands and feet, and who was this new man in glasses, this green man without a face watching her with tears in his eyes? Why was *he* crying? "SCHAEFER," she screamed, banging her shaved head against the padded table, "SCHAEFERSCHAEFER..."

A green woman entered her field of view, which was suddenly eclipsed by a great, soft, stinking rubber moon. "Schaeferschaefer..." her mind pleaded, sobbed, hopeless and alone. She heard the sounds of machines, of tanks; they had brought her back into the war, and Schaefer was still somewhere else in time, oh, Schaefer, where have you gone, *wo wo wo?* Despairing then, she and her hurt and disappointment and fear spun down and down and down, and into darkness.

PART THREE

1

IMAGINE A CLOCK that has been crushed into a soft trapezoid by a strong fist, flattened along the early hours after twelve, corrugated between nine and midnight. That is the general shape of Vienna. An odd clock, an odd machine for telling time. The numerals on its face—the numbered districts of the city—go up to twenty-three, but are not all in clockwise order; a perfectly predictable and appropriate difference, one might say, for Vienna. Number one is at the center of the dented face, the site of the old city that once lay within the encircling walls and fortified glacises bounded by the narrow curve of the Danube Canal, which winds through the northeastern quadrant of the city with almost none of the beauty of the Potomac, Thames, or Seine. The old walls have mostly vanished, replaced by the pretty, some say pretentious, deformed circle of the Ringstrasse, and the watching rooftop crowds of stone and metal figures, who stand, and possibly converse very quietly, among a tangle of microwave dishes and wiring. They are all refugees from other cultures, other histories, from old Greece and Rome, borrowed gods, muses, heroes, anonymous horse-tamers are everywhere.

On this cracked old clock, I lived a little before noon, just across the *Gürtel* in the eighteenth district, where the town begins its transition from the mercantile clutter of the former suburb of Währinger into broader streets of pastelle villas and large gardens, all lined with chestnut and sycamore trees, spotted with pretty parks. If I walked a kilometer north, up the hill on whose flank my building stood, I would see rounded hills banded by vines, with woods and mountains behind. Going the other way, down to the canal, to the inner city was a feasible walk of a couple of kilometers.

My flat was high ceilinged and white-walled, with light streaming in on three sides, a kind of well-illuminated garret of a place, its once-fine parquet floor covered by a grease-grey carpet that seemed never to have been another color. The place was furnished with the tacky castoffs of landlords I never met. My only contribution was a large bed, bought to replace one of those split-mattressed Austrian doubles, designed for just about everything except what beds are for. In late spring and summer, the flat floated in light, and the birdsong, drifting into the enclosed courtyard at the building's heart, had that lusty European quality that awakens but does not annoy, trills and whistles, in bold capitals.

The façades that filled my front windows were cheerful ones, white stone frames set in brick walls, or in white or pale yellow stuccoed ones, with Roman profiles in one tier of pediments, and cherubs in another, Greek masks, lions, wise heads and serious ones, a run of unicorns and Habsburg double eagles, all rising to crowded crowns and scrolls and shields at the top. Mixed in with these were live Austrian neighbors, immobile as caryatids, leaning on their elbows to watch the empty, idle streets.

The days turned predictably around the sounds of town and traffic, and sweeps of music, awakening like birds during the day, the piano in the forenoon, the flute just after lunch, and, later in the afternoon, from an Austrian middle school a block away, the sweet rising notes of a girls' choir. It was a neighbourhood of such sounds, without any litter beyond that of passing dogs, every window in every building shining, and, down on the main drag, the mingled flats and shops, shops with nothing but gloves, or umbrellas, or brushes, chicken shops, sweet shops, flowers everywhere.

A quiet life, then, in rooms where almost nothing was mine, a place in which one could bring in extra work to do, and read, and listen to Blue Danube Radio, and tune in the BBC World Service on the small Sony 2000, which for a time had been my best friend in Vienna. ("Get one," Dexter had urged, "get one so you'll be able to hear an English voice at any hour of the day or night, or you'll go daft in this place, utterly daft.")

All the Russians lived there. It was the site of the Russian school, mandatory for their children, closed to others, and where they went about in small clusters, I suppose watching one another, but I think also dreading the return to a homeland where nothing quite worked, where life, unless you were young and idle, or powerful, was a hassle. You would see them make their preparations to leave, the purchased trailer hooked to the wheezing Lada sedan, a small mountain of everything tied on with bungee cords, the things they could not buy at home. And even then they could never take quite enough away. Not a looting instinct, really—it may be unfair for the Austrians to call the Soviet war monument the tomb of the unknown looter—but that flow toward a vacuum, the reflexive grasping of perennial have-nots.

Sometimes, on long walks, I would encounter Emil Dashko, escaped from the Russian woman who maintained him, cruising silently through the broad hilly turns of Türkenschanzpark, and we would greet one another, and talk, and be friendly. He went out in all kinds of weather, daring God perhaps, and also refusing to submit to his illness, or his nurse, which one imagines would have been a very easy, comfortable thing to do. Sometimes I came upon the narrow double track of his chair in a thin veneer of snow, and marveled that he would venture out in freezing weather. If asked, he would say, "Breathing clean, frozen air is the other thing I can still do." I think the cold reminded him of home, and youth, and lost vitality.

I often saw Trulov and his wife and the lunar daughter, Svetlana, at the local laundry, or at the Julius Meinl, which is Austria's Safeway. His superficial coldness toward me had vanished, and his greetings were once more hearty and funny and often physical; and yet, he seemed to me the coldest thing about our winter, I didn't know why. Odd justice, that gives one the same vivid sensitivity to others when we crack and when we heal.

The beautiful city slipped around me as comfortably as an old coat. And more. Arriving there had been in some respects like returning to my old whitewalled room at the avocado ranch in California, a room that had not changed, beyond the accretion of strata (the age of Teddy bears, of tin soldiers, of model planes, surfboards, scubas, girls, enlightenment) in my lifetime, a room where my presence lay, hands cupped behind the familiar skull, upon a broad, sagging, noisy metal bed covered with a formidably white candlewick cover. Returning there, I would simply slip into this waiting presence, a body returning to its spirit. I could return today to that empty, uninhabited ranch and there he would be, that spirit, waiting to be contained once more.

The sight of the Ringstrasse curving off among the chestnut trees and enormous ornamented buildings with their stony rooftop populations, the low autumn light warming pale towers, seen from a narrow street blue with dusk, even the earnest trams flying their jolly little flags and blue explosions of sparks—these produced what passed in me then for a leap of the heart. I chose to believe in the cheerful chorus of *Grüss Gott* at every encounter, of *Danke schön* and *Aufwiedersehen* at every departure, and ignored the rote quality, the possibility that these might be the sounds of robots, not of friends. I found warmth in them. I liked their ultimate willingness to relieve the mild catatonia of living in a country without speaking its language—the Viennese would always finally bring out their English, if they had any, and dust it off for you, and ease your isolation. I found them welcoming and pretty as flowers, and it didn't matter to me if the blooming I observed occurred in a kind of false spring. It felt like home and mother and the room in California to me, I suppose partly because I met my Uncle Stuka there.

His real name was Heinrich Braun, and he lived with his wife, Renate, and a Doberman bitch named Fee, in a grand greystone villa well out into the nineteenth district, where the city turns suddenly old and beautiful, and then ceases to exist along the boundaries of woods and vineyards. In summer the house disappeared in greenery as the garden became a fountain of willows and birches and chestnuts and spruces, and the façade grew its pretty mask of roses, a pink and white and yellow pointillist mask that made it seem that Beauty slept there. But in winter, even the mild winter of that year, at dusk the trees stood like black skeletons without their flesh of leaves, and the evergreens looked like great hair tails moving in the wind, and the brown hard fingers of the rosevines scrabbled on the cold, damp stones. In winter all the warmth of the place emanated from Uncle Stuka himself, when he met you and his big Bavarian face exploded into an enormous, rather carnivorous, grin, exposing the broad yellow teeth that seemed carved from cedar, crinkling the wise bird eyes of the aviator. "Schaefer," he would always cry out with surprise, even when he expected me. "I am so *happy* that you can come," and he would confirm this with a vigorous nod to himself, and grip my hand in the big ruined paw of a retired builder of homes, and give my shoulder a powerful squeeze, and then take me into his home—that was the sensation, always, of being somehow incorporated into the happy place he had made for himself.

Happy, but also flawed. Renate was dark and broad-faced, black-haired and coffee-skinned, so that he called her "my gypsy," and ignored the sombre look, almost one of mourning, she wore beneath a thin, destroyed gaiety. She was a pretty woman, a bit thick in the body, but with fine breasts and the possibility of resonant sexuality, which flickered dully in her heavily lashed black eyes. Her look, her body, her demeanor, all spoke of disappointment, the hot woman of thirty-five carried off by a lusty old knight not yet turned sixty, and then the hot love becoming perfunctory, and then a mere formality, and then an occasional touch, a goodnight kiss. There was that to be mourned, and she grieved for it in the tough, thin-lipped way of a Greek widow. After my uncle's big greeting, the first thing you noticed was Renate's heat, that suppressed flame beneath the grief. I found it hard to ignore, this bad news on sable wings.

Fee's complaint was easier to accommodate. Cancer had caused her right foreleg to be amputated that summer. Meeting me with Uncle Stuka, she would hobble nervously on the three that remained, the unconnected muscles in the right shoulder fumbling beneath the skin for a leg to propel. "Soon it go to her heart," he had told me sadly, and the dog seemed to sense the end was coming too. But where grief had turned Renate into a hot stone, it had produced in Fee that rarest of creatures, a reflective Doberman.

No, the warmth in the house of Braun came from my uncle, who had greeted me upon our first encounter there, in spring, and at each of my visits since. Because I liked him, because we were one another's last living blood relations, as he put it, I would have gone there more often; but I rationed myself to intervals a bit longer than a fortnight, to preserve my own anticipation, to keep the visits fresh and rare, and to steer around the smouldering ardor of his wife. But I looked toward these evenings with eager interest, for each one, beyond the greeting, beyond the sense of being yanked from a cold world into a warm one, was invariably different from the others.

In summer there were the afternoons around a table, with meats and chicken bubbling on a grill, and a great deal of red Austrian wine, and bread, and cheeses, and salad, and the small baked potatoes you get there, often with an apology from the hostess, who had heard of the potatoes of Idaho. Usually there would be a dozen of us, Austrian couples and the lone American, the droll guest who spoke no German, so that these get-togethers were performed mostly in English, as a courtesy to me. The garden rang with jokes and reminiscences, my uncle lead-

ing the proceedings always, his voice filling the yard, while
I sat, listening and laughing, and his wife brooded nearby,
feeding us. He would tell me about when he and my dead
father were boys in Bavaria, and about my mother, and
how his arm of the Brauns had lived for centuries in Kitzingen, a little town southeast of Würzburg, which he still
believed was the most beautiful land on earth, "... Austria is good, yes, but not *so* good." His eyes would look
back through time, then, to his youth, to his good old
days, and also to the war. And as he told me these things,
sprinkling them with anecdote and proverb ("Prussians are
saying Bavarian is like sack of flour, always you can beat
more out of them."), there would sometimes spread across
the wide terrain of his face a look of sadness, of loss perhaps, in which there was something intended specifically
for me. The big face seemed to say: *If only you knew.* I
would have to turn away from this, finding it incomprehensible, as so much was to me then.

But his Stuka and Messerschmitt stories—well, those
were something else. He would lean toward me, his old
enthusiasms flashing in the small blue eyes, and spin an
atmosphere of flight and danger and command that enfolded us. The tripodal dog sat nearby, not quite excluded
from our journeys through time and hostile skies, but the
wife would not come; one felt her recede from us, and then
be lost, although she still sat not two meters away. She had
not been his wife then; this chapter—this watershed—in his
life happened without her, and she hated it with the same
grieving hatred through which she viewed her own existence.

"The Stuka is big machine, but only one engine, you
see. On northern sectors we stop ships going to Russians
in Murmansk. Now, take off, it is time of winter, cold like
old love, and we flying three hundred fifty kilometers over
water, water so cold it kill you like this." He snapped thick
fingers with a *bang*! "We fly, and soon are ships, big convoy, destroyers, *many* guns...they see us, is shooting, flak
everywhere around as we start the dive." His eyes glowed,

then, as his hands began their flying. I could almost hear the big in-line engines revving up, screaming as the planes pointed downward, broken cloud strata rushing past... "To bomb in Stuka you must point her down, straight down, like so." A big hand, fingers stiff, pointed toward the dark grain of the wooden floor, at ships, at the cold, ice-strewn sea. "Straight down we dive then. Straight down into convoy. And then..." He looked up, his eyes asking if I knew what followed. I would always shake my head, causing him to give a big yellow flash of a smile. "At the bottom," he went on, hauling the hand out of its screaming dive, "we fly out *between* ships... we stay *below* the levels of the decks...guns cannot come down on us, we are too low on water..." He leaned back with satisfaction. "The Stuka, big plane for only one engine. We lose many of them and pilots and gunners too, to fly over Baltic in winter."

Not all of his tales were of combat. Stukas were where he began in the Luftwaffe, but later he led a group of Messerschmitts based in the north, and other groups, as the German forces contracted back toward their center. His stories of the early part of the war evoked a kind of aerial knighthood, though, an era lost forever now in which a fighter pilot, finding a weekend free and feeling some homesickness, would leap into his ME-109 and fly home, put it down in a pasture near town, spend the weekend, and fly back to war on Sunday night. I loved the image of the young officer-pilot landing his fighter in a field, and then helping out from the cramped piggyback position behind his seat a lovely young girl. "Oh, *not* my Renate, my first wife... hair like corn. A good Aryan girl, excuse the expression. Wonderful and happy, in her *Dirndl*." Here he would turn toward some unseen presence, tears standing in his eyes, and for a time sit in silence. That pretty German girl was with him still, and, one thought, his gypsy knew it.

His last return home had been that of a knight on the run, unhorsed, beaten, one of thousands of German pilots without airplanes, a staff officer baling out ahead of Göring's southward flight to the Tyrol that April. "This is then March 1945," he would recount. "I am fighting then since 1938. I see the war goes against Hitler, all is lost, I am not infantryman, but pilot, officer." A stern, faraway expression filled the big face. "I come home then on the road with no uniform, to be with the others...my wife...when end comes. Sometimes I think to go back, but Americans are in Kitzingen in April...they stay in *our* Gasthaus! There is no place now to go. I stay. I see it happen." And here, that look of agitated sadness would pass across his face, and tears would form, and I would look away.

My parents, according to Uncle Stuka, had left Kitzingen by summer of that year, taking with them a small hoard of gold hidden away when the war began. Posing as Jews (he shuddered when he said this), they had gone to California, and bought the decrepit ranch as if they must put both an ocean *and* a continent between themselves and what they had always called "the Nazi time." I knew, in his descriptions of their leaving, he left key elements unsaid. One reason for hearing them over and over, as one does with old uncles, was finally to hear those missing parts, the truth at the heart of my own existence. I don't mean I dreamed of revelations. I just wanted more detail for the outlines I already knew. But my uncle invariably took an undetailed course through these histories.

Tonight a cold night in late November, when the low sun had begun to lose its ability to warm the earth at our latitude, I'd found it pure hell to park my little BMW even within walking distance of the place, so that I finally ran it up on a sidewalk two blocks away and left it, hoping here would be no tickets. I arrived at his house and rang the bell from the locked metal gate in front. The buzzer let me in, and he had the door open when I reached the stairs. He and the dog stood in silhouette, and he wore his customary smile, and uttered his customary greeting. But the house was crowded. Coats were everywhere in the foyer, and in one of the front rooms. "I hope you not mind,

Schaefer," he said diffidently, "but tonight is night of our *kleine* Luftwaffe . . ." He grinned magnificently.

"You didn't tell me," I began to protest, wanting not to intrude upon a special gathering.

"I think you not come if I do," he countered. "But you love it, watch and see. Sit with us, listen . . . I am translate for you, come, come." And with that he led me into their large dining room, where a dozen assorted old men and women had arranged themselves like happy dolls among the odd blend of Bavarian, Tyrolean, and Viennese furniture beneath the necessary chandelier, which floated in a glittering sphere of light and refractions.

The faces that turned toward us as we entered were merely old, at first. And then, an instant later, I began to see, in the males at least, something of the smaller, younger face of the aviator, some residual flush of courage, manly fear, and the excitement of high-powered flight. My uncle was their putative leader. His big voice and manner dominated these monthly gatherings, his anecdotes and jokes filled their evenings. But the effect was not to suppress them with all this power; he drew them out, led them to a kind of happiness, and forced them to participate. Most of them had wives their own ages, women they had married during the war, women with whom they had shared picnics and junkets in borrowed observation planes, and even an occasional outing in a fighter, in those grand early days.

Renate would have stood out against this paler backdrop of older men and women, but she did especially tonight, for she had made herself splendid in an expensive purple and white *Dirndl*, which emphasized her large, olive breasts, bared her strong arms; instead of brooding she radiated sex, and power, and confidence. Yes, and she did it at me, saying, with her poised body, with her highly held chin, with her unblinking eyes, Take it, take it, don't be afraid . . . She had come to her point of decision. But, you see I was frightened of the trouble. I had the fear of the tempted, and would not look at her there, although I felt her aura like the spirit of sex in the room. I tried to concentrate on Uncle Stuka, who, beyond his occasional dutiful samplings of this wife, had attained immunity. He pulled me into the room with him and announced to the gathering, *"Meiner Neffe, Herr Doktor Professor* Schaefer Braun, *von Amerika."* The men stood and all reached across one another to shake hands, and nod in greeting, although no one uttered his own name. For a time, my presence in the midst of these old friends damped their activity. But then, as the wine flowed, they coalesced once more around my uncle and returned with him to the war. And, without a word, they switched to English for my benefit, although nobody there was quite fluent, and some struggled terribly with the language.

Having given me a half hour of English, they now returned to German, talking earnestly. I could only make out famous names—Göring, Himmler, Hess, Hitler—and places like Bremen and Calais and Salzburg and Linz. For awhile I listened attentively, like a courteous visitor from another planet, and then excused myself and left the room.

The house was an odd one by American standards, the rooms big and high-ceilinged, with lace curtains blurring the world beyond the tall, double windows, a house filled with cut flowers, but almost without books, the antique furniture rich and ponderous. It had no fireplace, and the old tiled stoves in the main rooms were no longer used, although they remained as ceramic antiques. An elaborate Japanese stereo played the sentimental songs of old Vienna, filling the room with nostalgia and that odd quality of resignation. I went into the darked-out solarium that faced their large, back garden, and sat down on a chaise, looking idly at the trees and the streaming greys of the night sky above the city. Stumbling upon the little Luftwaffe had left me feeling awkward and somehow unconnected, and restless, enough that I thought of a cigarette, as I had not in ten years. Abstracted and facing inward, then, it took me a long time to realize I wasn't alone. Renate had entered behind me, silently but without stealth, and watched me from the other side of the door. When I sensed someone was there and looked up she tensed slightly—you could just make out a shifting highlight along her throat, in the arch of her body—and smiled. "I no frighten you, Schaefer?"

I shrugged. "I thought no one was here." But I thought, Yes, you frighten me plenty.

"I not can hear more the men talking." She sneered, looking at the night. "The *men*! Sixty year, seventy year, eighty year, they not pretty year for a man." She looked at me. "You are a pretty man, Schaefer. A very pretty man." She sat down on my chaise. "Do that give you, what you say, *Verlegenheit* . . . ?"

"If that means am I embarrassed, I would have to say yes." Jesus, I thought, just look at her. Her warmth filled the air around us, she seemed almost to glow; and she knew it.

"And me, do you think I pretty tonight?"

"Yes, you are very pretty tonight, Renate." My throat ached. I wanted to be intruded upon now, and to flee— but, I'm afraid, not very much.

She leaned toward me and took my hands in her soft plump ones, and pressed them against the lower curve of her breasts, which felt hot through the thin cloth. "You not know how long is for me with no man, Schaefer," she whispered. "But these is good, doesn't they? Like *Melonen*. Feel from them . . . yes . . ." She moved my fingers down with her own, unhooking the embroidered bodice, and when her breasts were released and suspended between us she brought my hands in about them again. "Kiss me there, Schaefer . . . it all right, kiss me here, here, here . . ." She arched her throat back and brought my head against her bosom; then, freeing one hand, she explored me gently. "Yes, I like you, Schaefer, I like it much, I always know it . . . from first day." Her hands fumbled with my belt, unzipped my trousers. She said, "Yes, yes, I always know," and took me into her mouth . . .

"Schaefer?" boomed my uncle's voice suddenly, the large sound plangent in the hall. We could hear his footsteps and the odd pattern of the dog's approaching from some distance. I flinched but could not move. Renate began to hurry but did not release me, and I resigned myself like someone dying to the worst possible situation; the old man would enter, and we, paralyzed by pleasure, the giving and the taking of it, would be unable even to utter a salutation. But then I happily yielded everything up to the gentle warmth that seemed then to be the world. *"Du,"* she breathed. "Oh, *du, du.*" I stroked her soft black hair, my eyes closed for the slow fall through space.

"Schaefer, where *is* you?" asked my uncle, the voice good natured, happy to be searching. Fee's claws tapped close to our door.

Renate put me back in order, and kissed me with the salty remnant of my semen, then stood up and hooked her bodice into place, all just as my uncle and Fee burst into the sitting room and saw our silhouettes against the night. "Ah, there you is, come, come..." He turned, gesturing to us to follow, and went back down the hall. The dog watched us for a moment, sniffed the air, pondered the odors she discovered there, and hopped after him.

"You look happy, Schaefer," she whispered. "I never forget tonight. *Never.*" Her eyes shone, the brooding figure had become a pretty gypsy girl again. "You funny boy. Think about tonight and it make you *hart.* Next time, we can be so kindly again... am I pretty to you now?"

"Yes, very pretty," I said, regretting the moment but also relieved to have had it happen, all that secret tension between us finally eased.

Uncle Stuka hurried back into the room, "Come, come." Had I heard anything in his voice? I thought it held a note of resignation, that his eyes, while not avoiding mine, now saw me differently. I still don't know whether this was guilt or reality. Of course, distinguishing between them is one of the big human problems.

The others were already gone; his urgency came mainly from its being time for our last brandy of the evening, a hint for me to follow the little Luftwaffe into the night. We drank this quietly, peaceably, as we often did, with Renate just outside our tiny circle of males, and Fee somehow included, which is a dog's right. But as he saw me to the front gate, while we were truly alone, he grinned and squeezed my shoulder, and said, "I think we are doing each other a favor. That is what I think." It took me a moment to decode: I know and I don't care, except...you are not creating any cuckolds here. Then, as I searched for a reply, he was deflected by the sight of a small white telegram sticker on his mailbox. "Oh," he said, *"oh,"* and removed the envelope as gingerly as he would have a vial of nitroglycerin. When he had the message safely captured in one great hand, he would not look at it. "Schaefer," he said then, "come back in please. I get such things only from America. But I have no people there. I worry. You read for me, please."

So, in the foyer that had been emptied of coats, in a house still and dark after its little Luftwaffe party, I ripped open the telegram under the hall light. "It's from the California state hospital at Camarillo," I told him—him, because he and I, as we did when he told his war stories, excluded Renate, who receded from us, resenting and puzzled by this nocturnal clutching at him of people and events so far away in time. "It says, 'We regret to report death of Ms. Lisa Braun yesterday at 11:17 a.m. PST. Surgery prescribed to ease her growing distress. Fatal complications incurred through no fault of medical personnel involved. Ms. Braun under our care since February 1947. Instructions from late Anselm Braun, father of the deceased, ask that we notify you of unfortunate demise.'"

It numbed me. Anselm Braun was my dead father. I had no sister...or was this lost, crazy person a lost one, a secret one? "Who is Lisa Braun?" I asked sharply. "Who is she?"

My uncle shook his head, and uttered a low moan of sorrow, his blue eyes dancing with tears, his huge face trembling, like a carved mountain about to slide. "Lisa," he murmured through lips gone stiff and unmanageable with grief, "Oh, oh, oh, *meine kleine* Lisa, oh, oh, oh..." Then this big wonderful old man shattered, and I gathered him into my arms while he sobbed. "Oh, Schaefer," he cried, gasping for breath, "Oh Schaefer, *unser schönes kleines Mädchen ist verloren*!" I rocked him while he sobbed like a broken child over this poor, lost Lisa.

After a time, Renate, Fee, and I helped him to his room, and into bed, removing enough of his clothing for him to be comfortable. He had stopped crying, but watched me now as though something had cracked within... ah, well, it was his heart, wasn't it? I told him to be quiet and to rest and that I'd see him the next day, and would check in, and when he wanted to talk we could. He only nodded, and watched me sadly.

His gypsy saw me out. We said our goodbyes coolly, and said nothing about what we had done that night, or where it led, or what it meant. As it was, we shook hands in the foyer, and, almost as an afterthought, I asked her, "Who was Lisa Braun?"

And Renate, restored not to the bitter, grieving widow of a woman, gave me a pitying look, and replied, "His wife."

2

SO THERE WAS UNEXPECTED DEATH, of someone hidden from my life for all those years in California, the golden-haired girl in a *Dirndl*, the girl imagined in the ME-109, the pretty Bavarian so vividly recreated in my uncle's tales of flight and war and homecomings. Lisa Braun. Not a sister, but my aunt, then, I would think, another figure on my desolate stage, a crazy one... but nothing to do with me.

My uncle recovered from the telegram slowly, and I spent more time with him, for at first he needed to explore what had happened, and it was that interval of his life he would not share with Renate. "Years ago...nineteen fifty, fifty-one...Anselm tell me Lisa is dead. Why he lie to me then?" He would lean toward me, the earnest question in his eyes. "Why he lie so?" And I would shake my head, and shrug, indicating wonder and total ignorance. Gradually, he began to piece together for me what he had not before, the odd tableau of three people and a crippled dog, sitting close together in their parlor or on the sun-porch, the old man's earnest voice the only sound, and I the only audience; the woman somehow beyond earshot, beyond the discussion.

"When I come back from war," he would begin, his hands fidgeting with one another with energy that, in such a large, calm man, unnerved the viewer, "Lisa is not how she is at the beginning..." His eyes clouded with revery. "Beautiful, *ja*, loving to me I think, but also...something is wrong with she. Something. I see it in her eyes. She wait for...something to happen. We have bad days then, days when I think she love me not. Days..." His eyes teared and for a moment he squeezed the high ridge of his nose, giving himself a moment's pain to keep from crying. Then, "Days when she crazy."

He told me how the old Lisa would awaken like a flower, in the wonderful Bavarian spring, with the land rolling off like a quilt of greens, and they had their good times, the maiden and the charming knight of the sky. But when he fled the war, all that had changed. "She cold to me, then, so cold." He was no knight, but a beaten soldier fleeing his side's declining fortunes. "In spring comes the American soldiers. I am caught out, I am deserter from German side, but I am also *from* German side, a man to despise, you see." His eyes slid away from mine, eternally ashamed of his desertion. "I am afraid to leave house. I cannot leave Lisa. Our life is more bad each day." Something had happened in April of that year, but he would not describe it. I knew it was there because of the detail around it, but all I could make out was a white shape. What? He would not say. His mouth drew into a thin line of determination. No, he would not tell me. And why? Because he was ashamed, even more ashamed of this untellable thing than of his desertion from the Luftwaffe. "In summer," he would say, leaping the April gap quickly, "she get quiet, as if . . . she wait for something . . . as if she sad about something." I visualized this Lisa, faceless as a snapshot in a dream, waiting in that summer, with the cities lying in rubble everywhere around her, and Hitler a suicide in Berlin, and the war ending—I envisaged her sitting somewhere, on a ridge perhaps, with the sun setting before her, and then in darkness; poor Lisa beginning to mourn the loss of light at the end of her day. "The war is over then . . . we should be happy . . . but still she wait, still she quiet. Anselm and his wife go to America. Lisa, she only wait, sad and quiet." Sad to think of him, seeing, tattered like everything in his familiar Bavarian landscape, this Lisa he loved, her wonderful white body animated and untouched, wearing a cape of golden hair; and then, to know a mad woman lived within, hungering . . . he would not say for what. "In October . . . I send her to my brother and sister in America. *Your* father and mother," he inserted here with odd emphasis. Lisa lived with them, he had believed, until Anselm's notice of her death in 1951. "They tell me she dead," he lamented, "They tell me so . . . I never marry *meine Zigeunerin*, my gypsy, they not tell me so . . ." If she were present at such times, Renate would take his big hands in hers then, as if on cue, as if about to sing to him, and tell him that of course he would not have insulted her in that way, she understood, he must not worry. The kind of talk one can follow without speaking the language. The charade was not easy for me to watch, even knowing it bore elements of real concern and affection.

Lisa's death altered the way he and I spent time together. I don't mean his stories focused entirely on the guilt of the gentleman deserter, or the loss of his golden girl,

although to a degree they did. Now, instead of taking me
vicariously to war, he took me vicariously, and not always
willingly, to a country war had nearly destroyed, to people whose lives had been shattered by participation in a
dream that had gone consummately ugly. It drained me, to
be with him in the ruined market, scrounging, at the
Bahnhof, straightening tracks, in the fields, raising that
unexploded bomb, in the diurnal minutiae of Kitzingen
and Würzburg and Nürnberg. And yet, here, as before,
there were gaps of detail, like white blanks on a chart of
South America, where suddenly all the contour lines and
elevations are gone. Crossing these in our conversations,
he would pause, and I would sense that he studied me,
scrutinized me, and not in any especially friendly way. His
small blue eyes would fix upon me, he would lean closer
and closer, as though I were a stranger, and he searched for
marks of recognition. Sometimes I saw the lights of hatred
in his eyes. I know now whom he searched for in this sudden stranger. But at the time it mystified me, this searching, or the disappointment he displayed, when at last he
would turn away, having failed to find what he looked for.
All I knew was that Lisa's death had changed his percep-
tion of me in some unfathomable way, had made me a
kind of stranger to be examined.

By early December, my visits had dropped off again—
there had just been a burst of close attention—mostly engineered by Renate, chaperoned by Fee, the woman having decided it was time I had an *Austrian* woman's touch,
and wonderful, clandestine sex, some sewing, a bit of help
with my flat, laundry, food, and barbers. Renate also decided to cast away her mourning, to be young and sensual
and in love.

Ah, love. *That* corrosive ingredient I steadfastly ignored, and it may be that on our first night we should have
talked after all. She could have told me then that our affair meant everything and led everywhere, and I could have
said, No, it means nothing but some warmth for us both,
and goes nowhere. The misunderstanding was fundamen-

tal. Except, really, she knew it would come to nothing, that it generated heat for us, not light—you could feel her waiting for the vessel to split and spill her out, back to her hungers, back to sexual grief. It made me sad, to see her fated to a failure we both saw, and to receive only warmth in return for her investments. A better man—a less lonely, wary one, perhaps—would have turned away from it, and, if it had taken the customary forms of affection I might have had the strength to do so. But Renate liked to *rub*, she would rub and stroke and caress all night long if she could, like someone born to serve, but in some specialty requiring both tenderness and endurance. And I...well I am the Caligula of rubbing. I would lie there, my face caught between her breasts, like a giant lying between tan hills, and she would rub, and rub, and rub, and I would drift and doze, contented as a child returning to some favorite dream while she gave me what she wanted me to have. Sometimes she would visit my flat and pick things up, and dust, and prepare some snack from the spinster's stores in the small, feeble refrigerator, and take me into her arms for a dessert of rubbing and giving and taking. Sometimes the three of us, she, the chaperoning Fee, and I would see my uncle to bed, and then retire to her room, from which she would affectionately evict us in the early morning.

I make no claims in this, for it was just the warmth and contact working; but it quickly made Renate pretty, drove her to stores for those loosely draped, long-skirted dresses women wear in Vienna, caused her weight to drop slightly, so that, lying naked in the pale illumination of the night, she had the look of a woman one would want to paint. Her affair with me was definitely what she'd needed, then, if not always what she wanted. But now and then she would see the flaws in our pleasure with particular clarity, and begin to brood, and fidget, and grow a little bitchy, wanting to test me in some way, fearing—no, *knowing*—that very much testing would drive me out. So it would take the form of responses to cues. Some night, when the atmosphere in the room we shared, hers or mine, suffocated with these rising storms of bitchiness, she might murmur in a neutral but edged voice, "I never see *Madame Butterfly*."

Caught at mid-rub, I might merely grunt.

Then, her hands anchored on my back, she might add, "I never go to *Staatsoper* with man before, never in my life."

Aroused, now, and warned, I might then rise on one elbow and say through clenched teeth, "Find out when it's on, get tickets, I'll pay for them, and we can go."

And, for a time, it would be rubs for me again.

But, flub your lines, and she would retreat into her inner shadows, and have to be retrieved, like some moody Eurydice. Sometimes I would retrieve her, sometimes I would not.

The problem was that the return she wanted, the only one, was my love. Or, rather, the love of a man she loved. Affection, good humor, contentment of a sort, and warmth, even *Madame Butterfly*—all that she could have, you see. But that other, wild, suicidal creature, love, was busy elsewhere, shaping another expedition to country more remote, beginning to explore what looked to me like the dead end of all dead ends—the affections of Valentina Ivanovna Orlovsky, whom I had greeted with the obsessed cry of: *Nancy?*

3

FOR A TIME, after Valentina Orlovsky joined us at the Centre, Dexter and I handled her diffidently, which he insisted was the craven western reflex when dealing with friendly Russians, each contact carrying a burden of awareness that we were separated by an ideological no-man's land, and there would be all those things one never talked about. Maybe so, but it was not a bad beginning, treating her as though we were agnostic boys and she a favorite, but unfortunately devout Catholic, aunt.

She dazzled me, even when I knew through and through that she was not some incarnation of my vanished Nancy. The same chord had been brushed, though, and tingled still, tingled eternally perhaps; and the melting of my spine drew me along. I observed her as though she were the last golden bird of a species, and I an obsessed ornithologist, who watched her move through her workday, watched her in the clusters of Russians with whom she lunched and traveled between the Centre and Vienna, and, presumably, had her outside existence. I was conscious, roaming the eighteenth district alone, that, somewhere nearby, somewhere up among all that Russian-occupied high ground, was Valentina. My Valentina, as I considered her, abandoning myself to folly. And how did she spend *her* nights? Who lay obscenely across her splendid white body, thumping away? My Valentina, under some goddamned Russian! So it went, not love, exactly, but obsession at first sight.

Her red-lipped mouth was too broad, her eyes too big and blue and prominent, her body too long, for her to be beautiful in any conventional sense—despite that initial, powerful evocation, she looked nothing like Nancy, she had none of those classic magazine-cover lines. Her hair was long enough to braid, and such fine gold it could not be braided without springing at every turn into little halos and clouds. Seen against a light, this aurora of golden hair gave her a slightly disheveled look. Later, I would discover that where she lived she left a soft trail of it, as though she were a spider who spun a fluffy golden web, and left it everywhere. She was so pale, so like a rose, that she had no outline, in the way a darker person has a very definite one. Her big round eyes were margined with greys and blues beneath this white field, giving her a sad, vulnerable look when seen in repose. And yet, at five eight and a bit more, trim and fit and well made, there was nothing frail about her. Really, she shone, but softly, and she went about her work quiet as a mute, at first, with the assurance of a blind person on familiar ground.

The conventional wisdom at places like the Centre for Analytic Studies holds that you must keep away from the Soviet women. They neither want nor need or even like Americans, and an American lover does nothing for a Soviet career. They are all spies anyway, it continues, or they would not be free to travel, they would not have been "let out." Forget them, we hear, forget them, it is doom and death and hard feelings if you don't. Usually this is an easy set of unwritten rules to follow, for there are at least as many ugly women, per capita, in Russia as in Maryland or Utah.

Yes, but . . . what about those shining girls who merely by being in the world have melted the base of one's romantic spine? Their Russianness is irrelevant. No, even these are supposed to be off limits. A gentleman does not mark his lady for the Gulag, does not, with his effusions, drive her to the bleak exiles of her homeland—that is, to cities other than Moscow. And, in fact, you have to understand that they don't *want* to . . . cultural differences, you *smell* funny to them.

Of course I ignored all the usual advice, the voices of other experience, ignored everything but the delicious spear in my side, and began a gentle pursuit of my rare Russian bird. I went at it, at first, with the desperate stealth and patience of a man in a minefield, but, on the whole optimistic. I resolved to avoid sudden starts, startling sounds, the display of strange objects. It was all about as subtle as Othello's fretting over a handkerchief, or Romeo's tragic crush. But it *felt* stealthy, you see.

On the mundane level of work, I believed—and Dexter secretly did too, although he grumbled—she added the perfect final touch to our project, and not merely by linking my watery domain with Dexter's aerial one. She ranged widely and well, and to a degree we had not expected, drew our research toward greater coherence. One hears that Russian slowness in developing supercomputers has preserved the ability of scientific brains to solve difficult problems, and Valentina was a minor proof of that. She had a wonderful memory and eye for interlinked detail, so that a patch of anomalously warm water in the North Pacific could trigger a memory of some matching satellite image, or a chemical profile across the same region, at about the same time. When you're studying interactions that range in scale from the molecular to the continental, that leap of the mind is invaluable. Neither Dexter nor I could do that particular kind of construction half so well, and we were very pleased to have a colleague of her quality. Of course Emil, after about a minute's conversation with this pretty compatriot, recognized a kindred mind and began spending more time in our cluttered office.

The work itself was quiet and persistent, like sewing, for we stood at that early stage when you must put into some usable form the salient elements of previous studies, and there had been a mountain of work on the oceanic carbon cycle. So we snipped and sorted and annotated, and fed everything to the Centre's main computer, and then, with that next iteration in hand, we proceeded to a finer sorting, a more selective cut through the data, and on, in that cascading way, moving from the general to the particular. The three of us knew that these menial preliminaries would grow into something more intellectually satisfying; but we also understood the need to build a platform of analysis and surveys to support any future jumps. So we occupied our office like three little old ladies, speaking in parentheses and asides, while we did our scientific sewing.

Gradually, Valentina became Val, I became Schaefer, Dexter became Gordy. While the other Russians still had her most of the time, we made such inroads as we could, stealing her now and then for lunch, when we would shun the castle's cafeteria for a *Würstel* stand, and take hot dogs into the park, among the yellow leaves, out in the blustering world of the Ukrainian crows.

"How do you know they are from the Ukraine?" she asked in her soft, full voice, slightly accented, fluent except for the small holes in idiom, in the grit of grammar.

Dexter looked mischievously at me and replied, "Bellorussian crows are white."

She smiled for him.

"Georgian crows cannot get a visa," I attempted.

Val laughed, then, a nice little crystal laugh that must have cheered everything within earshot. "Siberian crows are frozen to ground," she said then, embarrassed and diffident to be taking even this small feint at the Soviet Union while alone with two westerners. We all laughed together, to make her easier about it.

When a nearby *Heuriger* opened, we rode off to it in Gordy's Wee Froggie for our *Viertels* of red wine. The drink touched Val up just a bit, added color to her striking Russian face. She kept cautious, but in a relaxed way. You could see her making up her mind to trust us, but not entirely, not absolutely. The other thing I saw, that day at the *Heuriger*, was something in her lightly flushed face that told me she knew about my chord being brushed, and was both saddened and mystified by it. I wanted to say: Don't worry, it's going to be fine, wait and see. But I kept it light instead.

Often, after such outings, we would see her walking with Trulov, who was in some respects the Soviet conscience at the Centre, receiving an earnest lecture, Dexter explained, about the evils of lunching outside with an Englishman and an American. "*Especially* the latter." When she rejoined us, he told her, "Val, I think we shall have to begin leaving Schaefy behind." And to me, "Sorry, old chap, but it's the only thing to do. International tensions and all that." Val laughed shyly, behind a cupped (beautiful) hand.

"Bastard," I replied in the same cheerful spirit.

"Bastard?" asked Valentina.

"*Ubliudok,*" Dexter said, adding hastily, "That totally exhausts my Russian, except for tovarich." I was not sure.

On fine days, and we had these frequently that year, we took our project discussions into the park, where the three of us would stroll like a family and talk about the shape the work finally should have, the reformation of its goals, how we would publish and where. Around us, the odd mementoes of Maria Theresa at play loomed in the forest, bridges and arches over nothing at all, and the castle where the chairman and I had lunched. I told them about the village boys, playing in this forest during the Russian occupation years, how it had been a wilderness with these sudden royal surprises; boys playing knights. Saying the word, I thought of my poor uncle, and his poor dead Lisa, the descent from knight to deserter, from maiden to madwoman...

We made a fine threesome, walking together in that hole in time, she and I reasonably tall and slender, both light, almost in step, and then the great hulking bear of Dexter, amiable but, in some unstated way, a guardian as well. We must have looked, I thought, like a trio in a children's book, the boy, the girl, and the protecting bear, wandering from danger to danger through the magic forest.

She and I, when left alone without some element of work to bridge between us, drifted toward discomfort. I knew what I wanted to tell her, and no doubt she did too. But the time was wrong, it would send her flying away, this rare Russian bird. I think we both dreaded some displacing crack, back then, for we reflexed away from it in the same direction—we began to speak of the sea. It was from these deflections, really, that I learned enough of how she viewed the world to believe we had a chance of...anything. As I said before, oceanographers comprise a large population of people whose lives are cold. We talked sampling techniques and shipboard computers and how multisensors had made life so much easier, and how heavy and hard to handle all those early Nansen bottles and sediment grabs had been, and the dismal complications when a many-wired cast busted, tangling lines, losing cable, the sensors dropping away into the eternal night miles and miles below. We remembered to one another the long watches, when a line would drop all that distance to the surface of a drowned earth, and return eight hours later with a bucketful of muck from the seafloor, and how one froze waiting if it was winter, and burned if it was not, and dropped into one's berth afterward with fatigue. We talked of voyages on the *Vema* and *Lomonosov* and *Ob*, of *Atlantis II* and *Oceanographer* and *Gillis*.

Behind all the oceanography we were talking about something else—about the sun (she loved the sun, and made me think how she must look, her whiteness done to a faint coffee color) and the winter storms in which the water rose like buildings and the wind screamed madly and one rode it out, knowing the ship was indestructible. We talked about the cigarettes on empty decks, the feel of being on another planet, bereft of everyone and yet unlonely. The great world ocean swallowed ideology and obsession, quenched my selfish internal fires, eased her mind about this nervous American who poised toward her.

Dexter stayed clear of all this, although I knew he observed us, listening in his intense, analytical way, on the walks, on the lunches, on the long drives back to Vienna. "Considering she comes from a land ruled by bloody criminals, she's not half bad," he would say, by way of praising her. Then, noting blood in my eye, he put in, "I mean, Schaefy, that, for a Russian...and a woman...she's really quite...nice."

"Kudos," I replied. "You bastard."

"I mean, Schaefy, what I really and absolutely *do* mean, is..." He waited, inflated with jollity.

"Is?"

"I think she is happy with us." It may be that he loved her a little too. When he had seen how things stood with me, he began to leave us more alone, leave us to drift closer and closer, without touching. I don't know how much he knew, back then—more than I would have dreamed, but he never had it all, and never had it quite right—but he treated us as if our time were short. Looking back, I think he saw us as casualties of our encounter, and so he tried to give us that extra increment of time.

For, at that point, days were all we had. I describe our work and walks and growing together as though they occurred very gradually, over geologic sweeps of time, and that is how it felt, each day protracted, strung between my contacts with Val. But, in a way, that's just the deformed clock of Vienna. In fact, the day Dexter admitted to me that Val seemed happy with us was the end of our fifth week together, with the weather finally turning cold and the wind ripping around outside the castle, dark night at the end of our workdays, our office windows black mirrors, holding everything in.

Life proceeded at the Centre, as well—that is to say, we had a moving backdrop. The chairman, we heard, was back from Moscow, although we rarely saw him and then usually in the distant lunchbound clusters of directors and distinguished visitors from member countries. Pastukh and, always within reach, Andrews, the protégé, the "son." But the chairman's presence filled the castle like smoke, and everyone was conscious that our prime mover was upstairs. Trulov had returned from a quick trip somewhere, the grapevine said Bulgaria *and* Libya, and Lincoln was back from the States, still looking evil to me, still radiating his incomprehensible dislike, which he masked with a thin, clammy disguise of good fellowship. "I see you've found a pretty Russian girl, Schaefer," was all he'd had to say to me. That, and "Let's have lunch." One felt him there, an evil spirit, haunting us.

News media in Europe had picked up the story, which began in the States, that the Russians were using our computers to probe classified computers in the west, causing all of us to shake our heads and hold our sides in mock consternation. "Do you think they're that smart, Schaefy?" was Dexter's way of putting the story down. "With these antediluvian electrified abacuses they give us. Bloody nonsense." Although, you could also see in his gleaming eye the notion that the story was merely off the mark, that of course the Russians had something going on. But he gave the impression of not caring tuppence, an impression he did very well.

The Committee had passed its resolutions—the Carnival Project was in, provided another eastern scientist was added to the staff, hunger and energy would be trimmed; our carbon dioxide work was in, and everyone seemed glad to have it. The bad news was that Emil Dashko's sectoral modeling project had been cut to nothing, and phased out, the Committee calling it "intellectually barren," a term that hurt him especially because the Centre never gave Russians, its main source of income now, such slaps without concurrence from Moscow. "I find it very difficult to believe this," he whispered to us, but mainly to Val, "very difficult." Then, his head tilting up with a mad look, he added, "But nothing is immutable, eh?" and whirred out of sight down the corridors of the castle.

"He thinks he can turn it around," Dexter said. "But I doubt it."

"Not without nude photos of the chairman with a Shetland pony," I said.

Val had turned away from our talk. Now she asked, "If they say his work is not worth doing, then why do it?"

Ordinarily, Dexter would have responded cruelly with something about the Soviet mentality. But he bit his tongue, and looked at her with a melancholy expression that said: I am so sorry you are one of them. "Why indeed?" he muttered, and then went after Emil, his big face wrinkled with worry for a friend.

"I said something wrong?" she asked when he was gone.

"Not really. He is . . . strongly for Emil, that's all."

"What do you think of his work?"

"I think Emil believes in what he's doing. That makes his work as good as a lot of the stuff done here. Is it better to look for long waves in the global Carnival cycles, or to make primitive tools for city planners? I honestly don't know."

"Well," and she grinned. "Dexter was very kind with me."

"He likes you." Then, with my face tightening, "Me too."

"I think we make a good little team," she said, halting the drift toward affection.

"I think so too."

But we had become too conscious of one another not to continue the contact. We fiddled around with our papers, working halfheartedly, preoccupied, half hoping Dexter would return and save us, half hoping he would not. The silence crackled with the movement of paper, the clearing of throats, a hum. At last I laughed and turned toward her desk. "This is terrible."

"What?" She feigned surprise and mystification.

"Listen, Val, have you been to the opera yet?"

"In Vienna?"

"No, in Omaha, Nebraska . . . of *course* in Vienna."

"Not yet."

"Let me take you, then."

She blushed a little, and replied, with a smile, "Do you think that is such a good idea?" Then, she let her eyes reveal how thoroughly she understood me. "Do you?"

"I think it's the idea of the century."

"What a funny man," she mused. "Why ask me? Ask your girl friend . . . one of your girl friends."

"Girl friends?" I countered with vast innocence.

"Ah," and her tone filled with exasperation. "Don't tell me you have none. Ask one of them. A good western girl. *Play by the rules.*"

"I want *you*," I said.

"I know."

"I mean, for the opera."

"I know what you mean."

"I'm only talking about our going to the opera."

"I have known from the start, you show it for everyone to see. Trulov sees it, Emil sees it, Dexter. Everyone. So I know you . . . want me."

"Val, listen..." I wanted to take her hands, to touch her, to smooth away the anger I heard rising in her voice; my own had begun to shake.

She retreated to the black windows, faced the mirror of them. After a moment she said, slowly, in a voice that was cold and controlled, "You know the rules. It doesn't matter what *you* want. It is not for us. You know that." Sensing my protest, she added, "No, let me tell *you* everything now, and then we have it behind us.

"Two things. First, I am from Soviet Union and you are American. You have love affair with Soviet woman, perhaps you get a medal at home. For me is very different. They give me smaller job, in worse city, next they put me on *Vema* for another year of polar research. If I am *lucky* they do these things. They tell me about the affair as well, they ask questions about the American, what you do with him..."

"If we were careful..."

"Oh, what a selfish boy you are: 'If we were careful.' Perhaps 'If we were careful' *I* would not be caught, you mean. The risk is mine. You can have this big 'love' you wear on your coat for all to see, and you 'want' me. And for this thing you 'want' so much I can go back on *Vema*? What a selfish boy! But, wait," and she held up her hand again. "Wait. Even that, even the worst that can happen does not keep me away. Loving is important. Even this other bad thing with you, this invention that is not me, not Valentina Ivanovna, but somebody else, a mother, an old lover, who knows what? Even that false thing does not keep me away, if I love you. But," and here she tossed her head back and said not quite triumphantly, "I do not. I am friend and co-worker. But no love, do you hear?"

I nodded, sullen, unwilling to look at her, the seeds of bad temper sprouting everywhere within.

"Now... with that... do you still wish us to go to opera?" she asked in a suddenly softened voice.

"I still wish us to."

"Schaefer, I hate talking so rough to you."

"Me too." Pause, calculation, then off the cliff. "I love you."

"Ah, you love someone, something. But it is not me." She heaved her shoulders with a kind of tired resignation, and sighed, touching me to my obsessed, unhappy center. My impulse was to pull her against me, to lean upon her, to be close...

"I won't speak of it again," I told her.

"Then... I enjoy going to opera with you, Schaefer." Before I could reply, she said quickly, "I must go," and left me to the silence that rose around her footsteps down the long terrazzo hall, and the sharp discomfort of knowing everything she'd said was true.

A painful exchange, and yet, in the days that followed, the air between us clarified like wine, became new and improved, as they say. We worked easily together, as we had before, but that cloying crazy affection that had been trying to escape, now, having escaped, no longer had us in its shadow—the obsession, the nasty selfish part of it, lost intensity. Oh, she still compelled me, my affection retained that canine singlemindedness, but her cold candor had rinsed our atmosphere, and I, comparatively speaking, felt clean and cured. It was as though she led me back through the labyrinth of some illness. Perhaps she had. Perhaps she had shattered one of those distorting mirrors we carry deep within.

We went to see *Tosca* with good seats in the orchestra. I had almost no experience of this kind of music, had never heard anything quite so pretty as the soprano voice rising over, and through us; recordings had never conveyed the power of it. But the opera itself was merely the gem in our brilliant evening, for we had both prepared ourselves for An Event, and had one. The opera there began early enough that we had to dress in the showers used by running and tennis-playing scientists at the Centre, and then hurry into town in the bullet. Val wore a pretty dress of white wool trimmed with pale fur, and black boots, a very Russian costume that evoked evenings out in St. Petersburg with a countess on one's arm. I wore my one good winter suit, well cut in charcoal wool. Eddying among the crowd of people and pillars, beneath the lines of gleaming chandeliers, I caught glimpses of us in the mirrors of the opera house, a handsome couple, the blonde American and his tall, golden Russian lady, out for an evening in 1892. I loved to see us slip in and out of time that way. She was nervous during the interval, afraid of meeting people from the Centre and causing talk. I was surprised to encounter no one we knew, although there were a few, passing at a distance; Vienna is a very small town. And the gem itself—well, there is nothing quite like the *Staatsoper* productions, an elegant audience treated to that amazingly flexible stage, where whole civilizations can be transposed in a minute or two. The incredible beauty of the human voice trained as a musical instrument.

Afterwards, we preserved the old days by having drinks in the Blue Bar, and she, to my great pleasure, mentioned our stepping through time. "Did you see us?" she asked, her cheeks bright from the evening and the chilly wind of that December night. I nodded, grinning. "We could have been..." Her head rose, she smiled happily. "It looked like..." She could not bring herself to say it.

"Another time."

"Yes, an evening long, long ago. Oh, Schaefer, it is as if we have been to a ball."

"That season's right around the corner."

"Oh, that would be splendid... can we do it, though?" she wondered, suddenly troubled.

Then I spoiled it with an American shrug: "We can do what we want."

"How wonderful," she cried, but even as she said the words I saw her spirit slump. "If it were true." I leaned toward her, ready to argue the matter, but she put up that teacherly hand. "No, no discussion. I think of the opera."

But, you see, despite the rules, the big political shadows, her own nervousness, we had begun to be happy with one another. And more than that: seeing her happy was my great pleasure. Obsession had begun to cast its selfish skin, and turn to love.

Later, we walked by the pale mound of the illuminated opera house, down the deserted pedestrian mall of the Kärtnerstrasse toward St. Stephans, careful not to touch, cold, very happy. The only people we saw were scattered couples, and *Kurier* and *Kronen* paperboys from Turkey and Lebanon and Iran in their crimson and yellow slickers, and rose vendors from whom I bought my lovely girl a long rose. "They get them out of a freezer. It will barely last you home."

"Still, it is a rose, in winter."

It was natural, then, when Lincoln brought the invitation from Stockholm, that we would turn to one another, and to Dexter as well, and wish, in silent chorus: *Let's go together.* The invitation was for someone from the Centre to speak at a symposium on Baltic Sea processes. The letter bore Andrews' *Jolly good! Suggest we send carbon person!* to the director, who had scrawled boldly across the bottom of the page, *Doubly marvelous and great!!! Valentina, please try to do this! Wonderful!!!! MANY thanks!!!!*

Our impulse was to cheer and make grand plans right then, but, with Lincoln in the room, we lay low. Then, to our surprise, he said, "You know, it seems to me you should go as a team. Shall I recommend that to the director?" He asked this dryly, knowing it was what we wanted, knowing he could obtain it for us; and even then, in the act of doing us this favor, his hatred flickered like a flame.

"Yes!" exclaimed Valentina, beautifully excited and unable to hide it. I merely nodded, not wanting to spoil anything. Dexter did the same. When Lincoln was gone, though, we all let our excitement into the open. "I have never been to Sweden," Val said.

"Me neither," I said.

"But, they will not let us all go," she lamented.

"Of course they'll let you do anything you like," grumped Dexter. "The director has already gone to God on this, or, that failing, and better, to Chairman Pastukh, who is in town. But...I can't do it. It falls at just the wrong time for me. I shall be in London then. Damn!" His voice trailed off and I realized that he wasn't kidding. He really did not like having us go off without our bear.

We, Val and I, ignored his grumping. We were already worrying about what to present there, time was so short, we had less than a week's notice, the letter having languished for a month with Andrews. What could we do in a week? "Everything!" Val yelled giddily.

"An overview," Dexter said.

"An overview!" we shouted.

Lincoln brought the director's response in another note. *Baker's idea superb, all hands to Stockholm, look forward to full report after!!! Great!!!! Thanks!!!!* He lingered to watch us—in fact, he only carried messages to observe their effect upon the messaged—like someone mildly interested in how rats handle this or that section of the maze. Finally he said, "Well, that's good. Have a good time. I'm off to London tomorrow morning."

Dexter looked up sharply. "Are you? Perhaps we shall see one another there."

"I doubt it, but it would be a pleasure."

"Going for a meeting?"

"Yes. Some...architects."

"Ah, architects." Dexter grinned evilly.

Lincoln ignored him and said to us, "Not a bad thing, really, the two of you going out together. East and west holding hands, so to speak. Puts the lie to all this spy garbage in the papers. Don't you think so, Valentina?"

His banter bullied her, and I saw when she nodded that her happiness had begun to drain away.

"It's a stupid accusation," I said, angry.

Lincoln gave me a derisive frown. "Sure it is, Schaefer. We all know it is. *Adios.*"

Dexter growled from his side of the room, "*There* is a nasty piece of work for you." Before we could respond, the telephone buzzed and he answered, then handed it to Valentina. "And here's another... Trulov for you, Val."

You couldn't understand the Russian words, although Trulov's voice was loud enough that Dexter and I could both hear its rhythms, up and down in a mild tirade, then calming to the rhythms of instruction. When she hung up she was nearly grey with fatigue. "Maxim says that I have the necessary permissions from home... to go to Stockholm. We can go."

"But...?" I asked.

"Oh, nothing," she said quickly, not meeting my eyes. "He just asked me to bring him something from there." She shrugged.

"Something from Stockholm," mused Dexter. "That would be some granite, wouldn't it? Or, no, hmmm. I'd say bring back a fully equipped Swedish blonde except we already have one on the project..." She gave him a friendly glare. "Sorry, didn't mean to imply you were a Swedish blonde... but anyway... by George, I have it." Val's eyes widened anxiously. "He wants you to bring back a Russian submarine. Bags of them up there!" He went off into his har hars, and took us with him.

Quickly, then, we called the house travel agent and asked to book two seats on the afternoon SAS flight for Monday, and two singles for two nights. I looked up from the phone, wondering where. "The Grand Hotel," Dexter said, "Stay at the Grand." Afterward, stepping into the silence that had begun to form around us in the wake of such excitement, he said, "Stockholm in winter. Good Christ, but you'll be cold. All that ice roiling about in the Baltic. For awhile you think you've lost the ability to see color, everything's gone to grey and white, and there's no horizon in the cold fog... and then the stuff will clear and the sun will come out and by God if you're not in a city as pretty as old Leningrad. Prettier! Well, I shall think of you two up there on the ice floes." His enthusiasm merely

coated a species of grief, as though he didn't want us to go
after all, as though his spirit had begun to dissolve in some
secret dread. Perhaps he saw that Val and I, middling
young, middling handsome together, just beginning our
fall toward love, approached some outer rim of innocence.

The whole thing lasted most of a day, and a night, this
excited preparation, the dreaming. Emil drove by early the
next morning to report that the entire castle had heard of
what was being called "Valentina and Schaefer's Stockholm Trip." "It is not a scandal, exactly," he whispered
with a mischievous grin, "but very exciting for everybody."

Val looked at me in horror. "We said nothing."

"Oh, that never matters here," said Emil. "Rumor
propagates more rapidly here than in Carthage. I give an
example. At the *Heuriger* evening when the Committee
was here, I announce to one or two people that I remember the chairman from the war. Only to one or two people, you among them, Schaefer, Gordon, and Maxim
Trulov. I think that is all. Last night, guess what?" We all
raised our eyebrows for him. "I am approached by this
American, Lincoln, who expresses...what? 'Mild curiosity' about this memory. Memory is a funny thing, he tells
me, and I say, yes, very funny, and he wants me to explain. So I say, Mr. Lincoln, please, this memory is between me and one other person, only. I do not share it. But
then, I cannot resist. I give him a clue. The memory, I tell
him, is that I cannot remember something. It is the memory of nothing, you see. Perhaps this man will leave me
alone now. He was most angry. I do not like him."

Dexter leaned near the clever, destroyed face, listening.
"May I ask you something, Emil?" he said at last.

"Of course. But I reserve the right to be silent."

"You said you remembered being with Pastukh in the
war. That is the memory you speak of, isn't it?"

"Yes...or...yes and no. I also remember *not* being with
him in the war." Emil cackled happily. "Suddenly. The key

word here is *suddenly*. But *unezapno*, not *neozhidanno*."
He laughed. "All of a sudden, not a surprise." Emil made
a face then. "I have a meeting with Academician Pastukh
about 'intellectually barren'…and perhaps I explain to him
then. In general, I am hopeful. Well, of course, I am an
optimist."

"I see that," Dexter said. But when Emil was gone, he
spread his fingers on his face, the gesture of a tired man.
"It sounds as if Emil has those Shetland pony photos after all."

"Shetland pony?" Val wondered.

"Pornography of a very usual kind," Dexter replied. He
looked about himself with a worried frown, like a great
guard dog whose wards have begun to move outside the
circle he can protect. You expected a frustrated whine. But
he strode to the windows, where the year's first real snow
had begun, wrapping itself around the dark trees, putting
a thin white patina on the park, and the sidewalks, and
benches. We were all, the three of us, suspended for a time,
watching the darkness come down with the snow. "It must
have got damned cold out there," Dexter said, being the
meteorologist. "Nothing's melting. Wish I'd brought another coat." But he was away somewhere, thinking,
thinking—you could almost hear his mind turning something over and over, like a heart beating.

Outside, a solemn procession entered the framed rectangle we could see from our window, small figures, black
against the grey fall of snow, but with just a touch of
color—a fleck of red in a cravat, the flash of spectacles
turning as the man walking next to the wheelchair glanced
behind them. We could hear nothing but the rising wind.
But there was something agitated about the men, although they did not wave their arms or yell. Emil curled
into his chair, the snow dusting him, speaking earnestly,
while Pastukh leaned down to listen as he walked. Then,
minutes later, like someone walking on a softly illuminated stage, a third man appeared, and for a time the three
of them suspended in a cold, silhouetted tableau; then they

moved beyond the frame we could see, and the night that
enfolded us by late afternoon swept in behind them.

"I think Emil made his pitch," I said.

"Pitch?" asked Val.

"He's telling the chairman why his work should go on,"
Dexter said. But he had forgotten we were with him, and
thought aloud, "But why would he think he had any leverage?"

"Who was the other man?" I asked.

Val said, "Lincoln," and shivered with distaste. I knew
the feeling. We returned to our work, but Dexter looked
worried, and unable to concentrate. At one point, as
darkness grew, I think he would have gone searching for
Emil. But the director's message deflected him, and afterwards it was too late.

The message was carried down by his Dutch secretary,
a big masculine figure with enormous legs and bosom, and
that sliced off nose you see so many of in Holland. He had
scrawled it on his personal stationery, which bore his name
and the name of the Centre, and a reproduction of a
Japanese ink drawing of a tiger. "It's from the tiger,"
Dexter said, unfolding the paper. "Want me to read it in
dialect?" We shook our heads, apprehensive. Dexter read:

"Valentina, Schaefer, Gordon!!! I fear I have less than
good news now. Stockholm. This morning it seemed a
splendid way to give the Centre some exposure, which it
needs now very much. Your project was just the thing!!!
Also, it seemed good to me to have scientists from east and
west go together, because of CIA smear campaign. Now I
have heard from Academician Pastukh that he not want
you to go, but Andrews shall go instead. I regret this
change. I also ask that you help Andrews get up to speed
on project. Many thanks!!!!! VERY SORRY!!!"

Dexter flipped the paper on his desk. "Well...looks like
old Trulov must go elsewhere for his submarine, eh?" He
frowned for us. "But it's a surprise isn't it? I wonder
why...I mean, *really* why."

"Because," I said.

"No, I mean I wonder that the chairman himself intervened. I mean . . . why would he *care*? Interesting question
that." The phone buzzed and he, being closest, picked it
up. We could hear a female voice raised in some unintelligible question. "I don't know," he replied, his face
clouding. "I saw him in the park maybe an hour ago . . ."
He hung up then and said to us, "Come on, quickly now,"
and ran from the office, clattering down the hall to the
French doors that opened on the park. We followed,
bringing our coats.

Outside, in the darkness, he ran to where we had seen
the chairman, Emil, and Lincoln. The thin double track in
the snow had nearly filled in, you could just make out a
trace of it and shoeprints in the glowing darkness. We
tracked along the parallel grooves, tracked along them like
dogs until, at the entrance to a long mowed avenue between the bare trees the tracks disappeared in snow.

"EMIL?" Dexter yelled, and we joined in, yelling,
"EMEEL? EMMMEEEEL?" for the idea that had pro-
pelled the Englishman frightened us now—our immobile
friend could still be out in this suddenly changed, freezing
weather, thinly clad, and terrified.

"Emeel, *Emeeeel?*"

Farther into the field we found a short run of the thin
wheeltracks, where the snow had not covered them. We
plunged ahead, Dexter in the lead, running in a cloud of
breath.

We would have missed the chair, against the background of tangled, silhouetted trees, except its batteries
were not quite dead, and the trapped vehicle surged against
the slight tilt it had found in repose against a fallen tree.
Listening for some reply to our calls, we heard the faint
urn, urn, urn of the wheels slipping on the snow, digging
a shallow grave. Emil was there, curled nearly into a ball,
like a cold boy sleeping. His face had cleared of anxiety
and the stresses of illness; he no longer worried about what
happened to his project at the Centre, or whether the
Committee would call it "intellectually barren." Snow

formed tiny drifts in the sad, cold grooves of his face, the
folds of light wool that covered him; a stiff wind flapped
his thin trousers against withered legs. The control panel
of the chair dangled on its power cable just outside the
arm, just out of his reach. The stiff little fingers still
crabbed at it.

"Emil, Emil," whispered Dexter, tears standing in his
deepest eyes. "Ah, my friend, what have they done to
you?"

4

WHILE DEXTER waited like a dog on a grave, guarding
Emil in the falling snow, we summoned the Austrian police, and found someone with fluent German, and then all
of us went back out through the snow to Emil's body, followed by a small pack of vehicles with flashing blue lights.
The first wave of police were from the village gendar-
merie, self-important and fumbling, and perhaps diffident about this matter of tackling the problem of a dead
Russian. They touched him to make sure he was dead, and
then hurried about like tricked dogs, confused and offi-
cious, trampling the ground around the wheelchair into a
swamp of black footprints, which quickly began to go grey
with snow. Before long, a more senior team arrived from
Vienna, and the investigation steadied. When had it happened, could we tell them that? Why was he out here, in
such weather, with so little cover? Can you tell us that, *herr
professor doktor*, sir? We told them what we knew, and as
the crowd of people from the Centre accumulated in the
field nearby, swept there by the winds of rumor blowing
through the castle, the chairman appeared, bundled up
with only a small rectangle of pale, intense face visible between scarf and hat, to say he had left Emil there, over
there, no, farther, *there*, after their conversation. And
Lincoln? He had left him approximately there as well.

Where had Emil gone after that? Pastukh fixed the questioner with his magnificent eyes. "Here, I would think."

The senior Austrian detective, who wore the mandatory trenchcoat that reached nearly to his ankles rather than the grey overcoat and low-slung automatic of a plain cop, watched the proceedings with a full-lipped, slightly sneering smile, treating the event the way he would a death in an asylum, and a Russian death at that. He paced slowly, taking in and cynically reflecting the evening's ironies in the swirl of blue light from the cars.

Now a private ambulance and a black Mercedes sedan joined the parade of vehicles. A man and woman got out of the sedan, their broad, flat faces utterly closed, except for a quick, clandestine flash of something mean-spirited and empty. They were from the Soviet embassy. The Austrian detective greeted them, and quickly hid behind his pipe, his eyes scrutinizing them across the matchlight. They talked in low voices. Clearly an accident, perhaps he dared the elements, that had been his reputation; or perhaps the miscalculation of a brave but possibly imprudent individual. The detective sniffed and sighed, sucked on his pipe, let his pale, watery eyes dance with irony, as if to say: And after all, another dead Russian more or less does not make a hell of a lot of difference to Viennese law and order; one less to worry about, eh?

The emissaries smiled with richly metalled teeth, frightening to see in the spinning blue light and falling snow, and thanked him, complimented him and his men on an excellent response, they would certainly let it be known elsewhere . . . and extricated the incident, and Emil's remains, from Austrian jurisdiction. Like a broken centaur, Emil and his wheelchair were loaded into the ambulance retained by the embassy, and the flashing lights went scattering slowly back across the snow-covered field, and off through the village toward Vienna. Emil would find it droll, I thought, the suggestion that he would be buried, like an eastern king, with his favorite steed at his side.

The excitement past, most of the Centre people drifted back toward the light of the castle. But Val and Dexter and I stayed on, even though we were all blue with cold by then, like pilgrims on a vigil. Then, surprising us, we saw that Pastukh had also remained behind, and now came over. "A terrible business," he said. "I understand you discovered him?" He did not wait for our reply. "I wondered, when we talked, why he would come out on such a day. He seemed extremely frail. But he insisted, wanting privacy..."

"Did he get what he wanted?" asked Dexter, his voice weak but hostile.

"I'm sorry?"

"Did you give him back his project?"

"Ah. I told him...we would talk about it tomorrow, after I had given his proposal further thought."

"Then he *did* have some leverage."

Pastukh regarded Dexter evenly. "He had an argument that could not be ignored."

"I see." The big Englishman looked away, and then excused himself, but then we all moved together back toward the castle. The chairman said to Val, "Dr. Orlovsky...Valentina...I regret not having had a chance to talk to you about your work here. It is good to see you...although the circumstances are unhappy ones." He might have met her at a ball, except he watched her tensely, scrutinized her. I thought: She must feel that gaze like fingers on her face. "Yes," he said at last, breaking off his disconcerting study, "it is very good finally to see you again. We will have to have lunch, if you could."

When he turned to me, his eyes, even in the dim glowing snowlight, were bright with sympathy, but whether for the loss of our friend or my drift toward Valentina, I couldn't say. He seemed to know everything, this old magician of the castle, of the park. "You must be great colleagues at this point," he said to me, including the other two with a look. I nodded. "I was sorry to ruin your visit to Stockholm. An unfortunate conflict. But, I am sorry to deprive you of a beautiful city. Perhaps something else will come along. I believe there is something in January in London. Perhaps you should look into it, but discreetly, and let me know. Will you do that?''

I didn't feel much like talking to him, not with the memory of Emil like a broken boy, forever sleeping in the snow. I would dream of that, it would mix itself into my other nightmares. But I smiled for Pastukh, to indicate I understood the gift, and accepted for the three of us.

We began to break up at the French doors through which we'd gone out, all that long time before, to find Emil, but then Dexter held back. "Mr. Chairman," he said then, "could you tell me what Emil's argument was?"

A flicker of something hard crossed Pastukh's face, but the eyes held Dexter's. "I think this would be the wrong time. But, at some point, I would be glad to share it with you." He gave a short bow, and left us. We could hear his feet crunching the crust of snow long after the darkness had taken him in.

"Gordy," Val asked then, in a voice that said she'd been wanting to ask this all evening. "When we find Emil, you say, What have they done to you? Why?"

"Ah, Val...I was just speaking dramatically." He peered down the hall, not meeting her eyes. "To say it was anything but Emil's mistake is to put the following construction upon it. Emil applied pressure of some kind, possibly something connected to the past, on Pastukh. He may have done it in Lincoln's presence. So what does that give us? Emil killed by Pastukh? I doubt that. By Lincoln? But that sounds farfetched too. In the absence of anyone who would want Emil dead, we have to accept it was an accident, of the type he kept asking God to send him.

"You mean you think it was deliberate?" I asked, incredulous.

"Of course not." He puffed. "Emil would never cave in that way. But, perhaps to steer away from self-pity, he kept himself always at risk. Those lone winter rides around

Türkenschanzpark, for example. No, he didn't kill himself. But he could easily have miscalculated in some way, and then not been able to retrieve the situation. Something like that." That is what Dexter said. But when he faced us again I saw his eyes were hard and cold with hatred, and knew that his question to the dead Emil had been everything but rhetorical.

I would have pressed him, but his face shut and he stalked away from us, saying, "If you two need a ride tonight, Wee Froggie sails in two minutes." He didn't want to talk anymore.

"I would like a ride, Dexter," Val quickly volunteered. And I, to be with her, and also to keep away from my silver bullet that so hated snow, followed. In a few minutes we were grinding slowly out across the slick surface of the parking area, and through the village, following the cone of Dexter's headlamps, and the dancing white forms that briefly lived in them. We were quiet and reflective, the passing lights setting our faces into starkly relieved profiles, like people on dark coins.

After a time, Dexter said, "I think I won't be in tomorrow, chaps. There is some proper mourning to be done yet tonight, which should leave me in a condition that will only just permit my catching a London plane on Friday morning. Would either of you be interested in sharing such an enterprise, on our lost friend's behalf?"

Val said, "Thanks, Gordy, but I must get home. I am glad to take the U-bahn, though. Go to town, and leave me at any U-bahn station."

"No, madam," he replied, "we drop you at your door, or nothing. What about you, Schaefy?"

It felt like midnight to me, although it was not much past seven, and my brain and body wanted only sleep. But I knew when my friend needed his drinking buddy, and said, "Right on."

"Done," said Dexter grimly.

Then Val said, "I have one with you boys, to toast Emil, and then I take taxi home."

"Smashing," said he.

Traffic had nearly vanished from Vienna that night, in that weather, except for the trams and the taxis, which were always around, and we had no trouble finding a parking place behind the opera. The newsboys flapped around in the snow like brilliantly feathered red and yellow birds, and the brave whores of Vienna would be coming out on the *Gürtel*. Traffic may still, but commerce goes on. The opera loomed in its mass of light, and the sight of it almost tripped a memory... but then, trying to think what it might be. I saw Val in the snowy night against the pale stone and thought, Yes, only a few days ago, we saw *La Tosca*. The hint of something overlooked went away. Okay, we remember what we want to remember.

The three of us, arm in arm, rushed through the swirling snow into the Blue Bar of the Sacher, where, because it was after five, and we were tieless, we had to get our drinks in the pretty room outside the bar, where Dexter and I had our long, sad talk that night a century before, and where I'd seen Val glowing with happiness and cold and excitement after *Tosca*. We ordered martinis, for Val had never had one American style, and then got ourselves a second one. She acquired that pretty, lightly flushed look but could not retrieve her happiness—all of us were unable to see very far past the image of Emil dead in the snow—dead and then somehow withdrawn into Russia by those embassy keepers of the underworld, as if there had never been a small, sick man in a wheelchair. Finally Val said, mainly to Dexter, who had begun to look like a restless, mean old bear, "Gordy, I am so sorry to question the quality of Emil's work... when I know nothing about it, really. It was very unkind to do. But, you know, both of you, he and I were good friends."

Dexter smiled for her. "Don't worry, my girl. You did nothing to Emil. He loved you, as all of us do. Just don't worry. Do-on't worry."

She passed on the third round, and by the time we had our fourth decided to get a cab from the stand in front of the Bristol. "Will I see you tomorrow, Schaefer?" she wanted to know.

"Oh, I'll be there." Bragging.

We said our goodnights, and she gave Dexter a clean little hug, and hurried away. "God, what a lovely woman," he murmured, going a bit sentimental on me. "I tell you, Schaefy, if you were not in hot pursuit I should be."

"Thanks for leaving the field clear."

"Not at all. Glad to do it. What friends are for."

"Exactly."

Then, eyes gleaming, "To our little lost friend, Emil, again."

"To Emil," I replied.

"Murdered this night," he added.

"Come on, Gordy." But the ugly term raised the hairs on my neck.

"I plan to get terribly drunk tonight, old boy," he said then. "Before I do, let me make a promise. Before the vernal equinox...the *vernal* equinox...I shall know whether someone eliminated our friend tonight, and I shall know wherefore, I shall know if he slew himself, or was merely careless, or if he were slain by the one side, or the other...or the other. Hmm. How many sides is that?"

"At least three."

"Must be dozens. You know, they're like great spider webs, all interconnected, the spiders all rather alike, beyond some superficial differences. They sit on their webs, waiting for that almost imperceptible jiggle to signal the arrival of some bit of edible life on their web...but they also get faint jiggles from the other webs. So the American spider sits there and waits, and pretty soon here comes a jiggle. But the bloody Russian spider feels it too, and slithers out on his web. And the plucky old British spider, even *that* one, feels it too, and out he goes. Everyone...even the bloody *Austrian* spider feels it, probably. Christ, an *Argie* spider could tell it..."

"You're losing your thread. Or should I say, web?"

"Smart ass. Nobody loves one, Schaefy. But, anyway... when things are going along, you see, the webs are always a bit a-jiggle, like the beds in a low hotel, yinging away upstairs and down. You don't pay attention to that general sort of jiggle, not really. It's when you get this definite glumph! stick! thrash! silence. *That's* when you know the jiggles are not just the wind. It's something on the web!"

He tossed away his drink and we got two more from the hovering, mildly apprehensive bartender. "What in hell does he think we're going to do, start a fight?" grumped Dexter.

"Yep."

"Never seen a wake before, he hasn't. Anyway, I'm too bloody sad for fighting. And angry. Because that's what I think about Emil's death, I think it's something on the web. Which web? Who knows? But you can bet all the spiders are tiptoeing out to see." He shook his head. "Ah, I am so sad about Emil. I don't like the way the Russkies come in and whisk away their bodies, either, get everything reduced overnight to a few grams of ash and a memorial ceremony."

"Is there one?"

"Tomorrow afternoon, I think. Well, they have their ceremony, we have our little wake." He paused; then, with a thin smile, he said, "Trulov's going to be very upset. He loved Emil, you know. He's good, too. He feels the old web jiggling as though it's caught a flaming dirigible..."

"Gordy... are you a spider?"

He looked soberly into my eyes and replied, "Schaefy, I am the *queen* of spiders." Then he laughed, and made me laugh as well, as we had another martini and felt the evening begin to get slippery beneath us.

Finally, Dexter growled and grabbed my arm, and out we went, into the cold snowy night, or, rather, the cold snowy morning. "This won't last," he predicted, appraising the glowing grey sky. "Rain by forenoon. Ice by night." We walked toward the center of town, Emil's sad ghost whirring along with us in its spectral chair. "It wasn't enough, Schaefy, we're still walking."

I nodded, thinking it had damned near been enough for me.

"Well, old boy, I shall complete what we have merely nicked the surface of tonight. Emil deserves some sort of Christian delivery, and I shall attempt it. But alone. I think you need your rest, and your work, and to go out there and ogle your pretty girl." He smiled. "But do me one favor, won't you?"

"Sure."

"Keep the Stockholm business close. Just let everyone think you're going." I looked into his eyes. The glaze had fled, as though the alcohol had not touched him at all.

"If you want, sure."

"Good. God, I wish we'd done better tonight."

"You'll kill us, Gordy."

We parted at a cab stand on the Ringstrassse, said good night, and something caring about Emil, and even shook hands, which we had only done upon meeting that first time. Looking back along our trail I said, "Didn't know we had so many feet."

He laughed. "Take care of yourself, Schaefy. I'll be back in a week."

"Enjoy."

He stalked away into the snow and cylinders of light, and I watched him go, feeling that we had come to some kind of milestone, that in our drinking, our handshake, there had been an element of finality. I climbed unsteadily into the lead cab and told the driver my address several times, until I got to an acceptable German pronunciation of the street. When he dropped me off, he said good night, and thank you, in good English, and skidded off through the snow.

Then, as I stood in the cold luminous night, it came to me, what I had almost remembered when we first passed the opera—tonight had been the night for *Madame Butterfly*, Renate had tickets, a new dress, had talked about it for days like a happy child, about to receive some gift delayed. "Oh, shit!" With some slight difficulty, chanting my lamentation softly over and over, I found my entrance key, and the two keys to my flat's front door, and entered the building, heading for the wrecked marble of the stairs, and bed, and peace, and help for pain.

5

THE AIR AT THE CASTLE was dense with talk of Emil's death and wild speculation as to its real cause, for no one believed in natural causes where Russians were involved. In fact, the Soviet Union led all the nations represented there in this respect. A wife, dead of meningitis contracted, everyone said, from the infected ticks that flourished in the park, had evolved in this speculative way into a clever hit. A Soviet summer student had slashed his wrists, and died much later from a hospital infection; everyone wondered why They would kill *him*, so young, so untouched by the world, and yet ... People shrugged and hummed over such things, and rolled their eyes. A pleasant Soviet economist had a blood test made at an Austrian clinic, which gave him both a clean bill of health and hepatitis, from which one syndrome followed another until, suddenly, incredibly, he was dead. "Cancer," Trulov told me later. "He died of cancer." Sure he did. Our friend, Emil, joined this little procession of Russians dead from odd causes, and, by inference, the slightly longer procession that included those who had disappeared after falling from favor, or resigned after their networks had been blown, surfacing occasionally in distant conferences everywhere but Vienna. Given this atmosphere, given the further soiling of the inherently dirty event of death, it was natural for us to dread the memorial service planned for that Thursday afternoon in the village cemetery, where the Russian war dead had their monument.

And then, to add to my antsy condition, Valentina had not been on the bus but came stumbling in about tenthirty, after the expensive cab ride from town. She was contained and quiet, and sad about Emil. "How did Gordy do last night?" she asked, beginning to sort things out on her immaculate desktop.

"I don't know. I left him about four..."

She giggled. "What bad boys you are. Four! I am glad I came away." She looked more closely at me. "But you are all right. A bit tired looking. What recuperative powers, Dr. Braun."

"Thank you, Dr. Orlovsky."

The appearance through the door of Andrews' large anemic head brought relief. "May I?" he asked, as everyone did.

"Come in, come in." I gestured to Dexter's vacant chair and Andrews took it, sitting tentatively on its edge, the long legs bent like a grasshopper's. He was a shade over six feet, about my size, and reasonably well-made. When he spoke he gestured with the tiny hands of a nineteenth century English gentleman, and he wore size seven shoes. Although he was always running and playing tennis and squash, he emitted an aura of weakness that made one want to turn away.

"Jolly good," he said, caricaturing himself further, "glad to find you in, Schaefer," nod nod, "and you, Valentina," nod, "dreadfully sorry about this Emil thing, really bad business, that, but the Stockholm thing, regret that change very much as well, not my choice of whom to send at all, ha ha, still, if the *chairman*..." He left the portent hanging mysteriously in the air. "Well, no matter, I came by to get a bit more about your project, just enough to make me knowledgeable, you know, able to cope, able to comment in some broad context regarding the Centre's work...that sort of thing." His voice sputtered along like a Gatling gun, making him sometimes difficult to follow. "Not my field, actually, but I *am* technical, should be a quick study, know what I mean?" And on. I found myself holding my breath, listening to him. His reputation was mainly one of inexperience—he had never worked anywhere but the Centre, for anyone but Russians, so that he had lost his Englishness, except for the cartoon he offered of it, and no doubt lost his technical skills as well. Dexter had said, "God help him if he ever wants a security clearance in the U.K." His nervousness battered at one like the wings of a bird against a window, and I finally interjected quickly a sentence saying we were glad to bring him up to date on our progress and intentions, and promptly turned him over to Valentina, who, surprised, glared gently at me; and then, as expected, gave a briefing that was simply first rate, strung through that knack she had for interlinking disparate processes and events, of giving chaos, coherence. Although Dexter and she and I talked about our work, its quality (we often brooded over its quality, infected for the moment by word that the Carnival Project was bringing in twelve scientists and a large supporting staff), we had never sat down and prepared anything very concise about it. Now, here was Val, giving Andrews a look at our research that was highly focused, and that clearly demonstrated the successive, possible horizons of achievement.

When it was over, Andrews said with genuine admiration, "That was very good indeed. Thanks ever so for it. I shall go out to Sweden on Monday with a clear conscience, and something to say as well. Jolly good. Hate to take the trip from you. Chairman's office did it all, you see, even left me with your reservations, Schaefer...cancelled Valentina's, but kept yours. So I shall steal in among the Swedes as Dr. Braun...at least until I clear up the matter on the spot, like. Well, good show, appreciate your help awfully much, many thanks," and, babbling and babbling, he got up, "Grand show, very good, thanks, *ciao!*" and he was gone.

I gave a long, exaggerated exhalation. "Whewee."

She grinned. "He *does* talk."

"God, doesn't he? But the bastard took no notes. That wonderful presentation you made and he took no notes."

"Don't worry, I have it in my brain. Here." She pointed to her brain. "You are a disagreeable boy today."

"Not really. But I did like your presentation. For the first time I began to see that we could accomplish something. Sometimes it's kind of hard to imagine."

"Would you be here if we could not accomplish something?"

"I don't know. Would you?"

"Absolutely not." Her eyes widened and for a moment she was the blonde Russian girl on any youth pioneer poster, except her arms weren't filled with sheaves of grain or tractors or anything.

"You're magnificent," I told her.

"I have a confession."

"Mm?"

"It is like knitting."

We lapsed into our working silence again, both cheered, I think, at being able to chat, to laugh, against the memory of Emil. Except the ghost would not leave us alone, not yet. While we ate the two apples Val had contributed in lieu of lunch, I sorted through the mid-day mail, which always brought something from a journal or two wanting subscribers, and memos from the director's office with the usual excited notations along with memoranda from Trulov and Ivanov about changes in how the computers would be used, and material from personnel and rough drafts to review on the general subject of "alternative research thrusts."

Val looked puzzled. "Alternative research thrusts?"

"Like alternative religions, cultures, diets, candidates for office . . . it means something more acceptable to people who don't like the existing system. For example, I might be considered your 'alternative boyfriend.'"

She blushed. "Remember what I tell you."

"I'll never forget it. But I will probably make an offer anyway."

Talking about my favorite project, I didn't pay much attention to the envelopes but simply unwound the string on each one and spilled out the contents. That was how I came to open Emil's last message to Dexter. It fell out into my hand, a Xerox copy of a grainy photograph showing soldiers raising a flag on a building somewhere. Written above the soldiers, in red ink, in Emil's unmistakably distorted hand, I read

VNEZAPNO

13IV45

Puzzled, I looked at the envelope and saw it had been marked confidential for Dexter, and had not been mine to open. "Oops," I said. "I've opened something addressed to Dexter."

"What?"

"Something from Emil."

I handed it to her. She studied it for a minute or two, frowned, then said, "This is well known photograph. Everyone sees it in my country. Do you recognize what it is?"

I took the photo back and looked at it more closely than before. The seven soldiers on the building were Russians, wearing tunics with their medals and soft caps. One held a flagstaff bearing a big Soviet flag, the others raised their rifles and submachine guns in a victory salute. And there were other people...no, statues. Then it came to me: they were the stone and metal crowd on top of the Hofburg. "The fall of Vienna," I said almost too softly for her to hear, remembering Emil's telling us about the photo at the *Heuriger*. "But what is the word?"

"Suddenly." I felt her at my side, her warmth, the soapy smell. "But look, Schaefer, look at *him*." She pointed to the one on the right of the group holding the flagstaff. He was a tall, good-looking soldier, and wore his medaled costume well, with one of those submachine guns with the round magazines and perforated cooling sleeves, slung across his chest. "Look," she repeated. "Don't you know him?"

"Is it the old Emil?" I was just guessing.

"No . . . look at the eyes."

In the shadow beneath the visor you could just make out eyes that, seen across a street, across a century, you could not mistake. "Pastukh," I whispered with a kind of awe. "Amazing." Then, turning to her, "You know, Emil told us about the photograph with Pastukh, and I still couldn't see it. Amazing, to have a brain like yours. You identify people out of context."

She smiled, studying the picture. Finally she said, "And here is our lost Emil. Look."

Sure enough, standing fourth from the right, was a young man who, if you stripped him of youth, uniform, submachine gun, cap, vitality, of everything but a faintly squinting expression as he raised his head in exactly the attitude we had seen Emil assume from his wheelchair—if you did all that, yes, you ultimately came to Emil. "Val, you really are amazing."

"But why 'Suddenly'?"

"Who knows. Suddenly he remembers the photograph and looks for it. Suddenly they are brought together for a propaganda photograph . . ."

"Propaganda? Why? We *had* taken Vienna," she said stuffily.

"We *had* taken Iwo Jima, but the famous flag raising was posed." Then, "Suddenly. Suddenly what? What could have happened, there, on that day, that Emil thought would influence the chairman?"

Val shook her head. "I do not understand."

"April thirteenth is something. Something happened on that day."

"Soviet troops took Vienna," she said, not quite laughing.

"Thanks. What the hell is it?" Then it came to me. "I remember. They heard that Roosevelt died."

"You must learn the *day* all your presidents have died?"

"No, no...he died on the twelfth, in the evening. But it was a day my parents could not forget. They talked about it in hushed tones, made it important enough that I remember it too. Like Kennedy's. You just remember some dates."

"You should tell Dexter."

"I'll try." When I got an outside line I let the phone ring and ring at Dexter's flat, hoping to penetrate what must be by now a form of hibernation. The ringing gave the place an empty, forlorn sound, and evoked my friend still out in Vienna somewhere, no doubt in some street off the *Gürtel* in the seventh or eighth districts, a cluster of sleepy whores gathered halfheartedly around a great, unsleepy but terribly drunk bear of an Englishman, who, between tumblers of whiskey, winnowed his way through them, bitterly screwing himself to sleep—he'd always said they worked hard for their living. When his voice filled the receiver I jumped with surprise, and almost squealed, "It's Schaefer, Gordy." Silence followed. Into it, I said, "Sorry to bother you."

"Then...why...do it?" He had not been home very long.

"Something came in the company mail for you. From Emil. I opened it by mistake."

"Eh, something from Emil?" The sleepiness and hangover drained from his voice. "Something put in the mail last night, then."

"I guess. Do you want me to bring it over tonight?"

"Oh, no, don't take the trouble. But tell me what it is."

"A Xerox copy of a photograph that shows seven Russian soldiers..."

"Raising a red flag on the Hofburg, thirteen April, nineteen forty-five..."

"Very good. One of the soldiers..."

"Let me guess. One of them is Emil."

"You must have trained hard last night."

"No comment. Is another of them Pastukh?"

"I'm amazed."

"Don't be. I know the photo, and remember what Emil said. But I *am* surprised he sent it. There must be something else."

"It bears a message. One word. Shall I tell you or would you rather guess?"

"Guess." He hummed for a moment. "It would be...'Suddenly.'"

"Not quite," I said. "Try again."

"It *has* to be," he whined.

"Give up?"

"Yes, you bastardly sod, yes."

"'Suddenly' in *Russian*."

"Ah...damn me. Of course. 'Suddenly' in Russian. 'Suddenly' in Russian. I must think about that one. Anything else?"

"Nope. Sorry to spy on you."

"I'll send around kneecappers, teach you a lesson."

"How do you feel?"

"Don't ask."

"When's your plane?"

"Was tomorrow. I moved it up, leave later today. Back before Christmas. But listen..." and his watchful presence seemed to lean across the wires toward me, "I want you to be careful...cautious...till I get back. No big thing, but as a favor to me. I reckon the Emil business has me nervous."

"Okay," I said, wondering how such a big, strong man got to be such a little old woman, but also feeling that tingle of apprehension you get from warnings, even foolish ones; they are prayers to sleeping dangers. "Bye."

"Goodbye, old boy. Thanks for the call." He rang off, dropped into the electronic line noise like a parachutist vanishing into cloud. "He sounds surprisingly good today," I told Val.

But, having penetrated this far into the workday, we found ourselves waiting for the Dashko service to happen, and were relieved when three o'clock came round. Val said, by way of preparation, "I must . . . I will go with Soviet group. You understand."

"Sure. I'll see you . . . when I see you."

"Yes." She got into her coat and left, click-clicking down the tiles, away from me. I moved paper round desultorily, thinking to stay where I was until half past three.

I didn't answer the telephone until the fifth ring, and then only reluctantly, and ready to fight. "Braun," I said into the mouthpiece.

"Here is Renate," said a small, bitter voice in faraway Vienna, the voice of a wronged girl.

"I'm very sorry about last night, Renate," I said, feeling no sorrow at all.

"I think something happen with you."

"A friend died. A Russian. We found him . . ."

"We?"

"My partners and I." It made me sad, having Emil's death paraded out to soothe an angry woman.

"You have police."

"Yes, and people from the Russian embassy. Took a long time."

"And then you come home?"

"No . . . then we went for drinks. We liked the man who died. Emil. We gave him a wake."

"A *Kielwasser*?"

"No, a kind of party for the dead, to say goodbye. To drink to his memory."

"You drink much. You must like him much, Schaefy, to drink until morning." I let silence wash in around the hum of the line. "More than me." Silence. "Why you not call?"

"I . . . forgot." There, an honest man at last.

"*Forgot?* How you forget *me*?"

"Renate, I have to go."

"When I see you?"

"I am busy."

"Ho," and she tried a kidding laugh. "Not forever busy, I hope?"

"*Very* busy."

"You play game with me."

"I really have to go now."

"You unkindly to me. Can be I am unkindly to you."

"I really have to go. Goodbye." When the phone buzzed a moment later, I left it alone. It stopped after twelve snarls. Then, carrying Renate's unfinished curse, I grabbed my jacket and headed for the cemetery to say one last farewell to Emil.

Dexter's forecast had been wrong (I would say, looking back now, that he was often wrong with his predictions). The snow had thinned to blowing crystals, and the wind had picked up, but nothing had melted, and nothing had turned to rain. It continued bitter and sad, a world in which the castle was a yellow cake sinking in a larger, white one, the rectangles of buried lawn bounded by miserable trees, ornamented with the black puffs of grounded crows. There seemed to be no one in the world with me, just the crows, just the wind and waning light of afternoon, and a sun that, glimpsed through the ragged cover of cloud, raced along like a round ice cube.

I got there after the service had begun. The director had nearly completed a hollow, unintelligible peroration about Emil's real and imaginary manhoods, the converging symbolism thereof, the marvelous courage and remarkable intelligence—the usual stuff. Then others came forward to testify to some aspects of the man, to give anecdotal tributes, personal things. Trulov did not, an ominous sign, for he always spoke up at such functions. He had the shattered look of a widow on a bier, a father burying a child. His red-rimmed eyes narrowed when he saw me, and he wrenched away, full of hatred. Like Lincoln, I thought, wondering why. Jesus, *why*? I huddled, and listened, and squinted away the windbrought tears, and wondered what all this had to do with our little smashed friend, or his life, or his death...

When it was over, I found Lincoln next to me. "Nice," he volunteered, showing me his empty smile. "Nice tribute."

"Nice man," I replied, wanting not to have him around.

"Very. Odd, horrible kind of accident."

"Yes."

"I feel some responsibility. I wish we'd seen him back inside the castle."

"Me too."

"I felt he really didn't want us to. I think he wanted to be alone. Outside. In the weather."

"I hear what you're saying." And I think it's crap.

"He'd about lost his project. That would have been the end of him in real research."

"He thought he might turn that one around."

"Oh . . . I didn't know."

"That was why he was there."

"With the chairman, you mean. Of course. Must have been what they were chatting about. Went very quiet when I walked up." Lincoln ran along, his words rising and falling on a faint, false note, the carrier signal of lies. If I hadn't seen him with Emil and Pastukh I would have said he even lied about that. "But we left him . . . of course he seemed cheerful enough *then*."

"Emil didn't kill himself, Lincoln."

"Baker, please."

"Baker."

"Did I say he did?"

"I think so. But he couldn't even move that much, to put his control panel out of reach."

"Ah . . . you think there's something we don't know?"

"Like what?"

"You know, scratch a loose Russian, get a spy. Why else are they allowed out, eh?"

"A ninety-nine percent disabled Russian spy. I'll wait for the movie."

"Funny. But Dashko had his brain, his voice. What more does a good spy need?"

"I have a feeling you'd know."

He gave a cold chuckle. "Well, I read a lot." More metallic laughter. "And you?"

"I'm just what I seem."

"The naive American in search of the mysterious east? Do yourself a favor, Braun. On this Stockholm lark you've arranged with your Russian lady, watch what she does. Watch her pick something up, put something down, bump against somebody accidentally. Watch her go through one of those nasty little dances of spying."

I started to tell him there wasn't going to be any "Stockholm lark," but remembered being asked not to, and...ah, Christ, I remembered Trulov's call, those instructing rhythms in Russian, her having to pick something up for him there. Doubt clouded my confidence. Lincoln read it all, I think, for he said, "Ah, too bad. I seem to have struck a nerve. Sorry for that, Schaefer. I hope you see nothing of the kind, nothing ugly. But of course you won't believe that."

"Go lay your eggs someplace else...Baker."

"Have a nice day," he replied, mocking everyone.

Not wanting him with me, I lagged and let him walk away, saying his sarcastic goodbyes to the night. Then, chilled and lonely, I went back toward the low stone monument they had erected to the Russian war dead, to be alone, perhaps, or to be with some shade of the lost Emil. The snow had resumed, falling with its slight whisper across the watching crosses, assorted saints, and Christs. I stopped short of the monument itself, for Trulov sat on a slab nearby, his knees drawn up inside his powerful arms, his face buried in his coatsleeves. He cried and cried, like a heartbroken boy, there in the darkness and the snow, and I listened from the shadows, and finally backed away, trying hard not to be seen, not to shame him.

But he sensed my furtive movements, and sprang to his feet. He watched me from the monument, suddenly assembled, ready for anything, as unlikely now to shed tears over lost friends as a wolf is to sweat. "Schaefer," he murmured in a voice ragged from grief. "It *is* you, isn't it."

"Yes. I didn't mean to..."

"To what?"

"To intrude."

"Ah, to intrude." He advanced slowly, smearing the old tears from the corners of his eyes with thick hairy hands. "To see me at my lamentations, eh?" He gave a sniff that sounded vulnerable, coming from such a big man, and shuffled closer. "I had not meant to be observed. Such behaviour is very rare with me, it must come from the approach of middle age. But I had not meant to be seen, and not by an American particularly." Now he was well within reach, and I could tell it hadn't been all grief—he'd also done the first few laps of one of those incredible Russian vodka marathons, so that more rage than good humor flickered behind his eyes. I realized suddenly that anything was possible, and tensed, to flee, to fight, to meet the situation...

But, God, he was quick!

Before I could blink his two hands had me by my jacket front, swinging me back and forth, off-balance, so that my arms were almost useless, and then he lifted and threw me, very hard, against a large granite stone and held me there in a boozy cloud while air trickled back into my lungs. "I know what you are thinking, old buddy. Kick him in the nuts. Go for the eyes. The throat. Maim and kill, right? You do that. I will absorb anything. Shoot me with a cannon, I absorb it. Then I begin making you into kindling, into little pieces so small they will not burn." He pounded me against the stone. "Why is it always *you*, anyway? Why do I keep coming to *you*, Schaefer, you, *you*..." Bam, bam, bam. "Always you, the name coming back, always: *Schaefer*." Bam. "What is Emil to you, to any of you fucking Americans and Britons, what is my friend to *you*?" Bam, bam. While he was slapping me against the stone like a doll, I was punching at him, but feebly, with almost no weight on the ground. My best shots slid off his big chin, and he grinned, and said finally, "Ah, I am so fucking tired of all your cowshit."

"Bullshit," I corrected automatically, trying another haymaker, which he absorbed.

"Bullshit, then," he said. "What*ev*er, what*ev*er." The back of his left hand, the size and texture of a pine four by four, flew out of the night and slapped me on each *ev*, "what*ev*er, what*ev*er..." I could feel my face turn to hamburger and blood move across it like rain on a windscreen. Outside it was all stars, so that I wondered what happened to the snowflakes, where were my snowflakes? "What*ev*er." Whack!

"Maxim!"

Both of us tensed, hearing the voice, disembodied, floating on the darkness. Was it that little metal Jesus, or one of the stone angels with bad teeth? Was it God answering the prayers of old Schaefer Braun, now being beaten to death by this big Russian? We tensed like animals, both full of superstition, except you couldn't see our ears prick, our neckhairs bristle.

"Let him go! Now!" Pastukh came into view, then, another big man in the cemetery, but not as big as Trulov, and apparently unarmed except for his authority. But I could feel his presence, his force, working on Trulov's hands. The "what*ev*ers" ceased, the big hard hand stopped pounding, although he still held me off the ground, ready to smash me against the stone again.

"What do you care about this piece of shit?" he asked rhetorically, in English.

"Let him go."

The hands loosened slightly, I felt my feet touch the ground, my weight flowing into them. I could feel his reluctance, too, and I really didn't want anything resumed just then.

"Now!"

The hands fell away and I sank down on the horizontal surface of the tomb. "What is this disgusting game you play in the cemetery, Maxim? Is this how we remember

Emil Dashko, by acting the brute to his friend?'' The chairman advanced on Trulov, but carefully.

"To soshe s uma?"

Trulov moved clear of me, away from Pastukh, warily, angrily; he seemed all rage, a column of drunken anger the chairman controlled, but just barely. He growled something in Russian, Pastukh answered quietly; you could hear the prodding sarcastic question, the defensive, uncertain response from Trulov. But he trembled with rage, rage burned like a steady flame, no matter how he might retreat from the chairman. Suddenly he cried out, ''I can *prove* them!'' in a voice that seemed to shake the stones around us, and spun, lashing out with his left fist to smash it once, and then again, into a granite marker. The pain shuddered through him so visibly that I flinched. He poised that way, the good hand holding the hurt one, the rage drowned in the shock of pain. He watched us like a great animal calmed by its wound, and then he stepped back, his chagrin falling away from him, and said, ''I shall,'' in a quiet voice from which all rage, all vodka, had fled. Then, with balletic grace, he turned into the night. We barely heard his footsteps pad across the snow.

I still leaned against the slab Trulov had made memorable to me, wondering dully at the way my intellectual life style had suddenly got so physical. Trulov had wrenched me pretty hard against the granite, and my face felt like a peeled grape—the way it feels to the grape, I mean. And it had been humiliating, to be suspended and beat upon and so unable to do anything to stop it, like a puppet being dismembered by a mad child. ''I better read up on how to break that hold,'' I said as Pastukh came over.

''Maxim is an extremely powerful man. I would not want to oppose him.''

''Although, you did. Thanks.''

''Ah, my authority did. You can break that hold with authority.'' He added, philosophically, ''But I felt it weaken. I doubt I could stop him next time, or keep him from doing whatever it is he wants to do.''

"What were you saying in Russian?"

"He thinks you are involved in something. Things. Emil's death, perhaps. Perhaps he thinks you are part of the CIA smear campaign." He looked away, the eyes unable to ignore the disingenuous note in his voice.

It made me suspect him, for enemies had begun springing at me out of nowhere, for inscrutable reasons. "How long did you watch us?"

"Not very long."

"You could have stopped it sooner, then."

"I thought it would stop itself."

"With me in twenty delicious parts."

"Maxim would not kill you unless terribly provoked."

"Or under orders."

"I meant to say, he would not have killed you tonight."

"His simulation was impressive."

"Also...I did not want to show myself unless it was completely necessary."

"You didn't want to be the Russian saving the American if there were some official reason to beat the American into catfood." Pastukh didn't reply. "I'm going to make a complaint against Trulov. I'm going to fuck up his life."

"I would rather you did not."

"Why should I just let it happen?"

"A complaint will accomplish nothing. Who will act? The director? A complaint to him, especially one concerning a Soviet employee of the Centre, is not likely to get much support."

"What about you?"

"I intend to have the incident brought to the attention of those concerned at home. But quietly."

"The U.S. embassy."

"Better you drop your complaint into a well. Listen. This 'fucking up' of Maxim's life happens now without anything more from you. Nor does it matter if he attacked *you*, or simply attacked anyone, any American, say, he found within reach. The fact is he has fled. We will not

see him here again. He must now be considered by everyone to be a dangerous madman, a man on his own—a Soviet on his own outside the Soviet Union, and without our
support. He knows this, he knows he has nothing now, he
is merely loose in a world that does not trust Russians.
Eventually he will be taken home where he has a lifetime
of psychotherapy to look forward to."

"Are all of you spies?"

"Are all of you?"

"*Touché.*"

For a time we were silent. He stood over me like a be-
nevolent guard, the Prospero whose waning magic could
keep Caliban and the other evil spirits back for yet one
more night, perhaps one more season. At last he said,
"Schaefer, something dangerous and unstable is going on.
I am not sure what, but I know it is happening, and that it
will be bad for everyone. Everyone." He watched the sky.
"I want you to stay at home until your face is better. Stay
home for the holidays. In January go to London for the
symposium with Orlovsky and Dexter. Do all of those
things. But stay clear of Maxim, stay clear of strangers. We
have to get this thing . . . repaired. I shall do what I can to
keep it off you." His voice was low, his face very sad, perhaps already grieving for Trulov. He sounded oppressed
and melancholy, as though he bore a great weight tonight,
as though he were the last pallbearer in a world of unburied dead. "Come. I shall see you back," he said, giving
me a hand up. Then, together, our arms linked like
wounded soldiers, we walked slowly back through the
cemetery and the snow, toward the castle lights.

6

Schaefer,
Why you play game
with your
*   GYPSY???*

was folded and taped to my door when I got home, punc-
tuating what had been, in some ways, a perfect day—in
terms of pain, fatigue, fear, and shame, it rated very high.
I had left Pastukh staring after me in the darkness and
walked to the parking area, and, brushing two days' snow
off my silver bullet, spread some on my face, to numb it,
to keep the left side that felt like cracked porcelain from
shattering into a bunch of jagged shards that began to need
a shave. Who would I be if my face fell off? Interesting
question, enough to get me into the BMW and under way,
slithering along like a sixty-nine Buick on bald tires. My
little bombshell was wonderful under every condition but
slipperiness, when it presented a shade more torque to the
rear wheels than they could absorb; the car spent its win-
tertimes on the edge of spinning out, and had once, with
no damage beyond the shortening of my life.

Quickly, blindly, I wrestled the door open, cursing the
Austrian penchant for so fucking many locks (somewhere
hidden in the mountains is a complex the size of Mc-
Donnell-Douglas, where the Austrians build all their locks
and keys), and kicked it shut behind me. I sank down
against it and raised my knees into what is no doubt the
Adult Male Crying Position, and let it come out, the loss
of my old Nancy, the shame at being pummeled like a doll,
the hopelessness of whatever drew me toward Valentina,
my parents' death, my betrayed and busted Uncle Stuka,
Emil (Oh, God, *Emil!*), my grieving gypsy enemy, even
that poor lost crazywoman, Lisa. It left me hollowed out
and sad, trembling, ready to die of a deep and incurable
despair that seemed to thrive in me like some mould.

But, once emptied, I was then able to shake my head
skeptically, and whisper, through my stiff, cracked face,
"Come on," and slowly raise myself against the door like
a man scooting up a crevasse; then I pushed off toward the
bathroom. The mirror showed me a demon, a clown, a
man with a thin, high-cheekboned, blonde, and grey-eyed
half of a face, the other half oblate, bloody, and dark
purple, like an eggplant with a swollen, bloodshot eye

stuck on it. "Jesus Christ," I prayed. "But . . . *why*?"
Feeling a few balloons of sorrow still waiting to rise within,
I forced my feelings flat. No more out of control. Thing
you do, my man, you take something for the pain, and the
dirt, and . . . the pain, right. I let the bath begin to fill from
the overhead water heater, which came to life with that
startling *boomph* of exploding gas, and then shed my
clothes, but slowly, taking time to peel the mess off, taking time to hang up the bloody down jacket, slipping the
rest into the grey plastic commissary bag used for laundry. I poured a half-liter glass almost full of Chivas, and
dropped in two tiny ice cubes, and took these and
Wednesday's *Herald Trib* back to the bath. The hot water
took me in, a little healing ocean of heat, a kind of alternative pain. I lay there, my legs stretched out and up
against the white tiles, and soaked, and ran hot water over
my head with the hand shower, and hurt. And all the
while, my day played and replayed, like one of those film
loops from a weather satellite, the movement jerking from
morning till night, and quickly returning to morning.

Better. The tub helped. I thought of all the people whose
strength dwarfed mine, and of all those others who were
weaker than I. When the telephone buzzed, I let it.

Since sleep had not come when the second jelly glass of
Scotch was finished, I got up for more, and stood in the
dark kitchen watching the other windows that bordered the
Hof. Nothing seemed to live behind the lace curtains and
venetian blinds; the glowing light within might have been
a kind of phosphorescence. Street noises floated on the
night, the shrill complaint of smooth tires on slick streets,
the dedicated rumble of trams, a snowplow grinding along
Währingerstrasse, like an exotic orange predator, hunting
with bolts of blue light; once, the crisp sound of cars in
collision . . . a knock on my door.

It took a second for that sound to draw me back, and a
moment more for the reflex of fear to stabilize—Trulov
had trained me very quickly to flinch from the unexpected. I shook my head, lamenting my new jumpiness,

and opened the door without looking, taking whatever it offered, from a murderous Trulov to ... Valentina. She stared at me, her broad red mouth in a sorrowful O, her eyes flickering, not quite able to accept what they saw. "Schaefer," she whispered, "I was worried. I tried to call. I came. But, what happened?"

"Come in, Val," I said, realizing now that, compared to a normal person, I was a little unsteady.

She passed me silently as a ship, unable quite to take her eyes off the eggplant. I closed the door after her, and offered a crooked, painful grin. "Nice of you to come by." I took her fur-lined winter coat and round fur hat and folded them over a chair outside the kitchen.

"What happened?" Frowning, she reached a gentle hand toward my inflated cheek. I recoiled.

"Tender," I said. It had been hours since I'd spoken aloud, and the words came deformed and flattened out of a mouth that wouldn't work properly.

"You did not return to work. I worried. But this ... I cannot believe this."

"Trulov worked me over in the cemetery."

"Worked you over?"

"I mean he held me in one hand and beat on me with the other." I took a big mouthful of Scotch. "You know, like a rape."

"But he is so big. *That* cannot be worrying you, Schaefer. Of course he can manhandle you. He can manhandle anybody he likes. But why would he?"

"I would love to know. He went crazy. He told me I was always there, in the middle of it. God knows what *it* is." Then, realizing my manners had lapsed, I said, "Let me fix you something."

She shook her head. "I don't want to drink tonight. But what happened then?"

"Pastukh stopped him."

"The chairman."

"He came out of the shadows. I felt he'd been watching our dance for awhile. He came out and told Maxim to stop."

"And he stopped."

"Yes, amazing isn't it? Like a lion tamer."

"But Trulov must be mad."

"He was full of vodka. But he was sane."

"Where can he go now, what will he do?"

"Here's a famous quotation for you. 'Frankly, my dear, I don't give a damn.' "

She laughed. "Even I know that one."

"The chairman asked me not to make an official complaint. I thought that was almost as funny as Trulov's attack."

"But an official complaint . . . that would finish Trulov, even . . ." she broke off the thought.

"I know. Even in his line of work. Psychotic KGB is bad KGB, eh?"

She shook her head. "Not every Soviet citizen is KGB, Schaefer."

"Lincoln says you're all spies if you're outside."

"Lincoln is probably a spy himself." She raised her head and gave me that Lenin Youth look. "But tonight I only spy on you."

"How wonderful."

"Have you eaten?"

"Some cashews."

"Ugh. I fix you something decent."

I waved a hand at the kitchen, indicating the futility of any effort there. "Cupboard's bare. Except for booze, spinsterish crumbs." I tipped up the glass and drained the whiskey. "But there *is* plenty of booze. Won't you . . . ?"

"No, nor you either." She removed the glass from my sleazy paw and turned me toward the bedroom. "You lie down now. You don't know what you look like. Something ready to be dead. Lie down, I find something for you."

I lay down, feeling grand, the pain, blunted by whisky and aspirin, blunted further by the sure, caring touch of this adored woman. Imagine, someone taking care of me. No...imagine *that person wanting to take care of me.* "What are you doing now?" I yelled to her, suddenly afraid she'd gone, or been dreamed.

"Lie quietly. I come in a minute."

Smells emanated from the kitchen, and bubbling noises, adding fresh and unfamiliar life to my cold set of rooms. After awhile she entered with a dark wooden tray (where had she found a tray?) with mugs of hot soup and buttered bread and two more mugs with strong, dark tea. It smelled wonderful, and, after she'd got me propped up on my big down pillows, the comforter tucked in around me, I took my soup and sipped at it, feeling it cauterize the torn interior of my cheek. "Didn't know we had soup."

"Only one. Now you have nothing."

"Jewish penicillin," I said.

"How?"

I laughed. "That's what chicken noodle soup is called."

"Universal treatment? I wonder what is our equivalent?"

"Vodka, probably."

"I hate to admit it, but it is true."

We were both conscious, and perhaps a little nervous about, being warm and close and the best of friends that night. I could feel her hip where she sat on the edge of my bed, and her presence in the room as something infernally sweet and wanted and warm. There was nothing sexual in it. That aspect of me had more or less gone off the air. And yet, the sensation was strongly physical. "Tell them at work I have the flu, okay?"

"Okay."

"You could bring me some stuff to work on here."

"How long will you be gone?"

"The chairman told me to stay home until whatever is wrong is fixed. And I don't much want to show this puss..." Her eyebrows lifted. "This face at the castle."

"I bring some tomorrow."

"That would be nice. I mean, nice to have the work, nice to have you bring me things, nice to have you around."

"Careful."

"Don't worry. I wouldn't spoil this for anything."

"But talk like that could spoil it."

"Do you really think so?"

She did not reply. Then she said, "I must admit, I like it too."

The comfort, following the whisky, the pain, the trauma of the day, was finally too much for me. Sitting with my pretty Valentina in a tableau that simulated normal life and love and a small population of people who cared enough to call...it fostered contentment, and that engendered sleep. I heard her say, "Ah, you can barely hold your eyes open."

"Sorry," I mumbled. "A happy man is a sleepy man."

"I like you to be happy."

"I see that. I would like you to be happy too."

"Careful."

"Yes..."

"I go now, good night Schaefer..."

"You know, I would take a beating every day for this."

"Then it is *really* time for me to go." I heard her wrapping herself against the weather, and, as from a great distance, her goodnight...

"SCHAEFER?" Valentina asked diffidently, in the tone you would ask Hyde: Jekyll?

I started awake, sweating and frightened, and she pushed me gently back, and said, "It is Val...just Val...where do you go when you sleep? It is Val."

"Val." I tried to laugh it all off and my eyes brimmed with tears. When I could speak I said, "Welcome to Bedlam."

"Bedlam? I do not understand."

"An asylum. A nuthouse."

"I understand you are crazy *last* night, Schaefer. But now we have today. I am here." She held up a yellow Meinl bag. "With food." I nodded, tears beginning to spill down both my faces. "Please do not be so unhappy. Listen. Here we are. Enjoy it." Her voice was a song of fatigued vexation. She would not cry—one wondered how long it had been since she had—but you could hear the hurt in her voice, that I would not revive myself, and meet her, and let this good thing between us be just a good thing. Her eyes said: This is not allowed, I have ignored the all-important rules to be here with you, in your flat, on this winter night. "A Soviet hurt you. Now a Soviet helps you. I fix something to eat." She gave a brave smile, and held up another grey plastic bag. "And here is work for you. The ocean chemistry profiles from the Gulf of Alaska experiment. You will earn your food."

For a time, at least, we had the shadow of domestic life. On Saturday and Sunday, she arrived a little after six, we ate a spinster meal of tuna and tomatoes I prepared the first day, a wonderful goulash she made the next. We had a drink beforehand, and wine with our food. I kept my affection silent, the beacon of admiration turned way down, although she could not have missed them, leaking out in ready laughter, a hand that sometimes shook, a quick turning away.

We talked of work, compared notes on the Gulf of Alaska stuff, which promised weeks of simple but satisfying labor. On Monday she brought me gossip the way Cyrano carried court talk to the cloistered Roxane. No more rabbit would be served in the Schloss cafeteria. The food group had staged Hunger Week. The Carnival Project had been written up in *Time* magazine, and treated as a joke. ("How could they?" And she, laughing, "How could they *not*?")

The Centre's grapevine had assimilated Emil's death, after a series of rumors—he had been drugged and set loose in his wheelchair to die in the snow; he had suffered a heart attack moments after leaving Lincoln and the chairman; he had succumbed after a long fight with cancer; he had committed suicide, first of exposure, then of exposure with sleeping tablets, then by biting down upon the cyanide capsule "they all" carried somewhere on their person. "I wonder what his ghost must think of all this?"

She nodded, wondering too. "Why," she asked without expecting a reply, "do they look for the worst things, always?"

But Emil rumors had already begun to blend with Trulov rumors, speculation that the missing Russian had killed his crippled friend ("No, it was I he killed," I told her. Val grinned. "I come to *that* story later."), then fled. Emil faded quickly from this corridor history the way big news exits through the back pages of a newspaper. Soon it was all Trulov, his murder of Emil, but, no, his secret defection to the west, but, no, his running away with a secretary at UNIDO, but, no, he lives comfortably in San Francisco after a long career as an American double agent, but... On and on, a mythic Trulov, at large, hunting. "He's hunting," I told Val. "I don't know what, but he's hunting." Here my skin prickled with gooseflesh. "All I really know is he will be back."

"I hope not," she said, touching the hurt side of my face with the cool, gentle hand of a nun. "I truly hope not."

"Next time he'll have to kill me."

She touched my lips with a fingertip. "Do not talk so." We never acknowledged, in such asides, that next time Trulov would *want* to kill me.

Why?

The Centre's rumors came in with her, each night, always slightly changed from the previous day's report, never the same things two days running. Trulov had been reported in New York, in Athens, Lisbon, L.A., Rio. "You seek him here, you seek him there," I chanted, "but does anybody really seek him at all?"

"What do you mean?"

"I mean, if a KGB officer goes berserk and beats somebody up for no apparent reason, if he goes off like this on

his own, do They just let him go, or do They send someone after him?"

She shrugged. "How would I know about KGB?" Her
eyes held mine, defiant, waiting.

"Sorry," I murmured, with the memory of Lincoln
saying, *Watch her,* crowding in unpleasantly. "You know,
the chairman wants the three of us to go to London in
January. He said so the other night. He asked me to look
into it discreetly and talk to him about it."

"London."

"Have you ever been?"

She shook her head. "Have you?"

"Only to the airport. We could drive over."

"The three of us?" she asked warily.

"Of course. Dexter would die if we went to England
without him. He'd worry about us. Besides, I'd need a
chaperone."

For a moment her eyes sparkled with excitement. "It
would be splendid, to cross France, and the *Channel...*"
Then, the mood collapsing swiftly, "You know what I
think?"

"What?"

"I think it will be like Stockholm. We get to think of it,
but then it is removed from us. I will believe the London
trip when we are on the *Autobahn.*"

"When does Andrews leave for Stockholm?"

"He went Monday."

That night I dreamed we were back in the snow, running, running, all of us, Val and Dexter and the chairman
and me, all of us running, looking for Emil; and running
with us, off in the black woods, a great shape smashed silently through the trees. Trulov hunting.

PART FOUR

1

THE GLOWING FIELD of ice fractured ahead of the advancing prow, as though powerful unseen fingers walked ahead of them, depressing the frozen panes until they shattered into the jagged shards that bumped along the hull, rushing past in the ferry's translucent wave, pale and green, like drowned things. Trulov watched the ice spin by from the post he had taken on the boat deck, determined to ignore the wet cold that pierced him to his bones, forced tears from his eyes, froze his nosehairs, stung the fists he had stuffed into the pockets of his khaki trenchcoat.

The coat. Another mistake, another in what seemed to him now an endless series of mistakes, each worse than the last. He flexed his left hand, the one he had nearly broken on the American, and had definitely harmed on the gravestone. It had swollen badly, and was painful to touch.

The ferry engines mocked him: *dumb dumb dumb,* they went; *dumb dumb dumb*.

In an angry moment he had done all of those things one must never do. He had lost his head, smashed an American who looked to be the quintessential innocent bystander, and then, needing pain to quench his own rage, he had crippled himself. But it was even worse than that. He had signalled his suspicions and now there would be a move to silence him. There had already been vague stirrings around the Los Angeles trip, although he had paid for that one himself; they suspected him of something nameless. The incident in the cemetery would confirm their worst suspicions: he had acted on his own. Yes, the worst thing he had done was to go off on his own, for, doing

that, he moved outside his system, like a satellite saying
goodbye to the sun. But this was not the dark neutrality of
space. This was being Russian without Russia, in a world
that hated both.

They would come after him, colleagues from the Centre,
perhaps, or from home, and there would be the usual
oblique conversations touching upon matters of judg-
ment, stability, reliability, and then the two of them would
board Aeroflot for Moscow, and there say cordial goodbyes; and then others, and more talk. He would express his
suspicions. They would wink. Ah, shit, that was just the
trouble. Having given his enemies this example of insane
behavior, who would believe his extravaganza now? Did he
believe it himself? In the cemetery, the old man had merely
watched the beating. There had been no *reflex* to protect
the American, but intercession as a practical matter, from
a purely Soviet point of view. Perhaps he had got it wrong,
after all. Perhaps all this had to do with middle age, perhaps it was a wild gestalt that took one out and out, farther and farther from the truth, into the world on one's
own.

Except . . . *except* there was the fragment of proof from
the madwoman in California, and the further evidence of
her death within twenty-four hours of his visit. They . . . that
other They . . . had detected Soviet interest and had quickly
removed its object. And there was that thin trill of interest now from the British side. *Something* was there. He
believed he knew what it looked like, in the way a sculptor
sees the figure hiding in the stone. He had to keep hunting, and finally it would fall into his hands and . . . He
grinned. He could go home to more than psychotherapy,
perhaps, and his country would be served. You had to note
that, this matter of national service.

Ah, but he hunted only a few hours ahead of the pack,
and he had already thrown away some of that narrow
margin by his craziness in the cemetery. "Emil, Emil," he
whispered to the sea. "What are you to them, Emil?"
Another mystery, to go with his mistakes; a sauce of mys-

tery for a plate piled with mistakes. "Shit," he whispered to the cold Baltic, breathing beneath its coat of ice. He was burning himself out like a meteorite on a matter that required time, time for the brain to sort things out, for the unconscious to make its subtle connections. That was what intellect and intelligence were all about, linking apparently unrelated points through time, finding the picture among all the pointillist colors, the man in the painted abstraction.

He could see nothing but the water and the ice, for the night suspended like grey cotton from above. The low-lying lights of Copenhagen were swallowed up before they cleared the harbor, and Malmö was nowhere in sight. They might have been anywhere, on a pond, on the open sea. The only sense of motion was the slight roll of the ferry, and the passing ice; everything seemed to move but the ship. Yellow light streamed from windows, bars of it teeming with droplets, throwing illuminated trapezoids across the hull waves. Most of the other passengers had stayed in the light, in the warmth, had a drink ("Last chance."), as if reluctant to return to the quieter life of Sweden. One, a slender woman in her sixties with long white hair and a surprising figure, had joined him on the open deck for the first part of the trip, and he had watched her, this woman of formidable innocence, eyes bright with the excitement of crossing ice, in winter. She had stayed only a short time, though, before, red-cheeked and happy, she had gone back inside. He could see her through the window, sitting alone with a brandy glass in front of her, like a young woman acting an older one.

Trulov wanted a drink, wanted to be drinking in there with all those Swedes who, in his view, were incompetent drinkers anyway. It would be a secret way to show the flag, as the Americans put it. But he had preferred the open deck. The ride into town from Kastrup had oppressed him with a sense of arriving on a planet where he was the only person he knew, so that he had come here, into the cold.

"For us there *is* no cold," he told the night, and laughed softly, and gave a great shiver. Perhaps he was out here to prove that despite his crazy behaviour, he was still a good Soviet. And just then the first lights of Malmö broke through, flickering and disappearing, but connecting him to something besides this flat, black universe of ice and water.

All very good, he thought now. But why am I here?

Gambling, of course. Gambling like a wild man in a Dostoyevsky novel, like a Russian on his own. They always said that, the Americans: initiative fucks up the Russian mind, they can't think on their feet. Trulov smiled sadly. "I begin to believe you," he murmured. An eternity before, several lifetimes ago, he had been apprehended in the cemetery, beating the American to death . . . why? It may have been just to get his real attention. (How could he correct my English at a time like that? It was humiliating.) He had fled, like a boy. He should have confronted them then, pointed the finger, stirred things up, stood his ground with the slim proof already in hand . . . because at that moment, he realized afterward, *at that instant*, he held enough to excite others, for there to be questions asked, checks made. The situation could not have accommodated many sharp questions, he was sure of that. If only he had held his ground, he would be a hero tonight. Of course, holding one's ground is a definition of heroism, is it not? At heart then he was probably not much of a hero, for he had fled like a criminal, and now he gambled like a wild man. He had not even gone home, not even called Vera, who had no idea where he was, or Svetlana Maximovna. Ah, my baby, he worried then, ah, my precious baby, and his throat constricted around the sudden, vivid image of the pale, lovely face that was so much the face his daughter would have. Ah, God. When you begin thinking of your children, then you begin to lose. He had not thought of her once in California, not once, until he was back at the Vancouver airport, picking a gift. He gripped the rail hard enough to make his swollen hand hurt, and the pain drew him away from home, back to the night, back to Sweden. No one knew where he was. He had grabbed his briefcase, adjusted his identity to that of a German businessman trying to make a living, one of those drummers you discover on night trains and late flights everywhere, and he had fled on a westbound train.

But then, immersed in the suspended present of the traveler, feeling his new identity around him like a cloak, his mind had cleared. He had looked into the mirror of the window, a mirror broken by sudden spheres and cones of light, wriggling with snowflakes, and then the reflections of him and his companions, and outside the pale, indistinct contours of the embankments, rushing by. He had tried to think where to go, where to go, thinking with the carriage wheels that seemed to ask, *wheretogo*, *wheretogo*, *wheretogo*, through the night. And it had come to him: Stockholm. The next step, the next *thing*, had to be in Stockholm.

Now, watching the harbor lights of Sweden drift toward them across the water, he wondered why he had arrived at that impulse, which seemed so prescient on the train, and so foolish now. If they catch you in Sweden, my friend, they will read it as defection, and nothing you say will change that.

Well, there were compelling reasons. He hoped they were. Andrews would be in Stockholm, presenting some kind of paper, but also acting as his, Trulov's, courier for the music. Would he do it, knowing Trulov was on his own? Another detail caving in, another mistake about to be born. He would watch that closely, for it was one thing to be on one's own, dispossessed, possibly hunted, and something quite different to abandon a mission because of it. His reasons had been clearer on the train. But now he thought: it had something to do with the chairman's intervention, his tampering with routine travel to substitute Andrews for Braun and Orlovsky. Yes, it had been that anomalously personal touch that had turned Trulov toward Stockholm. He expected something to happen, another bolt of lightning to illuminate these things that live under rocks.

The ferry's whistle howled across the night as they slowed, wallowing through the shattered ice. Off to the left, swept by the beacon, the enormous shipyard crane stood like a metal quadruped feeding on the carcass of an incomplete supertanker, all veiled and medieval. The town lights swung off to the left as well, now, as they headed into the desolate industrial pier of Limhamm, the loud-speaker asking everyone to return to the vehicles, the ferry tacking toward the globes of misty light. Trulov abandoned his cold post with something like relief, like a fakir abandoning a bed of nails. But for the hour of heaving ice and frozen wind, he had not needed warmth or a human voice or any comfort. He remained a Russian, if a forsaken one, for whom nothing could be too hard.

He crowded with the others down companionways and back into the old bus, where it waited wedged between a few small cars and lorries. He took a seat well to the rear, to sit by himself, and look at his hands, which had begun to rub one another independently of him, the right one touching the swollen left one gently, inquiringly, with its fingers. The damaged hand throbbed and he worried that he might have broken it after all. It would make a big difference, for who had the will to strike with all his strength, on a broken hand, knowing the pain it would bring...blinding pain? It would make you hesitate in a bad situation. You could *die* from such pain. A thin dew of perspiration popped out along his temples. "*I* have the will," he murmured. He settled in to watch the busload of strangers, in a world that seemed to have no one in it he recognized. It made his heart ache, to be so cut off. Svetlana, Svetlana. His daughter's face hovered, a sweet, sad moon on the horizon of his mind. Trulov wrenched himself back to the bus, back to the strangers, whom he looked over now, deciding they had nothing to do with him, that he could in any case run through them like a hound scattering deer.

Across the aisle, the old lady who had come on deck glanced his way, and for an instant their eyes met; he saw something hard and direct in hers, which quickly vanished, leaving the blue sheen of inattention. Swedish, perhaps, although she seemed dark for that. American, then, with just a touch of that hard look you get in French women. He refused to turn away from this first direct human contact in more than two days, but stared her down, stared at her even after her own gaze had faltered, after she returned to the dark window which reflected her as an aging, still attractive spirit, flying through the shining streets of Malmö; and still Trulov watched her, letting her feel his force. A moment's cruelty, he thought. I had better begin to live for those moments of cruelty.

The town outside his window had that starkly medieval touch you find in Swedish cities, reminding one of tenth century winters. You could still feel the town walls encircling the place, although they had been gone for centuries, and the land outside, Trulov knew, would have a feudal pattern, centered on the city, on the fortified walls, the land distributed around the command posts of ancient battles. Not a bad looking town, though, with some modern buildings that, while plain, looked sturdy and well lighted and warm, and not so quickly constructed that their cement flanks had cracked. We could learn from that, he thought. We could learn to stop tossing up buildings as though we were Cubans, and having them begin to look like something discovered in the jungle after a year. Malmö was not deep in snow, although it looked cold and wet, and he knew there was a wind off the sea. Dark façades the color of rust and stone sweated and shone with water, as though the buildings perspired; the trees were meager, black, and bare. Really, he thought now, there is not much to choose between ours and theirs except, he added, watching a life-sized bronze statue of a man slide by outside, that they had let their winters, their northernness, cramp them. It showed in their monuments, which had something mean and pinched about them, not like those fine Soviet creations, in which giant figures seemed to step forth from great blocks of granite and steel. No, we have it all over the Swedes in monuments. He smiled. Natural enemies. They hate us still, and it has nothing to do with current politics—we are their ancestral enemies; to them, there has been no revolution, no Soviet Union, no socialist state, but only old Russia, the enemy.

The insight pleased him, suggesting as it did that he was still capable of thinking beyond his present situation, that, even when things became desperate, he could focus upon large themes. He was almost jaunty, leaving the Copenhagen bus at the railway station, carrying only a briefcase, his long legs driving him rapidly across the lightly populated floor. At a change window he turned his left-over California dollars (Shirley Morgan's, actually) into *kronor*, and then went to a ticket window, where, using the name of an Argentine colleague at the Centre, he bought a one-way berth on the night train to Stockholm. He had to ration his identities. The American, Cleveland Brown, had everything—passport, credit cards, even a shot record. But he had just sent Brown on a decoy trip to Madrid, from Munich. The German businessman had been used at the Austrian border and in Copenhagen, where he would appear to have made a connecting SAS flight to New York. Passport control between Denmark and Sweden was casual, so Trulov had used Brown's American one for that, gambling there would be no record made of his entry. The sleepy guard had desultorily compared the photo with the face, and handed it back. Now he was an Argentine, traveling inside a country, where no one would ask for anything unless he brushed against the law. Without denigrating his homeland, he acknowledged a certain skill in avoiding that particular web, especially in the "free world."

Since he had more than two hours to fill, he decided to spend it at the station with a newspaper, if they had one in English. But when he sat down on the long wooden bench with his *Telegraph*, he found waiting unendurable, as though, in the act of sitting down, he had broken the machine of time. A look at his watch and then another, and another, had the stroboscopic effect of making the hands seem to move backwards. He fidgeted uncomfortably, glancing idly at the paper, looking up at the small pulse of people discharged from an arriving train, at the thin current of them drawn to a departing one. The place was nearly empty, except for such tidal changes, and sterile, and...depressing. He could not wait there, which he took to be a sign that his inner discipline disintegrated. No lines of command hold me together, he thought sarcastically. "Fuck you," he muttered to the western world. The white-haired woman from the ferry looked up, hearing him, and appeared—for she sat nearly ten meters away on another, facing bench—to smile, although Trulov could not feel certain. Why would she smile? Had she not seen him on that frozen deck for the entire crossing? Had she not felt his moment of cruelty? Perhaps she was an American, and ignored it, turned it to affection. Trulov came quickly to his feet, his mind beginning to bubble with exasperation, and then flung out of the station. The town awaited him across a canal and a boulevard. There were lights among the ancient stone façades, and the probing headlights of moving cars—life. He buttoned his raincoat and put his head down a little and walked briskly toward them, coming, after a couple of blocks, to a large square flanked by medieval buildings of brick and stone. Some of the buildings bore large solid letters lighted from within; they floated ominously in the low ice clouds, mysterious and unintelligible, passing the cryptic message

HANSA

to a smaller-than-life equestrian statue of the tenth Carl Gustav, who rode eternally at the center of the square. No, Trulov decided, these people really did not know much about monuments.

Although he could see lights going off down the dark sidestreets, he decided he had found the core of the city, and looked around for a place to wait. What I need, he thought, is a bottle of vodka and a glass. Simple. Well, and perhaps not a glass, either. But this was not a drinking country, and he would have to be sedate. A cognac, then, to ease the chill that, despite his patriotism, folded itself around his bones.

Behind him, where he stood near the statue, was the Hotel Kramer, in the familiar Scandinavian style, the white oblong of the building set between corner turrets, tipped with lightning rods. "Like a pair of rockets," Trulov observed. A cake for cosmonauts.

The bar was dark, blood-colored cushions in booths of dark wood, with a narrow line of brighter booths next to windows that faced the empty square. Trulov hung up his raincoat and slid into one of the interior booths near a corner, his spirits quickly elevated by the warmth and the prospect of something to drink. The waitress was tall and full breasted and dark haired, and would have been pretty except for a doggy look about the mouth, and an absence of light in the eyes. "Hi," Trulov told her in his clanging American accent. "Like a cognac, please."

"Stor?" she asked, ignoring his English, and her own.

"A big one, yes," he replied, gesturing with his good hand. If she didn't speak English, did she know Russian? He shook his head unhappily. Nobody knew Russian.

While he waited Trulov discovered a forgotten Cuban cigar in his inside pocket, and removed it, pleased as a boy to have such a surprise, not even broken or dried out. Really, he thought, the cigar was a good surprise, a good omen. Then, frowning, he flexed the damaged hand. It grew worse with time. It would look like a mango by tomorrow.

Tomorrow. Tomorrow his money would have run out, and it would be time to load up with the German businessman's Eurocheck card, and Cleveland Brown's American Express, Diner's Club, and Visa. In a few days the alarm lights would begin to flash in Moscow, if they had not already, and his colleagues would come hunting him. He shrugged. With any luck a few days were enough. He might take someone home, and sweat them hard enough to extract the proof he needed. Something. And, if he needed more time, he decided now, warm and confident in the wood-paneled room, he would use the credit cards to saturate the system with spurious tickets, and leave... how? It didn't matter. On a fishing boat, a rental car, something. By the third day he would have turned into someone else. A Finn. He grinned. *Nobody* understood Finnish, it was worse than anything, and on the other side everybody up here spoke English more or less. A big Finn, with a little English, he thought happily, but not too big and not too much English. Perhaps a drunk Finn hanging about the ferry dock in Stockholm.

The waitress came by and he ordered another double cognac, thinking, What the hell, I have the hard currency resources of the KGB behind me, for the moment. Would they forgive him for spending their dollars? Perhaps. For going out on his own? Trulov shook his head. What the hell? For the first time since he'd fled Pastukh in the cemetery, he felt he had a future. He could see his life proceeding out and out past this night, past the train to Stockholm; then, rising like a bridge, there was tomorrow, Sunday, a day to be got through carefully, invisibly. Then there would be Andrews' arrival in Stockholm on Monday evening, probably a departure on Tuesday... except Trulov sensed there would be no departure. Something was going to happen in Stockholm. He would keep close to Andrews, watching for... "What*ever*." His heartbeat throbbed in the broken hand.

2

TRULOV COULD NOT TELL whether he had slept or not. The dark window held the usual lights, but widely separated here, as if no one lived in southern Sweden, a flat land that had begun to give way to terrain with more rise and fall to it, a world of granite thumbs and skulls and elbows poking through the soil among the black trees, and water everywhere, still as metal plates. He lay with his jacket off and his tie loosened and his shoes and socks tucked to one side of the tiny compartment, rocking gently with the carriage, feeling wrinkled and grimy, on a pallet too small for him, his head balanced on the tiny pillow in one corner of the polished wooden enclosure, his arms folded across his chest, his legs drawn up as if he were in pain. Ah, *pain*. He tried to flex the damaged hand, which moved its fingers a few millimeters in response to his command. It felt as if it should glow in the dark. The unhurt fingers tiptoed about on the swollen ones, like sympathetic, worried animals. Now and then he slept, and knew he did, but like a guard, awakened by anything. His head would snap erect at some sound, a creak or rattle in the carriage, the shifting pitch of the iron wheels where they ran through switchings.

Trulov slept, or thought he must have, for suddenly it was no longer a black two, three, or four in the morning, but grey predawn, past seven. Outside ravines whipped by, hillsides stepped with granite outcroppings, and high pines, wild and opaque, and tunnels cut through the spreading veins of cold Nordic stone. The beech forests and willows were mostly gone, although now and then he caught a pretty stand of birch rising from a steel-colored band of water, and once he saw something glowing white out on a brown rise, centered in the metal of a slough—a nesting swan, her wings stretched across the big pile of twigs, her mate cruising like a gunboat around her. Trulov shook his head in wonder; the beauty, though seen only as a frame flashed at the passing train, touched him deeply. "Svetlana, have you ever seen a wild swan, at dawn, on her nest?" he whispered to the air, his eyes filling. "I have," he told the image of his pretty daughter, "in Sweden, once." He wiped his eyes. The last few days there had been altogether too much crying. He pressed his swollen hand, let the pain sweep his brain clear of the daughter who haunted him, the simple memory of whom brimmed his eyes with tears. Then he looked determinedly out the window. It was all stone and water and wood now, like a Viking lodge. As the land streamed past the lightening window—a light that would never be more than the glow before the low, abbreviated transit of the sun—he began to catch an occasional touch of subdued color, an enrichment of detail, as when the granite slabs grew grainy in the light.

They were running now closer and closer to the sea. Trulov put his shoes and socks on and splashed his face with water from the basin, and went outside, where he could see the eastern sky, and intimations of saltwater. The conductor came through chanting, "Nyköping, Nyköping, Nyköping," a meaningless word to Trulov, and then, after an eastward dash, the train slowed to a halt in a small village, grey and dispirited, but also clean and well-made, set almost at the edge of Sweden, where the granite rise and fall of the land descends to the ragged estuaries. And out there, Trulov thought, is the Baltic, and the rising sun, and, if one goes far enough, home. If I leapt from this train and swam directly at the sun I would come to the Gulf of Finland, and if I kept on I would arrive at beautiful old Leningrad, and then, dripping wet and cold, lie down on my own frozen land and cry. I seem to do nothing but cry, like some king.

They were moving again, and turning toward the northeast, so that now and then the Baltic flickered at him, the polished stone surface of a calm winter sea, seen in the rising light of northern mornings, almost the light of a solar eclipse. More life outside, now, towns whipping past, and, to the east, the ragged seacoast, mounds rising into islands, like the backs of great fish, rimmed with sand, ragged with spruce. Trulov went down the aisle to the WC, relieved himself, and returned to lean against the windows watching quick flashes of ice and water among the trees, the land filling with structures.

The train swooped into a long curving tunnel to emerge suddenly balanced above rushing water that teemed with ice, and a medieval city wound around a low island hill on the right, and palaces, cathedrals, gleaming boats, across more water, flaked with jagged panes of ice, and then they slid into the central station. He felt like a man returning from exile. He stepped down with the crowd that scattered back toward the terminal. Just behind him, an unfamiliar woman's voice asked in English, "Did you have a good night?"

Trulov half-turned to find the white-haired lady from the Kastrup bus walking a step behind him. "Good morning," she said. Her voice was warm, with something tough in it.

"Good morning." He slowed to let her draw abeam of him, wondering what would happen now. What is this? he asked the new day, the new city, feeling a few cc's of adrenaline beginning to fizz within.

She laughed, a sound that reassured him totally—it was clear and certain, open and direct, and a little tough, too, like her voice. "I hope I haven't embarrassed you. I always feel kind of upbeat on cold, crisp mornings in a new place. It seemed to me we'd been traveling companions long enough that it would be proper to greet you."

"Very kind."

"I have hardly ever been in a place where *everyone's* a stranger. Whereas, *we* remember one another from Denmark." She laughed again.

"Yes, old friends by now," he replied, entering the spirit of her banter. She was American, after all, and pretty for a woman past sixty, still rather lithe, her face well-formed, her skin surprisingly smooth. In dark hair, he thought, she would not look fifty.

"Do you know Stockholm?" she asked. Her blue eyes were uncommonly clear and well-focused, and, as she waited for a response, you could *feel* her waiting, drawing out a reply. Quite remarkable, Trulov thought. "My first visit," he said.

"Mine too," she confided. "What do you think of it?"

"So far I like the station well enough."

"Yes, it's too early to say, isn't it?"

"But it looked a pretty city, coming in," he added.

"All that water."

"Like Seattle."

"You know Seattle?" He nodded. "One of my favorite cities. Do you live there?"

"At the moment, I live in..." and he hesitated for just an instant, feeling in her question that slight pressure of interrogation, but ambiguously. "...Vancouver," he said, without really breaking stride. Vancouver was fresh in his mind, he could borrow Vancouver. "And you?"

"Northern California...Stanford." Had she felt the same pressure, the same thin wind from him? Her eyes showed nothing. "My husband taught at the university there. He's gone, now, but I could not bring myself to leave the area."

"A very beautiful part of..." he almost said America. "Of the world."

"You know it, then?"

"A little."

"My mother was Swedish, so, after George died, which was not so very long ago, my family began to get after me to visit, and finally I simply had to succumb, although it's a very long flight over the Pole." Had she sensed his slight flinch at her question, then, and was all of this piling up of unsolicited information about herself intended to calm him down? "But now that I'm here, I'm happy I came."

"Why didn't you fly into Stockholm?"

She laughed. "No, and call me silly after a sleepless night. But the railroads are about dead in the United States, so I thought I'd give myself a little treat and fly into

Copenhagen, and then come up to Malmö and take the train to Stockholm. I miscalculated, though. I'd intended to see some of the countryside, and wound up traveling entirely at night." She cocked her head pensively. "I'll fly back from Stockholm, no doubt. To Paris. Or Vienna maybe." Nothing happened in her eyes, where something always happened, Trulov believed, if people were not what they seemed. She could not have said Vienna without some tiny fish of a shadow moving behind her eyes; she could not. Although he kept on guard, he could feel the killing springs that had begun to tighten slowly uncoil now. "Or," and she gave a soft chuckle at the improbability of this, "somewhere behind the Iron Curtain." No, he was sure of her now. No one could have looked into his eyes, knowing who he was, and said *behind the Iron Curtain*, without some signal. It was humanly impossible. "Where are you staying?" she asked brightly.

"I am not. My business is at Uppsala. I am just here for the day." He felt his American English not quite falling into place.

"Oh, too bad. I thought we might . . ." She blushed and turned away. "That sounds terribly forward. I suppose I am not yet accustomed to the subterfuges one needs among strangers. Do you know what I mean?"

"Of course." He knew too well. And, he thought, soon this pleasant old lady will go off and leave me and it will be like the last two days, my mouth thick with silence, my voice rotting down below. "What about you?"

"What?"

"Where are you staying?"

"At the Grand Hotel. It sounds very fine. I hope it is."

"So do I."

"But before I do anything I need my breakfast. My roommate on the train said the buffet breakfast here at the station is the best in town, and I am very hungry this morning." She looked at him with flat innocence, and a kind of finality, as though she had returned to decorum, having now entered the high central room of the terminal.

Would she ask him to accompany her? No, she forced him to do the asking. He smiled, for what more proof could he want that she was simply an attractive woman, grown old, on her own, like him. On her own. He laughed aloud, causing her to start.

"May I join you?" he asked.

"I would be delighted," she answered, pleased.

They paid individually going into the pleasant wooden maze of the station restaurant, and helped one another carry juice and coffee, eggs and Corn Flakes and meat and cheese, to a booth they found near the front, where one could look out upon the ice-caked streets, "Goodness," the woman said, "I've never seen so many *Volvos*."

"Like Ladas in the east," Trulov ventured. There, behind the Iron Curtain. He had immediately become interested in his food, and fed with canine intensity, stoking up the big, faltering furnace within. He felt her watching him, but, having decided she posed no threat, he could ignore her. His good hand flicked a knife through the top of a boiled egg swiftly and cleanly, and, he had to admit it, aggressively.

"Why, you do that like a judo chop," she said, and laughed.

Trulov grinned back, and chewed, and swallowed, pouring in the fuel for another day on his own. On the run. When she got up and brought them more coffee he smiled his thanks, and did again when she refilled their orange juice glasses, or brought him another pair of croissants, more brown bread, and butter and packets of jam. At last he leaned back on the green cushions of his booth and gave a large, happy sigh. "That was very good. Thank you for the..." For an instant his English failed, frightening him like a skip in his heartbeat. Then, "...tip."

She bowed her head with exaggerated pleasure. "Thank you for joining me." Now she looked around, birdlike, beginning to leave. "I believe I shall get a taxi to the hotel," she said to no one in particular, adding, to him, "May I drop you anywhere?"

"Thanks, no...I shall just muck around until the Uppsala train."

"Is that where they have the huge cathedral?"

"I do not know. It could be."

They were up, and he helped her into her overcoat, lamb covered with wavy black hair. When she saw his trench-coat she exclaimed, "Why, you're not nearly warm enough to wander Stockholm in winter. You'll freeze."

"Vancouver gets pretty cold."

"Of course. Hot-blooded Canadians."

"Yes." Then, "Here, I take your bag." God, how Russian he sounded.

"Kind of you."

He picked up the fawn-colored bag with the big belts and zippers folding it shut, grasping it in the same hand as his briefcase and walked with her across the waiting room. A handsome woman, with handsome luggage. Looking at her peripherally, she seemed very pretty indeed, what the Americans would call classy, but also well made, with good legs and an attractive curve of breasts beneath her expensive clothing. And she, as if she sensed his attention, resumed her own air of watchfulness, causing him to go once more on guard. Finally she said, "I hope I haven't caused you any distress, barging into your life this way."

"Not at all." He thought how it would be to undress this good-looking woman of sixty-something, of spending his time waiting for Andrews tucked between her good old legs, in her good old hotel...

"...lonely, travelling. Well, living can be too, I suppose." He wondered how long she'd been talking. But the force of his gaze made her look away, embarrassed. "I mean, if you were going to be in town, we could see some of it together. If you don't mind being seen with a woman older than yourself, I hasten to add."

"It would be a big compliment," he winked, still being the boy. And then, his alarm queried: what about her "relatives?" "What about your family?" His voice was soft and cold now.

"They..." She flushed, her eyes flicked away for just that crucial fraction of a second, and then she recovered quickly. "They won't come for me until tomorrow."

"Too bad. I really must be in Uppsala tonight." You lied to me, you American bitch, and God alone knows why. You are not what you seem either. If it is love you wanted, it is too late, you get no big Russians tonight. And if it is worse than that, if you are somehow involved in this shit that drags me down to hell...Trulov felt his blood run through him; his impulse was to kill her there and then, with a shake, like a hen, but... *"JESUS!"* he screamed. She had taken him earnestly but unexpectedly by his left hand, which she quickly dropped.

"I'm sorry," she cried, frightened by his shriek of pain. "I didn't know."

His face beaded with perspiration; he trembled. The pain sent the angry killer running. He gave a tight smile. "Bad hand," he said. "Of course you didn't know."

"I'm awfully sorry."

"Come...it is all right, I tell you." His hand throbbed. But his anger was returning too, he could see it behind the pain, like a big animal blocked for a moment by a shrinking wall of fire. "Come."

They went through the glass doors into the cold wind, slipping on the ice that littered the pavement. He handed her into the back seat of a green Volvo cab. "It has been very nice, Mr...you know," she said, leaning forward, "I don't know your name."

"Owens," he replied brusquely, the name appearing in his mind from nowhere. "Jesse Owens." Was that what he'd wanted? It sounded Canadian enough, and had a familiarity he could not place.

"Mr. Owens. Jesse Owens." Her eyes sparkled with mirth, as he shut the door, and she rolled down the window, bent toward him with a kind of fatal eagerness. "Named for the great Negro runner?" Her eyes crinkled at the edges, and she waved goodbye. To the driver, she said, "Grand Hotel, please."

"Wait," said Trulov. "What is *your* name?"

She laughed, that clear, glassy laugh he had found so distinctive, so pure, and the car fishtailed into motion. Trulov trotted alongside, watching the taxi, inclined toward her to catch her reply, until he hit a patch of ice and went down hard, unthinkingly breaking his fall with the bad hand. The pain brought tears, and rage, the desire to kill, to make the angry sounds of a bear or elephant or wolf. A horn honked immediately behind him as he hobbled clumsily to his feet, and he stopped and tore a long shard of ice from the ground with his good hand, then pivoted, poised to hurl it through the windscreen, into the angry male face that had begun to go pale and scared...Then Trulov, catching himself, dropped the projectile and moved aside, his spirit in the early stages of collapse, his hand pumping pain through him with each heartbeat. His anger nearly blinded him, so that for a moment he didn't recognize the green Volvo swinging out into the traffic. The woman in the back seat watched him coolly, evenly—contemptuously, he thought—from her open window. Then, seeing his look of recognition, she called, "Cybelle. My friends call me *Cybelle*."

3

TRULOV STOOD THERE in the cold, his left hand aching like something ripped from a hunter's trap, his head ringing like a bell with rage from this humiliating encounter. Ah, God, his rage raced around his brain like the plague infecting a medieval city, wanting nothing but piles of bodies, the end of the world...There, he told himself, there, there, there, and at last regained his control. Let us return, he told himself, pushing thoughts at his brain like a man gentling a very nervous horse, let us return to the old machine-like efficiency. You are making mistakes, and most of them come from this crazy anger; *you* are worse than a woman scorned, my friend, and that is no compliment. Come. Come. He could calm himself, but he could not resurrect his spirits. Even in California, where he had moved with great skill, using his time almost perfectly, seizing the objective he had set out to achieve, he had also lost the photographs, flashed that signal of external interest. Perhaps he had lost his touch, like an alcoholic pilot, the mistakes multiplying with speed until finally... He shrugged miserably.

The fall had dirtied him, smearing a black oily blot on his crumpled raincoat, splattering his pale blue shirt with a spray of ice that had melted into dark grey water. He went back into the terminal and found the men's room and tried to repair his appearance, for it was fatal, to roam a foreign city, a man of his size, dressed in a fine wool suit so wrinkled it looked stolen, the big face unshaven, a hand like a mango. It was fatal; they would pick you up, shake the various identities out of you, and, worst of all, call your embassy, who would call home and learn that you had run amock, wasted hard currency doing it, and, unforgivably, insanely, gone off on your own.

Trulov soaked his face and cooled the throbbing hand, hoping also to cool the wild rage burning within. It was good at least that he was sober. Thank God for making drink so hard to find in this... *cursed* town. *"Fucking socialists!"* he yelled to the empty lavatory. His big voice banged around the tile-lined room, childish and shrill. Trulov began to laugh, to laugh and laugh, hanging on to the white basin, watching himself in the glass, laughing and laughing, the evil spirits, the incubi, rising and flying out of him. A small Swede came in to piss, stood uncomfortably at a urinal, and fled. Trulov held onto the basin, and felt some of his strength return. Finally, he whispered to himself, the way one did when drunk on vodka, sharing secrets with the old friend in the mirror, "You are going to be all right. I know it now. I can see it."

Better. He felt steel within, where it was supposed to be. His head cleared, and he sighed. It had to do, he knew, with operating on one's own. Americans loved to improvise, for everyone always forgave them. He hated it, having observed little charity at home for innovative bunglers. But he was more the Trulov he recognized now, more the solid man, trusted operative, strong and venomous and calm, like a big cat, freshly fed. He bought a throw-away razor from a machine, and some soap, and paid his way into a coin-operated shower, where he shaved and soaped himself and let the hot water course across his skin, the islands of body hair, the large muscles, soothing his hand, restoring him further to the man he knew and loved. No, respected. You could love a clown.

Dressed again, his tie properly knotted, his face no longer blue with two days' beard, he began to believe he could tackle anything, even the mindless waiting he must endure to reach through Sunday to Andrews' arrival Monday evening, and the interminable Baltic Sea meeting—until what must be going to happen, happened. He needed now to vanish for a day, and rest, and get his hand working again if he could. And he needed a drink.

On the way out of the station he wrote a Eurocheck against the German's bank, then stopped at an information counter for a street map of the city. Outside, he got his bearings, and headed south, toward the rush of water. The low clouds had begun to fray, admitting the slanting beams of the sun, which coasted along not quite the width of a hand above the southern horizon. The morning sunlight had the color and texture of autumn afternoons at lower latitudes, so that the buildings shone, red bricks and yellow ones, stone and mortar and green rooftops, façades of marble and salmon-colored brick, all floating on water that was deep and dark and blue, as though the city suspended in mid-ocean, like some subpolar Atlantis. Trulov walked briskly to keep warm, heading east along a tidal channel that boiled like a flooding river, the slabs of shattered ice spinning and rolling, pale and ghostly in the translucent waves, lost souls . . . the ice nearly hypnotized him. Across this Norrström lay what had been the old walled city of Stockholm, rising on the low hill of its island, a labyrinth abutting the great pale cake of the palace. Trulov took one of the bridges over, comforted by the sounds of tires crunching ice, the hiss of water, the crisp day under a low winter sun. It could be home, this beautiful city, floating on its ocean. He climbed to the royal palace, and entered the maze of the old town, where, after the lonely walk along the tidegates, it was good to be part of a current of people, most of them on the young side, flowing through the narrow streets. A bundled guitarist, young and rednosed and runny-eyed, tossed long blonde hair and sang American country songs. Near the end of his sound, a string quartet warmed up, their hands crimson and raw in the cold, their Mozart filling the stone canyon. Even on Sunday, the street had the aura of a bazaar, and, deliberately quaint or not, he liked being there.

He stopped by a window filled with old porcelain dolls and doll clothing, and toy metal cars of the type he had heard of but had never owned, those wonderful bourgeois toys from before the Fatherland War—fire engines with ladders, metal six-shooters with pearl handles, old posters, a kit for making one's own lead soldiers, cowboys, and Indians. It was not just that the window held toys, but that they were the exact toys he had never had, *the exact ones*. The pleasure of this contact filled his eyes with happy tears, and he dabbed at them with a sleeve, forgetting for a moment who he was, or where, or why, the old dreams of a toyless childhood vividly before his eyes. He tried the door of the place, even though it was dark behind the glass, but it was locked. Tomorrow he would return, and enter. Perhaps Cleveland Brown would charge a hundred-*krona* porcelain doll, have it mailed to a certain beautiful daughter. His throat constricted. Would They forgive him for that? The thought of the bureaucratic deliberations over Svetlana's doll made him laugh softly, his troubles flake away once more. He would do it, somehow, in a way that would not have them ruining the gift for that lovely face, that moon over what seemed now to be all his good memories.

He broke away, then, ready to be in the open once more, and turned east, crossing through a narrow stairway out of the street bazaar, entering an old stone square, vanishing into the blue light of a shadowed alley farther on. Fire-colored rooftops and steeples rose everywhere around him. He walked past the palace and down to a boulevard filled with speeding Volvos, and finally crossed to the quay, where white boats, mostly tourist boats and restaurants, were tied up, their hulls sunk in smashed ice, as though they had dropped from the sky. Trulov stood there for a time, his hands deep in his pockets, his face wonderfully cold, and watched the water. A beautiful place, he thought. When I have to defect, perhaps it will be to Sweden after all. They have socialism but they also seem to have everything else, like the Austrians. And they have these low Nordic buildings and redcheeked people, and water. It was lovely, having such water everywhere, and the ice swimming in it like white seals. He shook his head with good-natured wonder, calm and possessed of a kind of joy.

Without thinking about it, he had turned back toward town, and crossed another tidal bridge, where he loitered, watching the roaring water spin its cargo of ice, excited when it seemed to clutch at him with an awful chill. Farther along, he saw the Grand Hotel, shining pink in the sunlight. Somewhere in there, Trulov thought, is the woman called Cybelle. Perhaps he should go in and look for her, continue their game... Bad temper flared briefly, and thoughts of murder. But, no, she could not be in this. Remember her eyes, saying *Behind the Iron Curtain*. If she could do that, and give nothing away, then she was either an accident in his life or too tough to tackle with only one good hand.

Trulov retreated, cursing himself silently for moving so far into the open, where those intermittent crowds of Japanese and Swedes and Americans and no doubt a few people working for the Soviet Union could notice him, identify him later, *place* him there, at that time. It was as stupid as having Cleveland Brown check into a first-class hotel, and set alarms jingling everywhere in the world within twenty-four hours.

This time he made for the city, across another bridge toward the opera, and an ice-free area where hot water discharged into the stream, and hundreds of ducks and swans floated, cadging food from old people and children who threw bread at them. Trulov had to stop and watch, drawn by the luminous swans, which evoked the wonder he had experienced, watching the wild swan on her nest. "Svetlana," he whispered, "between the old city and the new one there is water that moves like a ferocious river full of spinning ice, but really it is just the tidal current setting between a lake and the sea; and in this dark, freezing stream are hundreds, no, *thousands*, of ducks, and great crowds of the most beautiful swans, regal and wild, but not so wild they would not take food from you, my love..." His throat hurt, hearing in his memory his daughter's soft laugh of appreciation. After he defected, after it was clear that he had simply gone crazy after all, he would bring her to Stockholm in winter and they would feed the swans, and shiver, and laugh together. "Oh, God," he prayed in a small voice. His atmosphere reeked of burned boats. He was hopelessly cut off. Hopelessly.

Walking aimlessly now, merely toiling against gravity, he came to a central part of the city that had been entirely razed and rebuilt—it had the unmistakable look of urban renewal everywhere, a touch of warmth and clean-lined new structures, rich with glass and metal, but also that coldness at the core. But he liked the abstract monument, vertical, glittering with shards of glass and stainless steel, perhaps twenty meters high, centered in a silent, frozen fountain. Beyond this in one direction lay the central railway station, a parade of several small skyscrapers in another, and a broad sunken square in the third. Trulov started for the station, thinking to return to more familiar ground, then hesitated, and turned up an alley next to the square, which he now saw ran under the streets to arcades and shops and the granite caves of the Tunnelbana. The subterranean corridors, the pillars holding the pavement up, the courtyard itself, swarmed with the early crowd of young people, hippies, girls with hard eyes, boys with the look of killers. Trulov smiled, finally at home in the new city. He recognised the place as the locus of action in a city without much, where one bought drugs, where the whores waited, where the illegal activity of a nominally crimeless community had become concentrated. He watched them mill about from his vantage point on the railing above. Their inferiority to him was unmistakable; the sight of them gladdened his heart. He looked at his watch. It was just after noon, and the crowd in the square was sparse. Later, he guessed, even with the cold weather, it would become dense with pimps and whores and queers and the boys who preyed upon them. There would be dope for sale, guns for hire, false papers, outlaws dealing with outlaws. After I am forced to defect, I shall become the king of this shithole, he thought, smiling broadly. Forgive me Vera, forgive me my little girl, but this is my ocean, and I am its shark.

"It picks up at night." Trulov glanced down at the speaker, a thin girl with straight blonde hair to her waist, a cape of it, and visible ribs and breasts like tea bags. Her eyes shone like smooth blue rocks in tan earth, a face that seemed eternally disappointed by the hardness of the world outside, but still able to give him a twisted, tough smile. "Maybe we'll see you later."

"Maybe so," he said. "If I come back, who are you?"

"Inger."

"Really?"

"We have a lot of Ingers here."

"I bet you do." After a neutral interval, his voice relaxed into the American one of Cleveland Brown.

"What's yours?"

"Cleve."

"Short for Cleveland? *Trés distingué.*"

"I can be a very distinguished guy."

"I bet you can."

"Where do you come from, Inger?"

She shrugged. "Would you believe Uppsala?"

He laughed. "Or L.A."

"Really," she said, laughing too. It brought a touch of life into her eyes. Not a bad-looking girl, Trulov thought. Beneath the layered Icelandic sweater and wool skirt and boots he thought he could discern the well-turned leg of a skier, and after all tits were not everything. "Well...maybe we'll see you later."

"Wait," he said, afraid to lose this comfortable voice, "I was looking for a bar."

"Nothing till one," and she grinned with good white teeth. A pretty girl behind the toughie. "Is that an offer?"

"It's a proposition."

"I like propositions." She looked down at herself, and said after a moment's inspection, "Well, Bohemian but clean. You caught me on one of my presentable days."

"I wish I could say the same."

"You look delicious, Cleve." She frowned. "What happened to your hand?"

"Hurt it. Caught it in a cab door," Trulov fumbled along, surprised he had not formulated a story earlier. This lightning improvisation wore him down. Was he falling behind again? Was she part of something...? The anger stirred.

"You better have it looked at."

"Where?"

"I've got a friend who could."

"A medical friend?"

"Well, more or less. A midwife."

"A midwife." He could see the report: Trulov apprehended at midwife's lair. Did he have the clap? Was he also pregnant then, in addition to the insanity? "Is it far?"

Inger shook her head. "Come on. After Mother Russia gets through with you, we can get that drink."

"Mother Russia?" Was this another joke, like *Behind the Iron Curtain*? He looked into her eyes, found nothing.

"She's an emigree. Her real name is Eva Something-ovna Somethingelyich. Better we call her Mother Russia. Come on."

He lumbered after her, clutching his briefcase in the good right hand, holding the tender one against his chest, where only he could touch it. Striding along with this girl who, after all, had approached him, and therefore had to be regarded with suspicion, he exercised his abiding anger with thoughts of what he would do if she were in it, if she tricked him toward... what*e*ver.

But there was nothing in her manner, her step, her voice, that suggested anything but the young expatriate whore, waiting for the sun to go down. She guided him farther into town, where the renewed buildings quickly gave way to the mixed shops and blocks of flats that had always been there, drab and somber, the edges somehow harder, sharper, than in Vienna. After several blocks of this, she steered them into an entryway and up four flights of stairs, which to his disgust caused him to catch his breath. "We're here," Inger announced, and knocked on a peeling white metal door. Trulov tensed against the prospect of surprise. But the door was opened by a woman in her late sixties who smiled at Inger, presenting a face of complete innocence to Trulov, who saw that she smelled his slight odor of policeness. *"Vad är det här?"* she asked the whore.

"Amerikansk. Hans hand."

The old woman darted a look at Trulov's hands, and, like a bird focusing on prey, stared at the swollen one. "Good. I was afraid he was pregnant." She spoke the lilting English of a Swede, and the three of them laughed, although Trulov's heart was not in it.

"Come in." She left the door ajar for them and wandered away through the small, low-ceilinged flat, the walls done in the heavy blue and white checks of a cheap tablecloth, the furniture sparse, most of it prefabricated Swedish stuff. She waved them toward a kitchen alcove, and Trulov took a chair under a high window there. The place must be a clinic, he thought, for there was no clutter, or even a piece of bric-a-brac. No one really lived there.

Inger sat down next to him, and the old woman took the chair to his left. "You must remove your jacket." Trulov complied, easing his bad hand gingerly through the sleeve. Even that touch brought a line of perspiration to his upper lip, not from the pain, but from the fear that something might touch the hand. "It hurts," she said.

"You noticed," he replied with what he hoped passed for a brave smile.

He winced when she took the hand in one of hers, but there was no pain. Her fingers were dry and crisp and cool, the gentle antiseptic probes of all medical people. He felt a mad impulse to kneel at her feet, to rest his head upon her lap, to shut his eyes against his hand, the world, his expanding universe of trouble...

"You must have killed him," she said softly, feeling delicately along the swelling. "I hope you did, because he will get you next time. Your hand is broken."

"Who?" asked the girl.

"The person he beat with this hand, so," and the old woman imitated a sharp series of backhand blows. Whatever. Bam.

"Another man?"

Trulov nodded. "I thought he was...connected with the death of a friend. I had a lot to drink, and went a little crazy." It relieved him to utter one truthful sentence, for deception, familiar as it was, began to wear him out. He had been too many people lately, and, besides, the idea of being American, and not even a real one at that, depressed him. He looked into the brown, animal eyes of the woman. She read him, he thought. She knew it all, everything. She knew he was on his own, too. Mother Russia, help me for I have sinned.

"Hands are like fish, they are so full of bones. I cannot set yours without an X-ray. But I can put it almost in order, and bind it, and give you something for pain. But..." and she gave him a long, wise look, "you should be at home." Trulov almost sobbed, but controlled himself and merely nodded sadly. "With your family," she went on.

"Yes," he whispered.

"What are your children like?"

"There is only the one girl." His impulse was to share with this woman, those gentle hands gave such relief from pain, his haunting sense of his beautiful Svetlana, of the way he loved the child, of how she drifted across his mind, like a glorious moon, an angel. But the midwife's fingers brushed some core of the hurt that shocked him, cleared his mind. He looked at Inger, who watched him evenly; he had no idea what went on behind the flat, opaque eyes, only that she pulled back from him.

"Well, that is where you should be," the midwife said.

"But I am here, you see," Trulov countered, recovering himself. "The reasons why I would like to keep out of sight are obvious to you. You seem to see everything." It made her grin, this thin smoke of flattery. "Well," he went on, looking at the girl, "Inger and I are having something to drink, and perhaps I can talk her into dinner afterward. And that would be a kind of family outing, you see." He smiled at Inger, whose hard mask slipped a little. "The next thing to a family."

Inger laughed, then. "A *good* dinner, though, something special."

"Something special," he said, wondering if They would also forgive him something special.

The old woman had washed the bad hand in antiseptic liquid, anointed it with what he thought must be an anaesthetic salve, and splinted it with tongue depressors, which she taped in place and packed with cotton wool, and now wrapped with a long roll of gauze, methodically and steadily, like a woman weaving. "Keep this clean and stay out of fights."

"Yes, no rough stuff, please," echoed Inger.

"I am not a violent person," Trulov said humbly.

Both women laughed derisively. "And I am having my period," said the midwife. She shook her head. "You need a doctor for this, to get an X-ray, to make sure the bones are matched before they heal. I may have given you a claw."

"A claw." Trulov looked at the big white stump she'd left him.

"Here are pain capsules." She handed him a small plastic container full of red and white pills. "They are not strong, but they will help. Not too many at one time, and not while you are drinking. But...who can afford to drink very long in Sweden?"

"We will do all right," he told her, cocking his head toward the girl. "I think we will do okay." He swallowed one of the capsules without water.

"Good." She hesitated. "I have rather enjoyed this, for a change. You can give me what you will."

Trulov fished a hundred-*krona* note from his trouser pocket. "Is that enough?"

"It is generous. But not too generous." She stuffed the money into an apron pocket. "If the claw turns black, see a doctor."

"I will. Thanks."

Then, holding the door for him and the girl, she smiled around her bad teeth and said, in Russian, "I am sorry you carry such troubles, my son. God bless you."

The benediction stung him; and yet it comforted too. But he replied in English, "Thank you, Mother Russia." Her rat's eyes watched him, unwaveringly. She read him like a witch. "Goodbye."

He felt her staring after them down all the flights of stairs, felt her eyes upon them moving when they had regained the street, and were moving once more through the thin crowds on the sidewalks toward the glass and steel monument. "What did she say?" he asked Inger.

"I don't know. Something in Russian."

"Oh."

"But she's Russian, so why not?"

"Mother Russia," Trulov said. Yes, that was good, and in fact it was as if he had drawn strength from her touch, like Antaeus from Earth. The tablet he had taken deadened his hand, that and the wrapping and whatever she had spread upon it. He could not move the fingers. No doubt the bones would mend as she had left them, but he knew those cool, sure fingers would never shape his into a claw. Mother Russia. He had been touched by Mother Russia, then, and like a good Russian boy the contact had given him the strength to face and endure a dangerous, doubtful future. She had spun the illusion that he was not entirely on his own. He wondered if he could find her again, by himself, and looked back up the hill. The streets had already begun merging in his memory, it would take considerable luck now to find her flat. And perhaps that would be just the wrong thing, to go back. Mother Russia she might be, but you could not always count on her, not even her. At this moment those comforting fingers could be dialing the embassy, to report a big Russian in Stockholm on his own, a Russian who sounded almost like an American, with a daughter somewhere...

"I'm heading for Old Town," Inger said. "Do you mind the walking?"

"No, I am fine. You did me a big favor there. I appreciate it."

"*De nada,* Cleve. I don't often get these, uh, friendly outings, you know." She looked up at him and grinned like a child. "It's like you said, the next thing to a family. It's nice."

"I like it too." He did, he did so much that he forgot calls to the embassy and the parade of mistakes and the stupidly smashed hand. As they crossed the bridge he held his left elbow out so she could take his arm, and they walked along then like old friends.

They had their first drink in a dark, empty bar on the street where he had seen all the handsome shops, both of them having cold six-centiliter measures of vodka. Trulov looked at his for a time, and then, holding the narrow glass up to her, said, *"Sköl."*

"Za nas," she replied.

"What is that?" Suspicion crowded in upon him.

"Damn if I know. Mother Russia says it. I guess it means up yours in Russian. Or something."

"Za nas," he growled, tossing his vodka down and setting the glass empty on the table. Inger only sipped at hers. "That is how...*they* do it in Moscow," he said, "except their toasts are more elaborate."

"Have you been there?"

"Yes."

"On business?"

"Yes. Fitness equipment," he added, comfortable with fitness equipment, and the vodka, for a big man with muscles showing under his suit. Yes, that felt fine.

"That would explain your, uh, physique."

He grinned like a wolf. God, that vodka had been just what he'd needed. He signalled to the waitress for another round. "Jesus," the girl said, "I can't put it away that fast. At least, not for very long." But she drank hers down.

"I do not mind being a little drunk if I am among friends." Trulov leaned toward her. "Am I among friends, Inger?" She nodded vigorously. Too vigorously. Too vigorously? He believed not. "We shall have a special time tonight."

"Oh, I hope so, Cleve. I get so...tired. You know."

"I know."

"This is more like a date."

She led him across the old city, stopping at intervals for another drink, until at last they came to the water, the white boats, the Grand Hotel like a strawberry cake on the other side. The sun dropped away, the water glistened, the ice in it moving like dolphins. "Night has fallen," Trulov intoned, pleasantly aware that vodka had begun to put him on automatic pilot.

"Come on," she said, taking his arm once more. They walked in the cold for awhile, letting the mid-afternoon darkness spin its illusion of latest night. Trulov felt a stab of hunger, as if his large engine had suddenly run out of fuel. "I am starved," he announced. "All of a sudden, famished."

They ate upstairs at the Reisen Hotel, enjoying themselves like the other young couples, Trulov thought, as if she had no pimp waiting to beat her for not working, and he had no flock of KGB men about to unwrinkle his brain. "To pimps and police, everywhere," he toasted, downing the preliminary double vodka and ordering another.

"To Mother Russia," said Inger, and they drank to the old midwife, among other things.

Over shrimp cocktails, Trulov decided he *would* have to defect to Stockholm, beautiful Stockholm, where the seafood was so fresh and the view of the water such a comfort, and the vodka so cold. "To the removal of my prefrontal lobe," he toasted with their first glass of Pouilly Fuissé, thinking, That is what they will have to do, of course, remove my brain, the source of all my internal rot.

"To AIDS and herpes," she toasted then, "proof there really *is* a God."

"To..." he wanted suddenly to toast Svetlana, and could not. "To the Church, proof that there is not."

On their way out they stopped at the downstairs lounge, where an American of about fifty, a melancholy man with a failed look, played and sang the grand old songs. They sat in their big leather chairs and ordered cognac and Trulov bought a cigar, while the man sang of kisses still being kisses, and sighs remaining sighs, and stardust, and smoke in one's eyes. Afterward they walked along the quay, like lovers, Inger's head against his big arm. "Here is what I want," he told her. "I want you to take me home with you and for us to be together all night, and also for a late breakfast somewhere in the morning, through the day." Sensing her rising protest, he added, "Not to worry. I know you have to work. But tonight is your night off, and mine too. We can take care of each other. Good?"

She snuggled against him.

Inger lived in an unrenovated flat in the Old Town, out of sight of water or the city, the view from the single narrow window nothing but a yellow brick wall across an alley. She had only one room with a bath and WC down the hall. A coffee machine and electric coil sat with some china dogs on a sideboard someone had painted lavender and orange, and a torn upholstered chair brooded by the window. A double bed was neatly made with a light blue tropical spread, and she had hung some art on the walls, mainly silkscreens, Trulov believed, but real art, not prints. The wooden planks of the floor were covered with panels of wood of different colors, remnants and ends, a clever idea. The room had a slight, attenuated smell of sex and toothpaste. "Nice," Trulov said when they had entered. "Very nice," thinking: You should have seen the Morgan woman's condominium, it would make you feel poor, as it did me . . . and we are Europeans after all.

She sat on the bed and patted the mattress. "Sit here."

Trulov sank down on the bed, put his good arm around her and pulled her back with him. "It was a piece of luck, running into you."

"*I* think so." She leaned over him and removed his tie, smoothed his long black hair, and put her cheek against his chest. "A piece of luck," she echoed.

She turned out to have good legs, as he had suspected, and her breasts were nothing like teabags, but small and wellformed and pretty, the pure, bluish white skin going to rose at the nipple. Even favoring his broken hand, he could lift her almost out of bed in his arms, holding her body against him as he entered, forcing pleasure upon her, making her pant, forcing them to move with the coordination of a centaur, imparting an odd familiarity to the union. When they had finished and had been quiet for a little while, she bent down upon him and made him ready again, and pulled him back into her from the back, into all the softness. The drink and pain pills and loss of semen finally pushed Trulov into sleep, although he had no idea when. It was more like falling, the dreams anxious, varied, terrifying. In one he slashed at Schaefer Braun with his left hand, which was a claw, the fingers fused into a single long talon, covered with flesh and hair and blood, and turned then to find Svetlana watching him, her broad face twisted in horror, and then she ran from him, from her father, and he pursued but could not catch her...

He came awake sweating like a runner, like a famous Negro runner, he thought, and sat up. The girl was gone.

Down the hall the toilet flushed and he heard footsteps on the linoleum outside, and the door opened, showing Inger outlined inside a dark robe. She sat down in the upholstered chair, a match flared, and she settled back to smoke. Trulov could see the orange tip suddenly glow, then intimations of exhaled smoke, the pale gleam of her eyes.

"Can't sleep?" he asked finally.

"You either."

"I had a dream."

"Ahh hed uh dreeem," she drawled.

Trulov sniffed the air. It wasn't tobacco. "Can I have some?"

"Sure." She passed the joint to him and he inhaled deeply several times and returned it, and lay back.

She came back to bed and shared the dope with him. They curled up together. Then, finding him hard and her ready, they made love again, in that delightful easy-going way one does when stoned. Later, lying on her pretty little breasts, he thought again it had been lucky, running into her. The beast of rage had gone off somewhere, off into the birch forests. For the first time since the terrible moment with Braun in the cemetery, Trulov felt completely free of anger. He smiled. "Is there a telephone outside?"

He felt her shake her head. "No, why?"

"Just wondered."

"You want to call somebody? It's four in the morning."

"No. I wondered if you had."

"Who?"

"I don't know. Mother Russia?"

"But why?"

"To let her know I am still here. Asleep. Ready to be taken."

"Jesus. Ready to be taken." She laughed, the sound surprisingly light, and he joined in. "Who's after you, the CIA, KGB, the Argies, who?"

"Never mind."

"Anyway, there's no telephone. There's not even a signal lamp, or a set of semaphor flags, and all the carrier pigeons died of Newcastle's disease just last week . . ."

He slapped her with his good hand, careful not to touch any bone. "Enough," he said calmly, still without malice, the rage cruising out there in the forest, out of mind.

Tears sprang to her eyes, and she held the flushed patch on her cheek. Trulov could feel the bed shake with her trembling. He said, "You know, Inger. Sometimes I think you are exactly what you seem."

Again, her laugh surprised him. "Sure I am. What else would I be?"

"If you were bringing people in on me. If I thought it for a second . . ."

"Let me guess. You'd tear me apart."

"Worse."

"You'd rape me fore and aft, knock out my teeth, pluck out my eyeballs, break my bones." She took his member in her hands. "Better?"

"You're getting there."

"You'd kill me," she murmured, stroking him.

"There."

Stroking, stroking, she said, "With your big hand . . . with *one* big hand."

"One hand, yes."

"You'd kill me while you were in me."

"Yes."

"You'd press on my throat gently and shut off my blood to my brain, and the world would get grey, and my heart would begin to rush..."

"Yes."

"You'd feel me die around you, while you pushed in and in."

"God." Internally, privately, he recoiled; but the part of him she held had a life of its own, and flexed like a snake against the gently moving hands.

"Long life is *second* prize, Cleve." She leaned closer, to look at him, to lick his lips, and he saw the glowing opaque eyes, and greed, and craziness, the death's head in its cape of golden hair. "Let's start with the rape," she said, guiding him into her again, the pelvis gliding up and up... He embraced her, eagerly, even believing he held a powerful symbol of his own death, frightened and horrified, but also profoundly contented with this stroke of luck.

4

THE SAS FLIGHT had been held in Vienna against weather delays going into Copenhagen, and was late getting out of Kastrup, so that Andrews did not arrive at Stockholm-Arland until nearly seven Monday evening, not terribly late, but with the winter feel that darkness had settled in and matured; the feel of midnight. He was another hour on the bus into the city, bored and restless, the surrounding world occluded by his formidable self-consciousness, that put him squarely at the center of the universe, but also brought that itch of worry: Is this *really* the center? He felt the flick of any stranger's gaze, the peculiar focusing upon him of murmured, inaudible conversation, and wondered what these people thought, and said, about him.

For, beneath all his sureness, his relentlessly developed sense of personal achievement, lived a scared boy, waiting fearfully to be found out—to be revealed as having just the quality you would expect from the son of a stocky family

butcher, a jolly, strong, stupid man of London, and his
bovine mother, happy and unintelligent, and also of that
damnably low class. That was how Andrews perceived
them. He would shut his eyes against their memory, the
shabby gentility, the bloodspatted aprons, the paisley
dresses, the ordinary desires of small people. *In spite of
them,* as he snarlingly put it to himself, he had done well,
honors at public school, honors at Hull, suddenly, the
technical young man, all dressed up, uncertain where to go.
Then, fabulously, beyond his grandest expectations, a
school contact with the Royal Society had found him a
spot at the Centre, and away he went, as if shot from an
academic cannon, to Vienna, to the only position he had
ever held, or, he believed, ever would. He loved and believed in the Centre, in his bloodless way, took its people
and programs at face value, and enjoyed the internation-
ality of it all—the calls that came to him from Moscow,
Mexico City, Tokyo, Washington, and, more recently, even
Beijing; and the friendship and respect of Academician
Pastukh, the man, if one dared think such thoughts, he
might have picked for a father, that big, magnetic states-
man of a person, a man of character and influence in the
tough arenas of the Soviet Union. Why, that was proof
enough of something more than a veneer rubbed off upon
a butcher's son, proof of something latent, gentlemanly,
and fine. Pastukh would now and then intercede on his
behalf, hurl "anathema from the Urals," as someone once
said, even in small matters. Even this trip, engineered for
him because it required both scientific expertise and discretion. That was how the chairman had put it: scientific
expertise and discretion. One could deplore the tales of
spying, generated in the CIA to give the Centre what Andrews called a "black eye"—one could deplore them and
still undertake a "mission of discretion." Pastukh had told
him simply, sparing him all detail: "Go to Sergels Torg. A
girl will put something in your pocket. Some music. A tape
cassette, with nothing incriminating on it." Andrews had
accepted the assignment as a favor to this great man, tell-

ing himself at the same time that this was innocent, but
required his kind of discretion. No wonder the chairman
had substituted him for that churlish American, Braun.
You had to know whom to trust, and the chairman obviously trusted this young man, this putative...son.

The bus left him at the railway station, where he caught
a Volvo cab to the Grand Hotel, tense at the prospect of
being taken for an expensive and humiliating ride through
a strange city, relieved when the hotel appeared in its gar-
lands of lights, within a few blocks. Being a careful man,
Andrews had bought *kronor* at the airport in Vienna, and
paid with a solid eight-percent tip, shaving convention just
the slightest bit. The doorman let him out into the cold
winter air, the driver handed him his single small bag,
which he kept, through the double glass doors, up the
marble steps to the lobby, brilliant and well appointed and
full of people about to leave for dinner. He asked if they
had a reservation for Dr. Braun, hating it that the chairman, having done so much for him, had left it all in
Braun's name; then, once the reservation had been lo-
cated, Andrews explained in a low, embarrassed voice that
"there was a bit of a mixup, you see," the human contact
triggering his reflex to chatter, "Dr. Braun unable, know
what I mean, I came instead, intending to use his reservation, if you follow, irregular, of course, I recognize that,
but all quite verifiable," unable to stop talking, "but I assure you it's perfectly all right, ah, jolly good, bitter cold
out there tonight, good to come in, the old city looks very
nice indeed..." chattering away while the silent clerk
pushed a pen and registration card over, and left Andrews
talking and talking; but conscious also, that, at the center
of his flood of idle conversation, lay the mystery of himself. "Jolly good," he said finally, pushing the registration card back across the counter.

The desk man signalled a bellhop to take him up to his
room, which turned out to be a small single with bath on
the fifth floor, overlooking an air shaft. Andrews tipped
the man, and unfolded and hung up his bag, and bit his lip

with disappointment. Given his position at the Centre, he had expected something a bit better, possibly a view of the water. It went to show that one had to travel on one's own reservations, not those of a not-very-senior American scientist who probably would not have noticed the difference. Quality tells. He unsnapped and hung up his carry-on bag, and used the lavatory, mumbling away, and humming, and whistling fragments of half-remembered tunes. Andrews thought of himself as extraordinarily sensitive, and alive. In fact, he was a nervous man.

By eight-thirty, he stood outside the hotel, facing the Nordic winter in a lined khaki Burberry, the belt drawn up, the chest flaps buttoned across one another, the collar turned up around his neck and matching Burberry scarf. Even with the coat, though, and the fleecelined gloves, the cold penetrated to his deep interior. Bad show, he thought, mucking about like this, on a mission of discretion that he knew had more to do with Trulov than the chairman. To tell the truth, it frightened him to be doing something untoward for the Soviet Union.

Something inside said: You're theirs now.

No, no, he corrected swiftly. It's a *favor* to them. A favor.

He checked the simple blue and white map he'd found in the room and set off past the cab stands, thinking he would dare the cold and walk the few blocks to Sergels Torg, whatever that was. His route took him along the hideous black water, past a docking point where an old woman in a dark coat threw bread to the birds. At the next bridge, he turned north, into the city, glad to leave the cold waterfront, and that awful water, water, it seemed to the frightened boy behind the international executive, made for drowning.

The streets were nearly empty, the stores dark behind their lighted display window, ice everywhere, streaking the pavement, making it difficult to walk. When he topped the low hill, he decided *torg* must mean square, because here was one, and the sculpture his map called "Northern

Lights" towering some twenty meters into the air, light caroming through it, quite attractive, although a bit abstract...his brain rattled along like a loosely assembled vehicle. Off to his left concrete steps went down to a sunken square, where the Tunnelbana corridors carried people off into the ornamented caves blasted out of the granite world beneath Stockholm. Struck by a sudden sensation that all eyes turned toward him, that his arrival there had been universally noticed, Andrews struck a pose of enlightened interest and understanding, hands on hips, chin nodding. Must have been the devil's own job, digging this underground, he mused, his face pursed in mock reflection, but they did wonderfully well renewing this part of the city, really, a fine job, out of the top drawer, first rate, and all that. A perceptive fellow, after all.

Down in the square itself, Andrews felt less comfortable, avoiding the looks of whores standing enshadowed by the Tunnelbana pillars, the hippie musicians playing guitars with blue hands in woollen socks, the toes cut out to free the fingers. Far across the open area, a girl played a mournful cello, the pale face reflected in the curve of polished wood, to which she seemed to cleave for warmth. Andrews wanted very much to speak to her, to give her money, but knew he would not. Mostly the crowd comprised people going home to the lighted oblongs across the water and up the hills; violence, if it were present, moved invisibly among them, although Andrews sensed bad things about to happen everywhere. Another sound now joined the cello and country guitar that mixed on the winter air, a high, reedy voice interspersed with a guitar and rhythmic clatter and boom of drums and a tin horn, singing

> ... and for that great Shepherd
> Who rules our green pastures,
> Our frail loins to gird,
> We forfeit all pleasure

The voice rose from south London, almost unintelligible to anyone there but Andrews, or at least that was how it seemed to him; for a panicked instant he thought here, finally, he would be caught out, his Cockney ear exposed. The streetbusker approached Andrews, watching him with eyes that held no light—blind eyes. He sang into a mouth-piece mounted on a wire frame near his mouth, and plugged into a battery-powered amplifier strapped to his chest. His hands picked at a guitar that had gone drift-wood grey with exposure and, on a harness around his back, he carried a bass drum wired through springs and hinges to a pair of drumsticks and his right shoe. He could make a large boom by driving his foot sharply forward, or a series of smaller ones by striking his heel against the pavement. It was a lot of sound to issue from one small, scrawny man in a British field jacket shining with dirt, his throat wrapped in a long, filthy scarf, a black watch cap pulled down around his ears, his face healthy with winter around the stare of his eyes, his blue lips singing

> ... to yield up our treasures,
> That we match His measures,
> And Obey His word ...

Andrews threaded his way across the crowd, which opened ahead of the advancing streetbusker, large with his burden of instruments. But then he saw the girl, tall and sombre, a pretty girl with long brown hair and the pale, red-lipped look of English women. She did not seem to communicate with the busker, but, as he honked and boomed slowly through the assemblage, she maintained her position relative to him, as though she were a radiant moon to his ravaged little planet. Her dark eye caught Andrews' and held him where he stood. "Will you contribute to his mission? Thanks very much, God bless. Will you contribute...?" she uttered like a song, nodding to acknowledge the coins received from the people she passed, and yet, unmistakably, the orbiting pair made for

Andrews. When she hesitated before him, Andrews fancied that something passed between them, between the center of things and this lovely, subdued English girl, who was rather much too good for what she did, hanging around this lousy busker. Andrews flushed beneath her gaze, and when she asked, "Will you contribute to his mission?" quickly fumbled out a five-*krona* note, which he handed over with a sharp, miserly pang. "Thank you very much, sir," she said in her low, neutral voice, her eyes still on him. "God bless you, sir," she added, and began a graceful turn away; then, as she passed him, Andrews felt a small object drop into his pocket, an object that, reaching him clandestinely in this way, revived all his fears, as if the girl had dropped a pellet of plutonium into his pocket. She did not look back. The pair drifted away across the square, the thin voice lifted in its nonsense hymns, the girl like a satellite, "Will you contribute? God bless you, sir. Will you contribute to his mission? God bless you . . ." lost in the ambient noise of moving people, the scrabbling feet on icy walks, the murmur of voices.

Andrews peered around cautiously, positive he was under some scrutiny, surprised not to catch a pair of secret eyes watching him, weighing the odd transaction with the busker's girl. He saw no one, only the shadows along the sides of the place, shadows waiting for customers, shadows waiting for dope, shadows talking to shadows. He hunched his shoulders up and jammed his gloved hands into his pockets and strode purposefully out of the square, trotting he thought lithely up the concrete steps, where he turned toward his hotel.

Once clear of the crowd he removed the object from his pocket, and held it up to the glancing light of a streetlamp. It was a standard LP tape cassette with a badly printed label showing a cartoon of the blind busker and *The Further Hymns of Basil Michelson*. Andrews grinned and ran his tongue around the edges of his slick, red mouth. All of that secrecy for this? And if I play it, he asked the night, what do I get? I bet I get *The Further*

Hymns of Basil Michelson. How extraordinary of them, to want something like this. And the busker himself, what could he possibly tell someone like the chairman, or Maxim Trulov, about anything? Ah, but the girl...*that* was a different matter. Andrews could see her working out some code with the "hymns" reporting on...what? What was important enough to transmit in this way? What could be transmitted this way? Again he shook his head. I shan't ask, he told himself. I shall never ask.

Still, the transaction, the slight tangential contact with a world outside the one he considered to be real, had rattled him. He felt himself perspiring inside the Burberry, the moisture turning cold and clammy, a dead man's sweat, and he unbuttoned some of the flaps, let the air cut coldly into him, dry him out. He did not know quite what to do now he had done *It*. He toyed with finding a bar, but, as he walked slowly back toward the hotel, the ones he saw were too full of people who seemed too much at home— having just been slipped a coded message, he could not enter a crowded room where all voices would die in mid-syllable, all eyes would turn to him. He thrust his chin against his imaginary challenge from the crowd, and kept going along the icy walk, skittering now and then but retaining his balance. The opera rose on his left, now, and he thought how good it would have been to get to Stockholm earlier, in time for a night at the Swedish opera, something to chat to colleagues about at the Centre, opera here as against opera in Vienna or Covent Garden.

A bar slid by and he passed it like a blind man, his adam's apple working. The hotel would have a bar, and it would be more comfortable, it was his turf, in a way, so that his appearance would not cause any sensation, and he could take his coat to the room beforehand and use the toilet and wipe off some of the perspiration that clung to him still, like the cold, which had reached all the way into his skeleton...

"Please!"

Andrews spun around at the cry, a woman's urgent, frightened voice.

"*Var sa god* ... help, please, oh, help!" She ran toward him and he recognized her as the old woman he'd seen earlier, feeding the birds, but now her face was distended with what looked to him like terror (*Terror!* he thought, *Good God!*). Her neck was arched, the veins distended, her eyes shone wild and fearful, like those of a horse fleeing a lion. "Oh, help me, *please*," she cried out, reaching him, clutching at his shoulders. Andrews nodded dumbly, unable to say no, wanting to flee the...terror. But he could not; this might be his Moment of Truth. Her fingers grabbed his gloved hand and he felt a sudden sharp pain that quickly subsided, her nail probably, he thought, wringing the hand away, but then all sensation was swallowed up in excitement and fear, as she led him at a trot back to the seawall. Pointing down the narrow steps to a boat landing that teemed with ducks and swans and gulls, she cried, "There, *there* ... do you understand, hurt, *hurt* ..." He nodded and hurried down into the darkness, bent beneath this new challenge, as he saw it, this unexpected burden of responsibility fate had thrust upon him. The lights of the city were quickly eclipsed by the stone pier, the water rushing madly by, Andrews' heart pounding like a rabbit's, the air filled with glowing white birds, swans like pale ships on the tide, and ducks, as calm as stuffed ones, milling around, waiting for bread.

He could see nothing, and turned to the woman, who stood close behind him. "What?" he asked, gesturing toward the water. "Who?" She leaned toward him. He could make out the fine-boned face beneath the broad cap of white hair. "You speak English," she murmured. "Thank God for that!" and took his hands in hers.

"Yes, but..." He cocked his head anxiously toward the flood. "Is someone...?"

"Someone is hurt," she said, raising her voice above the roar of water. "Badly."

"Where?" he yelled. But even then, even then, he knew that it had come at last. Something was wrong. The trap had sprung. He flung around at the woman. Where was her terror now? He lunged for the stairs but could not reach them, feeling his blood race through him, through the growing numbness that made it difficult to walk, impossible to stand. He sank to the wet stone, his hand clutching spasmodically at his sides, the thin crimson line of his mouth gleaming with saliva. Oh, Jesus, it had come, a heart attack, a stroke, a trap...

The woman stood over him, the light wind rippling her black coat, her hair bright as a seagull on the night. Andrews wanted to tell her he thought he'd had a stroke, a heart attack, to find a doctor, that he had begun to lose control. But his tongue might have been a sausage, for he could not make it modulate the grunts he made. *Grunt! Grunt! Grunt!* God, don't you hear the urgency.

But, no. *She* had done this to him. She. The woman watched him, seemed to tower over him now, wind in her coat, a huge, powerful woman, a witch who had somehow brought this on him. The pricking of his hand. A witch, a poisoning witch, who had done this to him...because of the tape. Oh, listen, please, there's a dreadful sort of misunderstanding, do you understand me, perfectly usual sort of thing but bad for me, heh heh, but, honestly, I haven't the foggiest what those Russians are about, moving secret hymns around the continent and, I well, I am your original innocent bystander, know what I mean? *Grunt! Grunt! Grunt!*

He could barely see her, the dark shape of her, moving next to him, and felt her warmth, like desire, through his clothing, through his dead limbs. Ah, mother, mother. Mama. He heard her fidgeting, the rustle of plastic, and then, suddenly, her hand appeared, palm up, bearing a small cone of white powder. Carefully then she packed his nostrils with the stuff, forcing him to pant through his mouth, which had frozen half open; she clamped a hand, a hand as lean and warm as any mother's (Mama! Mama!

Bad DREAMS!), across his mouth, so that for a moment he thought he would suffocate, as though he were in the water, spinning down and down with the ice, and then he took a great breath through his nose and the powder flew in upon it.

"You're going out high," she said, and her face, as it moved across his field of view, smiled like a white planet, like the busker's sweet moon of a girl, Will you contribute to his mission? God bless you, sir, oh, God bless us, every one, the smiling woman, mother (MAMA!), the grand clatter of duck wings and long looks of swans and the water, and that rush now, that sensation of flying down the fall line of a steep slope, rocketing along, half excitement, half fear, flying...

He could feel the woman going over him, and thought wildly that this whole thing might be sexual, a kind of ultimate rape, and tried to laugh, *grunt, grunt, grunt,* while she forced something into his pockets, and then began shoving him across the rough stones, toward the *water*, her hands warm and somehow exciting but also somehow calming (Mother?), but the *water*... He cried out, he roared, for wasn't he the lion, and she just a woman, and couldn't he, with a flick of his paw, send her spinning away like a shard of ice? GRUNT! GRUNT! GRUNT!

"Shh," she said.

Oh, Jesus Christ Almighty God I cannot move, I cannot move or speak, my *grunts* are getting weaker, she wants to throw me into *that*, the Arctic Ocean, no, Baltic, it's all very well, know what I mean, jolly jolly good, no *bad*... His spirit let out a great, inaudible scream that came from its very marrow, a scream of terror and also of irresistible joy, in the way that falling from a high cliff would feel like flight, and drowning would make you a dolphin, for a time, a moment, leaping and diving.

"Bye bye, Raggedy Andy."

5

TRULOV HAD KEPT CLEAR of Andrews, not wanting to be seen, but not so clear that he could not exert some influence on the situation—on whatever came tonight. He was a new Trulov today, wearing the warm costume of an affluent Swedish fisherman, if there were such a thing, a dark turtleneck sweater and peacoat and corduroys, and boots for moving around the docks without slipping on ice, all courtesy of Mr. Cleveland Brown and his excellent credit rating. He looked both larger and less conspicuous, the fine suit on a hanger at Inger's flat, although he had kept the raincoat, rolled in his briefcase in a station locker.

Inger. He watched the crowd in Sergels Torg, wondering if she had returned to work, if she were there, waiting for him to notice her in the shadows. She'd said she would wait. "I guess I don't want you to see me."

He strained for a look at Andrews, who was obscured by passers-by for a moment, then visible again, then gone, like the moon swept by clouds.

She had said, "I guess I don't want you to see me." Trulov smiled. They had had a love affair. A small one, a largely physical, possibly crazy and death-directed one, but, given the constraints, a real honest-to-Christ love affair. They had made love. *You can make love out of anything, if you know what you're doing.* She had said that too. We shall never forget each other, he thought with satisfaction.

After a late breakfast he had taken her to the toy store and given her the money to buy Svetlana a pretty blonde porcelain doll with human hair, a Russian-looking doll, pale and glowing, dressed like a woman from Tolstoy. The store would send it to her, to keep the KGB and others away from the gift, keep them from spoiling it. Perhaps. It was hard to keep their hands out of things. But then, feeling good, Trulov had gone in separately and picked out a small porcelain doll in a clown suit, and brought it out for Inger, making the hard face soften, making her laugh.

"Someone to watch over you," he told her. Ah, God, what a stroke of luck she had been. He wished *he* could watch over her; he would like to reach out through the darkness and lift one of her customers into the air by his balls and give him a frightening, hurting shake, send him running... He laughed softly. A stroke of luck. That was what they kept telling one another. She had not mentioned money, and he had not wanted to bring it up either, so he left a few hundred *kronor* under her pillow to keep her from having zero income for the night, but not so much that she would remember it as the night she made a lot of money. No, it was their small, high-walled affair. She would never focus on money, this funny girl, this destructive, dangerous one. Not your proverbial whore with a heart of gold—but, still, a good girl, after all.

Andrews.

Where the hell had Andrews gone?

Trulov moved quickly, scouting the square until he caught his quarry once more, and went back to watching from the shadows. The busker approached Andrews, and the girl, and there was that faint brushing touch, and then they walked on, toward Trulov. No sign was exchanged as they passed, although he knew she had seen him; they had met on other tape exchanges. One was tempted to wave her a hello.

Andrews had moved again, and it took Trulov a moment to pick him out, going up the steps, leaving this bowl of whores and dopeheads and decadent youth. Where would he go? Trulov would find a bar where he could loosen up now the transfer had been completed. But he knew his man would not. Andrews would falter and fart around and find himself back at the hotel, the evening barely underway, and he might have a drink or two in the bar there, and possibly begin that kneejerk chatter of his to the bartender, for he was a terrible drinker, and if the moon and stars were exactly right and the situation fell into his lap, he might buy a girl a drink, although the Grand Hotel would not have much in the way of girls in its dull, fancy bar. Early to bed, then. Tomorrow the carbon dioxide overview presentation. A six-thirty flight back to Vienna. Finis. And nothing would have happened beyond that splendid night with Inger. Well, while They would never forgive him for it, it had been what he needed, yes, and what he wanted, too. A stroke of luck. Ah, and where are you, my girl? Trulov asked the night as he fell in a block behind Andrews. "Will I see you tonight?" she'd asked when they finished their meal (courtesy of the Eurocheck, which, at five banks, had brought Trulov five thousand *kronor*. They would never forgive that!), and he had hesitated before telling her no. It had hurt them both, for she had really been asking if she would ever see him again, and he had said no. It reverberated between them. For a time there were no smiles.

Now he regretted that, wondering where he would spend the night while Andrews slept like a boy in a comfortable room in the Grand, the water playing lights and shadows beneath his window, a good breakfast in prospect...

He followed Andrews as far as the opera, and then shrugged, seeing the tall, spare figure in the trenchcoat turn toward the hotel along the waterfront. What can they do to him in a couple of blocks? I could go back, find Inger, we could lie together one more night before the world begins to look for me. But he would like that, taking the thin, strong body back into his big arms, seeing her in the halflight of the room. Surely the world owed him one more night before it came for him? He smiled, thinking they would both be pleased, and turned back toward Sergels Torg. They would go out for a little drinking, as last night, and a dessert—she had turned out to have a formidable sweet tooth—and then back to her place again. One more night before he began his last run, a few hours ahead of all those hounds.

He stopped, cocked his head, listening. There was only the odd traffic, and, off beyond the opera, the roar of water pouring through the tidal gates. Had he heard anything, or was it just his skin beginning to jump? But...he would not go to Inger after all. She had given him, sold him maybe, everything she had, and restored what he had lost that night in the cemetery. She had left him strong, his instincts working like a wise animal's, and now he must turn her gift into something good.

There, surely, a cry!

Suddenly he was running, running awkwardly, even in his boots, skidding on the ice patches, almost out of control, but balanced, the white bandage of the left hand held out like a balancing pole, the other knotted into a big fist. He ran down the slick narrow road past the opera, no one in sight, the only sound that of the water, and the clatter of ducks and gulls, and *there*, something else. But it was amorphous, there was nothing directional in it. He stopped to listen. The sound could have been a child in one of the flats. A cat. Walking, then, straining to hear. Voices floated to him on the night, but the roar of water carried them away, made it impossible to tell where they came from, and with it all there was the feather rattling and earnest squabbling of hundreds of ducks, part of the water noise. He walked slowly, listening hard, across the bridge, almost to the Grand Hotel, which glared across the water in its frame of lights. Nothing, nothing. Every sound made Trulov's skin leap. Nothing. Andrews must have made it to the hotel more quickly than he thought. That thing, that incident about to happen, which had brought Trulov to Sweden, had not happened, at least it had not tonight. There was tomorrow to arrange, then, and tomorrow... He paused. Something was not quite right. Then he saw the birds scattering away from where they had swarmed around the warm-water discharge, flapping, startled by something he could not see, and then he was running toward them. From the quay, he heard, crisp as a witch's incantation, "Bye bye, Raggedy Andy."

His rage flared around that hated, remembered, witch's voice, and, yes, there, *there*, at the bottom of the steps, down in all the duck shit, there *she* was, kneeling on the ice, and there, in the water, the thin mouth gaping like a doll's, Andrews spun away into the night. Trulov had made no sound, but the witch felt him there, and now looked up, the fine ageless face expressionless and calm. She knew, she knew, and still would not give even that tiny flicker of animation which suggested fear. Wonderful, in a way. If you liked witches. He came down the steps slowly, his left forearm lightly braced against the seawall. The woman raised herself to the balls of her feet, and backed toward the corner of the landing, her eyes unblinking, stony, watching the Russian. You caught me at a bad time yesterday, he told her silently, you caught me hurting and depressed and out of confidence, wondering why I had come to Sweden. But this is why: to catch you at your killing. All the way to Stockholm, just for that. That, and perhaps to let you meet the Real Me. "Cybelle," he said. She recoiled, her nostrils flared. She showed no fear, but, dear God, where had he seen such hatred? "You are too old for this kind of work," he said. She made no reply. "Oh, I saw yesterday that it made you a bit high, to be back in the field. And it must have been exciting to do a job on that poor boy out there," that face, spinning like a round fragment of ice. "But you got it all wrong. You killed the wrong man, someone named Andrews. Pastukh saw you coming, you see. What do they say? He made a substitution in the line-up. And now you have been caught at it, by me. Old Jesse Owens, eh? Named for the great Negro runner. Where do you go from here, Cybelle?"

"Cocksucker!" she hissed and darted forward, swinging her right palm, quick as a boxer. He took the needle on his bandage, the pain exploding tangentially, irrelevantly, in the greater conflagration of his rage, and absorbed her karate kick with his right thigh, which would carry a great black bloody bruise in the morning; then he backhanded her very hard, very quickly for a man his size, sending her against the end of the landing. She crouched there against the cold stones, watching him like an animal. "Poison darts? Curare?" he asked rhetorically. "Back to basics, as

you say." He shook his head. "You are in deep shit, old
lady. Cybelle. Your being here proves everything to me. I
know what is going on, because of you. You cannot hurt
me. You cannot stop me from doing what I wish with
you...and you have some things in your head I need." He
stepped toward her, absorbed another kick with his thigh,
and grabbed her right wrist. And Cybelle, poised to strike
again with her needle, wilted suddenly, slumped to her
knees in vaporous surrender. Trulov balked momentarily,
releasing her; and in his instant of hesitation, she flashed
a look of victory and scraped the needle across the fine
blue veins of her throat. Blood and the brown drug
spreading beneath her chin, she said, "Fuck you, Jesse,"
and stepped into the current. The water swept her away,
something white, turning with the ice.

Trulov watched the white head sink, watched the water
carry her to Finland, Germany, or Leningrad, Behind the
Iron Curtain. The birds, sensing the excitement, had
moved on, taxied back into the warm patch, inscrutably
treading water, waiting for food, vaguely disappointed that
the big Russian offered none beyond the inedible woman.
He sank down upon the steps, stunned by how close he had
been to holding live, breathing proof of his worst suspicions in his hands. And he had lost her. Very well, at least
his doubts, such as they were, had been swept away. He
knew it all, everything. Maybe that would be enough. Except, God, they would be after him, the world would be
after him. He had run out of time. He was back on his
own.

A FEW HUNDRED METERS downstream, in a dinghy that
drifted in the lights of the Grand Hotel, another big man
dressed for fishing felt his grapple take hold, and drew it
toward him steadily, gingerly, towing the long, slender
form wrapped in khaki, the Burberry tartan scarf like a tail
in the water, and then the face next to the boat, a tiny face,
a face like a doll's, with a mere slit for a mouth. The
fisherman looked into the lightless eyes. "Poor old sod,"

he told them. Then, giving himself a large shake, he bent over the gunwale carefully, and checked the pockets. He felt the plastic bag of cocaine and left it there, and the wallet, and the keys, and the golden pen from the Academy of Sciences of the Soviet Union. He kept only the tape cassette, and when he had stowed it in his jacket pocket, he freed the grapple, cut the line, and let it sink into the stream. And then, as the current swept the body seaward, the fisherman lighted his meerschaum pipe, and pulled for the far shore.

PART FIVE

1

THAT WAS CHRISTMAS WEEK. Each day Val and I moved
imperceptibly closer, although, at the same time, we felt
the increased pressure of heightened risk. Loving her was
like loving a dying child, each contact sweet beneath the
certainty of death, the long shadow always our horizon.
The sickness was not in her blood, but only an ideological
one, and she and I automatically assumed it must be fatal. Well, why not? Ideology is more destructive than cars
or cancer. Of course we thought it was stronger than what
we might patch together.

My face knitted enough that I could venture out on that
Wednesday to forage on the Graben and Kärtnerstrasse,
looking for her present. I ended up with a cashmere turtleneck from Scotland, solid black, terribly expensive, very
personal, the kind of gift over which she would glare at me
and say, "Careful." And I took the U-bahn across the
Danube to the commissary at UN City, to get Dexter a
gross of blue-labeled Russian caviar, Uncle Stuka his holiday booze, Renate her French perfume, and myself more
liquor and some pink Russian champagne for such celebrating as Val and Dexter and I might do at my flat.

Through all of this, Val brought news from the Centre,
an oral journal from which Trulov had already nearly disappeared, replaced by vague word of Andrews. On
Wednesday she reported he had gone missing in Stockholm, and had not given his overview paper on Tuesday,
causing consternation and anger among the Swedish hosts.
Dexter had returned, and asked after me. We spent our
evenings leaning toward one another like affectionate

plants ignoring the approach of winter, never touching, being "careful." Still, it was a fine time for me; for her too, I think.

The two of them surprised me Christmas Eve, emerging radiant and happy from a wet, windy night, each carrying fat grey commissary bags, and Dexter dragging a scraggly little evergreen, plucked from God knew where. We greeted one another warmly, and while I prepared a set of drinks and something for nibbling, they set about putting my flat in holiday order. By the time I returned the thin tree stood in a corner, and Dexter had a tiny band of colored lights twinkling down among its sparsely needled branches. Val hung wooden ornaments and glass bulbs. "We stopped at Christkindlmarkt," she said happily. I envied Dexter's taking her into the jolly crowd down by the *Rathaus*, with all the kids and cotton candy and booths for everything under the winter sun.

"We've been doing nothing else the entire bloody day," grumbled Dexter, "and all for you. Jesus, what happened to your face?" Val shook her head almost imperceptibly, and he, noticing, told us, "No flaming coverups, either. What happened?"

"Trulov freaked out in the cemetery, after the service for Emil. I was within reach and he grabbed me. Very tough guy."

"Very," Dexter said, unable to decorate for a moment. "Very tough indeed. Any idea why he went for you?"

"I'm just an attractive guy."

"The hell you are. You don't know why?" I shook my head. "Bad news, that. Hmm." He looked at me with something like pity, then, and seemed to shake himself internally, and returned to the tree. "But you seem to be bouncing back."

"Resilient."

"So what happened to Maxim?"

"No one knows," I said.

Val echoed, as our Soviet spokesperson, "We do not know."

Dexter tossed her a skeptical look from behind the tree, which began to be downright elegant, "Pardon my saying so, Val, but I cannot imagine a KGB man on the loose like that. *Someone* must know."

"But *I* do not," she replied firmly, a note of strain in her voice.

"Ah, Jesus, I am sorry," he told her. "Let's have our drinks, and try to regain some of that Christmas cheer."

"Let's," she said with a grateful smile.

When we were comfortable as we could get in the flat—Dexter had the one chair large enough to hold him, Val had the other, and I sat with my legs crossed on the greasy-grey carpet—I asked, "How was London?" to change the subject.

Dexter looked up from his glass. "Bloody cold. Cold as hell. You know, that cold ring, the eighth, whichever, in the Dante thing."

"We've spent a quiet week," I said.

"You're bloody lucky you had Val to nurse you, old boy." He could not take his eyes off me, though. He had to *peer*, his eyes asking a question I could not read. "Damned lucky." Getting no response to his silent interrogation, he turned away. "Speaking of cold...some dreadful news today."

"Dexter," Val protested.

"Oh, I think our boy can take it. Nothing to do with us, fortunately. Has it?" A short silence. Then, to me, "They found Andrews."

"Good. Where?"

"In the Baltic. Some fisherman pulled him in with a bunch of mackerel. Poor sod. Well, what can one say, none of us knew him really. But a shame." He paused. "Odd thing, though." The illegible question again. Again, no response from me. "He was full of cocaine. Blood. Pockets. Everything. Never struck me as that sort of chap, doing dope. Quite a lot, according to the report I heard."

"They are saying he was killed," Val murmured.

"Yes, you know, one of those dope deals. Even in Sweden, democratic welfare state par excellence, and we get our distinguished member killed in a dope deal. Nothing is what it seems, children. Nothing, nothing. Ever." He took a long pull at his whisky. "But this is madness. Here we are, friends together on Christmas Eve, and we're talking about some poor criminal's murder. Come on now, we simply mustn't."

"The tree is beautiful," I ventured.

"But wait, just wait," Val said, trying to sound happy and excited again.

"You wait," I told her, going for the packages I'd wrapped in old *Herald Tribunes*. When I returned they'd spread out gifts of their own around the base of the tree: a box of Cuban cigars, a bottle of cognac, and, in a jelly jar vase of mine, a dozen little pink roses, and various cheeses and spreads and cans of nuts and dates and figs and apricots, and a record of *Evita*, which I'd once commented on in Val's presence. I was very touched, and handed them their gifts diffidently, with a kind of reverence—Christmas had become just another night alone, not a night you'd get drunk on, or go to town on either, just one of those interminable lonely evenings, with love everywhere but in your life. So, yes, I was greatly touched at these good friends, bringing their affection into my night, bringing warmth to one so cold. And then it came to me that, of course, the three of us shared this sense of holiday bleakness. We had all spent too much time by ourselves, had too many empty Christmases and New Years Eves and Thanksgivings and, God knows, Boxing Days and May Days perhaps. The difference was that their instincts were life-giving and warm, and brought them toward me; where mine drove me away, not wishing to inflict myself on the goodness of friends. What I am saying is that they were training me up for the human race, and that, in our little time together, they nearly turned me toward the sun.

Dexter let out a great yelp of pleasure when he unwrapped his caviar, and thanked me extravagantly before
heading kitchenward for bread and lemons. Val said
nothing when she opened hers, but spread the soft black
woollen thing across her lap, and smoothed it with her
fingertips. When she looked up her eyes were damp, and
accusing. "It is too nice, Schaefer," she whispered. "It is
far too nice. I ... I have never had anything like this."

"Please try it on." I flushed when her eyes widened.
"No, I mean go into the bedroom and try it on, and then
come show us. Please."

Smiling, then, she went out. I wrapped my arms around
my knees and put my chin on them, grinning like a boy.
My eyes weren't all that dry, either. I could hear Dexter
fussing like a bear in the kitchen, making us little caviar
snacks with part of his gift. Then Val returned. She always glowed, but it was something else, having her
wrapped in black cashmere, the high turtleneck empha-
sizing the sharp curve of her small, strong jaw, the long
neck, the broad shoulders, the soft curve of bosom. Ah,
lord, she was so beautiful! "You are so beautiful," I told
her.

She went red, still smoothing the cashmere with her fingers, and shook her head vigorously: *Careful.*

Hell, I thought, diving again off the Eiffel Tower. "I
love you, Val."

Her eyes brimmed, and still she shook her head, and bit
her lip. "No," she whispered.

"Once a year I get to tell you. Every Christmas."

"You will make me cry."

I sniffed. "Me too." We laughed together, then, and I
knew that, if we'd just been people on a planet, if there
were no nations, and no risks to careers and reputation, we
would at that moment have run into each other's arms,
and stayed there. But as it was, we settled for our quiet,
bonded laughter.

Dexter entered like the north wind, eyes aglow, nose
pink from the whisky, which he had decanted further while

fixing the pile of triangles of white bread with the crust trimmed away, piled with his caviar, bordered with wedges of lemon. It was lovely.

"You are a chef," Val cried.

"And just look at you," he replied, taking her in. "What a smashing jumper. Good God, Schaefy, you're not big enough to protect a woman who looks like this. Why, man, you'll have to get a bodyguard, a big Brit, perhaps."

"I'm tougher than you think," I kidded, although my heart wasn't in it—the talk recalled Trulov slapping me around like a rag doll.

"Anyway, eat up, chaps." He picked up the memory, and understood. Empathy flickered in his face.

"Jesus, Gordy," I complained then, easing us off our hooks, "where are the cucumber sandwiches?"

"The cucumber...?"

"What are you, some kind of impostor? I'm *veeerrry* disappointed."

"Boys, boys," yelled Val, laughing.

Dexter drew himself up to his largest size. "Thank you, Valentina. Schaefer, I fear your words mark you as a savage among sandwichovores. Try to remember the following. Caviar snackies belong in a holiday setting. But at tea on the lawn and cricket matches, *then* it's cucumber sandwiches."

"I see."

"You might write it down. You know, like which is port and which is starboard."

"I think these snackies need champagne."

"Oh, that would be marvelous," said Val.

"I thought the savage would never get around to it," said Dexter.

"Bastard," I told him, and went out to the little refrigerator for one of the bottles of sweet Russian pink. I opened it in front of them, and did it like a good waiter, with barely a pop, and no deadly projectile, and no foam running down my arm.

"By Jove, he's becoming almost gentlemanly, Val. Had you noticed?"

"No comment."

"Must be your influence, my girl. Hmm. Going to be a devil of a job, getting him into Russia with you when the time comes."

She went quiet, and I did too. I didn't want to be reminded of the illness that would take her away from me, our certainty of ultimate failure. Dexter smelled the gaffe, and retreated. "Or you into the States, for that matter, or me back into the U.K. when it comes to that." Then, seeing us still grim, he threw up his hands and cried, "Dash it all, I regret my silly mistake. Forgive me now, both of you, immediately, and we can get to our famous toasts, for God's sakes."

We relaxed for him. I raised my glass and said, "To the carbon persons."

We drank to ourselves. Val toasted, "I salute my two good friends," which was a sombre toast indeed for a Russian, and would have wounded us except that her eyes were warm and bright with friendship.

Then Dexter sounded like a whale into his gathering seriousness. Raising his glass, he intoned, "Here is to gravity, which keeps even small solar systems going despite all the forces trying to rip them apart. To my friends, to our fine friendship, at Christmastime." All of us got a bit thick-throated at that, for he evoked once more the spectre of eventual dissolution, of good comradeship tattered by those corrosive enemies of everything, time and distance. Even if I hadn't fallen for Val, it would have made me sad.

After an interval of silence, in which we retreated to our own preoccupations—I to thoughts of other Christmases, when my folks and Nancy were still alive, and the odd warm holidays of southern California, and Christmas Eves spent on watch somewhere at sea. I wondered where theirs took them. Val, perhaps, to that solitariness of hers, to memories I knew nothing about, and Dexter...God only knew where his thoughts drifted. But suddenly he burst back into voice, declaring, "Well, it isn't Christmas without music."

"I'll turn on the stereo..." and I began to get up.

"No, no, no, something a bit less...secular. Here," he went on, and fished a cassette from his jacket pocket. "Let's try this on your tape deck."

"What is it?" Val wanted to know.

Dexter held it up and pretended to have difficulty reading the label. Then he said, "The Further Hymns of Basil Michelson." His eyes had a cunning light, and the look he turned on Val was a probing one. What does he want from us tonight? I wondered. "Do you know them, Val?"

"I?" she replied mystified. "Why, no."

I saw him scan her for more, and come up empty. He asked me, "Do you?" I shook my head. "Well, no matter, you soon will. They are absolutely, perfectly...dreadful." He dropped the cassette into the tape deck, which he had switched on. The tape ground along with a faint preliminary buzz and then we heard a slight, high male voice, backed up by a guitar, tinny horn, and bass drum:

Are you riding on the
Motorbike of faith,
Or hiding from our
Lovely, Holy Wraith?...

"Jesus, Gordy," I protested.

"Exactly," he replied.

"But we don't have to hear this stuff, do we?"

"No, but listen for a minute longer. It's a peculiar tape. The singer is what we call a streetbusker. A one-man band, drum and horn and mike and guitar, all wired together."

"I have not seen such a thing," Val said, her voice containing an element of wonder.

"Not many one-man bands in the Soviet Union, my dear. Anyway, here he is, this Basil Michelson. Blind. Has this 'mission,' you see, and his girl . . . a super-looking girl she is, too . . . takes up the collection.''

Val and I leaned toward the speakers, listening to the chanted:

> *Mind you hold your tongue*
> *Against the urge to boast*
> *Of all the good you've known*
> *Since you've known the Holy Ghost . . .*

I shook my head. "The hills are alive with the sound of drivel."

But Val held up a slender hand for silence, and cocked her head toward the speakers. "Are they typical?"

Dexter laughed delightedly. "Oh, Valentina, I would love to hear you pose that very question to a minister. Oh, dear."

"And the recording itself is not very good I think. There is that grinding, whistling noise under the music. Almost a harmonic." She shook her head. "It must be the hum of the recorder, or static of some kind. Noise."

I could hear the sound now, too, a high-frequency squeak superimposed on a very-low-frequency rumble, that seemed to be under the melody, without interfering with it. "Trite lyrics, bad melody, low-quality recording. I'd say this one has it all, Gordy." And what else did I hear, down in all the noise? A familiar kind of static, the sounds you get when you're trying to radio a distant ship or shore station, and the satellite frequencies wander, and, down in the noise you hear those electronic ghosts and lost voices.

"But it's odd, I mean, being *so* bad," Dexter said. What was he looking for?

"Maybe it's meant to be listened to while stoned," I said.

"Stoned?" asked Val.

"High on dope," Dexter said.

"A lot of rock music, you can't really hear the whole thing, all those internal layers, unless you're smoking grass."

"I did not know that."

"Stay with us, madam," Dexter said, "and we shall teach you the World."

"I do not think I need the World, thank you."

We slipped once more into our bantering, jovial mood, the tape forgotten, the busker whining on and on until the thin voice died and the tape drive gave its terminal *clunk*. We switched to *Osterreich Eins*, where they were playing the world's most beautiful music. "Ah," sighed Val. "That is more like it." The room filled with voices raised in prayerful song, and we, without pretending to believe that Christ was ever born, let our spirits rise with the music. We sipped at our champagne, happy friends together.

Near midnight, Val began making sounds about leaving, and the three of us picked stuff up and carted it out to the kitchen. Then, far too quickly, she was in her heavy coat, telling us goodbye, wishing us a happy Christmas. Dexter went back to the living room to contemplate the tree, and I took Val to the door. "That was a fine Christmas you gave me," I told her.

"We enjoyed doing it. I did."

"Merry Christmas, Val."

"Thank you. The sweater is..." she shrugged. Then, as we suspended in the door, she leaned in and kissed me lightly on the lips, and, as quickly, touched the spot with a silencing finger. "Good night." She hurried away. The hall lights went on with a click and I listened to the timer switch tick back down to darkness as she descended the old marble stairs. The front door of the building opened, shut. The lights went out. I returned to Dexter, who had gone pensive.

"You don't mind my staying on for a little while longer, do you, Schaefy?"

"Course not."

"I'm getting a whisky. Can I get you something?"

"No, thanks."

He poured himself a jellyjar full of Scotch, added about half a teaspoon of tap water, and came back, still too restive to sit down. He looked out the window, at the blind eyes of the enshadowed lions and Romans across the street. Finally he sat back down, and gave me a sad smile. "I have a great deal to tell you, Schaefy, I am trying to get it into some sort of order." A heavy pause. Then, "You are looking at a man who may be about to make the mistake of a lifetime. Everything in my experience tells me to keep mum, you see, to let things unfold, to watch . . . but, Lor' 'elp me, I am mired in friendship." He smiled unhappily. "God, but I hope you are what you seem, Schaefer Braun."

"What do you think?" Was I what I seemed? Everyone wanted to know, and now even old Dexter had asked.

"If you *are* tainted I shall never forgive you, my boy. Not *ever*." And then, with the wry expression of a man who embarks on the mistake of a lifetime, he revealed himself to me.

2

"REMEMBER THE NIGHT Emil died?"

"Sure." I dream about it.

"I gave you my lecture on spiders and webs?" I nodded. "Well, without going into sordid details, let me say now that I really did know what I was talking about."

My spirits slumped. "The queen of the spiders."

"Nothing great and poisonous, I assure you, but more the sort of one you might expect from Great Britain. Nonpoisonous, but clever about things, traps prey, that kind of spider. Bags of cunning. Fabulous webs."

"Now, back in November, not long after the Committee meeting, the webs began to jiggle, just a bit at first, and then like a Richter magnitude eight sort of a jiggle. All the spiders ran out to see whose web had the morsel, and, well,

I was out there with the rest, wasn't I? And what did we find? A kind of noise. Noise of the sort you heard on that tape tonight. Noise with a kind of order in it. All of us took a look. Some of us—because some spiders are more equal than others at this kind of looking—found odd behaviour. The Americans were sweeping back and forth across a trail we could not even see. You can always spot someone sweeping, but not always why. Russians were all of a sudden in agitated motion, an experienced field man like Trulov suddenly out there like a mad dog. People who had not seen one another in years began to meet in out-of-the-way places. And the killing..."

My resistance had been building. Now I raised a re-straining hand. "Gordy, this isn't for me. I'm not in it. I don't want it in my head."

"But you *are* in it, that's the point." He paused, watching me with something close to pity. "First there is one Shirley Morgan. Know the name?" I shook my head. "Killed accidentally in a gas explosion and fire, or so the death certificate says. We are less certain, because the Morgan woman was a hospital attendant, linked to Lisa Braun."

The sound of the name chilled me. It came out of no-where, but also, hearing it, I could feel myself being drawn across a line, into the world of spiders and webs, insanity and violent death. "Lisa Braun," I echoed, unable to do more.

"You know about her?" He sounded surprised.

"My uncle's first wife. Camarillo...that's the..."

"I know about Camarillo."

"They cabled my uncle that she'd died."

"Ah." Dexter peered into his glass, which he wrapped in both large, hairy hands. "I shall give up sex and alco-hol if we find they knew there was still that Austrian con-nection, and left it in place. Sex *and* alcohol!"

"They?" I hated the paranoid ring of it.

"They. Just pretend it doesn't make us sound mad to use the pronoun of the persecuted. *They* are trying to keep something contained. So, something happens that makes Lisa Braun, and even her hospital attendant, dangerous. God knows what, poor women. Some memory, some discovery. And both are silenced. By whom? I know Trulov, yes, our very own Maxim, was there, at Camarillo, within a week of the Committee meeting. Probing . . . something. Perhaps he killed the Morgan woman. Perhaps he set up the killing of Lisa Braun. Or perhaps they were liquidated because he somehow signalled his interest. Russian interest." Dexter sighed. "Emil knew something about the chairman. *'Suddenly' in Russian*. He makes it known, and then he's dead too." He swished the Scotch around his glass. "Everybody is being killed. They . . . this They of ours . . . are destroying memory, but they are unlucky with it. For every one they rip out, two grow in its place. Killing Lisa Braun brought her back to life, in a way." Then, abrupt as a hammerblow, "Schaefy, how did Nancy and your parents die?"

I swarmed with gooseflesh. "Car accident."

"Single vehicle?"

"A truck hit them," I whispered, suddenly seeing the murder in it, seeing the three of them for the millionth time spinning through space into the sea.

"You know," Dexter said in his kindest voice, "it all seems to focus on *you*. It doesn't ever quite touch you, but goes on all about you, as though you were the eye of the storm."

"That's what Trulov was yelling at me, in the cemetery. He said he kept coming to me. But *why*?"

"I don't know."

Then, somewhere in that distant shopping mall, a crowd walked across my grave, and I shivered. "Andrews."

"Yes, him too. Set up, it looks like, loaded with cocaine and launched upon the Nörrström. I was there, Schaefy."

"Jesus Christ." I got up and walked to the window, watched the voiceless crowd across the street. "You know, Dexter, you guys play this crazy game, where bodies are just meat and the really interesting part of it all is how the jolly puzzle fits together, fancy this piece here, try this one just there, how shall we spring this one . . . on the meat! Jesus Christ!''

''Listen. *All* the spiders are out there trying to reckon what touched the webs to set them jiggling so. Some of them try to estimate where the next jiggling event will happen, and a couple pick Stockholm. I do. Trulov did, I saw him there. Why?'' I shook my head, tired of this short, unpleasant contact with the arachnid world. ''Because the Stockholm trip happens around *you*, Schaefy. *You* are in the middle of it, and so we expect great things.''

''But *why*?''

''I don't know. But . . . listen. I didn't *see* Trulov kill Andrews. I saw Andrews in the water, and Trulov on the quay, and that was all.'' He looked away, embarrassed about what followed. ''Then I, um, got the tape off Andrews, and, um let him drift away.''

''Oh, *shit*, Dexter! You're too much.''

''He was dead. At least he felt so to me. Couldn't have been too terrible, dying with your nostrils filled with coke. Trip of trips.''

''I don't want any more, Dexter.''

''So, we, you and I, have to ask ourselves,'' he went on, sweeping past my objection like a parent determined to finish a gruesome bedtime story, ''Who is this They of ours? The Americans? I see activity there, the sweeping over of trails, the odd meetings. But for the life of me I can't read a motive. The Russian presence is better defined. Trulov in California, Trulov in Stockholm. I would say the Russians are doing the killing except I don't think they would kill Andrews that way. They wouldn't care how he died, I mean, and so they would not go to all that trouble to criminalize him. No, you know what happened. Schaefy?''

''No.'' But I did. In my heart, I did.

''Andrews sprung a trap that someone set for you.''

My heart thumped crazily. "Trulov wouldn't have made the mistake. He wouldn't have killed Andrews instead of me." But I knew he had wanted me that night in the cemetery; he had brought murder close, then, and made it credible.

"That only means he didn't do the murder. It doesn't mean he didn't lay the trap. He may even have tried to stop the thing closing on poor Andrews. Look, I've tried putting this together without you in it, and it doesn't stand up."

"But why fill me with dope? Why not plant me in a building foundation, like Atlantic City?" Still, my heart drummed at a foetal rate, almost hummed, with the fear and excitement of being someone's prey. High on fright.

"I think, to discredit you. To make it unequivocal that your death arose from your own criminality, from something wrong with *you*, rather than some external, possibly political source. They wanted to convince somebody." He shook his head unhappily. "You know, staining you only makes sense if you're an agent. But you say, and in my heart I do know, you are not one."

"Nope, I really am not. Maybe I should have been."

"But one thing is sure."

"What's that?"

"You're no longer in the eyes of the storm, old boy. Although . . . I don't see their going after you again any time soon. Andrews' death has set all the alarms flashing, for sure, east, west, everywhere. The person with whom they want to discredit you is not going to believe anything, not flu, not old age. As far as that person is concerned it is impossible now for you to die of natural causes."

"I never see anybody anyway."

"You see Valentina."

"Christ, Gordy . . ."

"The *Russians* are killing people. That's what I said, the *Russians*." I wanted to put my head in my hands. "I love her dearly too," he said gently, "but this is a dangerous, uncertain situation. Worse for me than for you, now I've left my cover lying in small bits over your flat. For what it's worth, I think she is clean."

"You bet your sweet intriguing arse she is," I yelled back at him.

"Take it easy. I shall also keep close."

"Old non-poisonous you."

"Himself." He smiled. "You know, I am not your only friend at court."

"Tell me about all my friends."

"The chairman. God knows why. But if that trap in Stockholm were meant for you, as I think it must have been, he saved you from it. Why?"

"You're saying he sacrificed Andrews to save me. That really doesn't wash, Dexter." *They say he is like a son to me.*

He shook his head impatiently. "That's the trouble with this thing. I can't get the edges to stay down, east with east, west with west. The pieces don't move as they should. There goes a king streaking across the board like a flaming queen. The horses have wings. The bishops are weak as pawns."

"Why did you take the tape, Gordy?" *Let's talk about the common thief side of all this.*

"That's my job."

"Going through the pockets of dead men?"

"You have such a way with words."

"Really, why bother with the tape?"

"The tape is irrelevant."

"Then why bring it here tonight? Or was that just to show Val you had it?"

He would not meet my eyes. "The tape is another matter altogether. I thought you might want to know what they are actually doing."

"Who?"

"The Soviets, at the Centre."

"Oh, Christ, *real* spies now." I held my head.

"You're being wicked. Listen..."

"Let me guess. That wheezing twelve-year-old Model T computer at the Centre is probing the British Crays. Getting all those secrets you people are always selling the Russians anyway." And, suddenly, my spirits lifted, switching to a subject that had the immediacy and importance of a video game. If he were stupid about spies, he was stupid about murder, murder in general, and mine in particular. Another bad prediction from my spook meteorologist.

"The newspapers are off the mark, of course." He had begun to huff and puff.

"Everybody calls it a CIA smear."

"Oh, that's just part of the growing Russianness of the place—everything bad is a CIA smear."

"You think we're probing classified computers?"

"Of course not. That's just the media trying to explain something obscure in obvious terms. We live in a world where a government will spend a million pounds sterling to destroy a five-pound oasis. You can't expect readers to understand the importance of an operation that looks, sounds, and feels like a medium-sized computer peripherals company. It just ain't proper spying, wot? I mean, we need those fast cars with built-in grenade launchers, midget jets, all the mod cons, and women everywhere." Then he grinned. "But there's always *something* going on, you see. It isn't a smear, no, but just everybody smelling something a bit evil, and having difficulty describing what it is. Odors are very difficult to describe, you know. You always have to say something smells like something else."

"Well, over the years, the Russians have done their odd bit of spying from the Centre—you know, running an agent or two here and there on the continent. All small stuff, compared to some operations, but effective, in a small way. But, you know, we see less and less of that old-timey spying now. It's become a kind of dead issue. Why, it's all a decent spy can do to keep up with what's available in the open literature. And people in the east are often less interested in western military secrets than in western

technology. Any lunatic can build an A-bomb in his garage now, if he has the right materials, and money, mechanical aptitude, and schizophrenia enough to do it. No,
it's mainly a listening kind of job now. Things have
changed in the, um, profession.''

"Sounds like the oldest."

"Oldest but one, you nasty sod. Oldest but one." He
took a great mouthful of whisky and swallowed slowly,
thinking, I supposed, about the old days of this "profession." Then, "So we have other ways . . . other *vays* as ge-
stapo say in the cinema. One is to use the networking
abilities of the Centre to probe other people's computers.
It's almost a national pastime in the States now. You can
get into hundreds and hundreds of computers quite easily,
as you know. All you need is somebody—somebody who
can be just about anywhere—to give you access to the
computer you want to probe, and to keep your own system out of the probe itself. It's no good if a light goes on
in Washington or London saying, Oh, oh, those Russians
at that fun farm in Vienna are trying to screw us again. No,
you have no direct probing from the Centre, but you filter
the stuff probing turns up. And, of course, you only crack
those tough computers once, because they can feel you
sniffing around inside. Rather a sexual thing, electroni-
cally speaking. In a very short time, then, your agent is
blown, the necessary operational changes have been made
to negate your find. It is one of those fabulous opportunities for espionage that take you hardly any distance at all.''

"Seem to be a lot of those fabulous opportunities in
your line of work, Gordy."

"Stay with me," he cautioned, holding up a teacherly
index finger. "Try to learn something for once. Now we
fall back to the second most obvious thing."

"Second prize."

"Yes, two nights in Philadelphia. The networks we use
at the Centre are global, and they bypass the various
national telecommunications systems. There are always
scientists chatting via the Centre's computers to scientists

somewhere else. You know, commenting on manuscripts, saying hello, Andrews' office asking Moscow if they can use the loo. That sort of thing. Here, you get encoded material mixed into the regular flow of trivia from the Centre eastward. Doesn't matter where your terminal is. Los Alamos, Washington, Bonn. The network, through the Centre, wires you directly into any interested institution in the Soviet Union. Like having your very own secret radio station, you see? Makes you think it was invented by spies."

"Was it?"

"Oh, no more than invisible ink and the book code."

"So where does the tape fit in?"

"They use the tape transfer every now and then. Usually it's something they don't want to transmit in the usual way. Their source under surveillance, perhaps. Something fragile to begin with, like the signal from a distant space probe...a tiny scrap they feel is of great importance. So, for one reason or another, they want to portage the information back to the wise old Centre, repackage it, and pass it back to Moscow. The message is down in the noise."

"What do the noise say, Bwana?"

"You can be very annoying. Here I am, illuminating the very colon of modern espionage for you, and you're acting bored. But I shall not let you off. Pay attention and learn." He leaned toward me, confidential and pleased with himself. "What does the noise say? It says things like here is the telemetry from a space weapons test, here are radio-frequency emanations that tell you what the new American Cray is thinking, and how. The Russians listen like children hearing supernatural tales at midnight."

"They listen the way you listen."

"Yes. But, more often than not, they're listening to a tale. Know what's on the Michelson tape, Schaefy?"

"What?"

"A chemical signature of the *Trident* submarine. A bit of hydrocarbons of various kinds, whiffs of titanium off the hull, a neutron or two off the warheads, a bit of this, a bit of that." His eyes gleamed with evil mischief. "All you have to do is build equipment that can smell one of them, and your detection problems are over."

"But it has to be garbage!" Years and years ago, the Navy had wanted chemical oceanographers to begin working out the submarine signature problem. We found the chemistry involved took you way, way down into parts per billion and parts per trillion, down where the equipment was handmade, and operated by a talented chemist, and the results always a bit uncertain—a passing fish could defecate some trace metals and destroy your measurement. "You need a very sophisticated lab to make the measurements. Not something you can deploy a hundred or so of in the open ocean. It's shit. Everyone knows it, too."

"Ah, not quite everyone. That's the wonderful thing about it. The Russians trust our technological knowhow. Can you imagine the amount of time and money it will require for them to establish that this 'signature' is just planted shit?" He chuckled. "Nothing is what it seems. The Russians spy on us, and we let them do it, and tell them lies. No doubt they do the same when we penetrate to one of their computers. It's a two-way street, Schaefy. A game. A carnival." He gulped a mouthful of Scotch. "Thing is, most people don't see that an operation like this doesn't have to be something gigantically important. The idea is to run a successful small business, where your government invests a certain amount of money, and you give them a reasonable return. The Soviet Union puts about three million dollars a year into the Centre, the cost of a small rocket, perhaps, or a couple of tanks. And they take out profits in various denominations—time and money saved in developing new technologies, avoiding blind avenues, that sort of thing. Some conversions, possibly, although western scientists are onto a pretty good thing without the help of Lenin. So we believe...we, the United Kingdom of Great Britain and Northern Ireland...that they take out profits of ten or twenty million a year. The investment made by our side?'' He chuckled. ''*I* am about what Her Majesty's Government thinks such stuff is worth, if you see what I mean. America does a bit more by way of sabotaging the Russian profit margin. A few things like the chemical signature of *Trident* can eat up a lot of profits. Interesting relationship, what?''

''Gordon Dexter, master spy.''

''Don't sound so bitter, my boy. It's fairly innocent, by some standards. Just look at us, at me, at them, as if we were competing firms, on a capitalist model at that. The Soviets want a reasonable profit. The U.S. want the competitors bankrupted by false leads. All I want to discover is what form their profits and debits are taking. Secrets? Technology? Shit? What?''

''What indeed?'' But I had lost interest. No one was after me, it was just an old spy's mirage. Dexter was bored by this computer probing and noise-monitoring, the trading of lies, masturbation between superpowers; he missed the murder in his life, and had begun to fabricate it. Shirley Morgan died accidentally, and had nothing to do with me. Lisa Braun died on an operating table, and had nothing to do with me. Andrews had made a stupid, dangerous deal involving a lethal combination of money and dope. My people died in a highway *accident*. There, goddamn you, Dexter, there. These things have nothing to do with me, the killing is all in your head, the death of grey cells, your brain eating itself. I felt the storm drift out of my life. ''I think you're full of shit, Gordy, to use the polite expression. I think you're reaching for murder.''

''Schaefy...there is interest in you. *Russian* interest. *American* interest. *British* interest, if I may humbly say it. God knows *who* wants to know where Schaefer Braun is going next. You are the most exciting thing in years. This computer probing, this business of picking up spurious tapes to screw the competition, is damned boring. Nobody ever killed anybody for one of these tapes, or some exhalation of some computer. Nobody ever did much of anything for that kind of thing. But here we have something better, something with grand, old-timey overtones. Nations, flaming *nations*, maneuvering around one man. No one knows why. But everyone is learning. You are going to be a star, my son. A star. Because the thing all of us sense, that every spider feels, is that you represent something better than our piddling little carnival, something classical and important, something over which we kill one another. Of course it would excite us, of course we would want to see that thing, that element in this, that we...I mean you and I, now...are not seeing.'' His voice was low, level, and angry. ''The reason for telling you all this is obvious. I am your friend, we are bound by friendship and exchanged confidences. I am here to inform you that the world is not just this little nightmare alley of concessions, not just a little carnival of people looking into one another's *computers*—there are spies out there, and they have an interest in you, a real honest-to-Christ interest in destroying you. We are a bunch of very tough, very nasty, very determined and competitive people, Schaefy, and we are getting bored. And I do not wish you swatted like a bloody blackfly. God help me, if you were anyone else, I would see you go down without a quiver.''

''Like Andrews floating out to sea.''

''Do you never listen to your friends? Jesus, you are such a shit, and we try so hard to save you. Go to hell, then, go to hell.''

''I'm sorry, Gordy. I know you think you're doing me a favor. But I hate and resist the idea that someone wants me dead. It doesn't make sense, there's no reason.''

''There is, there *is*. We just aren't to it yet. But we shall be.'' He sloshed his whisky about and studied its amber seiche. ''Let's go back to Trulov in Stockholm. Let's assume this for the moment...he is not there to kill Andrews, or you. He's just there to find out what in hell happens next. Well, this makes no sense, unless we assume something else: two sets of Russian players. And then it begins to parse. Let's call one set the Trulov-

Pastukh group. The Stockholm trip is propitious because they need to pick up one of these tapes. Valentina is slated to go. But then you sign on as well. The Russian spiders are not crazy about an American on the scene, but plan to go ahead with the pick-up, using Val."

"Keep her clear of this, Gordy."

"Oh, Lord, nobody's accusing Val of anything. If your government asked you to let somebody drop a cassette tape into your pocket you'd damned well do it, and don't tell me you wouldn't."

Would I? I wasn't sure initially, and then I remembered the FBI coming around at La Jolla, asking if a visiting Chinese scientist had at any time left the premises during a conference there. I told the man with the yellow shades I couldn't remember, which was the truth, but my reflex had been toward cooperation. What if he'd asked me to carry a plain package to a music store? Enough said. "Go on," I said to Dexter, ruffled at being read so easily, and also beginning to hear a kind of mad sense in what he told me. If all this were possible, anything was, including the idea that someone had tried to kill me in Stockholm and got Andrews instead.

"Good boy. Very well, then, Pastukh sees something coming, steps in and changes the batting order. The chairman does this himself. He puts Andrews in for you and takes Valentina out altogether. He wants to protect you, that's the imperative here. To keep you safe."

"But Pastukh couldn't know about it."

"Oh, very well. He *suspects* it. But the tape is important, the bloody chemical signature of *Trident*. Must pick it up at all costs. So he gambles with Andrews, who will get the tape if that is all that's waiting for him—for *you*, Schaefy—in Stockholm. And to take what you Yanks refer to as the fall if a trap materializes. Pastukh felt the same thing I did about Stockholm, you see, the same things Trulov did. He saw Stockholm as the setting for whatever was going to happen next. Yes, that's how it must have gone."

"But whose trap was it?"

"Their trap. Our They. I think it's Russians from another Soviet camp who know nothing, or do not care, about the tape business. But they are interested in you, because, as you said about Trulov, they keep turning up this mysterious Schaefer Braun."

"Why?"

"I don't know. There is something missing, something we cannot quite see. We almost can, but not quite. But I tell you, the trap has to be Russian. The Americans may be involved in feeding the Soviet listeners shit on the *Further Hymns of Basil Michelson*. But I don't see why they should have any interest in you, much less want you out of the way. You carry no memories, no information, do you?"

I shook my head. "My life is an empty book."

"An open book, you mean."

"I mean an empty book."

"This is grinding you down, my boy."

"Oh? Is it?" Christ.

"I think it's Russians. You must know something about them, without knowing that you do. Some inadvertent contact. Something like that. But they want you put away in some apolitical context."

Looking at him then, this blustering, sorrowing friend with the worried eyes, the frown of a puzzled, determined bear creasing his face, I felt my heart go out to him. Poor old Dexter, telling me all this, opening up a life he had kept sealed all his career, and doing it because he was sick with friendship in the same way I endured the malaria of love. We were ill-equipped for life on the third planet, I thought, *really* poorly prepared. "I'm surprised you've lasted as long as you have, Gordy."

"I'll tell you, I am half giddy with this secret chat of ours. First time, honest."

"A spider's lot is not an easy one." But I understood how wrenching it must have been for him, the trained observer suddenly unable not to intercede, to change the progression of events, like a wildlife photographer who finally cannot let this animal die under his lens.

"I have no regrets. We shall see you through."

"Val..." I began, wanting to bring her in.

"Val hears *nothing* about this," he snapped. *"Nothing."* He relaxed, then. "Sorry for the martial tone, but I think it really is the Russians doing this to you, and she *is* one of them, whatever we may want to think."

"Christ."

"Don't be morose. We have a journey to London in January. We shall all go together, we can even drive it in your forsaken silver bullet."

"We can hit you with a tranquilizer round before we start."

"Excellent. So we have that to do, you see, and you will have your Valentina nearby, along with your husky old bodyguard and cheery guide to London. Should be grand fun. But..."

I looked up apprehensively, hearing a new seriousness. "What?"

"I daresay she will return to Vienna with a replacement for their missing Michelson tape."

Too much. He made me mad. "That's a crappy allegation, Dexter."

"So it may be, and I am sorry to make it." He regarded me sadly. "But watch her when we're in the big city. Watch and see if there is not that busker on the scene, and some brushing contact or another. It is the way of the world, my friend."

"You begin to remind me of Baker Lincoln."

"I have often wondered if he were not an American colleague."

"You could count his legs."

"Touché. As always."

We had come to the end of our evening, the friendship strained by the encroachments of death less than by this new tension over Valentina. I wanted her kept out of it, wanted her clean, and we seemed now to be dirtying her. "She's not in it, Gordy."

"No doubt you're right. Must go. Not a very happy Christmas for you after all, I'm afraid. Very very sorry, sorry to bring you bad news, sorry to cast suspicions. But, you know, we had to talk it out, even if it made you hate me, whatever it did. I really do not want to find you dead."

"I know."

"I think you've also got a code name. One hears it down among the, uh, webs."

"Rumpelstiltskin?"

"Raggedy Andy."

"Distinguished." But I lied, and thought that our They must be Russian after all, because it had been a Russian who'd held me up against a gravestone and pounded my face to pulp a week before. Like killing a doll, for him. That time.

"Bye bye, Schaefy," Dexter said, moving toward the red switch, starting the light and timer going. He was bundled up again, and carried the remnants of his caviar in a plastic bag.

"Night, Gordy. Merry Christmas." I listened to him descend the stairs and pass out into that grey morning, and then leaned against my door to shut it, and locked it with everything the Austrian lock fetish had given me.

For a time, I stood at the window, watching the slight glow of dawn lighting the east, watching the thin blonde man with the bruised face reflected back at me. I believed Dexter now, I believed They wanted to kill me, and that They were Russians. But where I should have felt fear and an urge to flee, I felt only sickhearted: it made me feel so *sad* to have someone want me dead. Seeing me observe him, the man in the windowpane smiled ruefully and said, "Merry Christmas, Raggedy Andy."

3

THE KEEN, breathless sense of danger barely sustained itself beyond that night, devoured by the banality of unrelieved hazard and the absence of action. My life, in a small way, imitated life in Belfast and Beirut, where one must fatalistically accept that every car may be a ticking bomb, every plane a bomber, and where the endless round of frisks and searches induces boredom so dense as to blunt one's sense of personal risk. By Tuesday, when Vienna returned to work, I felt no particular threat from the anonymous folk in passing cars, grim-faced Slavic women with baskets, big men in leather coats. My hand neither trembled nor perspired at the moment of ignition in the BMW, opening the door to my flat did not evoke tripwires and fuzes. There had been what I imagine is the usual decompression to flee these troubles for my avocado ranch in California, to that old room in that old house—and then, the realization that this sanctuary was where my people had been murdered. Location was irrelevant, then. Inevitably, the ability to think about such things reduced to a cretinous, Yes, somebody wants to kill me, but, no, it is not very important; that, and a Micawberish expectation that something would turn up.

One adapts. The reef fish discovers safety in the poison forest of anemones. Normal life returns, there is food to buy, laundry to take out, garbage to empty, work to be done. But there is at the same time a larger consciousness of externals: the knowledge that someone wanted me dead illuminated the realities of others. Thus, the risks that Valentina took to be with me became sharp and real and dangerous, another aspect of this Russian penchant for murder. They did bad things, to me, to her, to anyone. She sensed the barely perceptible change in my attitude toward her, and suspected it derived in some way from talking to Dexter on Christmas Eve.

Val had dropped by the day after Christmas, a few minutes after Dexter called to wish me, and her, if I saw her, a smashing Boxing Day. The two of us had wandered over to the Bürgerhof for some scampi and the desserts she liked. While she ate I watched her, took a gentle, clandestine peek into her eyes, thinking it was madness, to love a Russian woman, but a fundamental madness, ancient and incurable, and secret. And then, as in a reversing tide, the cynic proclaimed in the vast hall of my paranoia: scratch a Russian, scratch a spy. She looked up, her eyes met mine; it was eerie, as though she heard my voices chanting within. "Are you all right?" I asked inanely.

"I? Certainly. Do I not look fine?"

"Sometimes I worry about you."

She laughed. "It is about time."

"No, I mean I really do."

"I was only being funny. Do not worry. We are all right so far. It is an innocent friendship between colleagues. Nothing...*intimate* has happened." My throat constricted, hearing her quiet stress upon the term. "I am not with you overnight, and seldom until very late, by Soviet standards. It is still all right."

"You're no good to me on *Verna*."

"No, or to me either." She shrugged. "I usually take a taxi home at night, even though it is a pretty walk, and not a long one. I generally carry something in a Meinl or commissary bag, to show I have been somewhere definite. I do not invite you to my flat. And..." and her eyes flashed at me, her voice flattened, "my loyalties are well established. I am a respected scientist of the Soviet Union, and member of the Communist Party of the Soviet Union." I felt ideology enter our world like ice filling a winter sea. It made me sad, and put me on guard. Of course, she smelled my defenses going up. We began to end bursts of conversation on cold notes like that one, having nowhere else to go with them, once my guard came up, spooked by a sudden look at her ideology. I hated it—I mean, ideology, and what people will do in its name—and when it surfaced in Val, I hated her a little for letting it swim around in her. Sometimes my reaction went the other way, so that I longed to start from zero, take her aside and hold her and stroke her and tell her everything about everything . . . but that compromised Dexter. I began to wish Dexter had kept to his professional code of silence. And I began to wonder if his confidences didn't carry just a slight stink of manipulation. As I said, one's sense of personal danger becomes blunted; one's paranoia takes flight.

Despite this rough edge between us, Val and I were unwilling to forfeit our quiet time together. Perhaps, we thought if we could just pull along, the rip would mend itself. For, I realized with great pleasure and mild surprise, it was good for *both* of us, to meet at the Bürgerhof or to sit over a cognac in my flat or go through the Gulf of Alaska data she'd brought me that first day. We had attained another plateau in our careful relationship. Now, during our evenings together, I began to tell her about my life, wanting her to know more about me, encouraging her to talk about herself, a life she had thus far kept closed to me. I told her about growing up in southern California, fast cars on the coastal highway, surfing, diving, living near the Pacific; about life on the avocado ranch, probably the last one left in the crush of land development; about my parents, older people, gentle and loving, now dead (Killed, by Russians? There would be a flash of suspicion, and regret, and we would somehow get things as they were, and talk, although the rough edge had sawed through again). But I could only go so far. I gave her Nancy as a quick addendum to this call for the dead. I could not bring myself to tell her of those dreams which returned me panting to the world, or of my dull fears of assassination, for wasn't she, after all, a Russian, and mightn't she, after all, want merely to push my buttons? Okay . . . I talked to her, giving what I could, spinning an illusion of openness to ease the tensions of withholding, of being guarded, with this woman.

For her part, I will say only that I think she tried. To speak to me at all of her real life at home, of friends and parents and people and places, she bucked the deeply rooted national reflex toward secrecy. Russia has never been a society in which one turned openly and confidingly to one's fellows. You had to be careful. Yes, that was the operative term. *Careful.*

She was thirty-five, so that her earliest memories were of the hard life after what she called the Great Patriotic War. Her home had been in Moscow. Her father was a librarian, her mother a dietician, both in the Party. There had been a brother, who died in the late 1960s. Her father had died in 1974, her mother three years later. She had been graduated from Moscow University, and had always worked at the Institute for Oceanology of the Soviet Academy of Sciences.

Her account came to me without anecdote, almost without place and date of birth, lifeless and limp. Nothing lived or happened there—except, I knew *she* had, and wanted to know more, and pressed her gently. When she spoke of her father, I broke in. "What was he like?"

"What do you mean? He was my father." She shrugged.

"No, was he big, small, did he have a moustache, did he smoke a pipe, play the horses... you know, details?"

"Well... he was tall and slender. He always dressed neatly. He did not smoke. He had a beard but no moustache, in that old-fashioned way. He always had a book."

"He loved his Valentina."

"Of course." Then, shyly, "He was my father, after all."

"What about your mother?"

"Oh... a gentle woman, although sometimes brusque. She was the businesslike person in the family."

"Blonde, brunette?"

"Blonde. She and I were fair. My father and brother were dark."

"What about your brother?"

"What about him?" Apprehensive, guarded.

"Tall, short, how many legs, arms, heads? Come on," I laughed, ignoring her mild distress. "I want to meet your family!"

"Tall, like my father. But not quiet. A very loud boy, for Soviet ... sometimes ..." and she stopped. "He was tall. He read a lot."

"Adored his sister."

"Adored?" Her eyes brimmed. "Oh, yes. I would say he did. And I ... I also liked him very much." She would not go further.

Then our conversation would swing back toward the less troublesome world of Schaefer Braun, which had in it only murder and madness, and Russians hunting, all beneath the facile brightness of the California life style. As I say, Val *tried* to tell me about herself, but without much success. Perhaps her familiarity with the deep silences of the world came from losing her family, but I knew there was more.

Much later she did allow me into her life, after, as she put it, "you have points of reference, so that it is not just a cartoon to you." In this later telling, her childhood unfolded in the hard times after the war, but not in the city. Life had always been hard in the country, except there is the sky and land and distant horizons and the sense that one's squalor is one's own, not a cooperative mess. She came from the village of Mikhaylovka, south of the Dnieper River and Zaporosh'ye, a cottage among orchards, very simple, a land with modest winters, for Russian ones, the rolling, arid land turned green with water. (Listening to her I remembered that California, without water, is a desert too.) A few miles to the north, when she was very small, the Dnieper made a great curve to the west, creating the rapids and dunes and sinkholes of a huge flood plain. As a very little child, that had been both the ocean and the Sahara to her. Now it all lay like Atlantis, lost in the waters behind a great dam. By then her father had moved the family to Moscow, into a one-room flat whose walls were stained with years of tobacco smoke and cooking grease, but where the plumbing was inside, though shared; and where the pretty, powerful bitchiness of small-town Party officials was replaced by the possibility of midnight knocks on the door. That had been too much for her father. The possibility, I mean.

Ivan Ivanovich had taken his degree in literature, always a mistake in a book-banning nation, but especially so for a man who, Val said, had deep cracks of sensibility threading through his character—an easily shattered vessel. The Fatherland War had left him full of frightened anticipation, waiting for the next final, crushing event. It never came. The NKVD ignored him, the web of Stalinist Russia never touched him even lightly in Mikhaylovka. His job in Moscow was a good one in those days. Leaders came and went. There were no ruinous interludes in the Gulag. But he was broken by their possibility. Her eyes bright with memory, Val told me, "He could not love anyone, he had no feelings beyond that single one of waiting for the next bad thing. He spent his life tending books he dared not read. He breathed in a world where he was afraid to live. He would look at me with his sad, empty eyes and my heart would break."

Natalia Yashinovna had also been destroyed, but in a different way. Where the father dreaded what was possible in the post-war Soviet Union, she welcomed every possibility, pursued them, and was largely thwarted in her search for the place and power she thought belief would bring. There had never been, in Valentina's memory, that gentle woman of the first telling, but always the Party virago, a desert of a woman, embittered by the frailty of her husband, and by the scorn of the system she resembled and loved. "She spoke like a man, like a bad sailor, you know. She made the world dirty with her curses. One could not bear hearing her. I have seen her strike my father so that his nose bled. But he did not look up, or even move."

Yevgeny Ivanovich, the brother, had filled her life, and covered her with his skinny wings against the mad yelling of the mother, the violent and somehow collaborative erosion of the two adults. "He called my father Gregor, you know, from the Kafka story. Our big insect. My mother he called the Nazi. 'Gregor, where is the Nazi today?' he would say, coming into the house. 'Nazi, have you seen Gregor?' She tried to harm him, but she could not touch him, really." He and Valentina shared a bed and he would lie there, seven years her senior, a child of the war, streetwise and fearless, and hold her in the bony cradle of one arm, and tell her of the world. "He would whisper to me, 'Valentina, you will experience the ocean,' and then he would tell me of great castles, rivers, forests, knights on horseback and ladies in veils and how it was in Turkestan and Siberia and India and Japan and America." She shook her head sadly. "He, who had never been even to Smolensk, told me all. But with his eyes shut, holding me, he would come back always to the sea. 'Valentina,' he would whisper, 'You will see the ocean.' " Val could not speak of her brother without crying, and at first I thought it was the echoing of grief. But when I asked what had happened to him, she replied, "I do not know. I know he is dead or destroyed, like my father. It was for him I went to the ocean. When I look at it, I look at him." And then she would smile and say, "Now there is you. The new Yevgeny." And, hearing the loneliness begin to close around my Valentina, I, the new Yevgeny, would scoop her up, hold her against the possibility of grief. But that was all much later.

Now, in that little interval after the Christmas that followed Brezhnev's death, and preceded my own, she tried to tell me about this destroyed family, and gave me only cutouts and lifelessness. If, from what she told me then, I had constructed Scenes from Valentina's Life, it would have unfolded in a small, neat flat, the father a loving scholar with one arm about a pretty daughter, the mother serious and gentle, attended by a humorous son; I would have given you the softly laughing group around a plain kitchen table, drinking sweet tea and eating cakes in a cloud of cabbage smells, intense, happy afternoons in the country, all somehow intact under the familiar Soviet shadows, intellectually bracing when scholar friends dropped by—sentimentality fleshed out her cautious sketch.

Dexter descended upon us on New Year's Eve, another Friday, the two of us seated on the floor, with chemical profiles from the Gulf of Alaska spread out between us, and each with a glass of very cold vodka, and some commissary cashews in a bowl that we passed back and forth across the little sea of paper. When he knocked it was unmistakably Dexter, for he rapped a virtual tattoo upon the door, letting me know it was he, not someone less welcome. I expected him to be changed, to be more of a spider now he had confessed to me. But when I opened the door, in danced the same old St. Bernard of an Englishman, shouting his hellos to us. "Happy New Year, you two. By GOD I should have been angry to find you alone here, Schaefy, and then had to track down the lovely Princess Orlovsky."

"Hello, Gordy," she said, pleased to see him, but, at the same time, wary, knowing he had said something that altered me.

His eyes noted her wariness, then asked me if I had let his cat out of the bag. I shook my head. "Come," he boomed then, "I have brought all sorts of good things for us. Do you know what tomorrow brings?"

"The Rose Bowl?" I ventured.

"Rose bowl?" asked Val.

"The *Rose* Bowl!" He leaned aggressively toward me. "I ask if you know what tomorrow brings, and you respond with a Rose Bowl? A flaming American football game? Jesus, God, and Mary too, I cannot believe it. Do you really not understand the significance of January first? What happened on that day, damn it all?"

"Let's see. The stone was moved back?"

"Oh, shut up," he raged playfully.

"But he saw his shadow, so it's six more weeks of winter?"

"What are you boys talking about?" Val laughed at us, for Dexter was doing his excellent imitation of a stymied

Colonel Blimp. She said, "In a moment he pops and we have candy everywhere."

We all collapsed in laughter. After a time, Dexter said in the ingenuous voice of a small English boy, "Tomorrow is my *birthday*." He glanced away, feigning pain. "Knowing what I should have done had the situation been reversed, I knew you would wish to celebrate."

"Your birthday!" cried Val happily. "Gordy, how wonderful!"

"How easy to remember," I said.

"Nor is it just any birthday. Schaefy, have you a calculator about?" I fetched it from under the North Pacific printouts. Dexter had removed a bottle of pink Russian champagne from a commissary bag and was stripping the gold foil off the seal. "Now," he said, seeing me ready for mathematical action, "subtract from the number one thousand nine hundred and eighty-three…" He looked at us with mixed pride and melancholy. "…the number…"

"Would you like us to leave the room?"

"You could write it down and we would never know, Gordy," said Val.

"Don't be beastly. From that first number, you subtract the number, one thousand nine hundred and twenty-three…"

"Thirty-nine," I said, completing the function.

"Twenty-nine," Val added, "But I did it in my head."

"Ah, my patriotic friends," said Dexter, denting the ceiling plaster with the cork and leaking pink foam everywhere.

"Glasses," I yelled, running for the kitchen.

"A towel," cried Val.

We soon had it cleaned up and the champagne poured and were all sitting around on the grey carpet, quiet and happy. "You know," I told Dexter after a time, "You give us hope. Turning sixty tomorrow. Spry as a man of… I don't know… seventy."

"Fifty-eight," said Val. "At *least* that spry. And he looks not more than . . . fifty-nine."

"Sods," grumbled Dexter, terribly pleased.

"But as bad-tempered as a bear of eighty," Val said.

"Ninety."

"Sods," muttered Dexter. But he had come to the right place to have his birthday—we had got him across one of those ageing crises. "Now," he said, suppressing his rising sentimentality, "to some business."

"Who can talk business at a time like this?"

"We can," Val declared.

"To the business," Dexter said. "We have exactly two weeks and a day to prepare ourselves for the Eighth Annual Symposium on Biospheric Modeling." He pulled a sheaf of forms and brochures out of his pocket. "Begins Monday, 17 January, Royal Garden Hotel, London. Ends Tuesday, 18 January, at seventeen hours. Fees. Hmm. Rooms. Ah, papers. We shall need a paper."

"I could let you have a couple *Herald Tribs*."

"Hush. We need to think about what it will say, who shall present it, and all of that. Val, *you* give the paper."

"Good!" I said.

"I could not."

"We insist," said Dexter. "Schaefer cannot, he still looks like the Phantom of the Flaming Opera. I cannot. My reputation is such that any mention of me, beyond the usual written credit as one of a team of scientists, causes a stir of recognition that . . ."

"I will give it," she said.

"Thank you."

"Anyway, you stopped him," I told her.

"I have taken a few liberties, anticipating all of this," he now confessed with feigned diffidence.

"Alerted the media?"

"Worse. I have made the necessary arrangements."

"But we do not know if they will let us," Val said.

"Oh, but they will. Among these liberties . . . well, damn it all, a birthday boy of my, um, calibre, is entitled to a few liberties. I put the matter directly to Pastukh and the director, and have received their concurrence in the form of a written, signed, and dated memorandum." He took a giant slurp of champagne. "I have here visa applications for you, Dr. Orlovsky, for Germany, France, Belgium, Switzerland, and Great Britain. I regret their necessity, but as the Soviet Union remains outside the Common Market, you see..." He shrugged with Gallic disbelief. "They are completed. Simply check over the vital information on the forms, and sign where I have put the small red X." He handed the forms to her. "Finally," he went on while Val scanned the applications, "I have booked us into the Royal Garden for late Sunday night, giving us a weekend of transsonic driving in the silver bullet. Unless, of course, you prefer a full week's driving in Wee Froggie?"

We shook our heads emphatically. But he had pushed Val, with the forms, the completed itinerary, as though testing her; and always, when our freedoms and her constraints were compared, it introduced tensions between us. Ideological tensions. "I must hear from my embassy," she faltered.

"Of course," he said. "But the chairman has already helped with that. I think, by gum, you darling carbon persons, we are on the way. A veritable Yalta Conference." But he watched her a shade too closely. Once you knew what he really did, nothing was quite innocent again.

Val smiled finally, I think deciding not to care about the tension, the differences, anything. "You know," she said slowly, "I have never been to any of these countries. I have not crossed the Rhine. I have never been to Paris."

"The Channel," I added.

"Yes. London. None of these famous places." She touched Dexter gently on one of his huge arms. "Gordy, all of this is mad and irresponsible, you know, but it is very exciting for me. Understand how grateful I am that you would force it to happen...for me, I think."

"For us all, my dear lady, for all of La Petite Yalta." He blustered, but I knew she'd reached him, and I thought,

There, you eight-legged bastard, there, raise your phoney flag and draw a genuine salute from this good girl. His eye caught mine and I saw he had been touched.

I raised my glass. "To Little Yalta."

"Hear, hear," said Dexter, eyes averted.

"Za nas," Valentina drained her glass. "To us."

"All right," he said then, "what shall we give them in the way of a paper?"

"Well," I said, "I've got a whole bunch of chemical profiles for the Gulf of Alaska."

"Good, very good meteorology on that. Val?" It occurred to me then that we always looked to her for innovative ideas.

"I think we can develop something. We have interesting Soviet material on atmospheric gas mixing into surface layers during frontal passage in the North Sea. We could combine one frontal passage and perhaps have one rough algorithm for vertical mixing."

"That's good, Val," I said.

"You know, Valentina," Dexter put in with mock seriousness, "Your colleagues will cease to love you if you make it so unflinchingly clear your brain is better than theirs." He said it gently and lightly, but, because of that peculiar tension, it held a threat as well.

She heard it, and flushed. "I hope my colleagues . . . will not cease."

"Oh, dear, she's taken me literally again. Of course they won't, my dear, my God, we look to you for intelligence . . ." He bit his lip, eyes shining. Jesus, how had he stayed alive all these sixty years, being so sentimental? (When I asked him that later, on the road, he said there were times to be sentimental and times to be not. Period.)

"We can call it 'Further Proofs of the Yalta Interaction,'" I said, wishing us back toward laughter and silliness.

"I prefer 'The Orlovsky Proof of the Dexter-Braun Effect,'" said Val. "Or perhaps, 'The Braun Proof of the Orlovsky-Dexter Effect.'"

"No, the Dexter Proof," he said, "and the Orlovsky-Braun Interaction. I like that."

But Val and I were embarrassed; hearing ourselves hyphened together evoked all kinds of impossible things. I chanted, "'The Dexter-Orlovsky-Braun Interaction Applied to Ocean Chemistry Profiles from the Gulf of Alaska, Transmogrified by the Addition of Certain Soviet Surface Layer Mixing Data and a Frontal Passage that Shall Remain Nameless.'"

"Schaefy, I'd no idea you were such a classy colleague. You must run for a seat somewhere."

"'Carbon Dioxide Mixing in the Oceanic Surface Layer,'" Val announced quietly and firmly. We nodded like poor students, grunted our support. "Done," she said.

"Here, now, we've only just begun," he roared abruptly, sailing into heartiness again. He got up with his glass and stormed the stereo. "A little birthday music," he said, sinking back to the carpet. Soon the thin voice of the busker filled the room with

. . . that great Shepherd
Who rules our green pastures . . .

"Come on, Dexter," I complained.

"I miss the Word," he replied, but his eyes had gone hard, telling me to watch her, telling me she was in it too. I glared, warning him off. "What do you think of all this, Valentina?" he asked.

She knew a gauntlet was down, without understanding why he had thrown it. She gave him a cold look, the eyes clear and unshadowed, eyes in which there was not a tremor of deceit. "I think we have heard enough of this music."

"Ah, well," he muttered, returning to the tape deck and turning it off, "I suppose I think the same, Val. I suppose I truly do."

"I must go," she said.

"You must not," protested Dexter. "It's still the old year. I am still young." And his expression told her something more: I'm very sorry, my dear, I hate the suspicious reflex as much as you do. Good, I thought. *Good.*

She smiled for him. "I stay until you grow older...until we all do." When I caught her eye she let me know that it would be no good at all, our beginning the new year apart. The three of us let the old year die, the new one pad toward us like a big silent cat, while we waited, frozen, half excited, half afraid, and let it come.

4

I SPENT THAT NEXT WEEK drawing out selected chemical profiles from the Gulf of Alaska data, still working at home, still what Dexter called "Lon Chaney as to faces." My two partners worked their sides of the carbon cycle at the Centre, and used the computer there to begin melding and shaping the chemistry, meteorological data, and surface mixing. At night we would get together at my flat or at the Bürgerhof, or downtown, closer to Dexter's apartment, talking animatedly over coffee at the Hawelka, as excited as the crowds of students who hung out there. It was exciting because you could see something take form, not a breakthrough, but a tidy, well-substantiated sample of the kind of sequence we wanted. You could see, in this emerging composite of ours drawn from two oceans, what happened chemically—especially to carbon concentrations in seawater—during the passage of an atmospheric cold front. By expressing this mathematically, and by applying some of Valentina's mathematical sandpaper to the many rough edges, we got a very primitive predictor for what should happen during any frontal passage in any northern sea. Okay, it is almost as exciting to hear about as somebody's gallbladder operation, I know, but it was damned exciting to the three of us. We were going to have an actual tool—the equivalent of a sharpened stone tied with vines to a stick, perhaps, but a tool nevertheless—that was also the prototype of what we would be developing on our project. It meant that we went to London carrying a completed first step of our study. Not bad.

"Not bad?" Dexter yelled. *"Not bad?"* He turned like a supplicant to Valentina. "Tell the boy, Val. Not bad. Indeed. Damned good!" He beamed. "Imagine, coming to Vienna on a carbon dioxide lark and then actually *achieving* something!"

"But would you have come to achieve nothing, Gordy?" she asked, whipping him back into line. My spiderish Brit hung his head. "I thought not," she said.

We were at the Bürgerhof, eating lasagna and chipping away at a liter of Austrian red wine. It was a new year, we were doing better than we'd had any reason to hope, and just ahead of us, approaching like a ship, was that trip to London. The tensions had healed, or perhaps been papered over with an unstated truce between Val and Dexter. And I had stopped worrying, or even thinking, about hunters, like an out-of-season stag. They were irrelevant. I almost never thought of Trulov, although now and then the big, violent figure would burst into an anxious dream. In fact, my world had narrowed to the three of us. Fixed in that way, the invitation from Renate to their *Faschingsfest* had surprised me, as if it were a message from another solar system. While we waited for coffee, I told my partners about it. "She claims it will be the bash of the season and says I can bring anybody I want. It's the twenty-second. We'll be back in town then, well rested, well traveled, full of French food. And I refuse to go without you two."

"But this *Fasching* . . ."

"Ah, Valentina, my dear," Dexter began, embarking on one of his sweeping racial estimates, *"Fasching* is the Austrian pre-Lenten carnival season. A time of balls and parties."

"Balls?" Her eyes glowed. "I should love to go to a ball."

"But mainly it is a time for disguises. Disguises going on. Disguises coming off. All of these staid people you see here, having spent the day attending to their dry cleaning establishments, bakeries, and such, after a visit to the mistress and dinner with the wife, who has no doubt spent part of her day with *her* consort... give us only their contented exteriors. But inside, demons roam, setting fires, causing fights, committing murder and mayhem. *Fasching* liberates the demons for a few weeks. At *Fasching* time you are promised everything in the way of earthly delights, but very little is actually delivered. It is," he intoned now, "a model...a simulation...of wild abandonment. It is Austria's Carnival Project."

"But it is fancy dress," Val protested. "I have nothing like that."

"Nonsense," said Dexter. "We shall go as the Yalta Conference. I'll get a cigar, bowler, some Winnie props, you see, and Schaefy here will need a cape and crutches..."

"You're ultragrim, Dexter," I growled.

"Val can be Joe Stalin. Think you can sprout a walrus moustache in two weeks' time, Val?"

She laughed, and so did I, thinking of her in a Stalin moustache. "I cannot go as Stalin. But I think it would be fun to go as something."

"Let's call it a night," Dexter said. "Wee Froggie waits without. May I drive you people home?"

She glanced at me, hesitated, then nodded. "Thank you."

"Ride, old boy?"

"No, thanks. I'll walk."

We filed into the mild, misty January evening. I saw them into the Froggie and waved as they pulled away, driving almost at stalling speed up Gentzgasse, following the bright curve of the tram tracks. Then, subdued and alone and, I supposed, intact, I turned for home, but slowly, thinking... what? Nothing much. Some aspect of the Gulf of Alaska data, perhaps, the final shape the paper might take, something like that; nothing to do with the

murderous games Dexter had handed me on Christmas
Eve. So that it took a moment for me to realize that the
large shadow by my door was a man.

Even while my adrenal gland was screaming *Trulov,
Trulov* like a destroyer honking *sub, sub, sub,* my brain
knew the figure was not that big, that its slow movements
were calculated not to alarm.

"Schaefer," Pastukh said, moving into the light. His
voice was low and soft, even conciliatory. "I am sorry to
intrude this way. Did I startle you?" he asked, noting I was
not quite myself.

"For just a moment, I thought..."

"That I was Maxim? Well, that is a compliment, but I
am not so big as that. Or so dangerous, I hasten to add.
May I come in?"

"Of course." I unlocked the door and ushered him in,
locking up behind us. Because he had acted as if a nocturnal visit by a ranking Soviet scientist was routine, he tem-
porarily removed the mystery from it. "Can I get you
something to drink?"

"I will take a cognac, if you will join me." He had
walked into the front room, and stood there taking it in.

"Standard furnished flat in Vienna," I said.

"Very nice." He turned and fixed me with his remarkable eyes. "How is your face?"

"Okay."

"May I see?" He came closer and, with a touch on my
chin that felt proprietary, turned my head to put the damaged side in light. "He hit you very hard. I am surprised
you lost no teeth. No broken bones."

"I have a hard face."

He laughed. "You must have. But I would not be surprised to learn Trulov had broken his hand. If not on you,
then on the gravestone."

"I hope he broke it off." I handed him his cognac in a
snifter and gestured toward the one large chair. He sat
down, still watching me in that peculiar, intense way. I
took the smaller chair. "Cheers," I said, lifting my glass.

"Cheers," he responded.

Silence filled in around us. He seemed not to notice, but it made me jittery, as his visit did, and his odd possessiveness. "I don't mean to be rude," I began.

"I am sorry. Of course you wonder why I am here. Of course." He studied the amber fluid in his glass. "I have been concerned about you, and have not been able to speak to you since that bad business with Trulov in the cemetery. Trulov is an extremely dangerous man at the moment. To you, obviously. But, for reasons I cannot go into..." he raised a placating hand, "*not* because I do not trust you, but because I do not want to put anything into your head that would make anyone wish to destroy you."

"Thanks." Intended to be ironic.

"Trulov has disappeared since going crazy and beating you. He leaves a big trail of stolen money, however, and ultimately he will be apprehended and taken where he can be...fixed."

"A trail through Stockholm?"

"Ah, you know about that, then? It surprises me."

"It shouldn't."

"No, I meant it surprises me that your English friend has been that open with you. He must be a friend indeed, because he will quickly compromise himself, letting people in on such things."

"I didn't get it from Dexter," I lied.

"Please. I understand your motive for doing it, but never lie to me. I cannot bear a liar. Liars should be drowned." He gave me a long, penetrating look. "Of course we know about Dexter. He knows about us, to a degree. From what you have just told me, I can also say the English have peeled away more layers than I imagined they would. It means that I...that we...are running out of time."

"We? There isn't any *we*." Why did he always grapple me into his situation? Angrily I went on, "I don't understand why we do this, why you keep coming on as the original mystery wrapped in an enigma, or whatever the term is. We have this inscrutable, personal talk in the park, and we have these encounters. You can't *do* this. We don't know one another, we're *nothing* to one another, and yet there is this interest of yours, this 'concern,' this bizarre sacrifice of your *'son'* Andrews..."

"That is very rude."

"I'm sorry to be rude. But why protect me? What does one more American more or less mean to you?"

"Please. Trust me. You have to trust me."

"I don't have to do anything."

"I meant to say that it was imperative that you trust me. I sensed there might be a trap for you in Stockholm, yes. My instincts are sharp. I did not believe Andrews was in danger. I did not think they would be so easily deceived..."

"They. Who are They?"

"It does not matter."

"The hell it doesn't. It matters to me. They're trying to kill me, Mr. Academician."

"For the time, let it just be an evil pronoun. Please."

"*They* killed my parents. *They* killed Nancy."

"Did your English friend tell you that? Perhaps they did."

"*They* killed Lisa Braun."

His eyes flickered at the name. "Lisa Braun," he said in the same sad voice. Remarkable, what he could absorb without flinching.

"Who's doing it?"

"It doesn't matter now. Later, we can talk about who, and why. Now we have other problems to tackle."

"Dexter thinks it's Russians, killing everybody."

"Ah." That was it: Ah. Then, after a short silence, he said, "Listen, and try to trust me. Now..." and he smiled shyly, that odd diffidence again. "Tell me how you feel about Valentina Orlovsky."

I laughed derisively. "I don't answer questions like that." I got up for more cognac, gave us each another fin-

ger of the stuff, and said, "After this I have to say the place
is closed."

"Trust me."

"Trust you to be inscrutable, prying, what?"

"You see a lot of her. You are often alone together."

"She said a Russian beat me up, so a Russian should put
me back together. Is today your day to watch me?"

"I remember your first encounter with me. You said,
'Nancy,' as though she were someone else."

"No comment."

"She evoked someone who used to be important to
you."

"No comment."

"And when you first saw Nancy, you felt that same in-
stantaneous recognition, didn't you?"

"I've said more than I wanted to already." But then I
remembered how, when I had stared, stricken, at Valentina, I had glanced at him and read his perfect knowledge
of my feelings. I had to ask, "How do you know that?"

"Let me tell you part of a story. When I was a young
man I met a lovely girl, one who did not look very different from Valentina, a beautiful girl but, it turned out, a
very fragile one too. That first sight of her touched me
deeply. It was as though some prophecy had been ful-
filled, some witch's charm completed...something of that
kind. I still think of her, after all this time, for this happened during the war. I still wonder what exactly was the
source of that sensation of discovery. I ask myself, Who
was that woman, really? My mother, a grandmother, an
old forgotten nurse of mine, someone from another incarnation? Or was she what she seemed, *that person*, who
had waited for me to come upon her in just that way."
Avoiding my eyes, he went on. "I saw it happen to you
when you saw Valentina. I know we are not close, that we
are nothing to each other. But I have seen *you* experience
a shock *I* have experienced, the same *falling...*"

He was irresistible. "I love Val," I whispered. "She
strikes a deep chord, I don't know what. Nancy did too. I

don't know why she did either. But with Val I think ... I begin to hope ... there's more to it than just some obsessive thing. It's ..."

"The real thing?"

I nodded. "Except ... it's impossible."

"It must seem so."

"She's a real honest-to-God Soviet girl, you know. She has a good career, she's serious and brilliant. She believes all that ..." I stopped myself.

"Horse shit?" he offered, twinkling.

"Thanks. She's a believer. She would never leave Russia."

"Perhaps you will have to come to her, then."

I laughed. "I'm not a believer."

"But you want her."

"Yes, I want her."

"And she?"

"I don't know. She risks a lot to spend a few hours with me. That's a large gift. Maybe she wants me too. But I make no claims."

"It would be so strange," he mused, hardly speaking to me now at all. "So strange if this thing ... whatever it is ... this thing that *could* happen, *happens*. It would be a wonder of the world." He uttered a short, happy laugh. "A wonder of the world."

"What did you decide about your girl? Was she a surrogate for someone else, or was that the real thing?"

"Oh, it was the real thing all right. I never reached a conclusion as to why, and I only saw her that one time, that one day. But it was the real thing. I suppose we have to take such encounters at face value, and not worry them to rags."

"But you still think about her. Why didn't you stay with her?"

"The war."

"But after the war ... ?"

"I could not ... work it out."

"It was important, though."

"Yes, it was terribly important."

"Did it alter your life, meeting her?"

His eyes sparkled at me. "A few months ago I would have answered no, that it did not. I mean, not beyond the cherished memory of having encountered *that person*. But in the event it has altered my life considerably. That is something I have begun to think of more and more, how this contact, brief as it was, was vital nevertheless. Vital in the strict sense of the term. It makes me think that perhaps we had all we were intended to have, after all."

We both lapsed into silence, like two men waiting until our women—our feelings about them, our memories of them—left the room. After awhile, with a look of terrible chagrin, he pulled a beige plastic package out of his jacket pocket, and passed it over to me. "Take this as a gift from me," he said. I unwrapped it and found an automatic.

"What is it?" I asked, shaking my head with wonder.

"Makarov. Standard Soviet army issue. I know you find it humorous, this sudden gift of a gun. But it is no joke. We know they want to kill you, and they will try it when they think they can get away with it. Or when they come to the end of their belief that any of us is worth saving. They are nearly there."

"They."

"They. A few very cold, very tough people."

"Who?"

"Just a pronoun."

"Lincoln?"

"Lincoln. Interesting you would think he was the type. But, yes, be careful around Lincoln if that is how he strikes you." He frowned. "But be a little careful of everyone. Your British friend seems solid, but I know he has not got so far along by behaving like a big puppy. I would not tell him about our talk tonight, for example."

"And Valentina?"

"No. I think Valentina is what she seems. I would consider her a separate department."

"Amen." Then, "And you?"

"I?" He grinned broadly and raised his glass to me. "I am an old magician. I may be at the height of my powers at this moment. But I also know my powers are on the wane, that I am running out of time and strength and...*power*. We felt it that night in the cemetery, my bare ability to control Maxim. I could feel it slip away. But let *us* pretend that I am still the powerful magician, as before, that I can hold off these hunters you have heard about, that I can keep Trulov outside the circle of my incantations, that I can give some helpful magic to you and Valentina, that..." and he gave his diffident grin. "That everything will come right. Let us pretend all of that, and see where it takes us. And let us pretend that we are friends."

"But you're saying that we—you, Val, and I—are somehow tied up together."

"Yes. *Yes.* That is just what I am saying."

I looked into his remarkable eyes. Then, unable to escape the sense that what he proposed was not merely positive but inevitable, I replied, like a man hypnotized by this incomprehensibly friendly, powerful magician, "Then...I will pretend that what you say is true."

5

AS THOUGH SUDDENLY, the three of us were on the road to London, high as kites, even the cynical spider who filled the back seat, his eyes squeezed shut against the high-speed collision he eternally foresaw. Valentina had the copilot's spot, her hair loose and flowing gold, rising and fanning when we got a blast of mild winter air through a lowered window. We carried a cargo of secrets. Only Dexter and I knew we hurried across a land where murder waited. "They'll be out there somewhere," he said at one point along the route, when we'd stopped for fuel and idled around the car. "They will. Trulov will. Because you're here, you see, and everybody, They, Trulov, I . . . all of us know that if you're around the next thing is probably going to happen. You know, you just may be the storm. Are you sure you've told me everything?"

Not everything, Gordy. I haven't told you that we travel under the protection of a great and powerful magician.

Tell me how you feel about Valentina Orlovsky.

I love her.

There, the words had been loosed in the world, uttered, and even now he casts his bones and chants his eerie songs, keeps us safe, brings the whole impossibility somehow within our grasp, everything to a good end. I gave old Austria a broad smile where she ripped past us, the day merely cool, and hazy, the traffic thin, as though exhausted by the recent spurt of holidays. Oh, they were out there, one felt the whole merry band of murderers speeding along, spreading out, greedy for the Next Event. I didn't care. We traveled in a field of magic.

We boomed along like a small, quick aircraft, in a manner and style that the speed limits of America have destroyed there. The BMW held a steady hundred seventy kilometers an hour on the autobahn, and a hundred and forty when traffic let it on the roadways in between, for three hours at a leap, the little car steady as a great ship sailing a quiet pond. The towns flew by. At Linz we turned north, running along the Danube to a fuel stop and our first frontier crossing at Passau, where bemused guards handled Val's green diplomatic passport like a hot coal, and flagged us along. The Russians are coming. Then we were off for the bergs...

"Regensberg, Nürnberg, Würzburg," we sang, happy as city kids in a stolen car.

The German countryside flowed past, even in winter a quilt of greens under a pewter sky, patches of yellow, slashed by sudden stands of black pine, dark as wilderness, the ornamental villages, the odd church spire like a spiritual lightning rod, the only human object raised above the treeline, and here and there a stone quarry, like a grey tear in the fabric. And also, there in Germany, we brushed

the eternal war, passing camouflaged tanks in their leafy
nets, like the captives of steel-eating spiders, being ferried
along the *Autobahn* on flatbed wings; now and then,
through one of the grey, rain-green valleys, an F-16 would
flash, lethal and sudden as a mammoth wasp.

Frankfurt for fuel and a lunch that was like an indeli-
cate Austrian one, and then we descended toward the flat,
grey wash of Belgium, the haze turning to fog under a
white sun. We leapt the River Outhe...

"Drink of these waters and forget," Dexter mumbled.

"You mean the River Lethe," said Val.

"Sorry."

...and the Meuse, the darkness coming down now, the
winter murkiness of the place, lowlands, sweating and
steaming, the constant battlefields of Belgium, still dank,
still evocative of trenches and hordes of silent men disappearing in flashes of fire and pillars of smoke. I glanced
around at Dexter as we crossed this sorrowing land of
graves and monuments, and saw him, in that unguarded
instant, as old and melancholy. Aside from this lapse, he
had accommodated the journey well, scarcely referring to
what he regarded as our "barely subsonic" velocity, except for occasional sarcasms: "Wonderful, the way you
run under the enemy radar." Or, "I say, have the clocks
begun running backwards yet?" That kind of thing.

Val looked at every budless elderberry bush, every tiny
wilderness of pine, every steeple, *everything*, drinking it in,
like a bird on her first migratory flight, enraptured and
free. It was wonderful to see her loose, to see her wings.

West of Mons the weather began to change. The darkness trembled, the silver bullet rocked in gusting cross-
winds, and veils of blowing rain swept us, getting harder
as we left the fast road to thread through the towns between us and Calais. And there, in the early evening, out
among the dunes where the ferries dock, we bought our
ticket and had a snack for dinner ("Not exactly your
bloody gourmet flight, this," grumped Dexter.), and
booked for the next Sea-Link boat for Dover. Even wait-

ing in the line of cars, the rain sweeping us, we could hear the sea, plangent and menacing, and the channel wind, blowing up a gale. "Oh, Schaefer, listen!" Val whispered to me, her eyes bright as flames. "We have a *storm* to go across in!"

We waited an hour, queued up with the other cars, the storm shrieking around us, the radio playing BBC ("At last, we are within FM radio range of civilization," Dexter announced.), the warm, talented English voices doing us a ghost story, anguished Jekyll, merry Hyde. Val glowed, Dexter sulked but listened; I watched the howling night and thought of powerful magicians. A spell had been cast, then, to free me of all apprehension, to clarify my love for this flowering Russian woman at my side. When had I felt so fortunate? Ah, sad to say—the day Nancy had entered my shipboard lab, a hundred years ago.

Farther north, that night, a ferry capsized and went under like a baby *Titanic*. We had only the wild beauty of a channel storm, the tempest, and the wonderful light it kindled in my Valentina's eyes.

Dexter endured the voyage, but only just endured it, going grey the instant we cleared the point of land with its fossil pill boxes and fortified hills.

Val and I made the crossing on the boat deck, open to the crashing waves and screaming wind, but in the lee of the superstructure. The storm turned her golden hair stringy and then made it curl; our heavy coats soaked up the icy water. We stood at the rail; excited and happy with our storm, and, gradually, gradually, became enfolded, our arms around each other's shoulders, like sailors lashed together for the ride.

The ferry turned toward the yellow lights of Dover, the cliffs a low grey slab, like cloud behind the slips. Gingerly we sailed through the breakwater and the ship pivoted to back into her berth, and faltered, unable to hold her bow against the wind. And, even as she poised uncertainly, across the water came the valiant tug. "Look," I yelled to Val through the wind. "Look!"

She flashed me a delighted face, and I grabbed her hand and led her up another ladder to the open deck lined with orange benches. The rain had stopped, but the wind made it bitter cold there. We could not take our eyes off the tug, pitching wildly, maneuvering toward the bow of the ferry, almost colliding but somehow holding a few meters clear, and then the lines flying across the narrow, violent space between ships, while we drifted slowly, inexorably toward the small lighthouse on the jetty. Then, at what seemed like the last possible moment, lines were across and the tug quickly took up the slack, holding our bow against the turning forces of the wind; our unseen captain backed us in against the slip.

"Jesus!" I whispered enthusiastically. I was grinning like a boy, soaked with spray, giddy with sharing the adventure with Val, who looked up at me then, her hair tangled, her eyes lighted from within. I gathered her into my arms, as it seemed I had wanted to do forever, and felt her come to me, her whole body leaning into mine. I held her and held her, afraid to let her go, my heart cracking with joy. "Val, Val, Val."

"Do not, Schaefer. We do it, but we must not talk about it." She leaned back from me, still clutching my arms, and took a long, careful look, and then she grinned broadly and came back against me. "But it *is* good, is it not?" I only nodded. Good? Yes, my fine girl, you could call it that.

We found Dexter standing like a poisoned bear on the boat deck, grumpy and embarrassed about his seasickness. "Good God, look at you two," he complained. "You're soaked, you'll catch your deaths."

"Old salts," I said. Val nodded her vigorous agreement. We barely noticed that we still held hands.

But Dexter saw everything, as always. His big hooded eyes took us in, read what had happened, and, in a quick gesture I may have imagined, gave a kind of limited blessing: Congratulations upon reaching true impossibility. "I would like to suggest something," he said then, resuming his miserableness. "I would like for us to stop at Dover tonight and drive up to London tomorrow. We are hopelessly delayed now. I am not myself. It will be past midnight if we make the drive tonight. The weather is abysmal..."

"And so forth and so on." I looked at Val. "How does it sound to you?"

"I would like that," she said. We could not stop looking at each other.

"Good. Good." His voice carried traces of a moan.

The British woman at passport control looked us over, and, after a careful reading of our passports and landing cards, stamped them and handed them back, almost with a shake of her head. Her face said she thought us a droll lot, the soaked Russian and American, and the green Brit in back. I laughed aloud and Val, understanding me, did too, and then even Dexter had to come in with a few hars. "Lor' 'elp us, we *do* make a strange group, at that," he gasped.

Customs waved us through and I pulled off into an Exxon station on the English side of the barricades to tank up. Dexter joined me at the pump, alert now, the sickness expertly suppressed.

"There," he said, "across the roundabout—do you see what I see?"

It took me a moment to understand what Dexter wanted, and another to recognize the big Russian standing just outside the ring of light. The man was so unlike the Maxim Trulov I had known, even at this range of more than fifty meters—the Yves St. Laurent suit had been replaced by a heavy turtleneck and anorak, and boots; he was dressed for the sea. His beard was sprouting then, and he wore his hair very short, almost a crew cut, the combination totally changing the broad oval of his face into a pale rectangle between blocks of dark hair. Our eyes met. The contact made me nervous, like a boy before a fight, but my nerve did not fail. I thought, There, you see? The magician is with *us*. I grinned, pleased with my reaction, raised my hand, and, with Dexter gasping his disbelief, gave Trulov an upright and unmistakable finger: *Fuck you!* For a time the Russian looked at me, his face frozen, the eyes hidden in beard and brow; but I felt his rage come across all that pavement like a hot wind, felt it rampaging around inside his head, because I knew it—*it*, not Trulov, had picked me off the ground one night and beaten me pulpy.

The Russian still watched from his post by the curving motorway ramp, imperturbable, ready for anything. For all he knew we could be calling Scotland Yard. "What does he want?"

"I don't quite know," Dexter replied. But he did, or I believed he did. Outside, I told him so.

"Very well, here's my best estimate. We have to assume he's not simply gone mad, and if we do that we ask ourselves, why has he put himself in such a desperate situation vis-à-vis his own side? I mean, I don't believe he is operating under orders at this point. No, he's on his own, a dreadful state for a Soviet agent, operating independently, living off bogus credit cards and false passports, staying just about one step ahead of his own people. He knows if they get him now, it's bags of psychotherapy, of a very damaging kind. But what would keep them off? Proof. Of something. He knows something, you see. But knowing something, even down in your bone marrow, is no proof. If he can't get proof, then he will have to get a shield." He frowned at me. "I have a feeling he looks to you for both."

"He could have got to me in Vienna. Much harder to do here." I had begun to sound very professional.

"He wants to see what happens. I don't think he's our They. Whoever goes about killing everybody in your university classbook, or whatever. A killer, oh yes, and a bad boy, and all of that. But he wants to know who They are too. Maybe...maybe if he learns that, the proof he needs will drop into his hand."

"You know, Gordy...you sound as if you know the beginning, middle, and end. Have you seen this flick before?"

He laughed. "God, I wish I had. I am rather far along, for an underfunded, superannuated spider who's arrived late on the web. But the pieces are still a bit unpredictable. I doubt I've got as far as Trulov has done."

"We could call the police on him." The yard, Inspector; let's call the Yard!

"That only sends him back to the Soviet Union. As it is, he's almost a scout for us. He needs to find our They almost as badly as we do. Besides, I'd rather have him loose and hunted in England. Keeps him properly miserable, keeps ninety percent of his brain tied up with survival housekeeping, you see. And we can outsmart that other ten percent. Or I can do."

"Thanks." Then, "I don't want Val to see him."

"Not to worry. Unless I am very mistaken, he'll be out ahead of us on the London Road." He chuckled. "Sorry, Maxim, but it looks like a long night on the road for you, watching for cars that never come. We're stopping in Dover." But when Dexter turned to me all humor had fled. "I have to say one thing that will put you in a rage, Schaefy. I would have had to be blind not to notice that you and Valentina coming off the ferry were not the same pair as boarded at Calais. I think that is perfectly grand. But I ask you to hold one thought. We have mounting evidence that our crazy pronoun, They, is Russian. Not American. Not British. *Russian*. We have only two Russians in this panto at the moment. Trulov, we are reasonably sure, is an outlaw, and if They are Russian, They are going to neutralize him."

"The other is Val."

"Yes."

"You're right."

"What?"

"It puts me in a rage." I went back to the car and had the motor going by the time he squeezed past Valentina into the back seat. She regarded me curiously and I told her, "Sorry to be so long," hoping to prevent discussion.

"I do not mind. I enjoy watching the traffic. Everything is backwards."

"Inside out," Dexter corrected. "Rumania and El Salvador, they are backwards. Great Britain is inside out."

Trulov had disappeared when we came out of the station, and we drove down the seawall toward town, turning off at the Holiday Inn. I was glad not to be driving farther, and there was an odd sense of security in pulling into something so familiar. Dexter guided me around to parking that could not be seen from the street. Then, wet and more or less hearty, and grand good friends again, the three of us trooped inside and asked for rooms. Despite delayed sailings and bad weather, they were running less than full that night, and could give us three singles on one floor. Dexter apportioned the keys, giving Val and me the two adjoining rooms at the far end of the hall, and himself the one which put him between ours and the structural column containing elevators and stairs. Guard bear. We agreed to meet at eight for breakfast and told one another goodnight.

The rooms were your standard Holiday Inn models, large and rather well-appointed by all but the best European standards, and an odd, plastic comfort to an American far from home. I hung up my folded bag in the closet to let the clothing unwrinkle, and dried off as best I could. The minibar yielded a Heinekens and some peanuts. I unlocked my side of the connecting door and settled in to wait for Valentina, whose eyes had held that bright, willing light on the ferry. My mind chanted the mantra of the lonely: O please please please, while I lay back on the big bed with my wet shoes kicked off, sipping the beer. O please please please.

Nothing happened.

I wandered around the room, had a second beer, and watched what I could see of Dover. The rain had resumed, the wind slapped the window with sudden bands of water.

The town was just a few points of light. I thought of Trulov, out there in the cold, windy rain, waiting for us on the London Road, and of how his rage would roar tonight while he waited in vain, remembering that saucy middle finger of mine. I looked at the connecting door, opaque and unmoving as a great slab of stone, and decided that holding her on the ferry was all one got, and that, in some respects, it was more than one had expected. The only other Russian in the panto. I wished people would stop poisoning my well. We had put in nearly eighteen hours, including the long wait for the ferry and the delayed crossing, and I was jumpy with fatigue, and ready to give up on Val, whom I had so much wanted to hold through the night . . .

I must have dozed off, for when she touched me gently I was fathoms deep in another dream of death, and thrashed around while she whispered, "Schaefer, Schaefer." A long, breathless kick for the surface, then, and finally I managed to get up on one elbow, dazed and disoriented. "Val?" Or had the voice, the touch, been part of the horror of my dream?

"How can you be asleep *tonight*?"

"I had given up," I told her, coming almost fully wake. She sat on the edge of the bed, a dim light from her room flowing in behind her, haloing her hair, showing her silhouette through a thin gown. "I thought you'd decided to be careful."

"But on the boat . . ."

"I know. God, I *wanted* you to come. But . . . look at you. You are so beautiful."

I pulled her down into my arms then, and for a time just lay there, cradling this cherished person. We kissed, her gown fell away, so that I could touch her gently, and tell her, "*So* beautiful!" and stroke her with hands that shook, as we made, built, constructed, tested, fabricated love. We came together as nervous and compelled and shivering for one another as birds, mindless, focused, drawn from the ends of the earth to this single time and place, and fluttered at one another, mating on the wing. Then, with her head warm against my chest, her golden hair fanning over me, I was moved to say, "I love you, Val." But halfway through the phrase her finger appeared upon my lips, and pressed me gently back to silence. There is this, said the silencing finger. There is this; it may be all we have, take it, take it . . .

Toward dawn we slept, and then I awakened from a nap to find her gone, the door closed to her room, the window going pale and pink. She lingered in my mind, as much like a dream to me as my dreams were like memories.

At breakfast she was fresh and radiant, her cheeks flushed with pleasure, a beautiful woman's compliment. I suppose I radiated something too, that morning. Dexter looked a hundred and fifty, perhaps because the seasickness had robbed him physically, but also because I knew he'd spent a nervous night listening to strange sounds, waiting for that *thing* which happened when I was anywhere around.

After coffee we retired to our rooms to wash up and pack, agreeing to meet in about an hour. That wonderful connecting door, more a veil than a stone slab now, opened again, and there she was, lovely, and hot, presenting her body so that one simply had to undress it, and touch it, and smooth its light yellow down, and taste it.

We were late meeting our grumpy, sickly guard bear in the lobby. Late but very, very happy.

6

THAT WAS THE AXIS of our London trip, then, this mad lovemaking—this raising of an entire city of it, and adjacent farms and airfields, ports, railroads, Wall Streets, Ringstrassen, Santa Monica Freeways, and Embankments. At the Royal Garden Hotel we found ourselves once more in connecting rooms, with Dexter down the hall, blocking, as he put it, the usual approaches. We took our meals, and did some sightseeing and saw the O'Toole play, in which everyone seemed a little drunk, but which we all enjoyed immensely, especially Val—"superman" she may have been, at that. We saw *The Beggars Opera*, and disagreed about its ideology; disagreed, and quickly put the matter away, not wanting any hard surfaces between us. Between outings, and even between sessions of the Eighth Annual Symposium on Biospheric Modeling, we made love. For we could not keep apart any longer; we had done that. Even a twenty-minute coffee break, if it caught us at one of those urgent moments when the other's gravitation stretched like an unseen web across the meeting room, was enough to make us grab another interval with the other. Or I would go alone, suddenly itching and lonely for my Valentina, and there she would be, expected, wanted, but also the beautiful surprise, standing in the connecting doorway, naked, glowing, pretty as a doe. It was very sweet for us, and very sad, for we understood tacitly that it was meant to last us all our lives, this one great flowering intimacy. All our lives.

The other large excitement came that Monday afternoon, when my lovely Russian girl mounted the podium and delivered, in her pure, slightly accented voice, "Carbon Dioxide Mixing in the Oceanic Surface Layer." It had the effect on me, and on Dexter too, despite his black hunches, that the sound of a child's voice rising in song would have produced. I was stupefied with pride. There she is, I thought, there she is, and . . . she's *mine*.

Afterward, during the coffee break, we leaned together, the three of us, proud of ourselves for offering good work. The questions had sounded interested, there had been a response, which is everything when you give a scientific paper. Between the podium and the table with the coffee urn, Val had been approached by an Indian asking for more of our rudimentary model, and a Canadian who wanted to talk about his work on the Mackenzie River delta, and then, while Val and Dexter and I huddled with our coffee and hubris, an American came over, compact, sixtyish, assured. "Very fine paper, Dr. Orlovsky, Dr. Dexter, Dr. Braun. My name is Carney." We all shook hands. "I very much liked the way you mixed oceans. Not the obvious sorting at all." He buzzed like a somnolent bee, and I wondered—I guess the others did to—why he had bothered to come over. His small, broad face watched me, though, and there was that gleam of a predator's eye; I wish everyone had not looked so predatory to me then. A closer look at this Carney made me decide he was probably retired military in business, electronics perhaps. The type abounded in the States. Except, goddamn it, he did watch us all too closely. I felt obscurely the panic of an antique savage, having his identity swallowed by the white man's camera. "Fly over?" Carney asked.

"We drove," I told him.

"Of course. You must own that silver BMW downstairs with the Vienna plates." I nodded. "Fantastic machines, pity we don't make something like that at home." He chatted a while longer, then gave a slight bow. "Hope to see you again before this thing is over. Pleasure meeting you. And my compliments again on your paper."

Dexter watched him go, his brow knitted with suspicion. "Pull the other, it's got bells on," he muttered after the small, trim figure.

"Is he, They?"

"He has the odor of a They," Dexter said. "But is it our They? Deuced difficult to tell."

"Now what are you boys talking about?" Val asked. Laughing, high on her delivery of the paper, the attention, the freedom of this first migration. But not so high that she did not watch Carney closely too, noting as he disappeared among the crowd, "He reminds me of someone. Someone I do not like."

That night we celebrated with a fine dinner in the hotel's rooftop restaurant, with a view across the Royal Kensington Gardens of the sparse London skyline, the skyline of a city not yet built, like Chicago a century ago. Between dinner and brandy, Val and I danced to a funky

American quintet that played everything but rock. We were clumsy together, at first, and then grew graceful, dancing as though we labored on that city of love we had under construction.

"Val, know why the Baptists banned lovemaking standing up?"

"No."

"Because it's too much like dancing."

But, lying with her late at night, the only sound the muted roar of London and the even breathing of her sleep, I would think of Russians killing everybody, and of there being only two in this panto, and of Trulov out there in London, walking his rage, waiting for proof... of what? What did he suspect that was so difficult to prove? That the world was round, the planetary orbits heliocentric, market forces smarter than economic planners? What? Into this peaceful but untrusting mental neighborhood would come, eventually, inevitably as the ghost to the banquet table, the untimbered voice of Basil Michelson, the inane *Further Hymns*, the drum going boomity-boom, the bogus secrets: *Trident*'s chemical signature. And what other kind of nonsense did America transmit to the Soviet Union aboard old Basil's hymns? Trips to the moon on gossamer wings, snake oil, Brooklyn Bridges for sale cheap, superconductivity that did not conduct, Basil hymns of the republic...? Ah, *that* went too far! I headed back toward deep water, thinking of how bad information would be goading to any nation, but almost unbearably so for a country that hated being kidded as much as Mother Russia. Call her anything but less-developed. Did I really care how they felt about being fooled in the east? Nope. I care about my Valentina. Pastukh had said: I think Valentina is what she seems. He *thinks*. Watch her, Lincoln said. Watch her, said Dexter. Then I would look down at my sleeping Russian, my brilliant colleague and partner in building a megapolis of affection, and silently ask: Valentina, are you what you seem?

The shadows never entirely lifted, you see. And then, on Tuesday, they began to close around our idyll, as I suppose shadows are intended to do, and idylls intended to be.

The shadows crowded in when she said, "I need to run an errand this afternoon. Do you mind?"

"Shall I come with you?" I asked her knowing everything there was to know about her errand, with unexpected heat rising like flame behind the words.

She shook her head, hearing the anger. "I shall go soon after lunch," she said, unable to look at me. "And be back before dinner. Please, Schaefer, please..." Tears stood in her eyes.

"Okay." Bloody okay. She was swept away from me then by a Japanese scientist to talk about frontal passages observed in the Yellow Sea. It seemed perfectly symbolic, her being taken from me. Christ, I felt like Othello on a bad day, then, crazy and alone, guilty in the certain knowledge that she was the sweet voice of life, and the whisperers were the voices of death, and yet I could not turn away from their: *Watch her.*

Dexter came over to say, "Judging from your pallor and spoilt boy expression, I gather Valentina is making her run today." I nodded. "Sorry about that, old boy. I truly am." He shrugged. "But I imagine you don't want me wringing my hands overmuch in front of you, right?"

"Right again."

Val left after lunch, and a quick, clandestine brush of my hand, and then out into one of the black cabs of London. I watched her out of sight, and then went in for the afternoon session. Dexter stayed close to me, like a St. Bernard knowing how we sometimes lie down to sleep forever in deep snow.

When the sessions ended we filed into the bar with a bunch of others, and began to experiment with the Royal Garden's martini. I had not been this sad since Christmas Eve. By nightfall, Dexter had gently extricated me from the place, and taken me upstairs to sleep and dream of death and crazy women. And then, as on that first night in

Dover, the connecting door opened, the shadowy figure advanced, stood over me. I cried out at her touch.

"Schaefer, where do you go when you sleep? It is like visiting a prisoner." Still, she held onto me until my heart sounded like a pump again, until the frightened eyes had focused, and the dreamer understood that he had been miraculously restored to life. "Where do you go?"

"Don't worry, don't worry." But, awake, I saw her face, drawn and unhappy, and I knew she had been given a tape, and seen it was the one Dexter had played for us (played it just so she would know we shared this dirty little secret of hers), and understood that we therefore must know all about the errand she'd just run for her side. "Where did you go?"

She shrugged. "Leicester Square, I think."

I thought of Leicester Square, imagining trees and theatres, and restaurants and queues, everywhere, queues. "What's the weather like?"

"Drizzle. But not very cold."

The streetbusker approaching her through the fine rain, then, singing his ludicrous "hymns," and the girl, Dexter had said there was a girl, dropping another tape...where? Into her coat pocket? Into her pocketbook? It worried me not to know. Ah, shit, I mourned within. "Glad you're back."

"Yes, I am back."

Who asked you to do it? Pastukh. Did you have tea with Trulov? "We had a few martinis," I told her. "Made me sleepy."

"I know. Here. Put your head on my breast."

"Ah, Val."

"Yes, yes, your Val." She rocked me gently, and soon I slept, gliding down a narrow room to nurse, and yet not frightened, the protagonist and dreamer finally united in hungry complacency... I shook myself awake. "I best get up."

"If you like, yes." Her face was tense with secrecy, her eyes spoke of secrets causing pain.

"I love you, Valentina. Whatever comes, okay?"

She put her admonishing finger on my lips. "I love you, Schaefer Braun. I love you and I love you. Now...we find Dexter, and we go to eat. But in a moment." She held me against her breasts, like a giant baby grazing pink-tipped hills, the happy man with the sick heart.

Dexter had returned to the bar, and we found him waiting for us to appear, a little drunk, and, as ever, tentatively bristling. "A man could get a liver as big as a wine cask, drinking while you two burn." He waved a conciliatory hand. "Sorry, that was disgusting of me. Very sorry. I shall make it up to you with a grand fish dinner, the best in town. Come." And off the three of us went, old spies and young, for an evening in the narrow rooms of Wheeler's.

By the time we emerged, almost too full to walk, I had decided that the kind of spying our countries asked us to do (although mine had not yet asked me) was mostly of the silly variety, and that it was madness to make the tape pickup important. *A.*, it was no big thing to do what your government asked you, unless it is destructive and immoral, like burning a village. And, *B.*, the *Trident* signature was a load of crap anyway. So, bursting with lobster and good wine, I was perfectly happy to have the Russians tangle themselves in what Dexter referred to as their Silly Code, and spend the careers of a few good men and women discovering you can't make real-time measurement to smell missile submarines. Rots of ruck, tovarich. And, *C.*, Val and I were the important thing that was happening in London, and one must not forget it. She felt me relax, I think, for our hands began to touch, we could feel the night ahead of us, more flights, more matings on the wing.

The American, Carney, joined us at the elevator, looking meticulous and bland, as contained as a granite slab. "Evening," he said easily, his sleepy voice friendly and casual. We nodded our greeting. "Well, that's it. How'd you like it?"

"The symposium? Fine."

"You people staying on for awhile, or heading back to Vienna?"

"We leave in the morning."

"Paris?" I nodded. "Then on to old Wien. Very nice. Have a good trip." He gave us a modest salute on his way out two floors before ours, and we ascended.

We told Dexter good night outside his door, but he gestured for us to wait, and went inside for something. When he came out he handed me a sealed manila envelope. "No great mystery, and I want it back when we're in Vienna. But for now...just hang onto it for me, if you would." Then, embarrassed over raising dismal possibilities, "If anything should, um, befall me, so that you cannot return it, the contents are yours. *Both* of yours. Not riches. Just a few pieces of a game."

"Night." I took the envelope to my room and stuck it into one of the thousand and one pockets of my bag, and tried very hard to forget about it. Below my window London roared with late night traffic—I doubted the city ever got quiet, as even New York does, finally, very late, or very early. I thought about poor Trulov's rage, the brutal creature who made him want to kill and kill, and Dexter, suddenly worried about death.

But even clinging to such externals, I could feel my heart cracking like a dried nut around the prospective loss of Valentina. We had only tonight, and tomorrow night in Paris, and probably that would be it, that would be our lifetime together, an interlude like the one Pastukh had described: brief, the real thing, vital, in the strict sense of the term.

I was far away and bitter about impending loss when I heard the connecting door click open.

Valentina entered and put her head against my shoulder. I put my arms around her. "Don't worry," I said, not knowing what else to say. "We'll be okay."

"No...no, we have a lot of trouble now. I thought that for just a day or so we could avoid the...I do not even know how to call it...the *sides*." She shuddered against me. "But we have this other thing instead. We have this thing in which everyone but Valentina is allowed to know we have seen Maxim Trulov in Dover." She put a finger to my lips to block the rising protest. "We have spying, violence all around us no doubt, and everyone trusted except your Valentina. But Dexter, what is he? No, do not tell me. And you, what are you?" She peered into my face. "What are you?"

"The eye of the storm."

"But why?"

"Let's leave it."

"Even now, you *still* think I am in it."

"It doesn't matter what I think. Listen. Listen. I love you. I can't turn it on and off, like a stove. There it is, it goes on and on, and when I think you're in this cruel business my stomach begins to hurt. But the love goes on and on. And when I know you are not in it...and I really do know you are not...then it goes on anyway. A lot happens around it, but nothing essential changes. I love you. Whatever comes."

"But I am *not* in it. It is no good, your not believing me."

"I believe you. Of course I *believe*. But then something will happen, some bloody-minded Russian thing, like Trulov beating me half to death...and even though I know you aren't in it, I doubt my knowledge. Like a priest trying to reconcile murdered babies and just gods."

"So, at this moment, you doubt."

"At this moment, I am damned happy to hold you in my tired, sad old arms, my girl. That's all." I touched the blue shadow of her cheekbone. "Stay with me?"

She nodded "We have so little."

"I know."

We clung together against that single certainty, that we had too little time.

Dexter met us downstairs for breakfast, after some calling back and forth, and then we paid our bills and got our bags out of the rooms. None of us had much to say. We were sad to be leaving, sad that there had been a kind of failure of trust within our ranks. Before I left the room, I self-consciously stuffed the Makarov into an inside pocket in my parka.

We took the elevator down to the garage and began looking for the BMW, which had languished here these several days. It appeared in the line of cars at the same instant that we heard the scuffle, the sound of men working on each other, grunts and fleshy thumps, and then we saw them, poised in combat like a statue of David and Goliath, the smaller one bent back over a red Ferrari, his silhouetted face gleaming with blood, but nothing passive about him; his thumbs groped for the big man's eyes, and from the breathing you knew both men were working hard. Suddenly the small man twisted himself so that one leg kicked free, and he brought it smashing down on the big man's bandaged left hand, and, in the second that bought him, ran into the darkness, fast as a pursued boy, his footsteps echoing away down the other parking levels. The big man leaned against the car, holding his left wrist, as though by shutting off the blood he could also stop the painful message. He did not try to follow, but straightened up, and then saw the three of us, as calmly as a tiger seeing hunters in his grove. "Wait, Max," I said, and against all instincts, drew out the Russian automatic, cocked it, and pointed it at his chest.

"He has armed you, then," Trulov said quietly. He stood about ten cars away, his back to the bright slit of light that marked the exit. We could not quite make out his face, but he could see ours, read my intentions, tell the type of gun—it had a peculiar sweptback look, as though carved by children.

"Time to talk," I said in an uncertain voice.

"Who was he?" Dexter asked. "The one who ran."

Trulov shrugged. "How should I know? Strong little devil. Resourceful and well-trained. But I know he is one of *them*."

"A Russian?" I asked.

"An American. The Americans are killing everybody."

"You're wrong," Dexter said, the meteorologist clinging to his prediction, "It's not you. But it is Russian."

"Stupid people." Trulov's voice rose with impatience. "I had one of them in my hands, and you intruded, and now he is gone. I need proof to take back, and I have it, and then you burst in upon me and I lose the goddamned thing." We heard his rage stirring, the howl within, which he barely suppressed. "So many stupid things are happening," he continued in a low, controlled voice. "And now I come upon this American... yes, *American*...tampering with your car. No doubt I have saved you from your stupidity. I am less fortunate. I am running out of time to make my case. So I shall tell you this one thing, you, Braun, and you, Valentina Ivanovna. I must find another one of them to take home with me, and if I cannot, I shall take you. And I shall do it. Warning you may put you on guard. But," and he emitted a shrill, unhappy laugh, "I see in your faces how much good that will do you." He turned and walked toward the lights.

"Max...wait...I'll shoot." I said this knowing there was not the slightest chance of my squeezing the trigger at this man's back, and also knowing that there was even less chance of my hitting it if I did.

"WHAT*EV*ER!" His scream filled the garage, and for a moment he looked back at us, swept us with his hatred and rage, then fled like a great bat into the pale light, leaving only his echo.

Dexter said, a trifle doggedly, "It isn't the Americans."

"Why not?" asked Valentina. "We have one here with a Russian pistol."

"Where did you get that?"

"Pastukh."

"Gunner Braun," he mused, finding it droll. But then he forgot about us and frowned at the car, troubled and oddly resigned, like Hector, seeing how the scales suspended. It was frightening to see. "Of all the many things

I hate, I hate *these* bloody things the most," he said to no one in particular. "Schaefy, I'll need your keys." I handed them over and he stepped toward the BMW, signalling us to wait where we were.

"Gordy, call the bomb squad."

"Schaefer's right."

He shook his head impatiently. "At the moment I don't want to bring a lot of curious people into our lives. Something gigantic is floating in this little pond of ours, and I almost know what it looks like, and I don't want it all buggered up with other people now. Besides, you can't have your bomb squad without the press." Gingerly, then, he opened the passenger door and leaned across to unlatch the hood. The *bong* of the catch releasing made Val and me jump, and look at one another, and utter nervous chuckles. We watched Dexter lean into the engine compartment, gently feeling his way along electrical leads, running fingers along the crevices below. His face dripped with perspiration. He wore a look of absorbed fatalism.

Val said, "How does one know you are not in it, with your Russian pistol?"

"Another doubter?"

"I see how doubt begins."

"Anyway, I'm not in it. I mean, I'm not one of Them."

"Prove it."

I handed her the Makarov. "There." Then, "Your move."

She handed me *The Further Hymns of Basil Michelson*. "There. They were to be given to Vera Trulov." Her eyes held the light of Right Triumphant.

After a touched, embarrassed moment, I said, "Val, let's get through this together."

"I think you are right, we have to be together. A few days in London, and a bit of Paris, are not going to last us forever. Besides, we are so thoroughly alone in the world, we have to keep together. For warmth."

"Babes in the woods."

"Not quite that," she huffed mildly, "but, yes, very much on our own. I believe Dexter, that Russians are killing people. But I also believe Maxim, that the Americans are. That leaves us very much on our own."

"Thank God we've got Gordy."

"And the Academician," she said. I thought, yes, our powerful magician.

Dexter had disappeared behind the car. We heard him scuffling around; then, grinning, he stood up and displayed an apple-sized blob of grey material with something like a spool stuck into it that sprouted colored wires. It was a shocking sight, for we had been drifting, with Dexter's noises those of a mechanic searching for a rattle, and now here he was with a bomb. "Jesus," I said.

"Detonate on ignition," he called proudly, like a doctor bragging to a father, "It's a boy."

"You are wonderful, Gordy," said Val. We stepped toward the car.

"Wait...wait, stay there, you two. Over there, between cars." Cautiously, then, he put down the explosive on the asphalt floor and slowly shut the hood. For a moment he leaned on the front of the car, then went around to the boot and unlocked it with my key, and peered and felt around inside. His face began to clear. Leaving the boot open, he unlocked and opened the driver's door, and carefully bent under the dashboard, a big hand reaching up to feel the wires there. Finally, apparently satisfied that all the wires went where they were supposed to, he stood up, rubbed his back, and told us, "I think that's got it. Quite good, but not *that* good, eh? I just want to crank it, and then we can set out, Carbon Persons." He swung himself in and settled onto the driver's seat, and we heard the engine cranking and that other, ripping sound...

In that instant time crystallized about us all, cracked at its edges, splintering inward and inward. We heard the skittering noise, the quick race of fire behind Dexter's feeble, *"Damn!"* as the world dissolved in fire and smoke

and sound, flying glass and metal; as though the world had
ended.

As though the magic had failed.

7

THE FACE WAS NOT QUITE RIGHT. There was something
missing in the eyes, possibly, or the smile curved too much.
Ah, *there*: on either side of the red triangle of my nose,
straddling the apex, the picture showed two thin red L's.
Yes, adding them seemed to do it. That, and just a bit
more grin, and crosses at the end of my painted smile. I
posed before the mirror. Not a bad job. A checkered shirt
and overalls, a standard European sailor cap, vermilion
fright wig, white gloves. The real mouth behind the black,
uplifted curve sagged unhappily. There he was, I thought,
Raggedy Andy.

"You have to see this, Val," I called, and in a moment
she entered, and clapped her white-gloved hands, and tried
to smile behind her crescent of mascara. "That is quite
good." Then, "It is terrible, to be able to laugh a little and
still be so sad."

"We may always be a little sad."

"I know."

For we were like the parents of a lost, unburied child,
unrequited mourners; or dogs convinced of a dead master's imminent return. Time had shattered in some fundamental way during that moment when everything
snapped in the hotel garage. We were trapped in the instant, like bugs frozen in amber.

In some ways, Dexter's death had been like Emil's, for
every trace of it had been quickly removed, there were no
remains to view, no family to inform, nothing. *Nothing*.
There had been the flash and shock wave and immense
sound of the bomb, and the shower of glass and flesh and
metal and fabric through the garage. The blast had
knocked us down, and the barrage had cut us only slightly.

All the excited hotel employees had to do, once they'd
rushed into the smoky cave, was dust us off and cluck
hopelessly, waiting for the police. Then they had arrived,
bobbies and plainclothes detectives, with their polite,
pointed, irrelevant questions. And then they had begun to
go hopeless too, and milled about with the employees until the other men began to arrive, tightlipped, calm men in
Burberries no more like our lost Dexter than I was—but,
still, his other colleagues. Despite their differences, there
was something in their knowing look around the ruined
garage, in their eyes, from which all sentiment had fled,
that reminded us of him. We were sent to a vacant room to
wait, with a bobby at the door, I think for our own security. After all, we were the bombees.

Later, the closed, contained men had come in and asked
if we had any idea why such a thing would happen, enemies, that sort of thing? Had Dexter been—eyebrows
arched interrogatively—*preoccupied*? You worked together, the three of you? Scientists? Carbon dioxide?
Hmm. The unasked question floated in the room: Did he
tell you he was one of us? They would have to answer that
one without me.

This round completed, they moved to the softer side of
the incident, which made them squirm and scratch themselves, and rub their faces, and their eyes slide around like
bad boys'. Would we be staying on in Great Britain, perhaps to arrange something for the deceased? Purely symbolic, in view of the rather, um, great *dispersion* of the,
um, remains. Possibly a memorial service with colleagues? We understand he had no surviving family. They
went on and on, rendering our huge, lovely man into
smoke and ash and the gravel of old bones. And I thought,
No goddamn it, we are not going to punctuate him for
you. He roams the earth now, like a freed bear, you can't
see or hear; his spider days are over.

We had felt our enemies in the evening rush of London,
felt them staring down the carriage at us when we took the
Heathrow Central, where signs told us how to alert offi-

cials of suspicious, untended luggage. London has become a city where one must think about bombs, although not yet on the Lebanese model. In time all cities would be full of bombs, I thought, bombs as common as firecrackers used to be, the kids excited over that fantastic new grenade from Israel, or the old-fashioned three-stick dynamite classic, with the real sputtering fuze. Instead of eating a little video glyph, you could blow up a family. Grief trailed us, like a black bird taking its time, flap, glide, flap, calm as a British spy, ready to land on our shoulders and bear us down and down. After we had checked our bags and went to an airport bar for another drink, since it had become a drinking kind of day, and the early television news showed us the smoking garage entrance at the Royal Garden Hotel, said one person had died, great damage to cars within, the Angry Brigade had claimed credit.

"The Angry Brigade," I had murmured to Val. Biting her lips, eyes gleaming, she nodded.

Our black bird had pounced, then. We tried to hide in the crowded terminal, where people took wide detours to avoid us, not wanting to hear, or share, or, most emphatically, *catch* what we carried. We had been almost unable to speak even after we'd boarded the Austrian Airlines DC-9 that would restore us to Vienna, although after another drink and a long silence, we did, picking up the threads like people returning to a dream.

"Why did you tell them so little?" Val had asked finally, emerging from her own reflections.

"The police?" She had nodded, watching me. "I didn't want them picking over us. Dexter thought it was so important to keep them out that he gambled, on the car." For a moment I couldn't speak. Then, "I was just doing what I thought he would have done."

"But you know who put the bomb there."

"I didn't when I saw him. But, later, yes."

"The American."

"Carney."

"Yes."

"An American, or a Russian who sounds like an American?"

"He is not Russian."

"Okay."

"It is all so futile, not knowing who, or what, or why. But Trulov does."

"Yes, he knows. I expect he'll let us know, too."

"You told them nothing because you think I am a spy."

"No comment."

"Before the bomb, Schaefer, remember, we decided we were together. Are we?"

Dexter haunted me with his skepticism: Only two Russians in this panto. "Sure," I said.

"You have to trust me."

"I know." But I had to look away from her, then, out the scratched plastic oval of the window. I will try, Val, I will definitely try.

I had unpacked in my flat and thought of action. Gunner Braun. When I came to Dexter's envelope, I hefted it, then took it into the kitchen, got a giant vodka, and went to the living room, taking the big chair he would have taken, in a room which, on that evening, clanged with his absence.

As he'd said, it was just pieces in a game. We all work in our own way. I liked yellow legal pads. Val used unlined pads of an odd European size. Dexter worked... Dexter *had* worked... from three-by-five cards and printouts and scraps. The envelope contained a thin deck of these cards, plus notes on pages torn from newspapers and magazines, wherever he happened to be when some Gestalt struck him.

Emil's Xeroxed photo of the Soviet soldiers raising their flag over Vienna was there, with the inscription

VNEZAPNO
13IV45

and, in Dexter's expansive hand,

"Suddenly" in Russian
Suddenly in Russian
Suddenly Russian???

Another scrap carried a soiled, often-folded photograph
from the Centre's last annual report. It showed the chairman, director, his deputies, the committee members, perhaps twenty men, smiling white faces on dark suits.
Stapled to this was a three-by-five card that said

> *Schaefer or schäfer,*
> *name or noun?*

A six-week-old carbon copy of a letter from Dexter to
someone unnamed was folded into eighths. I spread it out,
and read:

My Dear Fellow,

I write to send the regards of your oldest, dearest
friend, and also, as you might expect, to ask a small
favour. I have a theory I wish to corroborate or destroy, and either will do, if it be well done. My theory
is that, if someone were made to vanish, so that, from
a given point in time backwards, he ceased to exist—
no memories of him, no family, not a toeprint in the
sand that proved he had ever lived—we, by which I
mean you, I, and Her Majesty's Service, could still
detect him if he had ever touched our island. I believe this because I do not think the vanishing I refer
to would have been coordinated among allies, and
because, in time of war, there is all that slippage to
and fro. But there is also that odd parallax one finds
when observing points from Britain that have also
been observed from another country. You and I both
remember many cases where people and events that
were quite invisible to others were obvious to us, and,
sad to say, vice versa.

If you would now lend me your considerable talents and machinery in this, I would like to find out whether you have in all that rubbish we keep eternally *any* trace of a male with the surname Shepherd, or that name in any other language—"Schäfer" in German, for example. The parameters of the search are that he would have existed (for us at least) only during April 1945, on which date every trace of him would vanish, along with him. In short, we are looking for a man who twinkled very briefly in the U.K., and whose existence has been erased everywhere else.

Of course all this is for your eyes only, Burn Before Reading, and other highest secrecies. I do not need a reply before about eight a.m. tomorrow. Many thanks. Love to Edna.

He had signed it *Dex*, which surprised me. Dex. It must have been a nickname at school or in the services. The reply, dated four days before we left Vienna, was stapled to the carbon.

Dear Dex,

Thank the Lord you need these favours, else you would disappear from our lives, and leave us destitute. An odd request, I thought, and an odd search, embarking on your "theory," so that it surprised me very much to turn up anything at all, and especially to turn it up so quickly.

One U.S. Army Captain Andrei B. Shepherd was in England overnight in April 1945. The trail is very cold now, but here is what we have reconstructed. He arrived in England (we cannot say from where) intending to march from one aeroplane to another and fly out again. But weather intervened, he had to find accommodations for the night, and he is noted as having passed the night of 10 April at RAF Waddington, departing the next morning. He saw no one, spoke to no one. But he *did* sign for his board and billet. (One wants to go Ho Ho!)

On the other side, there is *no* trace of him in America. No social security number, no security classification, no telephone or driver's license, no educational record, no family, no friends. We have seen none from here, and our rather solid sources over there (with whom I traded heavily on your behalf, I might add) have found none. At the same time, we have indications that our sweep has caused some small excitement, which is to say, they know we want to know and are wondering why.

If you are curious as to how we sorted through all this so quickly, we simply began with every American known to have been in England during April 1945 and checked for any previous history. Many of them required some extra digging for a previous history. But only one fell out as having never existed anywhere before a certain day in England. A further check shows he did not exist after that day, either. We have many sudden disappearances in wartime, but disappearing soldiers vanish less uniformly (no pun intended). Interesting error for our Allies to have made, eh? Well, it could not happen to a better bunch of boys. Some day you must tell me whether the fumble was merely red, or red, white, and blue. Please eat this letter after you have done with it. And note that, when you are hungry again, Edna and I *both* expect a night at Wheeler's. She sends her love, as do I, along with grudging respect for that incomparable nose of yours for secrets!

James

Dexter and his incomparable nose for other people's secrets. My spy.

Newsclips in the packet included one describing the accident that killed Nancy and my parents, another the death of a Camarillo hospital attendant named Shirley Morgan. A short notice about the death of Lisa Braun, one that no one could have read. "Good bye, Lisa," I whispered, sipping vodka. "Good luck."

And then I had come to something titled *Card of Names*, names carefully printed in little round bubbles, like the symbols on a PERT chart, or the spherical atoms in a three-dimensional model of a molecule. I was there, floating in my bubble. Val was in hers. Lisa Braun. Every Austrian Braun but Fee. Pastukh. Lincoln. Maxim Trulov. Vera Trulov. Emil Dashko, crossed out. Andrei Shepherd, followed parenthetically by *berger, Hirt, pastore, pastor, herde, schäfer.* (I remembered suddenly: "Why'd you and Dad name me Schaefer?" "So the Good Shepherd would notice you, son.") And more names: Raggedy Andy, Spendahl (*The* Spendahl?), had been crossed off, with the note, *Stroke, dead Bethesda Med. Ctr, 10 Jan.* Cybelle had been crossed out too, with a question mark at the end of the deleting line. The last entry on the cluttered card was: *Check Carney.*

There'd be no checking Carney now, old ghost, he's already trapped and eaten you. Not even meaning to, of course. The usual scattering fire, building a pile of bodies with the intensity, the determination, of a nymphomaniac screwing an out-of-town football team.

On the table with Dexter's scraps were a few bills and residual Gulf of Alaska data sheets, and the invitation from Renate. I had picked that up and read her note again.

Remember, bring who you want, Schaefy
we not have Russian here before.

And I had thought then, looking at the tacky card with its birds and bats and funny hats and masks and balloons around the edges, the card of a girl about to have a tenth birthday party, that Dexter's *Card of Names* collected people who had nothing in common except me. People who, with one or two exceptions, never met, never touched, never spoke to one another. Let Dexter's names be a rough guest list, then, get them all into a room together, and show them . . . what?

Show them you know they're killers.

Show them Raggedy Andy . . .

Val had asked, when I told her, "Who is this Raggedy Andy?"

"It's my codename."

"But who *is* he?"

"A rag doll." And then, in a memory as misty as a dream, I saw the big round happy face with its triangular nose and big smile and black eyes peering into mine from just an inch or two away. Where had he gone, my rag doll? My mother used to read me the saga of Ann and Andy, and once, rapt and full of fantasy, I had asked her where mine was, and she had . . . faltered. "You were so small," she'd told me, "how could you remember such a thing? Well, anyway, he went to someone who needed him more than you did." Had the memory shaken her? I began to think so. It did me, for it had the quality of that other memory that was a dream. "Raggedy Andy is the boyfriend . . . no, the consort . . . of Raggedy Ann, a rag doll discovered in an attic."

When I had told Val what I could remember of the tale, she said, "Then there is also Raggedy Ann. No doubt that is *my* codename."

"They aren't after you," I had protested. The pronoun had stopped sounding crazy to me.

"If they are after you, they are after me." She grinned. "If you go as Andy, I shall go as Ann." She had paused, then, and finally added, "But I tell you one thing. These are not Soviet codenames. We would call you Ocean Star. Chemist. Newton. Kepler. Something like that. We would never have such a whimsical codename. Never."

Now, adjusting her red-yarn wig, she asked, "Do you think they will come tonight?"

"I don't know. It'll be interesting to see who does and who does not."

She said, "Everyone invited, all of them disguised." And I thought, You most of all, the old real thing, dressed up like a rag doll. We had taken some trouble to find pictures of Ann and Andy, finally running them down at the Amerikahaus library in town, and then doing what we could to imitate them. Neither costume was quite on the mark. But Val had done a splendid job assembling hers from odd pieces. She had found a blue dress with red and white figures on it, and had added a round white collar to it, and then covered it with a white Ukrainian apron, fancier than the doll's little pinafore, but surprisingly effective. Her red-and-white-striped stockings also filled out somewhat better than Raggedy Ann's. Behind her disguise you could feel the excitement. It was going to be a dangerous evening, an evening tweaking the noses of violent men, and she could hardly wait for it to happen; like crossing the channel in a bad storm. The prospect of confrontation lightened her eyes, flushed her cheeks.

"What a doll!" I told her.

Val had come by that first night back, very late, breathless from the walk, and I fixed us both a drink and clung to her for a time. When she saw Dexter's puzzle pieces, she asked what they were. So, because Dexter had given us both the envelope, I spread them out for her, thinking, Okay, okay, here it all is, like someone walking defiantly under a ladder. She looked them over in her careful, penetrating way, that eye of hers making every connection, missing nothing—not the eye of a cop, but more that of a highly skilled film editor, making sense from a tangled universe of celluloid. Finally I asked, "What do you think?"

"He was looking for these killers?"

"The Russians who are killing everybody."

"But *I* am a Russian, and I am killing nobody."

"Somebody is."

She had heard that barely imperceptible tremor of belief in my voice, the imperfectly concealed failure to com-
mit. "I can feel you choosing, saying to yourself, For my
Valentina I shall dive from this cliff. You see me as a risk."
She faced me, smiling, eyes bright. "It would worry me,
except that I *know* I am trustworthy, that I do not spy, that
I do not kill."

"I'm sorry."

"No, do not be." She straightened, the young Soviet
woman of the Pioneer posters again. "I am not some
lightweight person. When I tell you I do not love you, then
I do not. When I say that I do, then . . . I do. It means that
from then onwards, everything in me is for us, not for the
Soviet Union, not for the United States, but for the two of
us. I cannot give you up. I cannot cast away what we have
discovered, no matter what it means for us, even if it
means always missing my beautiful Russia." My Pioneer
looked at me with her eyes full of tears, fatigued by this
superstitious man. "You ask me what I think, and now I
shall tell you. We have this man Shepherd existing in the
west, in England, only for one night in April 1945. Shepherd, in Russian, is *pastukh*. *Pastukh*, in English, is shepherd. I think about Emil's message, *Suddenly in Russian*,
and, because I have declared myself with you, I do nothing about it. Perhaps I turn my back on the existence of a
dangerous enemy of the Soviet Union. Or I think of Pastukh as Shepherd for that one night in England. Perhaps,
in doing so, I give you my countryman as a wartime spy.
Take your pick." Her lips quivered. "Trust me or do not
trust me, I cannot do more."

I had held her for a long time, rocking her, hanging on
to this woman who had come to me like some golden
snowbird out of Russia, mythic, the fulfiller of ancient
prophecies, a woman who felt like Fate to me, although I
could not know why, not then. I walked her into the bedroom and laid her out, tucked the down quilt about her,
and kissed her goodnight. And she, exhausted and sad,
sank quickly into a frenetic sleep, so unlike her, the feet

flinching, the jaw working on the somnambulistic question: *Yevgeny?*

OUTSIDE IT WAS SNOWING, the black rooftops and streets grey, the flakes tumbling through the cones and spheres of light. Our cab waited by the entrance door, the white flakes flickering in its lights, dusting the dark metal. "Snowing," I said, sticking the Makarov into my pants under the loose sailor's blouse.

She grinned. "I hope you do not dance too close with that in your pants."

"What a reputation I would have."

"Man of iron." She watched the snow. "I hope it snows two meters." Her voice longed for Russian winters.

"You're going to hate southern California."

"Please." We did not kid about going into exile. "When the time comes, I wonder if I shall be able to do it. I may spend my life missing Russia."

"Shh. We may have to go to Mars, or a Jovian moon, to be safe. Don't worry about California now." For it looked like a light-year, to me, the distance between this present moment and a time when we moved freely, made our own choices, discovered a life together—or decided there was none after all. Maybe two light-years.

I helped her into a fur coat, and slid into a dark peacoat of my own, and off we went, into the temporary light on the stairs that ticked away as we descended, bearing the flowers one always carries to one's hostess in Vienna. We crossed the pale sidewalk to the Mercedes cab. The driver, so big and soft that he filled the front seat like a bag of cotton, grinned at our costumes. We told him where we wanted to go, and he turned up the hill, slithering in the thin soapy film of new snow, bound for the nineteenth.

Tuna cans wrapped in gold and silver foil and filled with wax and wicks threw globes of trembling light beneath the falling snow, like fairy spirits leading the way to my uncle's door. He met us there, his large face made larger by a leather flying helmet and goggles. Fee looked festive in her three gold foil anklets and a white clown's frill; her tail bone quivered in a Doberman wag as she smelled me behind the costume. When he recognized me, he beamed, revealed his big yellow teeth, and embraced me, saying, "Schaefer, ach, I cannot tell you who is half these people," and gave his grand shrug. I introduced Valentina, and he bowed, clicked his heels, and brushed her hand with lips carefully held a millimeter off the glove. But when he looking into her face, when he saw through her makeup, his eyes gleamed, and he grabbed her in a desperate but fatherly hug of welcome. Then he swept us inside, into his life, which tonight had been transformed into a nursery for wild children, all balloons and streamers, and chandeliers and lamps swaddled in red and orange and blue crepe, so that the milling figures crept about in dim reddish light, like the crew of a submerged submarine in combat.

Fee nuzzled my leg and I scratched the stiff short hairs on her tough skull. "You must be Cerberus," I told her, "but they got you wrong . . . next time, three *heads*." And to Val I added, "And this must be hell."

Among the lost souls were witches and goblins and racing drivers and an American Indian, people in old-fashioned bathing costumes, black female cats in leotards and net stockings, clowns and Arabs, kings and queens, diplomats, chefs, friars, nuns, vampires, motorcyclists in menacing helmets and plastic motocross suits, a skinny Sumo wrestler, the demon barber of Fleet Street, Snow White, Rose Red, perhaps two hundred people, all masked, all hidden from us, no one what he or she seemed. We would have our little confrontation, we would take off our killers' masks among camouflaged strangers, in strangely lighted rooms, a place loud with a babble of languages and voices, and western rock thudding away like a malignant brain tumor. "Let's find a drink," I yelled to Val, who nodded through the din and trailed me toward the sunporch, where they had set up a bar.

The party was solidly in progress, as the Viennese abandoned identity and inhibition, and were stalked by the usual international crowd from the UN and OPEC and the embassies. Danes and Swedes from UNIDO, and a big German from the Centre who peered into every bodice, and the mandatory mad Hungarian who dominated every dance, and here and there Brits and Americans bent in solemn cocktail-party conversation, ignoring the riot around them, like colonists ignoring natives in revolt. Middle easterners were there, serious and sinister, watching the women like buyers for a distant stable, their wives quiet and miserable, frightened by the fun.

And fun there was aplenty.

The Austrian couples foraged madly, for they knew, as the foreigners did not, that the spell lasted only until dawn, and then it was back to spouses again. Those hot fannies in your laps, my men, those peachlike breasts, that furry mound steaming beneath your hand, those lips, those eyes, they pass your way just this once. When you meet them in Meinl's those same eyes will look at you like mirrors, without memory or warmth.

And there was that Austrian orderliness inside the madness, that leavening against chaos. Everyone would get sillier than all the Habsburg princes on wine tonight, but hardly anyone would get really drunk—New York or London drunk. An American or Brit, or a Russian of course, might be expected to overdose on alcohol. An Austrian would not. The occasional violator was treated with gentle despair, like the victim of a nervous breakdown, and laid to rest somewhere away from the revelers, to regain his senses, and, in time, to have full citizenship restored.

We took our glasses, Val's of red wine, mine of vodka, and wandered the place, trying to see a face we had seen before. Our hostess intercepted us in her evening gown, gave me a cold hug, and shook Val's hand, looking her over appraisingly. Her gypsy face was hard and determined under its thin, festive veil—she had the aura of a lady who's decided to set herself on fire. Don't, I thought. Whatever it is, don't. "I like your costume," I told her, bending close so she could hear me above the music and multilingual roar.

"*This* not my costume," she declared with an unhappy laugh. "Not *this*." Another bad laugh. "I put *my* costume later. You see." Her eyes frightened me, and I was glad when the young Hungarian danced her away, sent her flying back to hell.

"What do you say about a woman scorned?" asked Val.

"Hell hath no fury like a," I replied, adding. "But, please, don't."

"A gypsy."

"A crazy gypsy."

"That is redundant." She frowned. "But I do not like what I see in her face, Schaefer." I didn't either.

At first I recognized no one. It was just a crowd gone a little wild, writhing in this Martian light beneath torrential music. But it was also a crowd with people in it who wanted to kill me. Us. I was there, I realized then, for the same reason that Trulov had appeared in Stockholm and London—this was the next place. A house full of strangers, big men hurrying toward me, suddenly revealed as a laughing Austrian when the monk's cowl fell away, or the visor raised. A big motorcyclist came by wearing one of those plastic space wars costumes, the face hidden by dark glass, the hands gloved. I was certain it was Trulov. My blood went cold with certainty, and then he had hurried to the dance floor without seeming to notice me, getting it on with a pretty baby Canadian in a black cat outfit.

Where were the people from the Card of Names?

They were nowhere to be seen. I decided perhaps they had not come after all, for I found no Pastukh, no Lincoln, and no Trulov among the men at the party, although I saw people with their general shape, size, motions. I tried to keep some space between the two of us and all these wild, careening others, souls who were lost only for the evening.

I saw Lincoln then, or perhaps some epidermal sensor felt the sweep of his hatred, hatred like the blood-colored light in the room. He had come as a comic-strip diplomat, in tuxedo and red sash and pince nez. An Austrian girl I didn't think he knew clutched his arm hard against her breasts, wanting him to keep her afloat, dully waiting for him to speak. With a peremptory shake of his elbow, he freed himself, seeming to toss the girl back to the mob, and pushed through the people, his eyes fixed upon us, the glasses shining like copper coins. "Quite a party," he said, coming close enough to be heard.

I stepped back, keeping distance between us. "Everyone seems to be having a good time."

"Well, a time, anyway," he said. "Dr. Orlovsky." He gave Val's hand the fake Viennese kiss, and made her a quick bow, and fabricated a cold smile around the central ache of his dislike, and said, "Two dolls against the world?"

"Why against?" I asked.

"I don't know... you seem so *united*, I suppose. Sawdust across the Iron Curtain. Universal themes."

"We're just poor old Raggedy Ann and Raggedy Andy," I said. "No big thing." Nothing moved in his eyes, hearing the names. Nothing. They were like stones, like those still, silent movie glades that are always full of Indians.

"How was London?"

"Smashing," Val replied quickly. "My first visit." She gushed for him, responding to his palpable misogynism. But she watched him as keenly as a bird, looking for the liar's shadow. Although he gave back very little, we both saw his knowledge of everything. "Gordon Dexter is a joy to see London with," she added.

"I'm surprised he isn't here tonight."

"He was... otherwise engaged." Talking of our lost friend, my throat began to ache, and I saw Val's eyes gleaming.

"I think," Lincoln said, "we need to clear the air." His face radiated good humor and sincerity. I asked myself, Would you buy a used car from this man? But that was what he did, he became the salesman, the entrepreneur. "I don't understand your game, Schaefer. Academician Pastukh told me about Dexter. Terrible business, that random violence over there. But he asked me to keep it quiet, I don't know why." He turned to Valentina. "Are you Russians in it?"

She flushed. "We 'Russians' are not. I believe it was one of your men. A Mr. Carney."

Lincoln flinched, and so did I, because it came from nowhere—no, it came out of that odd, able film-editor brain of hers. She might have slapped him. His response put me squarely with my Valentina, where I was supposed to be. "Carney?" he asked in someone else's voice. "I don't believe I..."

"You must remember him," she went on. "Not a large man. American. Retired military perhaps. Sleepy-looking and cold, I thought. A bit like you, Mr. Lincoln."

"I'm afraid this is a bad joke," he muttered, his face pale as dough. "I know no one named Carney, much less anyone you could legitimately call *my* man. You must tell me what the game is, Dr. Orlovsky. Some Russian variant of Dungeons and Dragons, I imagine."

"Get Raggedy Andy," I put in. "Old Russian folk game."

"Raggedy Andy means as little to me as this Carney person."

"I know."

Val had made him look haggard and old, the doll on the offensive, the diplomat beginning to crumble, and retreat. "And your Captain Shepherd," she went on, her eyes blazing away, as certain of her rightness as Raggedy Ann had ever been. "What about your Captain Shepherd?"

"Jesus," he hissed at her then. And, to me, "Schaefer, you don't know what you're doing, what you could bring down."

"The *Americans* are killing everybody," she said, vindicated at last. One imagined all the other toys and farm animals and talking plants shouting: *Hooray for Raggedy Ann!*

"You're mad," he whispered, and backed away from her, into the crowd.

She let him go and turned to me, her face bright with combat. "I thought Shepherd was a Soviet, because Dexter was so certain my people were doing all this terrible . . . *shit*." From her, the ugly word could have cracked glass. "But I see it clearly now."

I didn't, not then. I was too far from forming that clear an idea from the information we had. Impossible connections were Val's special province, that recognition of unexpected, unconventional linkages that ignored context, form, place—all those elements which compel us to remember the familiar face behind the lunch counter, and to forget it on the street. It worked with interactions in the physical world. It worked with people, Carney seen as a function of Lincoln, Shepherd as the reciprocal Pastukh. A kind of mathematics, then.

We would have pursued Val's insight, but something had happened in the room—that abrupt stillness of the reef beneath the big passing shadow; the roar of voices dropped, then spread into pools of silence, until the only sound was the steady thumping of the stereo, like a heart beating in a dead body. Everybody stared at the doorway. There, with people moving aside for her the way they would have for a woman drenched in blood, was Renate. She wore a faded blue and white *Dirndl*, and a grotesque wig of pale braided hair, and advanced like some bizarre aryan ad for craziness and death. Her eyes were stony with booze and something else. And I, seeing this mad creature cross the floor toward me, heard my own internal chorus singing: Here, Schaefer, *here* is your real thing, sex dressed up as Bo Beep, familiar and horrible, the love of your fucked-up life, my friend, the essential truth about you; here is the repulsive object of your nasty obsessions. I watched her approach like a bird does a snake, stupid and hypnotized, unable to look away from this primitive Medusa, who had stalked down the long road of time to fix me with that ossifying mix of fear, and horror, and desire.

Val cried out, "Schaefer," but seemed lost even then, another stranger in this sea of them, someone else drowning in the wake of my crazy ship.

My uncle rushed into the room looking wild as Othello, and grabbed his gypsy, who wrenched herself away, smoothed her tattered *Dirndl*, and again stepped toward me. But he intercepted her, and slapped her hard enough to put her on her knees, to bring a black worm of blood from her mouth. He slapped her again, hard, *hard*. You could hear her spirit snap.

Without looking up, she murmured in the dull voice of the tranquilized, "I silly woman. Schaefer unkindly for me. So I unkindly for he." Now she raised her sad, ruined face. "I want him to see his mother." She sailed a yellowed photograph across the polished floor. I picked it up. And there, beautiful and blonde, was everyone I'd ever loved. "You *mother*!" Renate screamed.

I knew it was a picture of Lisa; oh, Lisa, the poor dead madwoman.

"Uncle?" I yelled, as the room began to slide, the dim red light go dimmer. *"UNCLE?"*

Someone had hold of me, and, God, I thought, gotta move, gotta get my act together, Val, VAL, and here I go to be nursed by my Lisa (Nancy? Val? Renate?) in that narrow room, old Raggedy Andy, always a ready smile... But someone held me firmly enough that my fall was arrested, and for a time I suspended, held in darkness, and taking comfort from it. Then, slowly, I forced myself back to the hideous room and its burden of realities, like a beginning epileptic coming off the frightening high of that first grand mal, back to the crowd of satanic figures, back to the throbbing music of the dance. "Uncle," I whispered, "my uncle..." I wanted to tell him that I had figured it all out, that I was his lost son and he my lost father, and we would go away, the two of us, in his ME-109...

I opened my eyes.

Uncle Stuka's huge face loomed like a planet. "*I* not your father," he said in the sad voice of an old man with too much going on in his life. "He...this man...whoever he is." His thick fingers gestured toward the man who held me, his remarkable eyes glistening with tears behind the black satin of his mask, the hidden visage beginning to crumble. My uncle said, "He take my wife and I do nothing. It is my shame."

"No," I whispered, sinking again, "no."

Pastukh murmured, "I am so sorry for this...I did not know...it was not what I intended." He wore a wine-colored Cossack blouse, tight at the collar, with broad, flowing sleeves, and baggy trousers, and polished boots. Disguised as a Russian, I thought, trying to laugh. But now something else had happened; he stared past me in a way that made me swivel around to see what made his eyes go so cold.

It was Lincoln, glaring his hatred at us, the architect, the spider. Lincoln, telling us with his calm, empty face that everything would have to be taken apart now; everyone would have to die.

But where was Val? "Val?" I asked, suddenly afraid, staring down the ranks of costumed strangers who suspended around us. "Val?"

Where was my person?

"VAL?" Fear slapped me awake. *"VAL?"*

Renate's angry face floated into view. "She leave," the hard voice trumpeted, "this woman you want more than me, this woman you love when you love me not...she *leave, leeeeeeeeevve*. With a *big* man, a man who not want his *mother*!" The gypsy laughed and laughed.

PART SIX

1

ANDREI SHEPHERD KNELT in the garish light, holding the wiry body of his son, a man almost to middle age and still a stranger, disguised as a rag doll, and as limp as one. Except, you could feel the bones and gristle and muscle beneath the costume; the *illusion* of a rag doll, then, in a world, a city, a room, where nothing was what it seemed, where one spent an evening or a lifetime disguised, as a doll, or a Russian. A young man, really, not forty, and no longer quite such a stranger as he had been on that awkward walk through the park, and yet, a stranger still, a man whose details he should know, a man whose face should still contain that of the boy, and crack one's heart. They had no memories of one another. They had only what they shared of Lisa, poor, lost Lisa, whom he had loved. The boy had known her, though; he remembered her at some deep, unreachable level. What was it like in there, remembering Lisa? A comforting maternal scene, baby upon breasts, light streaming through white muslin, affectionate sounds and touches? Or was it more a nightmare of time spent with a madwoman? All one knew was that the boy had still been a baby when Lisa had gone to Camarillo. He would have baby memories, whatever those were; and yet, Shepherd thought now, they were powerful enough that *this* madwoman could cut the world from under him. He gripped his son, this fine young man dressed like a rag doll.

Ah, but now, if one went by the pale rage in Lincoln's face, the masquerade was about over. Thank God. The boy trembled like a dreaming child, returning from wher-

ever the shock had sent him, returning perhaps from Lisa.
We shall make up what we have lost, if we hurry. We have
a little time. But thoughts of having time awakened the
pain, which, having visited him intermittently, had finally
come to stay. Now it flexed like a waking serpent, and
Shepherd grimaced, and tightened his hold upon his troubled boy, absorbing the wave that, a few weeks earlier,
could stop his breathing, bring him nearly to his knees.

He felt Lincoln watching all this, understanding everything. He could feel the American's gaze like a source of
heat in the room's furnace light, and if he looked up, he
knew, he would stare into the man's hatred of the boy, of
this innocent agent of destruction who had overtaken them
and their trivial charade. It almost made one believe in
God. Almost. For it had been Lincoln who discovered and
then produced him, all without the slightest impulse of
generosity. It was just another kneejerk of his propelling,
patriotic greed. He had always known what to offer Shepherd, that one inducement to keep the charade going, and,
yes, admit it, to keep it interesting, compelling, challeng-
ing. The money piled up in Switzerland, acquired a life of
its own, a little hoard of gold up in the grim mountains,
sunshine for the gnomes.

But Lincoln had been too skillful a puppetmaster to put
much on money. Knowing this particular puppet hated his
strings. Lincoln played on his puppet's secret wish to have
it all his own way—that secret wish to help both sides, to
constitute a kind of one-man third force, leavening the
Soviet loaf of secrecy and paranoia and bad planning and
corruption. Admit that, too: a Russian knight. Lincoln
had let him be the last of the Russian knights. God, and he
had told the boy *that* Russia no longer existed!

As Lincoln's "property"—Shepherd was aware they
used that pejorative, speaking obliquely of him—he had
become valuable beyond their wildest projections. They
had underestimated him because he had been willing to do
it in the first place, they thought it was innocence, courage, and their own type of greed that drove him. But, no,

it had been much simpler. He had wanted the adventure, at first, and then he had decided he had nowhere else to go. And meanwhile, they began to read him more precisely, or Lincoln did, and he had been given opportunities to play at knights. Because of him, Spendahl could tell this president that, yes, the Rosenbergs had spied for the Soviet Union, or tell that one, Russia would not go to war over the Cuban missiles, or tell the other that all the native soldiers in South Vietnam were not irregulars. Spendahl had been the first to offer Andropov as the probable successor to Brezhnev. He had developed quite a reputation, being prescient about Soviet intentions. But Lincoln was his puppetmaster too, so that when, through the channels of the international scientific community, Shepherd had received Spendahl's proposal for an east-west Centre, a kind of technical celebration of détente, he had known the idea really came from Lincoln, and wondered why. He even saw the hook for him in it, in the idea of a place where scientists from east and west could "discard ideology," as the proposal put it, "and exchange ideas and insights in a free and apolitical atmosphere." Until then, Shepherd had believed Lincoln could not read him.

"Of course," Lincoln had told him later, when plans for the Centre had congealed, "we must acknowledge that it has an operational side, as well as a, um, spiritual one." An operational side: masters and their puppets would mingle there, and run their ugly little plays. Still . . . it was going to be that place where ideology could be jettisoned, the atmosphere free and open, as advertised. Shepherd ignored the hoof prints the greedy ones left all around the idea, and proceeded with this monument to the discarding of ideology, the universal solvent. His own father had died of it, strung between the old Russia and ideas of revolution, trying long after he had emigrated to America to bridge between life and ideology; he had believed in the whole bag of tricks, as they say, and the steady betrayals, drawn from that same bag, had revealed the new icons as just another form of patricide. His heart had broken, he had died. His son survived him, not quite in his teens, suddenly alone beneath the low, grey eastern sky, the teeming continent behind him, running off to its exotic Californias and Alaskas, as bleak and barren to him then as the steppes of central Asia. So, yes, he would work to build a place in which people discarded ideology, and Lincoln had known it, and Shepherd did not give a damn. He loved the idea, the place, and, when the offices had been designed into the yellow shell of a Habsburg palace nearly destroyed by looting Soviet soldiers, he had been still more pleased—he liked the *fit* of it all. And it was in the park adjoining this monument to a lost father, this anti-monument to corrosive ideology, that he had first walked alone with his own lost son, this young man who lay in his arms.

Ah, but the park had also been where Lincoln asked him, in that sneering tone of his, "Did you know you have a son?"

Did he? He wondered now, as the boy stirred in his arms. Certainly he had wanted for there to have been something real outside his disguise, something offstage, actual, and warm. Lincoln's question, the stink of his greed when he subsequently offered to produce the son, had seemed almost careless. "There is something particular that we need, and I begin to sense your reluctance to go on and on with us. After all, it has been a long time. It would be unnatural if our demands did not begin to repel you. But this time I have something rather unusual to offer in exchange. Something ... unique." His face had radiated hatred, then, as he asked, "Did you know you have a son?"

A son. Well, everyone is greedy about something. Lincoln wanted his secret scraps, contacts within the Soviet system, a bit of this, a bit of that. And he, Shepherd, had been instantly greedy for a glimpse—no more than that, a *glimpse*—of this vital stranger. But, if he had a son, then Lisa ... He had looked up at Lincoln, knowing he raised an open, vulnerable, desperately questioning face to a

cold, destructive man. Lincoln shook his head. "Forget
the mother. She's catatonic. She's been in the California
state hospital since 1947. She's, um, lost her looks."

"When can I see him?"

"First..." Lincoln shrugged like a rug merchant, and
they had constructed still another transfer. "To meet your
ocean chemist, I shall need to dispose of some ocean
chemistry, something really spurious, using the busker
route. It's the worst kind of merde, a chemical signature
for *Trident* submarines. I doubt your people...I mean, the
Soviet Union... will be fooled for a minute. But I can't
resist the... *fit*." The joy of others curdled something in
Lincoln, and at the same time gave him an appetite for the
consumption of it.

And then, suddenly, there had been this young man, his
son, separated from him by only a few meters of carpet
and tables, and a handful of delegates. A handsome young
man, almost as fair as Lisa had been, tall, well-made,
brilliant in his scientific field, but also a man of the sea.
Shepherd had felt pride and something else—his latent
Americanness had almost suffocated him, his Russian self
rattling on him like an exoskeleton that had cracked loose.
He had tried to focus upon the death of Leonid Brezhnev,
while his thoughts leaned toward his son, to the fact that
they, he and Lisa, had in this way survived. He had known
the boy immediately. He had seen the predominance of the
mother coloring him, and he had felt paternal stirrings,
although he understood that one could manufacture them
for such occasions. But then, on that walk together, he had
begun to doubt. In speaking of lost parents there had not
been a word of Lisa, and no filial reflex toward him,
Shepherd, who could not resist believing that one would
have to feel *something*, and show it.

Nothing, there had been nothing. He had backed away,
emotionally dulled and angry that Lincoln would trick him
so close to his secret core, and saddened by the certainty
that his life had been as barren as it had seemed—an illusion, in which he had been made to vanish. But then there

had been the extraordinary shock of seeing Valentina Orlovsky, a shock for him, but the same kind of shock for the boy, both men the slaves of memory; it was just that Schaefer's was the memory of an infant, and more like a dream than his own. Although—his was very like a dream!

If they had not quite had him before, they had him then, for they had the boy, and hated him, this surprising creature who had sprung from their own creations, like life stirring in their petri dish of death. He would have to arrange a system of insurance like his own, to protect the boy from Lincoln and the others after the serpent won the argument.

He looked at his son. He stirs. He stirs. I feel his return to life, this man of nearly forty he kept calling a boy. Thirty-seven. A man of twenty-five is more a boy than this one. If Schaefer said to him, I have decided to spend the rest of my life living in an enemy country, but working for my own, he would say: You are not far enough along to take that decision. Was I, at twenty-five? He shook his head. He had thought so, at the time.

But back then everyone had been so young, so brave and intelligent, so ready for whatever came, that the whole business had been like a fistfight among friends: exciting, transient, without lasting effects. In retrospect, Shepherd had seen that Lincoln and the other architects had conducted a very careful search for just the right man to send over, someone who would let himself be assimilated by the Soviet Union, someone with an innate sense of a fatherland along with the belief that the Soviet *system* was the enemy; possibly they had smelled that faint Messianic odor on him as well. A tough, intelligent young man, then, but one with a crack, something you could manipulate. The off-handedness had been like the first steps in the choreography of psychoanalysis, or calming wild animals, or getting a man to give up his realities in the national interest. They had come to him the way others like them must have approached the best young physicists over cocktails in flats in Berkeley and Chicago. "How would you like to build a bomb?"

In his case, it had been a party in one of those narrow Georgetown houses, where, among the murmuring, self-isolated crowd of women in broad-shouldered dresses and men in suits and uniforms, Baker Lincoln had asked, "How would you like to go to Russia?" *Did you know you have a son?* The same sarcastic, minimizing tone.

"How would you like to go to hell?"

Lincoln must have known him well enough even then to know he had his man, and Shepherd knew himself well enough to know that he would go. It touched him on an unhealed wound, that single word: *Russia*. It evoked so much for him, the hateful, death-dealing system, the giant motherland, hope, despair, war, peace; so much. His mother lay in a Moscow grave. The Soviet experiment had been to his father what the headlights of a car are to a deer.

How would you like to go to hell?

Perhaps, if hell were Russia, he, Shepherd, would like to go. He wanted to escape Lincoln, though, whom he knew vaguely from school and the Pentagon corridors, this person who had uttered a word full of evil and compelling magic. But Lincoln, if he sensed this dismissal, kept close by. "What do they have you doing over at the fun fair?" Lincoln asked.

"Nothing much." Shepherd looked at the women, a big man of twenty-five, quick on his feet, and strong, and dark. His eyes had been brilliant and deepset even then, and he looked elegant in the pinks and greens of an army captain, wearing the crossed rifles of infantry. The women glanced back at him, the herd shifted self-consciously. That's what he ought to be doing, cutting one of them out, making an arrangement.

"Nothing much, with a physics Ph.D.?" Lincoln gave a snort of false laughter.

"Yep. They have me doing nothing much for the duration."

"Unless you go to Russia."

"That's right. I forgot about going to Russia." He had laughed. "I'm not going anywhere, Lincoln."

"Don't be too sure."

He had left Shepherd alone then, having pushed this Russian seed into rich soil. Shepherd could feel the fluent language in him like an embryo, wanting to be born in speech. He saw himself in great cities he now knew only from books, in comradely scenes from *War and Peace*, old Pierre dropping in... He laughed again.

"What's funny, soldier?" The voice had been clear as a musical note, low but melodic, with something hard at the center, reminding you of vibrating metal. The woman was pretty, black hair worn very long and braided across her forehead, everything held in place with tortoise-shell combs. Her fine bones were visible as slabs of pale blue shadow beneath a milkwhite skin, eyes blue as water, the body long and strong, like a swimmer. Shepherd had smiled his interest. "I mean," she said, "what's funny about going to Russia?"

"You heard?"

"Sure I did." She smiled back at him. "You could go as a Don Cossack."

"I thought they were cutting wood in Siberia."

"Somebody has to cut wood."

"I'm more the executive type."

"I know what you are. You're Captain Andrei Borisovich Shepherd, a soldier with some scientific job over at the funhouse."

"You'd be from the NKVD, right?"

"No such luck. Would you come to Russia if I were?"

"Everybody wants me to come to Russia. Did Lincoln send you?"

"My new, good-looking friend, nobody sends me anywhere."

"And who are you?"

"I'm Cybelle."

"Cybelle who?"

"Cybelle Cybelle Cybelle."

"Oh." He moved away. "I'm dry," he said. "Excuse me."

"Anderson," she said, handing him her glass. "Didn't mean to be rude."

"I thought you did. You do it so well." But he had taken her glass and let the black man at the bar fix him another martini, and her a Scotch and soda. When he gave it to her, he asked, "What does Baker have in mind?"

"Sounded like a trip to Russia."

"Sounded like more than a trip."

"You'll have to talk to him. All I know is that Russia's the next big enemy. Hitler won't last beyond the spring..."

"This comes from the Vestal Virgins?"

"Vestal, maybe. But no, it's just consensus, is all. Hitler's not winning anything. Stalin is. But the war with Russia won't be any four or five year ground thing. It will be..."

"Ideological."

"You make it sound dirty. But, yes, ideological, and cold, and eternal." Her eyes glowed at the prospect of eternal war.

Like you, he thought. And yet, he wanted her. "Well, then, we'll all be going to Russia."

"Only figuratively. I think Lincoln had something more realistic in mind for you."

"What does he do?"

"Something spooky. Over in the lower intestine of the Pentagon."

"I don't like intelligence work."

"Aren't you a believer?"

"I believe in our getting out of here."

"Hallelujah, brother."

Later he had made love to her on the floor of her apartment, with her naked on her spread mink coat, and beautiful, her body like her voice, all warmth and clarity, with something cold and hard within. She had pulled him into her without preliminaries, like someone committing suicide with a knife, and their affair had begun.

Cybelle and the others had kept the pressure on, although none of it was necessary. He had known immediately that he would go, if they didn't spoil it for him, and that it had nothing to do with bravery or patriotism or where the next war, what Lincoln and the others called the "real" war, would be fought. He had been captive of the plan from that first *How would you like to go to Russia?*, as he had been a captive to this trembling man he held now in his arms from the first sneering words from Lincoln: *Did you know you have a son?* The thought of going to Russia had made his heart race, he leaned toward it like a plant seeking light. It was an opportunity to visit another world, to be a kind of assimilated observer, Marco Polo disguised as a Chinese. The difficulties challenged him. The hazards were exciting. There were possibilities of doing great good; of playing at knights. He had seen the whole thing clearly, so that when they told him it was just a probing exercise, a year or two at the most, he had known they lied—they would never bring him in. He thought of the loneliness of having no one to whom he could confide, no safe vessel for his lethal secrets. He saw it all clearly, and nothing about it frightened him but Lincoln, of being tied to Lincoln. Lincoln had sniffed it, and once said, "You know, Shepherd, we underestimate one another."

"You underestimate me," he had replied.

Why had he gone, finally? Because...there were compelling reasons for, and none against. Spendahl had played his trump: a call from the moribund president, the fatigued, aristocratic voice asking this favor for his country. And Cybelle had done her part, with cries of "I wish to God *I* could do it, I wish I had the Russian to do it with!"

It had been Carney who finally moved him. Carney, the little son of a bitch navy commander who took over his technical monitoring department at the Pentagon, and who immediately began slapping Shepherd in that military way that tells you, Take it, or fight me; fight me and you go to the stockade. "Captain Borisovich," he would yell, "this is not a goddamned experiment in socialism, or some fucking tractor factory near Minsk. This is a military office in which we monitor the activities of civilians, *capitalists*, who are trying to swindle us out of animal fats, gunpowder, ships, and aircraft. It is a place in which it would be appropriate to refer to your commanding officer as 'sir' and to extend the other military courtesies. Now, shall we stop holding hands with eggheads and get the job done?'' Day after bloody day, Carney had sandpapered him this way. Finally Shepherd had applied for a combat infantry assignment.

Lincoln reached him within hours of the request. ''If you want to fight come with us. This war is over. Germany won't last the summer. Japan...well, Japan is in for an ugly surprise. It's over. If you want to fight somebody, then come in with us against these latterday Tsarists. I know you well enough to say you'd thrive on it.'' Pause, then, ''Come in with us or try to get through the duration without slugging Carney and drawing ten and a D.D. One way or another, my friend, you are leaving the good old United States.''

He had looked at Lincoln for a long time. ''Maybe if I take Carney and you with me it'll be worth it.''

''Okay, I'm sorry for trying to bully you. Jesus, Shep, this means so much, and you'd be so goddamned good at it.''

Still, it had been that little son of a bitch Carney who got him to go. That afternoon, he had screamed, ''Captainovich, this is not some frigging Black Sea *commune*...''

He had submitted to their training, to the replacement of fillings, to the Russian name he selected because it echoed his real one, and preserved some sliver of his old identity—and more than submitted: he had embraced the assignment with such integrity and clear purpose that Cybelle had fallen in love with him, so that, at the end, she had turned to him with tears standing in those tearless eyes, her refractory heart chipped by the ease, the familiarity, with which he put on courage. But it had not been love, for

him, and it had not been courage. He wanted *Russia*, and
worked hard to place himself in her, to be ready for this
moment of transition. While records of birth and medical
care, parents (dead early in the war), school, Party mem-
bership, military service, employment were inserted in
various fragmentary forms into the war-shattered ar-
chives of the Soviet Union; while orders were cut for a
captain of administration and quartermaster to join Tol-
bukhin's Third Ukrainian Front near Vienna—Shepherd
had transformed himself into this other, Russian man.

Often then, in Moscow, in Vienna, on safe, lonely
ground, he would move that man, that Pastukh person,
aside, and let himself become once more the American in
Russia, thinking in English, talking to himself softly as an
American would, letting himself recover the young captain they had sent out in 1945, the assignment a species of
hell, always rolling the rock of deception up the bloody
Soviet hill. And then, compelled like some secret Jekyll by
this other self, he would submerge again, English would
decline to a second, learned language in which he had forgotten how to handle articles and contractions. Once, in
the late 1950's, attending a United Nations conference in
New York, he had found his homeland a frightening
place—the cars, the litter, the anger and despair in black
faces, the noise. The terrible music, the Plenty, had been
too much. He had been relieved to return to his small,
modern flat in Moscow, the softly playing classical music;
a city with less of everything. For, really, when he went
over that April in 1945, he did not look back, not at Cybelle, or his country, or his forfeited life. He had never
looked back at anything, except . . .

"Uncle," the boy cried out, like a child fleeing evil
dreams. "My uncle . . ." Shepherd felt him stiffen in his
arms, try to rise. He thinks his uncle holds him, but, no, it
is his father, his *father*. Heinrich Braun leaned toward
them then, his eyes on Shepherd's, then darting off toward Schaefer, filled with shame and pity. "I not your fa-

ther. He... this man... Shepherd, Schaefer, whoever he
is... he take my wife. And I do nothing. It is my shame."

The young face whipped around and there, between
them, was that first look of recognition, the first look of
the son at the lost father. All Shepherd saw in those eyes
as grey and clear as Lisa's were horror and confusion. It
struck him like a blow. "No... no," the boy was saying.

"I am so sorry for this... I did not know... it was not
what I intended." He could no longer see the room, although he clung to his son, not certain whether he comforted or cleaved to him, the room glittering softly through
a prism of tears.

What *had* he intended?

He had looked back only at Lisa. She had been that unseen confidante and companion, through all the years
alone, all the close calls, the frightening nights when he
knew he'd been blown, the masquerade discovered by
some resourceful Trulov. She had been the angel to whom
he passed his silent, simple prayers, the trusted wife to
whom he could describe the cunning gambit, some success, some new prospect. Lisa had enfolded him and kept
him safe, protected him against the encroaching madness
of perpetual disguise, her single touch spreading through
his life until it became the central fact of his own destroyed reality. For she had entered and left his life just as
it had truly cracked apart, on the very day it ended—or
began.

RAF Waddington had not been his first temptation to
leave a faint, faint trail, but it was the only one to which he
had finally succumbed. His reality would end in a day or
two at the most, and he was not prepared to have this familiar figure, this Andrei Shepherd, erased completely.
Not yet. When he signed for his billet and food he felt like
a man blazing the trunk of a sapling, so that anyone with
an eye, a memory, would see his mark there on the grown
tree. Andrei Shepherd was here, on the tenth day of April,
nineteen hundred and forty-five A.D., and ate, and
slept... *here*.

The next morning they were off, the pilot a nasal lieutenant with a neutral face who knew only that he had this
infantry captain in ODs heading for the front. They ran
beneath the low scud of clouds remaining from yesterday's weather, out over the flat, rainsmeared landscape
toward the Wash, and bruised expanse of the North sea,
dancing with squalls. Another coastline I shall never see
again, Shepherd had thought, although without self-pity.
Another irrevocable step toward…*Russia*. The name still
brought a rush of feeling, now faintly tinged with fear.

The chubby little L-5 flew southeast, bucking gusty slaps
of wind and rain, never more than a few hundred feet off
the slabs of grey water. Then they were past the continental coast, hurrying over the Belgian lowlands. He had begun to see the war. The war, he thought, just ending. Their
war. Mine is farther east.

Aachen was the first destroyed city Shepherd had ever
seen, the western railway yards a violent pox of shell and
bomb craters, the center reduced to lines of nothing but
shakey façades, rubble-filled streets, and that look, ac-
centuated here, that nothing lived except the servants and
matériel of war. They landed for fuel just east of the ruined city, and stretched and then were off again, still running under the weather, the thin fabric of the fuselage
trembling against the rush of air. The rolling farmlands
and forests came toward them, wheeled past, pristine and
empty; and then there would be the devastated village of
chimneys and stone walls, and clustered trucks and tanks,
lines of infantry advancing, pods of prisoners, scorched
gun barrels poking from the charred carcasses of tanks. He
saw Frankfurt only at a distance, the cathedral rising from
its shattered city, from rubble, and then they were passing
Würzburg, still smoking from the final assault, the Main
River bridges swarming with tiny engineers, and, out beyond the city, tanks snorting and nosing eastward, and
more men, and artillery, destroying the horizon. It was the
eleventh of April, nineteen hundred and forty-five A.D.,

and Andrei Shepherd had been right *here*, at what the Germans called the western front.

"This is far's we go," the pilot said. "Courtesy Patton's Third."

Shepherd had looked down at the neat land of vineyards and fairytale castles, medieval walls cupping rubble, roofless ruins, where nothing seemed to live but war. "Where are we?"

"Kitzingen."

They circled a small grass field where other liaison planes, and a larger single-engined plane covered with camouflage netting, were tied down, amid a litter of fuel drums and tents with their sideflaps up for ventilation. They landed and taxied to one of these. The pilot swung the plane around and yelled, "Good luck, captain." Shepherd got out with his bag. The plane taxied into the wind and took off quickly. Soon it was just a speck, sliding across the pewter sky above the vineyards.

"Tovarich!" a familiar voice had said then, and Shepherd had turned, knowing he would find Carney, like a small graven image of an aviator, dressed for flight, standing there in the middle of this grey spring day in Germany, with a mug of coffee and a sarcastic grin. "I'm your driver."

Carney had been part of it too, then, part of the conspiracy of persuasion, one of those interesting touches Lincoln liked to introduce. Shepherd spat. "Where am I billeted, or do I sleep on the ground?"

"In town," Carney said quietly. "We've got some rooms, nothing fancy."

"Not with you."

"No, we're not even in the same place."

"Good."

"Look, if it'll make you feel better, go on and punch me out." He took a step toward Shepherd. "Come on."

"I wouldn't touch you with rubber gloves, old sport. But I'm very tempted to fuck up your operations. I may opt out."

"There's a war on, captain."

"Sure, but you've forgotten the argument. I'm not in *this* war. I'm in the next one, the eternal one."

Grinding his teeth, Carney had led Shepherd to a jeep and they drove through the old walls into Kitzingen, following the narrow cobbled streets that converged on the town square. "You 'opt out' and we'll make it hot for you, captain."

"Fuck you...commanderovich." He got out and trailed Carney into a yellow *Gasthaus* which stood in a group of buildings near the church, still not quite destroyed by artillery and bombs. Carney rattled off his rather good German at a man of about thirty, slender, with the hands of a woodsman, and one of those big Bavarian faces with horsey teeth and booming voices, although he had been quiet then, having Americans around. Defeated soldier, home from the wars, Shepherd thought, envying the man the fact that *his* war appeared to be over. Then he had let his attention wander to the parade of small antlered skulls on the wall, the ticking clock about to cuckoo at everyone, the wood and glass...

The girl wore a fresh peasant dress, like a *Dirndl*, a bit tattered at the edges. She looked at him with eyes of a perfect, transparent grey beneath plaited hair of gold and silver, a beautiful girl with lovely bare arms and intimations of sweet breasts beneath the bodice, a girl of twenty perhaps; he had known her voice would be mellow and clear before she spoke. She blinded him, not so much with the lovely exterior as with what he sensed within, what lived far down in the depths of her eyes; *that* had been blinding, *that* had melted his interior and softened his spine. He knew she had felt it too. They could not look away.

"Lisa," the man said, *"bitte."* She took the key and turned brightly, the brightness veiling the trance, to the two Americans.

"Go on," Carney said testily, "but he's her husband. Thought you'd like to know." His eyes twinkled.

But Shepherd's heart had left this quarrel with the hated little man; now it boomed and fluttered toward the girl, whom he had followed, and let her show him the bare room with its single bed and down quilt, and bureau, and basin, all very poor, all very clean. "Lisa," he said. "Lisa."

She had turned. *"Wie heissen Sie?"*

He had searched his meager German. *"Schaefer,"* he replied. It had been whimsical, a way of bridging between the vanishing Shepherd and the Pastukh about to be born in Vienna.

She smiled with small white teeth. "Schaefer," she said. "Schaefer."

Shepherd had realized suddenly he was trembling. God, what chord had this girl touched in him, to rattle him this way? "Who can she be?" he asked himself softly in English.

"What...do you...say?" Her voice recovered from that instant's gravity, and held a lovely peal of laughter, seeing his surprise at her English. "I...learn English...from school. It not *so* good, but..." and she shrugged.

He could not look away. "I mean..." He shook his head in confusion.

"What? Oh, Schaefer, tell me!" Then, "No, not now, later. You will tell me later." She touched his lips with her fingers, and hurried out, radiant and happy.

Shepherd had sat on the edge of his bed, willing the shaking to stop, almost drunk on his good fortune. It was as if she had waited here for him, waited for him at the extreme edge of his existence, and caught him before his fatal leap into...*Russia*. He looked up quickly, blushing with embarrassment: Carney had come in without knocking.

"Jesus," he said, "I hope you don't gather wool like that in Russia. They'll have your head on a pike in ten minutes." He dropped a gas mask on the bed. "Peace offering. Assorted rarities. Cigarettes, coffee, chocolate, canned meat, even some gourmet K-rations. Hate to see a guy go east hungry."

"Thanks, Carney," Shepherd said.

Carney scowled. "Don't let it seduce you, Shepherd. We fly out of here tomorrow at nineteen hundred hours, period. I'm landing you in Russian territory late tomorrow night, dead or alive I don't bust my missions, neither do my co-workers. What I suggest you do, comrade captain-ovich, is spend the next ... lessee ... thirty and a quarter hours getting yourself up and ready for the operation."

Shepherd had not replied, and Carney left him there. He lay back on the feather pillows and watched the grey sky outside his window, the vineyards dropping out of the clouds from wooded hilltops, the light beginning to change as the sun began the long eastward fall. Interesting question. Is it Carney or is it fear? He remembered that flicker of apprehension over the Channel. Was his agitation over Carney just a way of getting out of something that began to scare him? Ah, well, he knew he would go, for he had said he would. He had one day that would have to last him forever.

She had come to him in the middle of the afternoon, wrapped in a patched woollen cape, and touched his lips with her silencing fingertip, and whispered, "Come." And he, like a spirit beckoned from a body, rose and followed her, a dying man in a dream of life. She took him through the rough, narrow streets that curved along the hillside, and then out into the vineyards, the afternoon moist and sombre, beginning to grow cold. He felt festive and happy, and swung the bag of food like a boy on a picnic, trailing after this long-legged German girl who had waited here, in this medieval town, for him. For her *Schaefer*. He smiled. He would have to tell her his real name, and where he had come from, and about his life and thoughts; he would lie with his head in her lap and tell her everything.

They stopped near the crest of the hill, where the dusty aisle between vines, some of them chopped up by mortar fire a few days earlier, some crushed by passing tanks, gave way to forest. And there, before an outcropping of rock that opened upon the northern sky, he spread his poncho on the ground and they knelt together, their fingers intertwined. "Now," she said in a hushed, child's voice, "you will tell me."

"You are the girl of my dreams."

"The girl of your dreams?" Pretty frown.

"Seeing you . . . I thought, *there* she is."

"Ah."

"As though you have been waiting here for me."

"I feel that also, when I see you in *Gasthaus*. I feel, *he has* come."

"What can we do?" he whispered, his voice hoarse with wanting his life back, and wanting her, life's golden emissary. If only he could stop trembling!

"We do what we can do." She kissed his fingertips, and lay with him upon the poncho, their backs against the sharp slab of rock, and watched the northern horizon, huddled together against the cold, against the intrusions of the world. Off to the west, silhouetted near day's end, the castle at Würzburg lowered over the gleaming ribbon of the Main, reminding them of the time. Guns flashed and thumped to the southeast, and they heard the brittle clatter of small arms. "They are fighting now in Nürnberg," she said.

"They are fighting everywhere, tonight. Everywhere but here." He put his arm around her, pulled her closer. "You must be freezing."

"You not let me freeze." She gave a delighted laugh. "My *Schaefer* not let me freeze."

"No, indeed he would not."

"We spend the night here, and the day . . . when you go?" She looked sadly into his eyes.

"Tomorrow night."

"Where?"

He shrugged. "To the front."

"And when you come back?"

"When I can. When the war is over."

"What if you die?"

"I can't. I have to come back to you. I have to take you away."

"Away. I would like that you take me away."

"When the war is over." Then, "What about Heinrich?"

"I not wait all my life for Heinrich. I wait for you."

They had leaned into each other's arms, then, and he had stroked her, this gleaming woman, and then he had removed her apron and dress, touching her with hands that shook, marvelling at what a chance encounter had brought him. Them. Their bodies, when they joined, moved like a centaur, and as they could not stop peering into the other's eyes, their lovemaking never quite ended, but merely phased from marvel to marvel. There was something, he had decided later, almost frightening in that terrible wanting of one another, as though their sexuality occupied their bodies like a wanton spirit, causing them both to moan, to hum, until they would burst, and fall . . .

Then there had come a golden light over them, the sun descending into view below the clouds, scorching their forest with slanting amber light. Lisa shivered. "It is like September, this light," she murmured in a frightened voice. "Will you be here in September?"

"If the war is over."

"Tell me yes."

"Yes."

"That is more easy for me."

He had fumbled around in his clothing, and drawn out a wallet, and handed her a photograph Cybelle had taken near the Capitol. It showed the strong, young captain in khaki. "Here," he said, "I don't want you to forget me." She had said nothing, but took the photograph delicately by its corners, like a fragile talisman, and studied it as she had studied him.

Later, they picked up their clothing and she led him down to a spring that gushed from the hillside, pure and cold, and they washed, almost shy with one another now, but also bound. He brought out his food and they had chocolate and crackers and cheese from the K-ration, and she watched him smoke a cigarette. They had gone quiet, watchful of one another, as though, conscious of time draining away, of their having before them more waiting that had to be absorbed somehow, each had to imprint the other. Silence seemed to stop the grinding machinery of time. Afterward, when he knew what had happened to his Lisa, he thought, That was where we went instinctively, to silence. They were that alike. He had told her, "I love you, Lisa."

They had spent the night there, curled together on the poncho, covered by his field jacket and her cloak, and even slept a little, like babes in the wood. The war went on with cruel independence, far away. Dawn brought that same autumnal light, the sun rising between the land and weather, brilliant and golden, then ascending out of sight, leaving them in a world rinsed of color.

Late that afternoon they returned to the village. Her neighbors watched them from behind drawn curtains, as though the lovers harbored dread disease. Heinrich looked up with red-rimmed, angry eyes when they entered the *Gasthaus*, but there had been no recriminations, no words at all. She went up to Shepherd's room with him, and they had lain on the bed and held one another until the sun swept low again, filling the place with golden light. And then she had touched his face with gentle fingertips, and kissed his forehead, and said, "I love you and I love you, my Schaefer. Please come back when war is over."

"I will."

He had.

And still he lost her.

Ah, God, what *had* he intended? Had he merely wanted to keep himself alive in the memory of this girl?

No, no; it had been exactly what it seemed, the shock she sent through him had been genuine and unique. Ah...but he also knew that, pumping his semen into her, there must also have been the fragment of a thought that here, here, on the twelfth of April, nineteen hundred and forty-five

AD, Andrei Shepherd had conceived a new life within the woman he loved, a life that would live on and on while he went to his own death—no, worse, to a strange anti-life, an eternal masquerade. Yes, he thought now, conscious of the boy leaning away from him, the uncle hovering nearby, the costumed crowd of strangers, yes, I *did* intend you. *I had hoped!*

"Val? Val?" Shepherd felt the sudden tension of fear along the muscled back. "VAL? VAL?" The voice of a man about to lose *that person*.

The dark, round face of old Heinrich's gypsy wife leaned close to them, and when she spoke the crimson light showed flecks of spittle, red as blood. "She *leave*, this woman you want more than me, this woman you love when you love me not, she *leave, leeeeeeeevvvve*, with a *big* man, a man who not want his *mother*!" She laughed like a bird in the night.

Pastukh released his son and stepped toward her. "Hush," he ordered, "Silence!"

"Leave her," said Heinrich, pushing Pastukh to one side. "You do too much already." The three-legged Doberman danced awkwardly between them, like a bargirl crooning *Boys, boys!*

"Shut her up or I shall do it for you." The two men glared at one another. Finally Heinrich turned to his wife. *"Genug,* Renate. *Genug."* She heard him. Her surrender felt like a death in the room. He put his hand on her shoulder and led her away. The costumed figures watched them go, their voices rising in puzzled discussion, like music coming up behind a final curtain. Pastukh glanced nervously around, searching for his son.

The young man stood out of his reach, now, which was just as well. The urge to touch him was almost overpowering. "Sorry I got so vaporous," he said.

"People can be killed with manipulations. You absorbed a lot of pain tonight."

"We need to find Val." The voice had no force. It carried a hopeless sound, as though he had come to the end of everything.

"Lisa was your mother. Somehow you...your *heart*...remembers her. So does mine. It breaks with remembering her."

"But you left her. As you said, people can be killed by manipulations." Bitterness. "You never went back."

"But I did."

All the way over to Vienna, with every beat of that Russian engine, he had thought how it would be. He would do what they wanted, for a time, but when the war ended he would vanish, again, and Lisa would vanish with him. It would be magical and right. But it had taken him until November to get there, hiking it from Coburg as a civilian. She had gone to America, they said. From their place on the hill he had looked out across the road going down to Nürnberg, wondering what to do, now that his real life would not begin after all. "I began walking east. Lisa and I both went into exile, you see, into silence." They had waited all that time to meet; afterward, they waited for that one encounter to resume. But it had drowned in time. "It is quite sad, when you think about it." He looked at his son, whose troubled eyes were bright with tears. "The thing for you to remember is that when I saw Lisa, when my heart cracked with the first sight of her, there was nothing mechanical or neurotic about it. Nothing conditioned. Rare, yes. Good, yes. You have your Valentina. She is real. For God's sake, keep her by you." He gave a quick, diffident grin and clapped the boy on the shoulder. "You mustn't inherit *everything*."

"But Val is gone."

"She is Trulov's unwilling prisoner. I would worry, except I know he will not harm her. Believe me, he will not. He wants me, that's all. And I am glad now to give him what he wants."

"What about Lincoln?"

"I have dealt with Lincoln and the others since before you were born. It is getting late. May I wait with you until we hear from Maxim?"

"Of course."

"At your flat might be better. There has been enough excitement here tonight."

"I'll get our things."

I'll get our things, Carney had offered, a gesture of good will to indicate his relief that the bad captain had come back into line. Then they had left Kitzingen, and he had seen Lisa for the last time, a lone figure high up the hillside, between the vines and the forest. They waved, in that light, in that odd, timeless moment between two wars. Later, as he and Carney cleared the eastern Alps and turned toward the fires of Vienna, Franklin Roosevelt had collapsed in Warm Springs, and died at about the moment Shepherd had finally disappeared, at about the moment when Pastukh spoke to that first Soviet soldier the next morning in Vienna. He had always thought it an emphatic way for America to say goodbye.

WHEN THE TAXI rolled up outside Schaefer's building, Pastukh paid, and the two men got out into the fall of snow. He found it difficult to concentrate, so hard did this unaccustomed excitement grip him—it was worse than love, for it had that unevenness in it that prevails between the parental and the filial; the parent must ache, the child must merely love. And more: he was with his person, the man who knew he was his son. Of course he would be nervous and excited. "I am glad to have it over," he told Schaefer.

"I would be too." A guarded, preoccupied voice.

"Thank you for letting me come tonight." He must control that impulse to touch this young man. Careful.

"Look...this is very confusing to me. I don't know how to treat you. My instincts tell me to run away, from everything. But, as you say, Valentina is real." Then he smiled sadly. "You probably are too. I'm glad to have my life ex-

plained, to know who my people are. Were. Usually I lose
people. It's a new experience, this picking up of mothers
and...fathers."

Pastukh smiled shyly, sharing the difficulty of the term.
"Thank you," he said.

As they approached the entry door, the shadows there
seemed to divide, liberating the woman they shielded from
the whispering cascade of snow. Pastukh saw the pale,
broad Russian face behind the fur. "Vera."

"Maxim sends this." She ignored Pastukh, but spoke to
Schaefer in the dead voice of a woman whose husband,
though alive, is lost to her—the widow of a man trapped
underground.

Schaefer took the square of paper from her, and unfolded it. He read, "*Hauptallee, Cafe Holzdorfer, 18hrs
Sunday, Father & son alone. It's signed The Holy Ghost.*"

Pastukh smiled. "Maxim keeps some sense of humor."

"He is crazy. He is in much trouble." Vera Trulov's
hands wrung one another, and she watched the ground. "I
have visit from Soviet men looking for Maxim. And others." She gave a frightened, involuntary shiver.

"Others?" Schaefer asked.

"Never mind," she said, her voice rising with fear.

"Lincoln," said Pastukh. "You talked to Lincoln."

"He promised to help Maxim get away."

"Where is Maxim now?"

"I do not know."

"But you have seen him."

"Only for a minute...when he gave me this."

"We shall be there," Pastukh said. "But I think Lincoln will be there too. It is a trap for Maxim. Vera, why did
you tell them?"

"I did not..." and she bit her fist.

"The child...they persuaded the child to tell them."

"Maxim can defect," she argued uncertainly, like a
mother bird pretending injury, fleeing the nest.

"You have to warn him."

Her hooded eyes shone, tears destroying her makeup. "I do not know where he is. Dear God, what have we done to our man?" She whirled away from them and hurried toward the dim howl of traffic on Währingerstrasse. At the corner, part of another building's dark façade detached itself and merged with her silhouette. For an instant, Pastukh glimpsed the luminous moon face of the daughter, radiant and sad, under the lights and snow, the lovely echo of Trulov—Trulov without the rage, but bearing the same doom.

2

THE ROUND, glowing face startled him, like a soft light suddenly haunting his sleep. He jerked awake, his heart racing. Afraid, but of what? Trulov glanced around the dim, filthy enclosure. The Orlovsky woman was still there. She sat in the darkness, visible only as a pale outline of shining hair. What had he dreamed? He could not remember, beyond the sharp sense that his daughter had been close enough to touch him, and now was gone. Gone, like her father, he thought.

Well, it was nearly over, a fragment of a night to pass, and an entire day, and then, when there were only a few people among the bare chestnut trees along the Hauptallee, and one could see them all against a white backdrop of snow, he would finish it. He would give the woman back to the American, for all the good she would do him, and he would take Pastukh, his chairman, his old comrade, and together they would tackle the confession that had to be made. And they would return together to the Soviet Union, and Trulov would not merely clear his own name and rid his family of this present disgrace—he would be a hero. He went over his plans and over them again, worrying like a criminal that he'd forgotten some crucial point in a crime, or an animal foraging for food in a hard winter—like the proverbial Russian on his own. It made him ashamed of himself, to be always tracking back and forth over his own footsteps, as though his brain didn't work. It had worked well enough to get him this far, to infer there was a puzzle to be solved, and then to solve it. Why was his head full of cotton now? Because he knew so many things were wrong, he skated on ice that thinned and thinned. "Are you asleep?" he asked, suddenly wanting company.

"No."

He laughed harshly. "Here we are, speaking English. Hardly anyone speaks Russian anymore, not even Russians, eh?" Silence. "I would rather speak English. You know, I have so much of it in my head that I often think in English now, like an American. Perhaps I am turning into one."

"A gangster?"

"I am doing nothing bad to you," he muttered, hurt by the sound of her dislike. "We should be comrades, not enemies. It is *they* who have taken action against *us*. Against the Soviet Union." He paused. "Doesn't that mean anything to you?"

She did not reply.

"Do you put this affair of yours ahead of your country? I know your record. I cannot believe..."

"Leave me alone."

"You will have to choose. You cannot have both him and your life as a Soviet citizen, a scientist, a Party member. You will have to defect. Have you been to America?" He knew she listened, although she remained silent. "You will find it terrifying. All those cars. All that freedom they boast about. Freedom to be fired from your job by some entrepreneur who doesn't like the way you fix your hair. Freedom to lose everything. Freedom to be beaten and robbed in a city park. Freedom to make your brain a dead battery with drugs. I know what I am talking about. You will find it terrifying." He waited. Then, "You will have to defect."

"If we all defect, perhaps the murder will stop."

"What murder?" He filled his voice with an edge intended to frighten her. "What murder have you been hearing about?" He leaned toward her. "Tell me." He felt her fear, like an odor in the darkness. "Listen, when I ask you a question, just answer. Then we will not need any painful extractions. What murder?"

"Someone killed two women in California."

He laughed. "Funny. Someone did, eh? God, they know that, and yet, here I am, free as a bird."

"A bird in a dark box."

He peered through the gloom at her. "Would you rather wait in the snow?" She made no reply. She was being proud. In fact, he had been ashamed of the shelter he'd provided for them, the cold wooden shack behind an empty shooting gallery in the Prater, stinking of urine and old cigarettes and rats. The whole place had been destructive of his confidence, the desolate midway almost unlighted, the concession shacks padlocked against the winter, the gaudy mermaids and vikings and ghouls mere sad plaster figures now, like the saints in one of those baroque village churches, restored on the cheap. It had been embarrassing, for she was such a tough bitch beneath that pretty exterior. At the party he had put the muzzle of his little Walther PP under her left arm and told her to come with him, and she had given him that aristocratic Pioneer look you see in some of these professional Russian women, a real fuck-you look. So he had whispered to her, "Come with me or I will blow Braun's head apart." And she had come. A very tough bitch inside that rag doll costume. He waved a large hand. "This was the best I could do without reservations," he said, and laughed. She said nothing. Her eyes stared off into the darkness, as though she had forgotten him. No doubt she thought of her American. "Thinking of your American?" She shook her head, he saw the gleaming line of hair move slightly. "Then what are you thinking of?" The rage pushed into a voice he had intended to be calm. *Calm.* No marauding animals today.

Calm, to deal with all those calm people who will be coming after you.

"Leave me alone. Please."

He said nothing. Let her wonder what *he* thought, then. He could be as big a prick as any woman, actually, bigger... he chuckled. Except, you see, this was just the kind of wild, whimsical thinking that puts you into somebody's gunsight. You could be sitting in one now. Harness your brain or they will kill you. You must stay ahead of them, preserve this half of a step you still have on them. He squeezed his eyes shut against the prospect of failure. Failure meant the end of the world. It meant he would never again sit at his own table, which he had come to miss above everything but his daughter. His own table, his place, where he was master, something he had brought together with his work and intelligence. All of this running, scrounging, living like a derelict under hedges and bridges had distanced him from the warm reality of his *place*. Ah, God, how he missed it, terribly, terribly, and Svetlana, my little glowing moonface. "You would not believe it from this," he murmured, "but I am not a bad provider." There was only silence. Trulov put his face into his cupped palms, tired unto death.

It had been a mistake—mistake number ten trillion, he decided afterwards—to involve Vera and the child in this. For weeks they had only the most tangential links with him, a Swedish porcelain doll out of nowhere, a tin of butter biscuits from London, a stream of postcards bearing nothing but a heart drawn in blue ink. Then, last night, he had appeared on their doorstep, huge and mysterious in his motocross outfit and helmet, like a man from space, dragging this bad-tempered Russian woman in a rag-doll costume. He had materialized like some crazy apparition to his family, the raging ghost of a dead father. He had crowded Valentina into his small flat with all the IKEA prefabricated stuff in it, and hugged Vera (he still felt her warmth against him now, the comforting touch of this fat woman who had begun to be old, and missed her with all his heart) and then picked up his daughter and held her up and up, until her sombre face lighted in a smile. If things went against him tomorrow...well, they had shared that final moment, after all.

Then he had scrawled the note to Schaefer Braun and fled, dragging Orlovsky with him. His wife and daughter had watched him hurry down the snowslick streets as they began the walk to Braun's apartment building. At the end of their street the husband, the father, stopped in a globe of light that was alive with falling snow, and raised an arm in salute; then the two were gone, their footsteps fading into silence.

It had been a mistake.

Vera had been frightened, trembling, afraid of the people who came looking for him, she said, cold KGB people, colleagues, on the trail of their bad boy. But, no, it had not been just fear of them; *everybody* was afraid of them. She had been afraid of *him*. Someone had made her afraid of him, told her of deaths and something about the depths of his trouble. The Americans, then. What had she said? "If you went over we would be safe. The three of us." Yes, the Americans had been there and planted hope in this poor woman's heart, and in his daughter's.

"They are liars, Vera," he had told her. "They want my silence. They do not want me."

"They?" She had gone red. "I do not..."

"Can I not read your face, after all this time? What else did they offer? A job as a vice president of Coca Cola? Something like that?"

"No, nothing like that." She was altogether too afraid of him. He wanted to kill her fear.

"What did you tell them?"

"I know nothing. What can I tell?"

"What indeed? That they do not already know."

And so they had parted in the snow on this suspended scream of fear, with Trulov trying to bank the rage that swept him, his stupid wife, letting them...Lincoln, somebody... know he was back in Vienna, that he would make contact with her.

Had she passed his message on to them? Only God and a few murderous people knew.

Mistake number ten quadrillion. The orders of magnitude flew by.

And what if they had gone to Svetlana, and persuaded her that, for her papa's safety, she must tell them where he planned to be? What if they had done that? Trulov shivered with despair. Not even God had such a sense of humor.

He thought of the meeting place. The Hauptallee, running straight and wide for three miles down the centerline of the Vienna island, bordered by dense lines of chestnut trees, which were bare now, providing cover but little concealment. There would be no one around, in the snow, no bicycles, no traffic. He would draw them around him as a living shield, and he would tie the girl to him. The slightest tremor would make him begin to kill. That was the worst case. They would get him, but he would also get them.

Trulov smiled in the blackness. You bitch, he thought, wondering whether she had moved, you do not know courage when you see it. Can you imagine a man who can, without a twitch, acknowledge the real possibility of his death this way? No, you cannot.

It was bitter cold, although, he added quickly, not too cold for me. The cyclist's costume had been a good choice. Still, it was very cold. How much better to have the Orlovsky woman next to him, to have her light, soapy odor, a small dash of perfume; he could smell her in the stink of the room, like a flower in hell. He should bring her next to him. No, his rage whispered in its hoarse animal voice, just fuck this Soviet scientist of a woman who so likes to go with Americans, teach her something tonight on this filthy earthen floor, crack her pride a little, load her with a burden of shame to carry eternally. His member moved delicately in his trousers. Ah, are we waking up? Let's see.

Think of...Inger, Inger, our lady of everything, giving you
that touch, a lick, in a doorway, with the winter folding in
around us, and she... Yes, he had definitely awakened.
About time, too. He'd had fewer erections lately than a
man condemned to be shot. Is it true that nobody dies with
a hardon? No, never mind this dying business, nobody's
dying, go on, stay awake, look around, here, a little pat for
you, yes, and a little attention of the proper kind. Think
of Inger pulling you inside. He closed his eyes, willing the
young whore to appear upon his mind, but all he could see
there was the dark swirl of water, the rushing ice, the pale
face and white hair of Cybelle, swept away, that face, and
then, as in a dream, the bright, white coin turned, and it
was his Svetlana, drowning...

He jerked like a drowning dog. Had he dozed? The Orlovsky woman was still there. Still there. His friend dozed
too, weighed down by all this thinking. Try again. Think
of taking this long, blonde Russian woman here, think of
how silky her thighs must be, and then, her entryway,
going damp, going swampy...Trulov shook his head.
Nothing, nothing happened down there. His old friend and
companion had withered, become a stump, barely fit for
passing water. Strictly a fair-weather friend. He heard
Valentina shift position. "I am thinking of fucking you,"
Trulov said, immediately ashamed of himself for speaking that way, like a boy frightened by women.

"Then I shall be the next woman you murder," she replied in Russian.

He chuckled. Just the kind of response one would
expect. But even her resistance could not inflate it. If I am
going to ravage anyone, I will have to find something to do
it with, he thought angrily. Yes, yes, there is always the
anger, the rage. Perhaps that was everything now, perhaps that was all his brain and body remembered how to
do. Jesus, nothing but rage, and dawn only just beginning, a grey streak of light here, another there, the snow
still falling.

"It's growing light," he said, badly wanting to talk. She only watched him, the beautiful face wearing its crazy doll makeup, the broad mouth still. For you, it seemed to say, I have only silence.

Silence. That is where one went, finally, when all else failed. That is where she sent him, grimly, like a witch. If I could do it, I would fuck you to death, you Russian bitch. He stifled a sob. But I cannot. Had that been the dream, then, his daughter drowning in the Swedish tides, spinning away with the ice? No... it had been he, himself, and it had been Svetlana on the quay, watching with that glowing sombre face. It had been a dream of his own death. He shivered, and crossed his arms more tightly across his chest. He fretted back over his plans, uncertainly, nervously, the proverbial Russian on his own, his brain out of focus, filled with irrelevant thoughts: is it true no one dies with an erection? He said, "Once in Sweden, I saw a wild swan on her nest, out in the forest."

"It must have been very beautiful," Valentina replied, and when he looked at her he saw her eyes were wet.

"No, it was nothing." Touch me with kindness and I shall kill you, tear off your wings and fingers, rape you with anything I can find; keep off me with your fucking kindness. He summoned rage, for its warmth, for the movement it imparted to his blood, crying out within: They are trying to leave you touched, and afraid, like a mad dog petted tame again, and you must *not* be! Ah, there. That brought it out. His rage stood now like a great animal on the edge of a forest. Rage, rage. He might go down today, but by God he would take them all down with him!

3

THE TAXI HAD BROUGHT THEM as far as the driver dared,
with the snow unploughed here, and still falling. They got
out before the Hauptallee, southeast of the wheel, and
walked toward the bowling alley. Hardly anyone was out,
beyond the occasional old Viennese with a dog in its plastic muzzle. Pastukh shivered with cold and *déjà vu*.

Here, just here, he had vaulted from the back seat of
that IL-2 after Carney's groundloop, and here, just here,
he had watched the blue sparks of its exhaust rise and
vanish into the darkness. Then he had slung his submachine gun and knapsack and begun his solitary march
into occupied, or liberated, Vienna, slightly ragged as a
captain in another army, a flash of panicked self-
consciousness subsiding now they had arrived, now he was
alone, the airplane gone, like a ladder pulled back into the
sky. A few kilometers ahead of them the Soviet army
smashed the German holdouts backed against the Danube, one could hear the chatter of small arms, the occasional *drub*! of a point-blank artillery round, as he and
Lisa had heard them at Kitzingen, where the sounds of war
had been farther away. An eternity away. April thirteenth, nineteen hundred and forty-five, AD, and Captain Andrei Borisovich Pastukh was here, *here*, where a
day before had been the vanished Andrei Shepherd, the
former reality suddenly gone, like old smoke, the new
reality enveloping him. He had looked up, then, and seen
the remnants of the great wheel, charred by fires, its cages
destroyed, so that it was just a huge, flawed circular frame
rising from the flattened, shattered forest of the Volks-
prater, like a clock from which everything had been removed. It stood against the lighter sky, a shabby
monument to lost gaiety. It was at that instant that Pastukh had seen his first Austrian civilian, an old woman in
several worn coats, tied by a thin strand of rope to a small
Dachshund, who squatted self-consciously, like a man
might, caught defecating on the sidewalk. No one else had

seemed to care about this new captain. The Soviet army had taken him in, uncorked his fluent Russian, fed him a bit of thin meat stew and poured him out some vodka, and, ignoring his adminstrative insignia, put him with the infantry. It had been exactly as he had hoped, like being inserted as a minor player into some Tolstoy manuscript, the Russian army immutably the Russian army, Vienna immutably herself, even in those lean times. No, someone else *had* singled him out—later that day when he had found the inner city, an army photographer had insisted that he help raise the flag over Hofburg, officers and men together. There he was, then. Suddenly Russian, as poor Emil had put it. *You are never there, and then, suddenly, there you are, a visible man like you. How could I not have noticed you before? I remember, you see, not remembering you. And I draw the obvious conclusion.* Not a thing to say in Lincoln's hearing.

"See him?" Schaefer asked. His voice was frayed with the long wait, and worry, and nervousness—he so clearly wanted not to lose this round to Trulov that he was nervous as a horse.

"He is out there," he said. They had reached the cafe, which threw yellow panels of light into the snow, and bursts of muted conversations in German, odd words, leaking into the night. "We just don't see him yet." The difference between him and the boy was that he knew what to expect. He knew Maxim, he knew this kind of meeting, this kind of exchange, of information, of people, of whatever the national greeds required. It was a good place Maxim had selected, the visibility limited by falling snow, and yet open enough that the snow provided a contrasting background. You could see them coming at you a long way away, but you could also disappear into the bare trees quickly. Well, Trulov had always been better than good at his work. "There," he said then. He had seen indistinct figures, just for an instant, but knew it would be Trulov and the girl. He felt it with his skin.

They came out like contenders for a three-legged race. Trulov had tied her right leg to his left one with a strip of torn blue cloth. As they advanced, Pastukh could make out Valentina's face, the makeup streaked and splotchy, the makeup of a madwoman, or a child. Trulov kept his left arm around her shoulders, and for a moment Pastukh thought she had been harmed, for her face had a look of... violation. But, no, she was intact, merely angry and tired, and beginning finally to be a little bit afraid. He saw the boy touch the automatic concealed in his coat. "Don't," he said. "Not yet." He raised his eyes toward Trulov, gigantic in the scarlet and black motorcycling costume, like a man from the stars. "Good evening, Maxim," he called. It surprised him, understanding the possibilities, to feel so little. The pain had seasoned him like a nut, so that he was impervious to possibilities now.

"Come in very close," Trulov said in a low, serious voice. He moved himself and Valentina between them. "I want you for shields."

"We have set no traps, Maxim."

"Maybe you have, maybe you have not. I still want you close."

"I cannot speak for the Americans."

"I thought you were connected, Andrei."

"Ah, well, only as a minor executive."

"Not so minor. Not so minor. I *saw* that connection, you know, that thread between you and that Lincoln, and with Braun, here, although I understand he is simply a bystander. But I have got to know all of you, that Cybelle woman..." Rage flared like a furnace behind the bright dark eyes.

"Cybelle? You know her too?" Amazing. "Small world."

"She wanted to be the first woman to swim the Baltic in winter."

"She was always athletic."

"She threw herself away. I would have kept her."

"I bet so. She would have given you proof, if you had been able to extract it." Cybelle Cybelle Cybelle. Goodbye, Cybelle.

"But I have you. We can extract it from you."

"I doubt it."

"You will tell us everything. Or your son is dead, you get to see his brains melting the snow. And this woman here who wants to be what Americans call pussy. Your cooperation buys both their lives."

"A bad bargain. I cooperate, and then, afterward, you come in on them. No, I mean to keep them safe. Safe from the Americans. Safe from you. I have arranged their safety." Trulov glanced uneasily toward the trees. "Not by trapping you, Maxim," Pastukh added gently. "I have no wish for you to be destroyed. I will make an arrangement with you, though."

"You will do what I tell you."

"What do you think you have caught? A master spy? But how can that be? My friends are comrades in arms from the Great Patriotic War, I have fought in the Russian infantry against the Germans. I helped take Berlin. Is that your master spy?"

"They put you there."

"They offered me an opportunity to *be* there. Would anyone turn his back on his own life forever if he did not want to do it? Do you doubt my essential Russianness? I have been a Russian twenty-four hours a day since you were a baby—I have been more a Russian than you."

"You work for *them*."

"I help them. I help the two sides adjust to one another. I help the incurably violent understand the incurably paranoid. I am the man in the asylum, helping the other side comprehend what our crazy society is thinking, what it is really saying when it speaks. Do you think the two superpowers could survive without people like me in the Soviet Union? In America?" Pastukh felt the weakness of his powers now, they seemed like candles against the gale of Trulov's rage. Where had the *man* gone? Into the anger. How did one argue with anger? Down, Caliban, down! "Listen to that roaring in your own head, Maxim, and then pretend you are a great nation, blinded by all the fears and rages and suspicions you have now. *Anything* can happen. I help it not to happen. The rage is an aberration. Listen, what do you think I do for the Americans? Microfiche? Photocopying? The Centre... that is the kind of work I do. I give the two sides a place where they can forget their mad ideologies, their violence, their paranoia, and think coolly for a change. That is my kind of master spymanship, Maxim. Oh, there are the other kind as well. If we open an institute like the Centre, soon we have your *real* spies around. You must buy those tapes from the busker. Lincoln must ensure the tapes are false. *You* are the master spies, you boys wasting one another's time with that kind of silly behavior. But, come now, do you really think I have been such an enemy to the Soviet Union?"

Valentina watched him closely, clamped in the big man's arm. But Trulov had not listened, he had merely burned. "Listen, Maxim," Pastukh said then, "Hold your silence. I can fix your problems at home, I can explain them away, put you back in a proper order there. I am retiring now. I have responsibilities now, a small future. I want this quiet life, hardly ever leaving my *dacha*..." The voice held a pleading note, the tone was all wrong. He shifted to a harder line. "You have no alternatives, Maxim. They will never believe you at home, no matter what you force from me. I can still save you. But alone, you are powerless."

"Powerless?" The big hand swept in quickly and grabbed Pastukh by the throat and lifted him almost off the ground. The rage got past the man, he thought, and now Trulov would kill him.

Schaefer dived for Trulov, then, jammed his stiff hand beneath the larger man's breastbone. The bandaged left hand batted him away; he spun back, this time holding the automatic, which he whipped up into Trulov's crotch. The big Russian released Pastukh, and that was all; the pain dissolved in the cauldron of his rage. He looked at Schaefer like a mad animal, wondering not so much what he would do, but how...Schaefer held the gun on him, whispering, "Back, back, goddamn you, I'll shoot."

Valentina made a sudden effort to rip away and Trulov ignored Schaefer, turned away from him, and lifted the girl between him and the gun, pinning the hands that clawed him. He brought out the Walther, a tiny black toy in his huge fist, and pressed it into the lower side of her chin. "You *deal* with me," he panted, "you *try* to deal with me. I will kill you all, and make my peace in some other way. Who do you think you are? Don't you know what I am...?" He flung the girl away from him with such force that the cloth holding her leg against his tore with a snap. He spread his great arms like wings. "Shoot, you fucking cowards, shoot me a hundred times, before I rip your arms off." Trulov stopped, suddenly puzzled. *"Job tvoju matj!"* he whispered. He fell forward like a tree, the force spilling what remained of his head into the white snow. His pistol skittered toward Pastukh. The big legs kicked him after Schaefer, the last signals of his rage propelling him another meter forward; then he lay still.

Schaefer looked at the mess at his feet and pocketed his gun. Without speaking he went to Valentina and lifted her up in his arms, and held on, as though some interior wind were trying to blow them both away. Pastukh knelt and touched Trulov's shoulder, feeling it warm but empty, dense meat.

Poor Vera, he thought, making her clumsy attempt to save her man, dealing with the devil, and of pretty Svetlana without her big father. No matter what happened, there would be no comparable man. He heard footsteps in the snow behind him and said, without looking, "Hello, Lincoln."

"How would you like to go to Russia?" Lincoln asked, sneering, but also much older than a week ago. The work was wearing him down, Pastukh thought. We are all too old for it. But he did not reply. No more banter. "We have a very complex situation here, Andrei. We have a property whose value has just gone through the basement. We try to keep the situation contained and things keep popping loose, like the jungle taking over or something. Now see what we've come to."

"You would have to blow up the world to stop all memory," Pastukh said. "Of course, knowing you, that should not be too difficult to arrange."

"We can't protect our little firm any longer, Andrei. Now we are going to leave memory alone. Let it be one of those things people whisper about forever. Nobody listens when people talk. We've decided to destroy the property, but I wanted to tell you. I mean, we are either gentlemen or we are not." His eyes flickered from one to the other of the trio. "Before you break and run, let me explain something. Also, before Schaefer tries anything with that gun. We obviously have you covered by a talented marksman. Any moves and at least one, maybe two of you, maybe all of you, go down the way this poor old teddy bear has. So, Schaefer, if you want to gamble, give it a try. But it will make you sick to see your little blonde's brains in the snow."

Pastukh stepped between them and Lincoln, wondering where the sniper waited. "As Carney would say, you're behind the throttle, Lincoln. If anything happens to me, there are all those packets. *Pravda. The New York Times.* Premiers and presidents. People in your line of work on both sides. The whole apparatus goes off automatically. You light that fuze, my friend, and you suddenly have nobody on the ground east of Kitzingen. Yes, *Kitzingen.* You lose."

"You're bluffing."

"You are beginning to look run down, Lincoln. I think all of us are too old for this." He drew with a foot in the snow, letting silence come round them. Then, "Here is what you will do. You will clean up the mess you've made here, and you will be silent hereafter. The property, as you like to call it, is closed. Not demolished, just closed. And for this, at some point before I die...I *am* dying, you see, the place is full of termites...I will disassemble the system of insurance that protects me. You can stop worrying that your whole apparatus will have to be replaced. When I come to the end, I shall no longer be insured. But until then, we have a Siberian standoff."

"I can't buy that, Andrei. What about these two? What about all the people who know about you?"

"As you said, people will talk about it for a long time. But Valentina is not going to go against me." Well, he bluffed a little. Would Valentina stay with him or was he too great an insult to the Soviet Union? They would find out. "I know you too well, Lincoln. I know she is safe only when she is with me. And Schaefer...I am afraid Schaefer will have to die...figuratively, as I did. Somewhere in the traffic death toll in western Europe is someone of about his size and coloring. But you work out the details, Baker. It requires a number of falsifications, lies, manipulations. It is just your kind of operation." He passed a tired hand before his eyes. "Poor Maxim. This man," he told Schaefer and the girl, "this man used Maxim's family to trap him, persuaded a child to help with her father's murder. A nasty piece of work, as your friend Dexter would say."

"You come well prepared tonight, Andrei."

"You always underestimate people who are willing to have you around. It is a mistake anyone could make." Then, "Goodbye, Lincoln."

He felt an unfamiliar sensation in his breast, a bursting, that at first he thought was some new form taken by the serpent within, the devil in one more disguise. But then he thought: It is *joy*! The recognition brought tears to his eyes. He walked over to his tense, huddled children, and put one arm around the boney shoulders of his son, and another around the softer ones of his crazily attired daughter, and with them he walked away from death, from the silent Lincoln, the shattered container of Trulov's consuming rage.

"A biologist told me once that everything inherits more than it should. You may have inherited the propensity to disappear. Schaefer and I have talked a lot today, Valentina. He knows he must go the way of Shepherd, at least for the time. Both of you are only secure now with me, in Russia." He felt her protest rising and gave them both a fatherly squeeze. "No, no, you have to hear me out, and do what I say, for we go to an old, old land, where people must still listen to their elders, although they do not always do exactly as they are told. I have worked it all out. You will break my heart if you do not come with me, and let me have a few months' talk, and roaming the birch forests, and taking trains across that huge land, which one must love. One simply has no choice. I want you to join me in *my* Russia...what I once called Blue Russia, remember? Yes, Blue Russia." He gestured with a hand as though it held a wand. "You shall be yourself, my dear Valentina Ivanovna. And, Schaefer, as we discussed today—*you* shall be Yevgeny Ivanovich Orlovsky." He gave Valentina a squeeze. "One of those stormy, incestuous relationships."

"Yevgeny!" Valentina laughed, full of wonder, her voice relieved by all this talk of life, the relief, Pastukh thought, of young troops who have survived a bloody action. "Yevgeny Ivanovich. And we go home together, you and Yevgeny, and I!"

"Call me Gene," said Schaefer, beginning to smile.

"Valentina," called Pastukh.

"Yes?"

"Do you think he can learn Russian?"

"Yevgeny can do anything!"

The three shared a nervous round of laughter, walking and walking through the snow, and Pastukh felt that he would burst with pleasure. He said, "My children, my son, my daughter, my reward for not having been totally bad...we shall have a splendid Russia together, such a splendid Russia. We shall have a secret Russia, one that no longer exists ... but ... what other kind is there, for people like us?"

Ah, God, he was a happy man at last. They strode through the snow, the three of them, the two young ones under his broad arms, each step freeing them a little more from death, and memory. When they stopped to get their bearings, there was no sign of Lincoln, no dark form on the ground, but only the great wheel, hanging upon the bright blurred sky over Vienna, and the streetlamps, and the pale curtain of falling snow.

EPILOGUE

I SAY TO A TROUBLED LINCOLN, "He told me you always underestimated him. I begin to believe it." He merely glares, wondering how long it will be before the night finally goes his way. A long time, old sport. A very long time. "Pastukh knew if he dismantled his insurance early, you'd hear about it, and your greed wouldn't let you stay away. You'd brood about how terrible and compromising it would be, his dying drugged and out of his skull in a Russian hospital. But, really, you're just riding that same old murdering reflex. He read you. He put a new policy in place for me and Valentina—touch us and you still bring everything down." You set all those other webs jiggling, as our murdered British friend would say.

"Then *he* broke the bargain," Lincoln argues.

"You're incurable. But, no... he just sucked you back to Vienna. He staked himself out in a clearing, and me too, knowing you'd get the scent and have to do a little killing. The old magician needed your help tying off one last loose end, and so he waved his wand, and here we all are."

"What do you want us to say?" asks Lincoln in that sneering voice. "We're sorry? Okay, we're sorry." Carney is quiet, however, even reflective. I begin to think he sees what's coming.

"You don't *sound* sorry."

"Oh, but we *are*, we *are*."

Did you know you have a son? We must put an end to your insulting ironies, old boy. Try them on the man in the black mask. "How would you like to go to Russia?"

His face reddens as though slapped, but he is a tough man, and rides his situation down. "How would you like to go to hell?"

"Not much to choose between them, for you."

"But why me?"

"It's you or Carney. Only one need go. The other has to go back to the States and tell everyone how important it is that Valentina and I not be touched. We tend our avocados or gold or mushrooms or whatever, and everyone leaves us alone. No more property. No more killing over it."

"We could both tell them."

"That would be wasteful. We only need one."

"Sending one of us over will destroy your insurance," Lincoln says shrewdly, with a cold smile.

"That's strictly up to the sendee. A good man isn't going to tell all, is he? I mean, a man of your experience must have a pain threshold that's out of sight. Anyway, that's not my problem. If a good man goes over, your apparatus is safe. If he cracks quickly, everything comes down. What do you want me to say, I'm sorry? Okay, I'm sorry."

"Bastard."

"That too." They watch me, knowing I will use the automatic on them if I must, sensing also that I am not alone. They stand there nervously, like animals testing the air for odors of death, the cries of their kind. "But the selection isn't mine to make."

Lincoln tries not to hear me. His nerve has drained away, his face is very pale. But Carney has seen the others, drifting out of shadows, moving slowly toward us, their progress restrained, processional. "He's giving us to the squaws."

"Great traditions die hard," I tell him. Then, "Good evening, ladies." The women continue their slow advance. Ivanov appears then in his bold costume, cradling a Makarov of his own. We nod to each other.

Lincoln's expression cracks a little. Carney, perhaps finding the future already foretold, is impassive. He is ready to take what comes.

I tell them now, "Trulov got into great trouble at home, trying to expose your operation. His troubles have moved on to his family. Andrei thought that possibly, if they gave *their* side something...someone...their life would be easier." I gesture toward the women and Ivanov. "I think you know everyone." The light touches my Valentina, and the broad, grieving face of Vera Trulov, and the girl...yes, I remember now, Svetlana. Pretty Svetlana. "If we ask which of you should go, you'll give us the less valuable. It's your nature to cheat. So, Vera...you decide."

But she shakes her head. "At the end," she says, looking at the shining black ground, "they come to us, these two, wanting to find Maxim. I tell them nothing. I do not share his message, either. But they go to Svetlana, then, they tell her how they will save her father, on and on, so that finally she must do for them what they want, no matter what I say. She tells them Hauptalle. And then...they kill him anyway." She covers her child's shoulders with her arm, winglike and protective. "Which one shall go to Russia for Papa, Svetlana?"

The child with Trulov's pale, round face raises her dark eyes to peer into Lincoln's scalded visage, and into Carney's closed one. At last she points to Lincoln, tears streaking her cheeks. "He," she announces. *"He."* She cries, and one senses she had not cried away her father's ghost before this. And still her hand points at Lincoln. Relief flashes like distant lightning behind Carney's eyes. Lincoln looks blind. Afraid and blind. The wings of my pity beat futilely within; he is not mine to save.

We hear sounds from the cemetery gate, and see the black Mercedes there, its interior illuminated briefly as the doors flick open, and then shut. It is the same pair, the embassy's messengers of death, the ones who took Emil's remains away, who must have handled Trulov's when they were dragged from the Danube by a Hungarian tour boat, and those of Andrei Borisovich Pastukh, discovered at the wheel of a rented car at Schwechat. Now they approach what is left of Baker Lincoln, the man who liked to say he created all of this.

"British espionage at its best . . ."
—*New York Times Book Review*

murder of a moderate man JOHN HOWLETT

A trail of terror leads an Interpol operative to London and Milan
where he must untangle a web of deceit that surrounds an Iran-
ian opposition leader who is stalked by assassins.

Available now at your favorite retail outlet, or reserve your copy for shipping by sending your
name, address, zip or postal code along with a check or money order for $4.70 in the U.S.
or $5.25 in Canada (includes 75¢ for postage and handling) payable to Worldwide Library to:

In the U.S.	In Canada
Worldwide Library	Worldwide Library
901 Fuhrmann Blvd.	P.O. Box 609
Box 1325	Fort Erie, Ontario
Buffalo, NY 14269-1325	L2A 5X3

Please specify book title with your order.

 **WORLDWIDE LIBRARY**

MUR-1A

"*Cross Fire* is firmly within the genre
known as a 'page-turner.'"

—Philadelphia *City Paper*

CROSS FIRE

RALPH YOUNG

A man finds himself trapped in a conspiracy of terror after a top-level NATO scientist is killed and he discovers a complex plan to wipe out opposition to NATO deployment of nuclear missiles in Western Europe.

Available in October at your favorite retail outlet, or reserve your copy for September shipping by sending your name, address, zip or postal code along with a check or money order for $4.70 in the U.S. or $5.25 in Canada (includes 75¢ for postage and handling) payable to Worldwide Library:

In the U.S.	In Canada
Worldwide Library	Worldwide Library
901 Fuhrmann Blvd.	P.O. Box 609
Box 1325	Fort Erie, Ontario
Buffalo, NY 14269-1325	L2A 5X3

Please specify book title with your order.

 **WORLDWIDE LIBRARY**

CRO-1

A gripping thriller
by the author of The Linz Testament

LEWIS PERDUE

The world's most powerful bankers conspire to gain control of
the world's financial future. Only one man is prepared to stop
them, but he needs every ounce of cunning to stay alive...

Available in October at your favorite retail outlet, or reserve your copy for September shipping by sending your name, address, zip or postal code along with a check or money order
for $5.70 (includes 75¢ for postage and handling) payable to Worldwide Library:

In the U.S.	In Canada
Worldwide Library	Worldwide Library
901 Fuhrmann Blvd.	P.O. Box 609
Box 1325	Fort Erie, Ontario
Buffalo, NY 14269-1325	L2A 5X3

Please specify book title with your order.

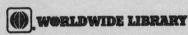 **WORLDWIDE LIBRARY**

ZAI-1